LOTUSLAND

A NOVEL

DAVID JOINER

PAINTED VEIL PRESS

Cover design by Kimberly Glyder
Interior formatting by Kathryn Guare

Quote on pages 288-289 from Henry David Thoreau's *Walden*, Chapter 18: Conclusion, paragraph five, p. 323-24 (Princeton University Press, 1971).

Painted Veil Press · Kanazawa, Japan
david-joiner.com/paintedveilpress

ISBN 978-0-9977155-0-7

Vietnam. Through the lens of that friendship, he's given us a dynamic, deeply nuanced portrait of a nation in the midst of profound change."
  - Dana Sachs, author of *The House on Dream Street: Memoir of an American Woman in Vietnam*

"An engaging and accomplished novel about contemporary Vietnam seen through the eyes of an American who lived there."
  - John Balaban, author of *Remembering Heaven's Face*, a memoir, and *Spring Essence: The Poetry of Hồ Xuân Hương*

"A rare, vividly rendered depiction of near-contemporary Vietnam full of details noticed by someone who lived in - and cares deeply about - the country. In *Lotusland*, David Joiner explores both Vietnam and personal relationships with welcome realism."
  - Michael Tatarski, editor of the *Vietnam Weekly* and host of the *Vietnam Weekly Podcast*

"Likely the most vivid novel set in post-colonial Southeast Asia that contemporary readers will encounter."
  - Garry Craig Powell, *Rain Taxi*

"An authentic account of expats struggling with love, money and trust in the realities of Vietnamese culture...[S]erves as an antidote to the conveyor belt of tired fiction about a war that ended more than 40 years ago."
  - *Oi Vietnam Magazine*

LOTUSLAND

FOREWORD

In 2015, we invited David Joiner to participate in a keynote session on "Vietnam, America – Past and Present" at an annual conference that we organize called Engaging With Vietnam: An Interdisciplinary Dialogue (EWV). This conference series is held in a different location each year, both inside and outside of Vietnam, and attempts to bring together experts from a wide range of disciplines, from both inside and outside of academia, to discuss and share all manner of ideas concerning Vietnam and anything Vietnamese. Founded in 2009, the 2015 conference was the seventh time the conference had been held.

Joiner's presentation at that conference was entitled "Writing *Lotusland*: The Reflections of an American Author Writing about Vietnam." His novel had just been published, and in his presentation he talked about the writing of the novel and his own experience of living in Vietnam for more than a decade. Reading the novel at that time, we saw that there was much about Vietnam that it reflected. Reading *Lotusland* again now in 2024, as we are preparing to hold the fifteenth EWV conference, we have the same sense, but also realize how much Vietnam has changed.

The main character in *Lotusland* is Nathan, a young American man living in Vietnam and struggling to establish a career as a writer. He falls in love with Le, an artist with a mysterious background who wishes to immigrate to the US. Nathan is friends with fellow American Anthony, who works in the fast-paced world of Vietnamese real estate development, and who is married to Huong, a young woman Nathan once dated. While the psychological and emotional energy that drives the novel is powered by the complex interpersonal relationships between these individuals, Joiner grounds the plot firmly in the Vietnam of the early twenty-first century.

Lotusland is thus a novel about a young American man in Vietnam. But more specifically, it is about a young American man in the Vietnam of the early twenty-first century, and that distinction is important.

Vietnam began to open to the world following the Doi Moi reforms of 1986. At first, its engagement with foreigners and foreign societies was limited. In the 1990s, for instance, one could find in the major cities of the country a small number of foreigners, including overseas Vietnamese, working for NGOs; businessmen from East Asian countries like Taiwan, Japan, and Korea setting up factories and investing in various development projects; and modest numbers of tourists. That period was beautifully captured in a film by Vietnamese-American filmmaker Tony Bui called *Three Seasons*, a film mentioned in *Lotusland*.

Given this limited engagement with the outside world, in the 1990s there were few opportunities in Vietnam for lone individuals like Nathan in the novel. However, such opportunities became more common in the first decade of the twenty-first century, as it became possible, for instance, to survive in Vietnam by teaching English, and from there, to land the types of jobs that Nathan and Anthony have in the novel. It is this world that Joiner wonderfully captures in *Lotusland*. That world, however, has now been largely overtaken by a significantly different reality.

While Nathan struggles to find American news outlets to accept his writings, today there are expatriates in Vietnam working for local online media outlets. While Nathan is in Vietnam on his own, today one finds entire families from around the globe working and living in Vietnam. And while Nathan falls in love with a woman who is attempting to immigrate from Vietnam, today his counterpart would more likely fall in love with a Vietnamese woman who is returning from overseas with a PhD.

Therefore, many conditions in Vietnam today are already significantly different from what Joiner depicted in *Lotusland* roughly a decade ago. This is also the case with issues surrounding the Vietnam War and its aftermath. Nathan is asked in the novel by Reuters to write a piece on the after-effects of the use of Agent Orange, and Le's sponsor for immigrating to the US is supposed to be an uncle who fled overseas after the war as a "boat person." In the early twenty-first century, when the novel takes place, issues surrounding the complicated aftermath of the war could still be encountered in Vietnam, but that is much rarer today.

We bring up these contemporary changes not to detract from the novel. To the contrary, these changes bring into focus the elements that were unique to the early twenty-first century, and which Joiner deftly captures and interweaves into his narrative. As such, like *Three Seasons*, *Lotusland* is another window onto a particular moment in Vietnam's ever-changing modern history – a distinguishing trait, as it remains one of the only U.S. novels set in Vietnam to portray expatriate and Vietnamese life during this century's early years. For anyone who lived or traveled in Vietnam at that time, there is much in *Lotusland* that they will recognize. At the same time, upon reflection, they will also realize how much has changed. The modern transformation of Vietnam is an epic story, and *Lotusland* offers a wonderful look at a fascinating moment in that unfolding tale.

Phan Le Ha and Liam C. Kelley
Engaging With Vietnam

1

Nathan tossed and turned on the hard lower bunk of his sleeper-class room, peering at his cell phone. It would take thirty more hours to reach Hanoi. He was struck by how things were always a long wait for him. Nothing was simple, and whatever seemed certain had a way of being turned on its head without warning.

The sound of the train was low and whooshing, like the winds of a relentless rainstorm. Whenever the train pulled into a station, the lull of stillness became just as loud, howling inside him, heightening his restlessness.

A premonition of endless night took hold of him. Unable to bear it, he left the room.

In the passageway a young man sat on a stool with his face buried in a copy of the *Army Newspaper*. There was nowhere else to sit, though at the end of the last train car an open door led to a small platform.

Outside, the night was cool; over the sound of the train's trundling, frogs and crickets trilled. Sitting with his legs dangling over the platform's edge, he watched moonlit fields emerge from a tangle of trees now receding on both sides of the track.

Hearing footsteps behind the platform door, he expected to see the man who'd been reading in the passageway. He was surprised when a young woman stepped through the doorway with a train-issued blanket draped over her head. It was an odd way to wander through a train, and coming outside alone and as late as this piqued his interest. As she considered the small space that Nathan occupied, or whatever was on her mind, he moved slightly so she could sit with him.

She tugged the blanket from her head. When she slipped into a shaft of moonlight, her hair appeared as pink as a rose.

Her age was hard to guess, though she was young, between twenty and twenty-five. The more he looked at her hair the more its shape came to resemble a rosebud: it enfolded her face so that the ends nearly met beneath her chin.

She wore loose-fitting pajamas and tatami sandals. She asked for the time – *Trời ơi, mệt quá...Bây giờ là mấy giờ rồi*? Her pronunciation – z's in place of y's and r's; ch's in place of tr's – was lilting and feminine, yet distinctly northern. There was something almost startling about the Vietnamese she automatically used, and it pleased him that she would.

He pulled out his cell phone and saw it was just after two. *Hai giờ rồi.*

Hai giờ hả?

The northern accent was easier for him because it distinguished more between sounds. Yet there was something cold and hard about the northern way of speaking, a wintry almost martial quality. But maybe it was only Hanoi's chill weather and thick cloud cover that bled the color from the streets, buildings, even the people's clothing, and made him feel this. For there was something warm and inviting about this pink-haired young woman.

"What are you doing out here?" he asked.

"I came outside to get a phone call." She rubbed her eyes. Under the dark sky he couldn't tell if she was merely tired or had been crying. "Why are you out here?"

He didn't feel like explaining his insomnia. "I can't sleep on trains."

They were silent a moment watching their knees sway back and forth. He pushed himself backwards until he leaned against the wall.

"Going to Hanoi?" she asked.

"Yes."

"Why didn't you take a plane?"

"I must've forgotten I can't sleep on trains. Where are you going?"

"The same as you."

Watching her yawn into her hand, he asked, "Do you live there?"

She shook her head, finishing her yawn. "I live in Saigon. But I'm moving to America."

Her plan to move to America stirred his curiosity. "Why are you going to America?"

"To make a life for myself." She turned away as if his interest made her uncomfortable.

It occurred to him that she had notably large eyes. Somehow they contributed to the disarming effect she had on him.

"Are you married?" she said, turning back to him.

Nathan held up his ringless hands.

The train came upon a crossing. Two streetlights stood opposite one another and bathed a strip of stony dirt yellow. An old man in a dark green uniform pulled a lever to lift the safety cross on each side of the railroad.

"You should go back to your room," the girl said. "If your girlfriend wakes up, she'll worry you're not there."

Her clumsy attempt to learn if he was alone amused him. "Maybe her snoring keeps me awake."

She glanced down the corridor. "It's late. I'd better go back myself."

"What about your phone call?" When she didn't answer he said: "In that case, why not keep me company a little longer?"

"It's late," she said again. She bid him goodnight and disappeared through the doorway.

The blue night suddenly telescoped, reduced to a receding square: a window onto a dream fading rapidly into nowhere. He grew colder in the chill night. For a moment he felt like he was traveling away from life itself. But in the next moment the feeling passed. He saw that the train had only entered a tunnel.

A high metallic wailing echoed off the tunnel walls; a moment later utter darkness curtained everything he'd just passed through.

"I thought you couldn't sleep on trains."

Nathan awoke to find the pink-haired girl placing a bowl of instant noodles beside him, followed by two small bananas. She'd changed clothes and wore an old knee-length skirt and t-shirt with a faded Đông Hồ painting of carps across the chest. Gold Chinese lettering cascaded down the side, sparkling in the clear morning light. It took him a moment to realize she'd spoken in English. Behind her, sunshine stabbed through mists which encircled the jagged mountains.

"You brought me breakfast?" he asked.

"You missed the delivered meal. This is better, anyway. I'll be right back."

Stretching to break up the stiffness in his back, he looked over the other side of the platform. Broken rocks lined the tracks, and between there and the near rice fields were ditches of stagnant water. It was a miracle he hadn't tumbled off in the middle of the night.

He pulled out his cell phone to see the time and noticed that his old friend, Anthony, had sent him a pre-dawn message: *Big week coming up. Not sure how much time I'll have for you in Hanoi.*

The message was not what Nathan wanted to hear. While his trip north was the best chance they'd had in three years for a reunion, Nathan also wanted to ask him for a job. He'd been preparing for several weeks to approach him about this.

Over the last few months, their correspondence had focused on the money he owed Anthony. In his last e-mail, however, Anthony mentioned that his wife, Huong, wanted him to forgive Nathan's debt. "Of course, you and I both know her idea is foolish," Anthony had written. "I guess that's just the not-yet-dead embers of a first love speaking."

The pink-haired girl returned with tea. A Lipton bag bulged at the bottom of the cup. Orange swirls rose from it, and steam from the tea's surface thinly veiled her face. He was conscious of a pleasant tightness in his chest.

"Thank you." He reached for his money but she stopped him.

"It's my treat."

When he hesitated, she told him, "Please, eat your breakfast before it gets cold."

"Your English is excellent. But I guess I shouldn't be surprised since you're going to America."

She smiled and turned to watch the passing scenery. The breeze buffeted her hair; it fluttered about her eyes until she tucked it behind her ears. He imagined it airy and soft in his fingers, like a silk scarf's fringe. As he thrilled over the prospect of touching it – absurd though the fantasy was – he wondered why she colored it. The Vietnamese language had so many ways to describe the beauty of black hair, he couldn't imagine why she'd dye it pink. The more he thought about it, he wondered if perhaps it were a wig. And why a wig unless she was hiding something, like a hideous scar or disease? But it was too morbid a thought; and besides, pink hair fit her.

"I like your hair," he said in Vietnamese. "It's like candy."

She laughed. "You speak Vietnamese like a Vietnamese," she remarked. "You must have a good teacher."

"I've never had one. They cost too much."

She looked at him skeptically. "Then you must have a *từ điển tóc dài*. People say that a long-haired dictionary is the best way to learn."

He shook his head again, not wanting her to get the wrong impression. "Vietnamese girlfriends are even more expensive."

Again she laughed. "But you're American. You never worry about money."

"That's a common misconception."

"What about your girlfriend?"

He had to think back to last night's conversation. "I said maybe I had a girlfriend."

He followed her gaze to the passing countryside. The land here was divided into paddies: a deeper green than the rice fields in the south. Far from the tracks, farmers stood knee-deep in the muck, like thin stunted trees, fixtures in an unchanging landscape.

When he'd eaten the second banana he asked her name. But she either didn't hear him or didn't feel comfortable telling him. The train's movement gently rocked her as she continued looking into the distance.

Her abstractedness allowed him to study the sharpness of her jaw line and the high bridge of her nose. When his gaze fell to her lips, where a tremor passed as if trailing a thought, it stayed there.

"I can tell you're from the north," he remarked, trying to draw her out. The term he used, *quê hương*, meant something like 'home village.' Its connotations were stronger than the English word 'hometown,' for Vietnamese roots ran much deeper than in America.

She turned enough that he could see her eyes. In them was a kind of wonder. "How? From the way I speak?"

"I didn't guess it from your clothes and hair."

"Last night when you first saw me, you must have thought I was strange."

Until suddenly you left, he wanted to say, I thought you were a gift. But he couldn't tell what she was after, so he tried to make a joke of it. "I thought you were a..." He stopped to recall the word 'stowaway,' but all he could remember was that it involved a lot of words. "...A deserter," he said instead, hoping to make her laugh. He carefully pronounced the words, as with these, too, he almost never had the chance to use them.

She smiled oddly and turned away again.

He thought he could smell the sea from here, an airborne brackishness so delicate that at first he mistook it for something sweet. Soon the near mountains fell away, and his eyes took in a wide blue sea. They were approaching Hai Van Pass.

The sea heaved torpidly while gulls circled the shore like specks of torn-off cloud. Together they watched the swell of the sea roll toward them.

"Have you had enough to eat?" she asked.

"Yes."

"Good," she said getting up. "I'll be back."

Once the clatter of her sandals in the passageway faded, a door slid open and shut, and then it was quiet.

He marveled at his interaction with her, whoever she was. The marvel came less from her having awakened him and brought him breakfast than from how comfortable she'd felt doing this, that it was all in the natural order of things. It gave him a sense that they'd long known each other and this was an established routine. He knew nothing about her, however.

For the next hour he waited for her, but she never came back.

He felt the train slowing. Soon the view changed from nearly empty countryside to the cement homes and paved roads auguring a small town. The train's brakes squealed as it pulled into a one-room station, whose yellow walls and orange roof-tiles glimmered in the crisp spring air. In the sloping roof's shadow, several stands sold cigarettes, bottled water, and items wrapped in banana leaf.

The station seemed deserted, but then he spotted several vendors under a grove of pepper trees, dozing in hammocks. The bright noon sun seemed to have sapped their entrepreneurial spirit. As the train came to a halt, they gathered their goods and trudged across the platform.

The pink-haired girl stood in the vestibule waiting to alight. He watched her step down and glide across the platform.

He headed for a drink-stand, keeping his eye on the vending area where the pink-haired girl was helping two elderly passengers sort through fruit. Her stillness in the presence of movement was a natural grace, he thought, like the sun shining through a midday downpour. The same could be said of her eyes, and the fresh, high color in her cheeks. It was something superior, an inborn quality he was certain she'd possess all her life.

The stand's matron approached him, pointing hopefully at a bottle of water.

"I'll have tea," he said in Vietnamese. "And a pack of chewing gum."

The matron quickly brought him a glass and a small pack of Doublemint, informing passengers already seated there that he spoke Vietnamese. But Nathan only sipped his tea, ignoring what she said. He knew that if he responded she'd ask him questions and distract him from the pink-haired girl. The matron eventually wandered off.

The elderly couple the girl was helping looked up and seemed to notice him. Nathan glanced away, not wanting her to see him gazing at her. But such a beautiful girl, and with pink hair – surely it was normal for strangers to watch her from afar? Looking back, he saw a vendor take from the elderly couple a handful of custard apples and set them on a scale.

The pink-haired girl was now moving between tables of dragonfruit only a shade or two darker than her hair. A moment later she disappeared into the crowd.

Left alone with his tea he realized that, while there wasn't anything unusual in wanting to meet a girl, his determination to do so now was pointless. Nothing would transpire between them on a train, and he had little confidence that much would happen with both of them seeking to leave Saigon.

These days he found his confidence in short supply. In his own case, he'd spent months looking for ways to better his life. But it was more complicated than he'd imagined. Nothing material needed to be jettisoned, but something else, something that oppressed him from within. There was no escaping the fact that his life had hit a dead end.

He knew there'd be no way out if he didn't soon change his life. After seven years in Vietnam he hadn't pushed himself in any noticeable direction – and, until now, without a clear sense of time having passed. While he'd enjoyed himself in Saigon for more than half a decade, he hadn't particularly accomplished anything.

"Do you want to be alone?"

The voice was familiar, and he realized then that someone stood beside him.

Nathan turned and saw the pink-haired girl smiling down at him. Unable to speak, he gestured to the chair opposite him. Quickly composing himself, he called to the matron for another glass of tea.

The pink-haired girl added a request for a cigarette.

The matron came over with tea and a pair of cigarettes on a plate, then fished in her pocket for matches. The girl took a cigarette and turned it between her fingers.

"Give me a light?"

He picked up the matchbox, glancing at the picture on the cover: a white dove with a rose in its beak, flying through a cloudless sky. Stamped along the top were the words Reunification Matches.

When he'd lit her cigarette, she leaned back and pushed her hair from her eyes. Not a trace of black was visible, not even when the breeze picked up and exposed the roots.

"Why do you have pink hair?" he asked.

"Because it makes me happy," she said, tapping cigarette ash onto the ground.

She'd spoken enough English for him to determine she had an education or had at least educated herself in the language.

"Why didn't you come back last night after you said you would? Did spending time with me make you unhappy?"

She brought her cigarette to her lips, which had formed a barely discernible smile at his questions. "I wanted my companions to know I was okay. Then I must have fallen asleep. Were you waiting for me?"

"You said you were coming back."

"I didn't forget. I'm here, aren't I?"

Sensing they were attracting the attention of fellow travelers, Nathan looked around. His eyes settled on the line of green, sun-beaten train cars. In half the windows, behind wire screens, Vietnamese faces casually observed them.

"Who are you traveling with?"

She pointed to the old couple eating custard apples in the station's shade. "They say I remind them of their daughter. Only she died a long time ago."

He wondered if this was why he found her sleeping at the end of the train last night. "Does that make you uncomfortable?"

"Not at all. They treat me kindly. Where are your companions?"

"I don't know."

She swirled the tea leaves drifting from the bottom of her glass. Clearing her throat, she set the glass down, tapping it against the table. Nathan sensed she had something on her mind, but rather than draw her out he was content watching her build up to it. Her large, petaline eyes sparkled and her lips moved slightly as if practicing what to say.

When she saw his bemusement, her face reddened and she straightened in her chair.

"When will you return to Saigon?" she asked.

"I'm in Hanoi for three days. I'll be back in Saigon after that."

"When you return, can you teach me English?" she said. "Just a few hours a week. Maybe we could meet at a café and talk."

The question was unexpected. "I think you'd get more from a class than from me."

"I don't have money for a class," she said. "Nor could I pay you."

He smiled to himself. He couldn't begin to count the number of times he'd been approached to teach English "as a favor." Now, unlike his first few years in Vietnam, he followed Anthony's practice of doing nothing for free. But before he could object she went on.

"If it's money you want, I understand. But I'm open to other arrangements..."

Her last sentence and how she delivered it – her voice trailing off, as if embarrassed to admit she couldn't pay him; looking down at her hands; her shy coquetry – aroused his interest. "Such as?"

"You could teach me English and help me apply for a visa to America."

Given the assuredness with which she'd spoken of her plans, he was surprised she didn't already have a visa.

"What's the rest of the arrangement? That's only half." When she lifted her eyes, he met her gaze.

"Instead of paying you money..."

She reached for the second cigarette and tapped it in her palm. Nathan struck another match for her. Smoke rose between them, and she sat back, holding her cigarette to the side.

"Maybe I could be your girlfriend."

Nathan blinked at her. He knew that a proposal like this meant sex. After all, what else could she offer when she knew him so little? In Vietnam there were no such leaps of faith – it was a practical arrangement, starting with the dearest thing she could offer.

"Only when you're free," she emphasized. "If you prefer money, I understand."

"No, no," Nathan said, rubbing at his chest. "Money's not the issue. I'm just not sure it's a good idea."

"Why not?"

He supposed that what in his eyes appeared to be trading sex for favors was in hers merely an expedient. He struggled to express this. "Because what you suggest – being my girlfriend – has nothing to do with love."

She looked at him strangely. "How can there be love? We only just met."

"That's exactly my point." He saw she didn't understand. "You shouldn't give yourself away like that. Don't you think that love–"

"But it's easier that way. Why should there be love if I'm only going to leave?"

He frowned. *What begins with love, anyway?* he asked himself. *Wasn't love cultivated over time? Didn't it require sacrifice, and involve some level of risk?*

The more he considered her offer, the more his sense of principle, and politics, gave way to a carnal appetite which Saigon, as seamy a city as any, had sown in him. Why not take what was offered and be thankful? Inside him, a quiet but penetrating voice issued caution.

"What kind of help do you need from me?"

"I have to go through the U.S. embassy for my visa. There's a lot to prepare."

"I don't know how I can help. I'm not in a position to persuade anyone or influence the process."

"I have a plan," she assured him. "You just have to do what I tell you. But if you don't want to, I'll find someone else."

"Let me think about it."

She smiled faintly. He could sense she was disappointed. "If I could pay you I would. But I don't have money."

"That makes two of us." He was the only one who laughed.

The train whistle blew, and passengers began dispersing from the platform. Nathan and the girl rose from their chairs and he paid the matron.

"If you didn't already know Vietnamese I'd teach you. What else can I give you?"

The ensuing silence unsettled him. "It's a long train ride. Let me give you my answer when we reach Hanoi."

"Sure. Thanks for the tea and cigarettes." She tilted her cell phone in the sunlight to see its screen. "My phone's in range," she said, obviously surprised. "I need to make a call." She started to leave.

"I'll walk back to the train with you."

"No, that's okay. I'll call from the station."

Her sudden coldness, he knew, came from his hesitation over her proposal. He called out: "I might be able to help you a little."

"Forget it. I'll find someone else. I should be more careful who I ask."

Frustrated with himself, he let her disappear into the station.

The matron cleared away the glasses and plate. Wiping the table with a damp rag, she asked where he was from. When he told her, she asked if he was married.

"Yes," he said. And then, he wasn't sure why: "To that pink-haired girl that just left."

"She's very pretty. Is she a famous singer?"

"That's right. But she's not famous like My Tam or Minh Tuyet."

"What's your wife's name?"

Nathan faltered, realizing that once again he'd forgotten to get the girl's name. He uttered the name of his employer – the first name that came to mind.

"Hang Ly? I'll ask my daughter tonight when I see her."

Nathan looked back to the station and promised himself he'd learn her name before arriving in Hanoi.

The train let out a second blast. This time only a dozen passengers remained outside. Vendors had abandoned their stands to make a final pitch of their goods beneath the train windows.

Nathan found himself walking toward the station, uneasy over whatever was delaying the pink-haired girl. Certain the train wouldn't give more than three warnings, he picked up his pace.

Near the doorway a uniformed attendant stopped him. "Where are you going?"

"Just inside the station," he said, pointing behind the man. "Someone I know is still there."

"No one's in there."

"But I've been waiting for her to come out."

Scowling, the attendant looked around the platform. "You better hurry," he muttered, perfunctorily waving him on.

As Nathan jogged through the door, he realized he might miss the train because of his growing obsession over this girl. What set her apart from all the other girls he'd met in Vietnam? Was it a reaction to her offer? It wasn't just a matter of engaging a pretty face, which was, quite naturally, his normal motivation for approaching a girl. He felt drawn to her for a familiarity, something about her he felt he already knew. And if he didn't know her, which was obviously the case, he felt he could, very easily, if given the chance. But maybe it was only the familiarity of a dream, of something long dreamed of…

Inside, two female station guards were snacking on seeds by a window. They showed no concern when he stepped into the women's restroom, which, aside from a dead mouse in one corner, he found empty. After poking his head inside the men's restroom, he asked the women if they'd seen a girl with pink hair.

"She was here," said one, cracking open a baked watermelon seed with her teeth.

"Did you see where she went?"

The woman pointed to a door that led behind the station. "Over there."

He looked and saw a clearing shaded by rubber trees.

"She made a phone call, then stood for a minute watching the cockfights."

Squinting into the distance he could make out the blue-black, bell-shaped bodies of two birds posturing with their wings in the air and hopping about a patch of dirt as if slowly being fried on it. The gamblers around them sounded like a small plane behind the clouds. They were too far away to shout to, too far away to receive a discernible reply.

"Where'd she go after that?" he asked.

The woman shrugged.

"You're going to be left behind if you're not careful," the other woman said, nodding toward the tracks.

As he hurried back to the train, the girl's disappearance made him consider staying behind. Unwilling yet to commit to such a course, his worry grew with each moment. He kept turning around as if she might suddenly appear behind him. When she didn't, he tried to locate her compartment window. It was unlikely she'd returned without his seeing her. Perhaps she'd come from the side, quickly, and then from the rear; but he hadn't felt she meant to avoid him. Maybe he'd been so focused on seeing her appear in one spot that he failed to notice any deviation from what he expected.

He turned around again once he reached his train car's vestibule. By now the only ones left on the platform were those not traveling.

Above the train's hissing were the cries of vendors discounting their goods. Nathan waved over a woman selling baguettes from a straw basket.

"How many?" the woman asked.

"Two," he said, deciding this might help. After he paid and the vendor handed him his loaves, he asked if she'd seen the pink-haired girl.

"Yes, I saw her."

"Did you see where she went?"

The train began to move, and he shot out his hands to the narrow walls to keep from falling.

The woman's finger seemed to indicate the sky.

"Where? I don't understand."

The woman, growing smaller as the train moved off, only stared at him.

"I'm afraid she's being left behind," he called out.

She tossed a square of old burlap over her bread and without answering watched the train pull away.

Down the hallway the pink-haired girl's door had its curtains pulled closed. Through the thin, pale green material he could make out the bright square of the room's outside window. Elsewhere inside were only vague, unmoving shadows.

The drawn curtains made him hesitate to knock. When finally he did and no one answered, he tried the handle but it was locked. He pressed his ear to the door. Suddenly he felt embarrassed that he'd gone to such lengths to locate the girl, especially if she'd been in her room from the time he set out to find her.

Back in his compartment, his fellow travelers were reading or napping. Nathan crawled into his bunk and sat with his back against the wall.

Outside, the small town had already disappeared. Tall, fern-like grasses grew wildly along the tracks. Beyond them stretched rice paddies pitted and filled with water. Several pits were thirty feet across – bomb craters from the war.

Seeing them made him think how in Saigon it was easy to forget that a war there had ever happened. A few months after he'd arrived, Anthony had shown him old bullet holes in the buildings they were passing. Since then, all the buildings had been renovated and the bullet holes were gone. Aside from a few war museums hardly anyone ever visited, the most salient evidence of the war was to be found within the people. But as the war wasn't something people liked to talk about and couldn't openly discuss if their views were critical of the outcome, that period in the country's history would slowly die with them.

As he watched one bomb crater after another go by, he thought again of the girl.

In the middle of a field, a water buffalo lay half-immersed in a boggy crater. Its crescent horns glinted in the sun, and its gray-black muzzle was turned toward a boy throwing sticks at it, trying to chase it out.

Shortly after the train rolled out of Phu Ly, passing a stone marker that showed only fifty kilometers until Hanoi, the passageway grew crowded.

Nathan stood beside a window and let the cool evening breeze bat his face. There was a point during his journey when the year-round southern heat had given way to spring. The crisp chill in the air and the greenness of everything – the breeze-blown rice fields, the bamboo clumped around villages, the unfamiliar trees carpeting low mountains – pushed Saigon to the back of his mind.

Several passengers had wandered into the corridor and were staring at Nathan, not bothering to hide their curiosity. Just as he was about to return to his room, his cell phone rang. When he looked at the screen, he saw it was Anthony.

"The train passengers are boring holes in me with their eyes," Nathan said by way of a greeting.

"I told you, you should have flown. The last time I traveled by train I bribed the conductor for his private room. The extra twenty bucks was worth it."

"I could take this train a thousand times," Nathan said, "and it would never occur to me to bribe the train conductor."

"I've always said you have a lot to learn from me."

The comment, tinged with something like vexation, made Nathan's smile fade.

"I've got bad news. Something came up at the Ministry of Property and Investment and I can't meet with you today. Since you'll be busy all day tomorrow interviewing people, that only leaves us your final morning to get together."

"I see. Today's an all-day thing?"

"If it's not, I'll let you know. But I expect it to take most of the day. Most of the evening, too, if I need to grease their wheels – which is what usually happens."

"It's no big deal," Nathan said, walking to the end of the train. Standing in the open doorway, he gazed at the stunted trees along the tracks and the weathered, quasi-modern dwellings visible through their branches. "Just save me the final morning I'm in town."

"It is a big deal. I've wanted to see you for more than three years."

Nathan didn't say anything, and Anthony asked if he was still there.

"I was just thinking," Nathan said. "This sort of throws a wrench in things, because I wanted to ask if I could interview at your company."

This time it was Anthony who fell silent. Finally he said, "You're kidding, right?"

"I'm completely serious."

"Since when have you been interested in real estate? For as long as

I've known you, you've always embraced the life of the poor, struggling writer."

"I need the money."

"I know you do. But you have a few things working against you. One, you have no experience. Two, I've got nothing for you. And three – and you said this yourself when I started my company and tried to get you on board – you're not a businessman."

"That was three years ago. I'm not the same person I was back then."

The train passed a pile of burning garbage beside the tracks. Acrid smoke filled the train car, and Nathan coughed and turned around.

At the end of the corridor stood the pink-haired girl. She, too, was talking on the phone, and from her expression he saw she was upset.

"You okay?" Anthony said.

"Yeah, there was just a little smoke I wasn't ready for. What were you saying?"

"I asked how long you plan on being in Vietnam. Are you still thinking of making a life for yourself here, or entertaining thoughts of cutting out?"

"I don't know. I'm not stuck here like you are."

"Thanks a lot. That's a flattering way to put it."

Nathan didn't apologize. In a recent e-mail, Anthony had admitted to being stuck, though it was true, perhaps, that it was for good rather than bad.

"I'd say I've become one hell of a success here, if I do say so myself. But you're right. I'm stuck. Sometimes, on one of my good days, I think things have turned out pretty good in a place where nothing's ever all that good."

The pink-haired girl, who Nathan had been watching, looked up and saw him. But when he waved to her, she hurried toward her room.

"Anyway," Anthony said, "we can talk about this more in person. Text me when you're settled in."

After hanging up, Nathan returned to his room and sat on his bunk. In a little more than an hour he would arrive in Hanoi and have to begin working on his article. Despite its importance to him, his mind was fixated on how to convince Anthony to hire him.

There was a furious push for the vestibule when the train pulled into Hanoi Station. It was a terrifically ugly place.

Nathan forced his way into the corridor. As he passed the pink-haired girl's room he looked inside. She stood at the window, a suitcase by her side, silently crying. When she noticed him she spun around, blotting her eyes with a handkerchief.

He'd presumed too much. The only thing he'd wanted was a private moment with her. She obviously had in mind a private moment, too, only it had nothing to do with him.

"*Chào anh,*" she said, turning around.

"*Chào em,*" he answered. "You keep disappearing on me."

"I do?"

"I thought you missed the train."

"Is that why you took so long getting back?" His look of surprise must have begged explanation. "I saw you from the window."

"I was buying bread."

"I heard what you asked the vendor."

He looked away as his mind rewound both moments. "I wanted to see you again, but your door was closed."

"You're too polite."

"What do you mean?"

"If there's something you want, why don't you go after it?"

He could hardly believe what he was hearing. "Sometimes it's hard to see a situation clearly."

A security guard stopped in the door to hurry them along. Nathan followed her to the vestibule. From the top step she peered into the throng of people on the platform.

"I have to go," she said.

Before he could ask if someone was meeting her, she reached into her bag and handed him a business card.

"Visit me sometime. I'll be back in Saigon in a few days." She pointed at the card she'd given him.

The next thing he knew she was hurrying toward the station lobby, leaving him behind. He glanced at her card.

Nguyen Van Le
Owner
Bac-Nam Gallery

A phone number appeared in the lower left corner, an address in the lower right.

Le, he thought. Her name is Le.

2

From the third-floor balcony of Anthony's house, Nathan gazed across West Lake. A breeze rippled the water's surface, and he stuffed his hands in his pockets to keep warm. At the bottom of one pocket, his fingers grazed Le's business card.

When he'd told Anthony about her, Anthony warned him to be careful. "I'm not talking about your so-called arrangement, either – that's just good luck. What I mean is that in Vietnam you're conspicuous simply by being a Westerner. But with a pink-haired local at your side, expect trouble."

Nathan was thankful he hadn't kept her card in his wallet, for he'd been pick-pocketed that morning on the bus back from Friendship Village, an Agent Orange care facility and training center on Hanoi's outskirts. In the crowded aisle where he'd stood, bodies collided as the driver swerved through the dusty, congested streets. Nathan couldn't recall when a hand might have slipped into his pocket. He hadn't even noticed his wallet was missing until he'd returned to his mini-hotel, worked on his article, and ventured out again for lunch. At a street stall, after ordering *bún chả*, he'd reached into his back pocket, and then all his pockets, and come up empty-handed.

The timing couldn't have been worse. He'd owed the hotel for two nights and was waiting to buy a return ticket to Saigon until he knew what class of seating he could afford. He'd gone a day without food before – three weeks ago was the last time – but he wouldn't arrive back home even on an express train for one-and-a-half more days.

So he'd called Anthony. "My wallet was stolen," he told him. Anthony had immediately replied: "Don't worry. I've got money lying around here. How does five hundred dollars work?" The amount was five times what Nathan had planned to ask for, but Anthony insisted that he borrow it all.

When Anthony had swung by Nathan's hotel, their first meeting together in three years began with Anthony saying, "It looks like you lost more than your wallet. When did you become so skinny?" Handing him the money, he'd added: "I should give you more to put some meat on your bones. And don't worry about the amount. Some weeks I spend more than that just on drinks."

A breeze picked up off of West Lake and blew Nathan's hair over his eyes. As he brushed it away, voices inside Anthony's house grew loud enough to overhear.

"They're your children, too. Tell them yourself."

"I can't."

"You never even try."

"Don't be stupid. Just tell them what I said."

"No," came the shrill reply.

Nathan twisted his neck to look inside.

Anthony and Huong were arguing from across opposite sides of the high-ceilinged sunroom, separated by a new set of furniture. Anthony was pointing at their children, Anh and Hao, who were grabbing Huong's legs and sniffling. The children's features were a shade between their mother and father's. Their dark blonde hair and hazel eyes made them look more Western than Vietnamese, but at four and three they were too young to suspect they were anything but the latter. As far as Nathan could tell, they barely knew English. They had English names, too, but never responded to them, no matter how often Anthony encouraged them to. Huong pried their hands from her legs and sent them away with the nanny, who hovered in the doorway, quietly observing.

Five minutes ago, Anh and Hao had charged outside shouting

Nathan's name. When Anthony nudged them back inside they fell, scraping their hands and knees.

Nathan turned back to the lake, trying to push away pangs of envy. Seeing Huong again had brought back old feelings he thought he'd gotten over; and seeing Anthony so careless with the life they'd built made him resentful.

Anthony returned to the balcony with a bottle of Bénédictine. He poured an inch into his coffee and stirred it. "French monks invented this drink five centuries ago," he said. "Life must have been much simpler back then, don't you think?"

"I don't think life's ever been simple."

Anthony slid the bottle across the table. "Help yourself."

"No, thanks. I prefer to get through my day sober."

Anthony leaned back and combed his fingers through his hair. He appeared about to say something but instead turned to the lake.

Nathan fixed his attention on the changes that had etched themselves in Anthony's person. Physically, the last few years hadn't been kind. Middle age had crept up, silvering his blond hair, adding several inches to his waist, and wrinkling his forehead and the corners of his eyes. Over six feet tall, he still carried himself well; not gracefully, but with enough natural authority that few would dare to challenge him.

A profound tiredness lurked behind his eyes, whose shadowy rings accentuated this. In the short time they'd spent together Nathan could count on one hand the number of times Anthony had smiled or laughed.

A door slammed inside the house, followed by the children's crying.

"If we had a dog," Anthony remarked dryly, "it would rank higher in this family than me."

"I'm sure they blame me for what happened, not you. After all, I'm the stranger here."

Anthony added more Bénédictine to his cup. "They think you're great because you speak Vietnamese. That puts you above me in their eyes."

It was true they seemed mesmerized by Nathan's ability to speak

Vietnamese. According to Anthony, they'd never met a foreigner fluent in Vietnamese before.

"But you're their father."

"Maybe it'd be different if they knew English. My complete lack of Vietnamese gives Huong more authority over them."

"When are you going to learn Vietnamese?" Nathan asked.

Anthony closed his eyes and rubbed his forehead. "Why waste my energy? It's only a matter of time before my kids pick up English. In a few more years I won't need to."

Nathan stared blankly at him. "A few more years is a long time from now."

"Of course, how can anyone predict language development at their ages?" Anthony raised his cup to his lips, then lowered it to add: "Who's even to say how smart they are? I have to take Huong's word for it because I can't understand anything that comes out of their mouths."

Nathan didn't know what to make of this. In Saigon there were plenty of bilingual children, and not just in bicultural families.

"Why don't you teach them?"

"Huong wouldn't like it."

Notwithstanding the notion of fairness, Nathan supposed there was no point asking why Huong didn't take on the responsibility. He couldn't tell if Anthony wanted to open up about this or if he simply found the whole subject distasteful. Nathan was going to ask why he didn't hire a teacher when Anthony's cell phone rang and he stepped inside to take the call.

Anthony wasn't the only foreigner he knew who couldn't communicate with his children. At least Huong's English was good, though it didn't seem like they spoke much anymore. When Nathan thought about it, he could recall several foreigners who'd married Vietnamese women with whom all they shared linguistically were a handful of words.

Nathan tried not to use Vietnamese around Anthony, who bristled at its sound – the rising and falling, the glottal stops, the broken tones – not unless the situation demanded it. In Anthony's own words, the Vietnamese language was like cold, hard rice. "No amount of money," he liked to say, "could persuade me to eat a stale grain of it." More recently he started calling it an acquired aversion.

From the side of the house came a sound like ripping cardboard. Huong's father stood behind a window, leaning over a blooming flowerbox. Twisting his thin face, he hawked and spat, then watched his sputum plummet like a sparrow's egg into the garden.

To Anthony's dismay Huong's parents had moved into their house. Huong had pushed him to accept this arrangement, explaining that it was her duty to support them now that they were old. He'd acquiesced after she went two weeks without speaking to him.

When Anthony returned he asked Nathan how they'd gotten on the topic of his family. "Weren't we talking about something more interesting?"

"I was begging for a job."

Anthony frowned. "That's right. You were trying to convince me that your lack of business acumen wouldn't be a problem."

"You recruited me once before," Nathan reminded him.

"Yes, but back then we were small, and I thought it would be fun having you around. I'm not saying it wouldn't still be fun, but three years have gone by. More's at stake now."

"Two years before that," Nathan said, "we were both English teachers in Saigon. You made a leap, and now I want to do the same."

"Things have changed, Nate. I need someone experienced."

"You know I'm a quick study. And I could take the pressure off you."

"No one can do that. If it's not work, then it's my life outside of work." He glanced toward the living room before taking a long sip from his glass.

Nathan saw that this was becoming a lost cause. "I guess I've said what I needed to. I just wanted to see where I stood."

Anthony watched him as if he expected Nathan not to give up this quickly. "And your writing career? What happens with that?"

"I told you before. I need the money."

"And I need *your* money. At least the five thousand dollars you owe me. Sorry, five thousand five hundred dollars."

Nathan nodded toward Anthony's well-appointed house. "You seem to be doing pretty well without it."

Anthony glared at him, letting the arrogance of the statement sink in. "I don't just give away my money, you know. I did you a favor. No – I've done you *favors*."

"Sorry," Nathan said, feeling ashamed. "It's just weird seeing how you live now. We were both in the same boat three years ago, struggling to get by."

Anthony lifted his glass, as if Nathan had given him a compliment. "Okay then. Just for kicks..."

Nathan waited for Anthony to finish his sentence, but he only sat there, gazing at the lake. "Just for kicks, what?"

"Just for kicks," Anthony said. "Sell me a house."

Nathan laughed. "Sell you a house?"

"Sell me *on* a house. The idea of a house."

Nathan laughed again, but this time over the blankness of his mind.

"Sell me on my house. Right now. I'm a buyer who's skeptical about this place. Convince me that it's perfect."

"Sell you your own house?"

"I haven't got all afternoon."

Nathan took a deep breath, and his mind focused, almost against his will. "First of all, West Lake's the most desirable place in Hanoi, especially for foreigners."

"You wouldn't say that to a Vietnamese person, would you?"

The interruption derailed Nathan, who felt like a fraud anyway, and he resumed at a different point.

"You can see that the design is unique; the Grecian columns in front would impress anyone."

"They're Tuscan columns."

"– and the size is ideal for a large family. You've got the Sheraton across the water, lots of privacy, a big yard..."

"You're merely ticking things off."

"– and a beautiful view."

"Lots of houses on West Lake have views. That's hardly a reason to shell out a million dollars."

Nathan cleared his throat, flustered and angry. But he continued. "The bottom line is, whatever price you're willing to pay I can get it for you cheaper."

"How?"

"Just leave it to me. If you want it badly enough, I'll make it happen."

Anthony held up a hand for Nathan to stop. "Okay, okay. At least you showed you can think on your feet, which is better than most."

They sat in prolonged silence. Finally, Anthony added: "Of course, Huong would love you to move to Hanoi."

Nathan was about to ask if Anthony knew of other opportunities in Hanoi, but his comment erased the thought. "Huong's changed a lot since I last saw her."

"She looks better than she did in Saigon, doesn't she? She's not the same person she was back then – not as vivacious or open-minded, not as hungry to please. As soon as we married, she decided to take charge of me. I used to think her sudden change defied explanation. But I don't anymore. She was like that the whole time but never showed it. Even with you she kept that part of herself hidden."

An awkward moment passed in which Nathan failed to keep from thinking of his past with Huong. They'd dated for six months, shortly after Nathan first arrived in Saigon. Anthony had spotted her on a beach in Vung Tau, but she'd immediately taken to Nathan when the two of them approached. Nathan stopped seeing her when his mother got sick and he flew home, the first of three long trips, to visit her in the hospital. When he returned for good to Saigon, Huong had already taken up with Anthony. "I asked her to help me open a real estate company," Anthony had said, "and that changed everything between us. If you'd been here, I would've asked for your okay. But I didn't think you were coming back. Anyway, you told me she wasn't what you were looking for."

Huong was Nathan's last serious relationship, although several women, both local and foreign, had filled up a lonely month or season since then.

Anthony's phone rang again but the call only lasted a few seconds.

"That was my driver," he said, glancing at his watch. "He just pulled into the driveway."

A shadow passed in front of the white furniture inside. Nathan turned and saw Huong approach them. She was barefoot, her tan legs disappearing beneath the high-thigh hem of her shorts. Her toenails were painted a liverish red that had started to flake off. Seeing this, he remembered how she used to paint her toenails after sex. Sitting naked on his bed, she would sing to herself and paint them gold. "It's my lucky color," she told him when he'd asked about it. Gazing at her feet he wondered if she still did this. He couldn't guess what that deep red color might signify to her.

She sat between them and looked at Nathan warmly. "I heard you talking," she said. "You surprise me, Nathan. I never thought you'd want to work in real estate."

"Right?" Anthony said, glancing at Huong appreciatively. "He just wants to pay me back. Which is good. But I need someone who wants to build up my company, someone with a genuine interest in real estate."

Huong laughed. "You've told me hundreds of times you're the only one at the company who cares about it."

"In three years, not a single employee has quit. I was really talking about their incompetence."

"Anyway," Nathan said, "I am interested in helping your company."

Anthony shook his head as if he didn't believe him.

Huong clicked her tongue at her husband. "Who have you ever hired that was qualified?"

"All my staff know something about business. I make sure of it. But Nate here's a writer. He has no business instincts. And what would he do? I'd have to pay him for something."

"You said yourself that you spend too much time at work writing reports and communicating with clients. Just hire Nathan to do it for you."

"It wouldn't work," Anthony said. "He knows it as well as I do."

"Give me one chance," Nathan said. "A trial run or something."

"We'll see." Frowning again, Anthony glanced at his watch. "We'd better go."

Huong held on to Nathan as he followed Anthony inside. "Don't give up," she whispered in his ear. "Together we can change his mind." She hugged him quickly before he left.

He followed Anthony into the back seat of his Land Rover.

Nathan couldn't understand why Anthony opposed him joining his real estate company. If there was no position to offer, that was one thing, and if in the past Nathan had proved himself unreliable, then that was another. But Anthony never mentioned these as reasons. It seemed more like he didn't want Nathan around. Perhaps he mistrusted Nathan's past with Huong, though it should have been clear that Nathan had no interest in her now. Besides, she and Anthony had two children and a home together. Nathan's life was such a mess that no woman, especially Huong, would give up all she had for him.

He could only hope that Anthony changed his mind. Nathan needed the money, and the pickpocketing had made him more desperate. For it wasn't only Anthony he owed. Creditors in the U.S. were clamoring for money he'd borrowed to pay his mother's medical bills. He'd lost track of the amount he owed, but by now, with interest, it was several times what he owed Anthony.

Hien, the driver, said, "Train station, sir?"

"Train station, then back to my office." He turned to Nathan. "You sure we can't drop you off at your hotel?"

"No, thanks. The International Red Cross is near the station and I need to pick up some Agent Orange material from them."

"It's a free ride. But suit yourself."

As they drove through Anthony's neighborhood, something on the lake caught Nathan's eye. No more than fifty meters from shore, several people treaded water while holding what looked like butterfly nets.

Late March had in fact brought out butterflies: clouds of them, orange and yellow, fluttering around the weedy border of the lake and blown like confetti by the breeze.

The people in the lake fanned out from one in front, like migrating birds in a flooded sky. Above the water's black surface, their conical hats bobbed.

As the road turned, Nathan asked Hien what the people in the water were doing.

"Catching snails. The market for them this time of year is good."

"I didn't see anyone out there," Anthony said.

"With the weather warming up, they're there every day, sir."

"How much do you think they make?"

Hien suggested a figure approximating a dollar per pound.

Anthony shook his head in wonder. "It can hardly be worth the effort."

As they approached Ba Dinh Square, Anthony took another call – the fifth, at least, in the hour Nathan had spent visiting his home. Half a dozen years had gone by since he and Anthony lived in the same place, and again Nathan was taken aback by how his friend handled himself now. Nathan never could have predicted the changes he saw in Anthony. Nor could he have predicted his success as the head of a real estate company.

And yet Nathan wasn't surprised that Anthony had succeeded in business. He was clever without having had a conventional education and was better read than almost anyone Nathan knew. He was able to incorporate the most useful aspects of what he'd learned into how he lived, and on several occasions Nathan felt nothing short of enlightened after talking to him.

Listening to Anthony was fascinating; he was astute and entertaining. Extemporaneous by nature, it was nothing for him to gather together a group and string them along for half an hour. But that was the old Anthony. Though still brilliant, this Anthony was more subdued. He was part melancholy, part resigned, and part plain angry at the world around him. It was an Anthony he'd never known. And the newness of him made Nathan question how much to trust him.

Nathan looked out the window at Ba Dinh Square. Here, at the end of the Second World War, Ho Chi Minh had declared Vietnamese independence.

Anthony pointed to the towering monolith of Ho Chi Minh's mausoleum, before which a line of people waited to see Ho's body embalmed behind glass. Guards in white uniforms stood before the marble building, rifles at their sides, staring straight ahead.

Spread in front of the mausoleum were plots of grass where elderly people performed tai chi, parents played badminton with their children, and vendors sold kites painted as dragons and fish. The open space here and around West Lake was as much of a contrast to Saigon as the cool spring weather he'd enjoyed the last three days. Even Hanoi's traffic flowed in currents less swift, less dangerous, less overwhelming than in Saigon.

Absorbed in thought, he didn't hear Anthony speak.

"You with me?" Anthony waved a hand before Nathan's face. "I asked what that writing job in Saigon pays."

"It depends. Usually one hundred dollars per piece."

"What are you getting for the article you're here to write?"

"One-fifty. For a thousand words that's decent money."

"They're taking advantage of you."

"Money's not why I do it. Anyway, if they like what I write they'll want more."

"Money should be why you do it, considering your financial situation."

"That's why I asked you for a job. One-fifty's okay for one article, but it's not enough to get ahead."

"You're worth more than that," Anthony said, scowling.

A few minutes later Hien pulled up to the train station, forcing food vendors and cyclo drivers out of the way. Nathan dragged his suitcase to a spot of unclaimed asphalt.

A crowd of onlookers quickly gathered. Foreigners evoked strong curiosity in Vietnam, and in Hanoi people had the same tendency to stare as the Saigonese, though the latter were more muted about it, more polite. Turning, Nathan found Anthony waiting to shake his hand.

"Use some of the money I lent you for a first-class room. I hate the thought of you sitting for thirty-plus hours in the cheap seats."

"Thanks again for helping me."

"Forget it. By the way, is your employer reimbursing you for the travel or is this another case of them taking advantage of you?"

"They'll reimburse me. At least they said they would."

Nathan reached for his suitcase but Anthony stopped him.

"How serious are you about working for me?"

"I'm serious."

"I may have an opening coming up. It won't be anything glamorous, but it can't be worse than what you're doing now."

Someone in the crowd imitated Anthony's speech, causing titters all around. Nathan saw annoyance crimp Anthony's expression.

"The advantage you have," Anthony went on, "is that Huong's on your side. But I'm not going to promise anything."

Nathan was tired of talking about a job he felt he had little chance of getting, and Anthony's jibes were hard to ignore. "I understand." Nathan hesitated. "I guess it goes without saying that I owe you."

"Let's not talk about that now. You better buy your ticket before the night train sells out."

After shaking hands again, Nathan hurried into the station.

By the time he'd bought a ticket, a light shower had begun to fall. A taxi driver spotted him in the station entrance and waved at him. Nathan ran through the rain and hopped in the back seat.

As the taxi pulled away, Nathan looked at the sky above the station. Over the rooftop were layers of gray clouds and vertical lines of rain. He hoped the shower would continue as long as possible. It had been almost three months since he'd seen rain.

3

Nathan had a few hours to kill before his train departed. Rather than work on his article, he made the short walk from his hotel to Hoan Kiem Lake, in the center of Hanoi.

Although the rain had let up, the sky was threatening again. Gum tree canopies along the lake's perimeter shook in the gusting wind. Hoan Kiem's surface trembled, making the pagoda on the lake's grassy island seem isolated and frail.

When a few sprinkles started falling, Nathan hurried to a store and bought its last umbrella. Just then it began to pour. There was nothing to do but seek shelter.

As he passed beneath the long overhang of connected buildings, he came across several galleries. A horn blared as a motorbike splashed onto the sidewalk where Nathan walked. The driver parked in front of a gallery, and a young woman ran out to help him with the cardboard packages tied behind him.

Rain had turned the cardboard dark and limp, and the girl asked the man why he hadn't covered his delivery.

"I thought I'd beat the rain."

"You'll be in trouble if they're damaged," she scolded.

"I'm wet, too. Why don't you show me some concern?"

The man laughed when she called him foolish. She, too, was smiling as she carried a painting inside.

Nathan stopped there while the rain continued, lashing the sidewalk where he stood. His umbrella didn't help much and to stay dry he stepped inside the gallery.

While the motorbike driver and girl leaned over the counter filling out a delivery form, Nathan casually inspected the paintings on the wall. The gallery was upscale, though not the most upscale he'd seen. The quality of its paintings was comparable to those he'd encountered elsewhere, and even the style of the works was similar.

A second girl he hadn't noticed approached him.

"You want to buy Vietnam lacquer painting?" she asked.

"I'm just browsing."

When he'd finished looking at the paintings and was staring out at the rain sparking off the sidewalk, the girl touched his arm. She pointed at the delivered items, still wrapped in cardboard.

"You want to see?"

"That's okay. There's no need to..."

But she'd turned and was commanding her colleague to unwrap the paintings. With a cutting knife, the other girl sawed open the wet top. Nathan watched her slide it down one side and then the other, knowing he was obligated now to feign interest.

With the driver's help she pulled the painting from the cardboard wrapping. A protective layer was affixed to the picture, and she squatted down to remove it. As she scooted aside to let Nathan gaze at the image, the driver cut into the other covered paintings.

The painting was of the Vietnamese countryside, its colors deep and rich, the whole suffused with green. The second was a landscape, too: a trail of H'mong women carrying firewood on bent backs down a mountain. The third was of Hanoi, though it wasn't a good likeness. To him it was merely a series of old Vietnamese houses transported to a Western street.

The room fell quiet, and he looked outside again. The rain had let up as quickly as it started, and he didn't want to stay longer.

"Thank you," he said. "I have to go."

"Wait. Only one more."

The girls snapped at the driver to hurry up. He was having trouble cutting the cardboard, and in the end he ripped it apart. The girls clicked their tongues in disapproval.

Nathan waited patiently, ready to decline their final sales attempt. He was looking again out the window, where the only sign of rain now was what kept dripping from the overhang, when his cell phone rang. The screen showed it was Anthony. He answered and said hello.

"Well," Anthony said, "you won."

"What are you talking about?"

"You wanted a job at my agency, didn't you? I'm calling to offer you one."

Nathan stiffened in surprise, then walked closer to the gallery window. He couldn't be sure, but Anthony's words sounded slightly slurred. If he was drunk, Nathan would have to question the genuineness of his offer.

"I didn't think a position would be available right away," he said. He stopped short of admitting that he never thought he'd be given this chance.

"The need became more urgent after Huong forced the discussion."

Anthony took his time describing the position. Nathan's responsibilities would be to help give a public face to the company and to manage the other employees. The Vietnamese staff and the subagents he had to go through would take care of the grunt work. Nathan just had to make sure they got it all done. And the salary, not counting bonuses, would be more than double what he'd ever earned in a year.

"What changed your mind?" Nathan said.

"You've lived in Vietnam a long time. I never gave proper credit for your experience here. Besides, Huong thinks you're the best candidate. And since the agency's registered in her name, I have to give her a say once in a while."

"I guess it's easy being the best candidate when I'm also the only candidate."

"You weren't the only one. I had three or four others in mind, too. But compared to them, she thinks you'll be a better influence on me."

"Then she's crazy."

"If she's crazy then so am I. I'm not offering you this just because she wants me to."

"Then why are you?"

Anthony paused before answering. "I have big plans for you. For you and me both."

Squatting by the painting she'd helped unwrap, one of the salesgirls tugged Nathan's pant leg and invited him to take a look. He held up a finger to indicate he needed a minute. On the other end, Anthony was still talking.

"I love my work, Nate. I love making good money. But it's hard to meet good people here. You know how the expats are all either on vacation without admitting it or are just wandering through life. They have no stakes in the relationships they make."

Something reminded Nathan of Anthony's refusal to learn Vietnamese, but Anthony didn't give him time to develop the thought.

"I'd really like to have you in Hanoi. I don't need a partner in crime to be happy, but..." To Nathan's bewilderment Anthony took a moment to compose himself. "Things would be better with you around. You know what I mean, don't you?"

Nathan said that he did. It was like that for him, too. Still, he felt wary about this flattery. Anthony had a particular talent for being persuasive. In others this kind of persuasiveness might verge on bullying – he knew because he'd seen it so many times among people desperate to get something, from more attention at a seedy bar to loyalty from friends – but in Anthony it showed his commitment to their friendship. He wondered why none of this had come out during his visit. Was it because Huong was always within earshot?

Still squatting, the salesgirl, perhaps impatient with Nathan, turned the painting so he could see it in full view.

A feeling of sickness washed over him. The painting was of a nude woman standing in a flooded field; rain was falling, and women dressed from head to toe in straw outfits were bent over planting rice.

"It's her," Nathan said, stepping closer. The nude in the painting looked just like Le, though her hair was black and her neck grotesquely long.

"Hold on," Nathan told Anthony, pressing the phone's mouthpiece into his chest. He bent down to inspect the painting. In the lower right corner the artist's name was stamped illegibly in red ink. He grabbed scraps of cardboard off the floor and searched for some clue as to where the painting had come from.

"Only five hundred dollar," the salesgirl said. "I think you like?"

"Who painted this?"

The girl pointed to the name in the corner.

"I can't read it. What does it say?" Could Le have painted this? Her business card indicated that she owned a gallery, not that she was a painter.

The girl squinted. "I can't read it, too."

Anthony's voice drifted from the phone. Nathan stood back up, half in a daze.

"You okay?" Anthony said.

"I think so," Nathan said. "Sorry, what were you saying?"

"I asked if the job offer was generous enough."

"It's incredibly generous."

"Good. I should probably give you a couple days to think it over."

"I don't need a couple days."

When Anthony spoke again, his tone was admonishing. "I don't want you saying yes now and then telling me no the day you're supposed to come up."

"It's yes, Anthony."

"I need you to be certain."

"I am certain."

"Then I'm glad, Nate. Really glad."

"When do you need me to start?"

"It's up to you. The sooner the better, though." Thinking about it he concluded: "Let's say a month from now. Six weeks if you absolutely need the time."

"All right."

Anthony let out a long sigh, as if he were relieved. "I can't wait to have you up here. Like I said, I've got big plans for us."

As soon as Nathan hung up, he bent down to see the painting again. "I know her," he told the salesgirl, pointing at the painting. In

Vietnamese he said, "Can you tell me who the painter is and how to contact them?"

His switch to their native tongue surprised them. The girls looked at each other and then at the driver, who stared at Nathan as if he couldn't fathom how Vietnamese had come from his mouth.

"I'm sorry," they said in English. "We cannot tell you."

"Why not?"

"We cannot because if you buy from them direct it bad for our business."

"I don't want to buy anything," he said, refusing to revert to English. "It's just that I know the girl in the picture..."

"You know her?"

"Yes."

"And you want to meet the painter?"

"That's right."

A confused look came over the girls' faces. "I don't understand."

They looked at Nathan expectantly, then suggested again that he buy the painting.

Nathan smiled, trying to control his frustration. "I just want to meet the painter."

The girls came together to discuss the situation. The driver continued staring at Nathan, then suddenly pointed at him and laughed.

"I'm afraid we don't know who the painter is," one of the girls said.

"Don't you have a record of where your paintings come from?"

"Only our boss has record."

"Then can I meet your boss?"

"He very busy. He go Hong Kong two weeks."

Smiling anew at one girl and then the other, he silently counted to five. "Why don't you speak to me in Vietnamese?"

They laughed but didn't answer. Eventually they started sweeping up the cardboard pieces. The driver took two hand-rolled cigarettes from a tin case and offered Nathan one.

Nathan shook his head. "Thank you," he said. "But my doctor says they cause impotency." He watched the man shrug good-naturedly, then stepped through the door and outside.

He visited all the galleries on Trang Tien Street to check for paintings of Le. An hour later, on the corner opposite the Opera House, he realized the time and hurried back to his hotel to check out.

He couldn't get Le out of his mind, and planned to visit her gallery the moment he got home. Somehow the mystery of the painting excited him even more than Anthony's job offer.

By the time he arrived at Hanoi Station, dusk had fallen, and the sky was low and filled with storm clouds. The rain this time was harder and lasted all night.

4

Nathan parked his motorbike in front of Bac-Nam Gallery and approached the entrance. He was excited to meet Le again, and eager to ask her about the painting he'd seen in Hanoi.

Inside, like something chiseled from one of the portraits on the wall, Le stood in a corner of the gallery with her clasped hands pointed down her body. She wore a denim skirt and sleeveless white sweater with a neckline that dipped midway down the slope of her breasts. The gallery's light emphasized her high cheekbones, the warm shadows of them, and turned her pink hair reddish. A blooming warmth went off inside him.

Beside her a customer gazed at a painting of a river and bamboo forest. He was speaking to Le, but her eyes were focused on Nathan.

Crossing the gallery floor, Nathan looked at the paintings on the wall. Few had women as their subjects, and in those that did, none resembled Le.

The gallery was unlike others he'd seen, particularly those along Dong Khoi and Le Loi streets that catered to tourists seeking expensive re-creations, often crude in subject and material. Here were no bare-breasted maidens bathing in a river or lying in hammocks with babies suckling from them; or girls dressed in traditional *áo dài*, glittering parasols in hand, carved into a jade-green countryside. The paintings here were something else. Immediately one caught his eye: a portrait of a girl in a pink summer frock.

The girl's features were blurred, her face like something viewed through a heavy downpour. The fragility of the lacquer, the delicate eggshell limning the soft edges of her clothes – the rare beauty captivated him.

Le skipped up to him when the customer had gone. "I wasn't sure you'd come. I thought you might break your promise to help me."

He stopped to remember if he'd promised anything, but then quickly determined that he hadn't. He'd been careful with what he said on the train. It was possible that she was manipulating him, but it seemed more likely that she believed what she wished to believe.

"I can help you learn English," he said. "But your visa's a different story."

"What do you mean?"

"I mean I have no influence at the consulate. I'm hardly worth their trouble."

"But you said you'd help." Before he could protest or clarify what his position had been she added: "We had an agreement."

"I'm being honest. I don't know that I can do much. But I'll try."

She hugged him quickly, then demurely looked down and smiled.

"I spotted you in Hanoi, you know," he said.

She looked back up in surprise. "Why didn't you say hello?"

"You wouldn't respond to me."

When she gave him the look of confusion he was waiting for, he told her about the gallery where he'd seen a painting that looked just like her.

"Why didn't you buy it? I would have liked to see it."

"But was it you?"

"How can I know? I wasn't there with you."

Before he could question her further, she asked what he thought of her gallery's paintings.

"They're impressive. I especially like the one of the faceless girl."

"There's one in back I think you'll be interested in."

She glided through a door where several paintings leaned against a wall, crowding two easels and a wheeled table filled with paintbrushes, paint tubes, and colorful plastic jars. A painting in front showed a lotus pond full of red-crested cranes, their black tufts flowing, their beakless faces those of Vietnamese women.

When she came back, she turned the painting she'd brought out so he could see it. It was a profile of a woman in a long white dress. Her neck was long and stem-like and stood out grotesquely between her collar and expression of calm. Her face tilted upward and to the side, as if looking through the gallery door. A line of trees stood behind her, black as after a fire.

His eyes went from the painting to Le. "Turn your head," he said. He lifted the painting so he could see her and the portrait side by side. "It's you." When he realized this, the grotesquely thin neck disturbed him more.

"But I have pink hair. The girl in the painting has black."

"It must have been black before it was pink."

"Actually, it was blue."

He laughed but turned serious again. "Did you paint this? And the one in Hanoi?"

She smiled, saying nothing.

"On the train, you didn't tell me you painted."

"Why would I have told you? Besides, you never asked."

It was true; he hadn't asked her. But by shutting herself away in her room, she'd hardly given him the chance to get to know her.

She gazed with him at the painting. "If it were in an American gallery," she said, "do you think it would sell?"

"There's no predicting taste, but yes, I'm sure it would." The more he studied the painting, the more her skill astonished him.

"How did you become a painter? And is that storage closet back there your studio?"

"Sometimes I stay after work and paint. As for how I learned, why don't I tell you tonight over dinner?"

There was a charm behind her way of talking to him, and it drew him closer to her.

"I'll be back at seven."

"I close at eight."

"I'll be back at eight then," he said, smiling at her.

As she carried the painting back, he gave it a final glance. He could barely make out the girl's thin neck, and her head seemed to float above her body as if about to fly away.

"Look at that," Nathan said, pointing over the side of the boat.

Concentration nearly drew Le's eyebrows together as she laid her chopsticks across her rice bowl and turned to the river. "Look at what?"

At first he thought she was joking. Then he thought she'd gone blind. "That enormous boat with yellow lights. It's decorated to look like a shark."

She looked again. "Not a shark. A giant fish."

"Whatever it is, it's ridiculous."

"It's clever," she said in all seriousness. "But I prefer this boat. I like live entertainment."

In her wide, lustrous eyes he could see the lightshow unfold behind him. It almost seemed like the music was meant to distract passengers from the boat's late departure.

On the landing, dozens of people huddled together to watch the boats come and go. Although the bright downtown towered behind them, none of the people looked like they belonged there. There was something distinctly un-city-like in how they dressed, and in their faces was a bewilderment he'd known when he first arrived in Saigon. It was unsettling to recognize a part of himself in these people, who'd been staring at him and Le since they were seated.

Looking beyond the crowd, he thought it was better that night had fallen. Night masked the city's filth. On the busy streets and sidewalks, all the neon drew one's attention away from it. Saigon was almost beautiful at night.

Their boat finally lurched from the dock, its engine popping from the exertion. On the opposite bank, among billboards shining brilliantly over the water, Nathan spotted a giant Eurowindow advertisement. Across the bottom looped the words *Cửa sổ nhìn ra thế giới*: Windows looking out onto the world.

Bats skimmed the river, their angled wings absorbing the advertisements' reflections, before corkscrewing away into the night.

The city slid away. Boson Port emerged where District One became District Two, and soon they passed huge ships and petrol islands and tall derricks rising into the sky. The boat's music echoed off the steel hulls they drifted past.

"This is more than I expected," Le said. She reached across the table to squeeze his hand. "Thank you."

"I just want to know you better."

Reddening slightly, she released his hand to refill his beer. "You don't have to woo me. I'm true to my word if you're worried about that."

Her matter-of-factness took him aback. Didn't she see the value in what they were doing?

"I'm not the one who needs to worry." He waited until he had her full attention before continuing. "If our arrangement means we have to be strangers, you'd better find someone else to help you. I never agreed to that."

She looked at him in surprise. "I don't want us to be strangers, either. I just meant that you don't have to second-guess me. When I say something, it's true."

A waitress in a teal-green dress, and so much powder on her face that she resembled a caricature of a Chinese opera singer, replaced their empty rice dish with a full one. The boat was graced with a few minutes of tranquility as the singer stepped off-stage.

Le leaned forward and pointed to a docked cargo-carrier they were passing. "I like that ship."

There was nothing special about it as far as Nathan could tell. Anyway, what was to admire in a cargo ship?

She pointed at the French flag atop it. "It's beautiful at night, billowing in the wind."

When asked if she had a particular affinity for France, she shook her head and said her heart was set on America.

"You don't have apprehensions about going there? It's a big change to leave Vietnam and move to America."

"What are you asking?"

He chose his words carefully. "What I'm asking is: how do you uproot yourself from the only life you know and move to America? And how do you afford it?" It felt gauche to ask, but coming from Vietnam it was practical to think about money.

"I don't know. Maybe the same way you did when you moved to Vietnam."

"That's different."

"How is it different?"

"America's expensive, for one thing."

"Everyone knows that. Anyway, I can survive on less money than Americans can."

He cleared his throat and went on with a softened voice. "It's a lot more complicated being an immigrant in America than it is building on the life you have here."

"You managed to do it."

"Le," he said, staring at her across the table. "First of all, it's easy for me to make a living here. English teaching jobs are a dime a dozen. And second, I didn't immigrate to Vietnam."

"Isn't what you're doing the same thing?"

The absurdity of her question annoyed him, but then it shocked him that he could be so dismissive. For all intents and purposes this was in fact his home. The difference was that, while he might choose to live in Vietnam, he'd never relinquish his citizenship. "I'm living here," he answered, "not immigrating."

Her voice, once she'd regained enough composure to respond, was defiant. "You don't even know me. The only difference between us is that you were born with privilege. Me? I was born in a dirty hospital with no electricity, no medicine, in one of the poorest cities in the world. People here were starving when I was born. That's the biggest difference between us. That, and your passport lets you go anywhere."

If this was to be their first fight, he hoped it wouldn't unfold before so many people. He picked at his food, feigning equanimity.

"But because I'm from America," he said gently, "I know it's often hard there for newcomers. Making a life there isn't as easy as people think."

"I've heard all this before from my uncle."

The word she used – *chú* – rang hollowly in his ears. Was she referring to a blood relation or someone who simply fell under the category of "parent's younger brother"? Everyone called Ho Chi Minh "Bác Hồ." Although *bác* meant "father's older brother," it was, in this case, only a respectful form of address. The term she used with him, *anh*, meant "older brother," just as *em*, the term he used with her, meant "younger sister." There were more than twenty forms of address in Vietnamese, and he still hadn't figured them all out.

"Your uncle?"

"He lives in Los Angeles and is sponsoring me."

It was unexpected. Nathan believed her and yet he couldn't digest it right away.

She extracted several pieces of folded paper from her bag and slid them across the table.

"What's this?"

"Since you insist on talking business over dinner..."

He glanced at her before taking up the papers. She was smiling but looking at him challengingly. He read aloud the large print at the top of the page: "Immigrant Visa Procedures. Consulate General of the United States of America."

"I made a copy for you this afternoon."

"You want to do this now?"

"No," she said sharply. "I'm just giving them to you."

"I suppose you want me to fill these out."

"Not everything. Only the lines I marked with an 'X'."

Flustered, he re-folded them and stuffed the square he'd made in a pocket.

"The paperwork is half-finished," she added. "I've even had a first interview."

He knew he should congratulate her, but his own feelings, growing more complicated by the moment, got in the way.

The boat slipped beneath a bridge. Yellow light illuminated the underside of the arch, where the scrawled names of lovers had faded into oblivion. It was like entering a cave; a chill swept over him, and the buzz of traffic overhead grew muffled.

The boat returned quickly to the open river. There were no tall buildings here, no docked ships. On both sides and straight ahead there was only teeming darkness.

He broke their silence to ask about her family.

"What do you want to know?" she said, staring across the river.

"Whatever you want to tell me."

She wiped her mouth with her napkin. Then she slowly shook her head and said something he couldn't hear.

"What did you say?"

Again, she didn't answer.

"Do you have brothers and sisters?"

When she looked at him there was something flinty behind her eyes.

"My parents might have had more than one child if my father hadn't died," she said. "Most of my aunts and uncles are dead, too. Some from the war, some because life was even harder after it ended. My mother ran away to escape a sad life. I wasn't a joy to her, but a burden on top of other burdens. For all I know, she's dead, too. Dead like the leaders of my commune who raised me after she left. I've been on my own since I was sixteen."

He felt ashamed for having pressured her about her past.

"My uncle's my last family, and I've never even met him. Still, he's promised to bring me to America. That's all you need to know."

Just when he thought his chance to get closer to her was lost, she reached across the table again and grabbed his hand. The warm look in her eyes was unexpected. It wasn't that she was forgiving him, for he was sure she understood his sincerity. If anything, she seemed to be imploring him not to give up on her.

"When will you go to America?"

"I don't know. It's harder now than ever before to get an immigrant visa. But I have faith in myself."

"I didn't realize you'd done anything concrete to make it happen."

"I haven't told anyone. Some people, if they know, will get jealous."

He thought about this and smiled. "Then why did you tell me?"

"You're different," she said.

He didn't push for more. The evening would be too easily lost, and the river cruise was something he wanted them to enjoy.

As a gesture, he removed her visa application from his pocket, flattened it out beside his plate, and began to examine it.

Le didn't like his suggestion to follow up dinner at a riverside café in Thanh Da, or at a jazz club on Le Loi Street downtown. When he asked what she felt like doing she said: "Can I choose?"

"Of course."

On his motorbike, leaning into him from behind, she directed him through traffic to a building lined with Klieg lights. A small army of young women in tight red tank tops and yellow miniskirts crowded around the entrance, handing out Red Label promotions.

"You come here a lot?" Nathan said, amazed by her choice of destination.

"It's been a long time."

Before he could stop her, she paid both their entrance fees. She handed him his ticket and drink coupon.

"Let me pay," he said.

"That's okay."

"But you paid for dinner."

She shook her head. "Business was good today."

It wasn't strange to be treated to dinner by a Vietnamese, who often took pride in the public transaction, but here, with a local woman, it was different. He was too slow at this sort of thing.

"You make me feel like a bad date," he said.

"Date?" Trapped in her face was a laugh. "Is that what this is?"

Remembering their earlier conversation, he was reminded of the difference in their expectations. "To me it is."

"A foreigner once told me that a date means there's an obligation between a man and woman. But I knew he was trying to take advantage of me."

"I'm sorry that happened to you. Anyway, I didn't mean anything by it."

"No obligations?"

"No obligations," he said.

"You're funny," she said, releasing her long-held laugh.

He followed her into the disco. He'd been here once, back when Anthony lived in Saigon, but now he hardly recognized it. It had been remodeled since then, with a new floor added and the stage enlarged. The atmosphere in these places tended toward seediness, with bar girls keeping their eyes peeled for foreign men. This obviously hadn't changed. Fake smoke curled around the women's high heels as they sauntered between tables, trying to sit beside customers. If they succeeded, an exorbitant "conversation fee" would be charged when the customer tried to leave. This had happened to him and Anthony. Even back then Anthony had paid the bill blithely, finding the whole scam humorous. Perhaps it was because the girl had given him her number.

On their way to a corner table they passed a group of old, well-dressed men who broke into smiles when they saw Le.

"We haven't seen your pretty face in ages," one of them called out. "Pink hair looks good on you."

She ignored their invitations to join them.

"You can see your friends if you want," Nathan said when they sat down. Doubting that these men had bought paintings from her gallery, he was curious about her relationship to them.

"I used to work here," she said nonchalantly, handing their drink coupons to a waitress. Le looked at him, waiting for his response.

"As a table girl?"

"At first I painted wall designs. Then I drew pictures for their menu. But when that ended I made drinks behind the bar. Sometimes I worked the floor after a girl got fired or walked out."

Scattered throughout the disco were easily forty girls, many of them picking at their suffocating outfits. He had a hard time imagining Le working in a place like this.

"When was that?"

"I quit two years ago. I was trying to make enough money to open my gallery."

"You made enough here to open a gallery?" he asked incredulously.

"No, I made decent money here, but it was dead-end work. Some customers offered to help me, but I didn't trust their motives."

"How did they try to help?" he said.

"With envelopes stuffed with money. But the bills were so small that it never amounted to much. Fifty thousand *dong*, one hundred thousand. How can you open a gallery with so little?"

"Then how'd you manage?"

"My uncle," she said after a moment. "My uncle lent me the money."

She seemed a rare combination of artist and pragmatist. If he had only half her pragmatism, he might not be saddled with so much debt. But maybe the difference between them was simpler than that: she was willing to take risks.

"I haven't met many artists as pragmatic as you. Most of them want to do nothing but their art. They're poor, but happy."

Her expression tightened, as if the word 'pragmatic' offended her. "The gallery is a means to an end. If I weren't planning to move to America, I'd devote myself exclusively to painting. It's probably the only thing that would bring me back to Hanoi, in fact. Vietnamese lacquer painting is a northern tradition, and Hanoi's full of poor but dedicated artists."

"What will you do in America? As far as I know, Vietnamese lacquer painting doesn't exist there."

"I don't know," she said curtly. "The world will open up for me there. As a painter, I can do anything."

The waitress returned with their drinks, hovering behind Le afterward as if trying to determine if her pink hair was natural.

"You don't seem to know any of the girls working here," he said.

"I worked here a long time ago, and places like this have a high turnover."

"Did you like working here?"

"No. But sometimes I like to come back. It puts my life into perspective." Her expression became contemplative. "You've asked me many questions, especially about when I was young. But there's a lot I can't remember. I've forgotten so much about my childhood, for example, people say I'm like an old woman."

"Why do you think you've forgotten?"

She shrugged. "Some things aren't important to remember. Other things I just forget. But that's not always true. I remember sunsets, the

fields I played in as a child, and festivals in my grandparents' villages –
yet I can hardly recall my father's face."

At the mention of her father, he began to speculate on her reluctance to discuss her family. He feared that her earlier reticence
stemmed from a desire to protect him. Maybe he was only paranoid
about his country's history here, but she was from the North, and the
possibility existed that a few decades ago American bombers had killed
them.

From his own experience learning about the lives of Vietnamese
friends, he'd heard personal accounts about family members killed by
American forces. And although these accounts weren't as guilt-
inducing as My Lai, they were still devastating and silenced him on the
spot.

He couldn't ask her to tell him more than she already had. A time
would come, he hoped, when she'd raise the subject herself.

She stood and gazed at the dance floor. From a gentle rocking, her
body began to sway.

"I like this song," she said. She reached for his arm and pulled him
onto the dance floor.

She moved with a grace and prowess that seemed suddenly
unleashed, and he saw that everyone in the disco was watching her. She
didn't notice them, however, nor couldn't, for her eyes were closed as if
to keep everything far away.

Dry ice from the stage sent white smoke across the floor, slithering
around their bodies and screening them from the audience. From the
disco-balls overhead, flashing colors caressed her body like a madness of
hands.

But before the next song ended he felt something was wrong. The
feeling had nothing to do with where they were, or who was watching,
or what words he imagined were being spoken about them. Rather, it
had to do with Le's eyes, which she continued to keep shut. He felt
that he, and everyone watching her, was intruding on something that
would be better kept private. There was an air of intimacy to her movement, a sense of freedom not quite appropriate for this place and these
people. Her movements were neither awkward nor unfamiliar, yet he
felt like he'd never observed this way of dancing before. As he peered

around, the expressions of people in the crowd seemed to confirm this. He pulled her off the floor.

"I don't like us being the only people dancing," he told her.

She looked around but didn't acknowledge that there was anything strange or uncomfortable about the way all these people were watching them. When she spoke, her irritation was plain.

"So, do you want to leave?"

"Yes."

"Where do you want to go?"

"I don't know. But I don't like this place."

When they passed a section of tables filled with glaring Vietnamese men, she kept her head down, as if she felt they were collectively chastising her, or as if she'd come to realize that as the only interracial couple here they were a spectacle.

It would be the same wherever they went. They became a spectacle again when they were back on the street and stopped at a traffic light.

"They're all looking at us," she said.

"Do what I do every day and ignore them." He rearranged the mirror over his handlebars so he could see her face. "And look at me all the time instead."

It was past midnight when Le's cell phone rang. Rather than respond to the question he'd asked her – if she lived with friends or alone – she dug through her purse to answer the call.

She stared at her phone's screen. The transformation of her face to unalloyed pleasure dismayed him. She took the call breathlessly, not with the standard "*A-lo*?" but with something longer and familiar, as if she were continuing a conversation.

Without looking at him she rose from her seat and hurried down the sidewalk, away from the soup-stand's noise. Even from twenty feet away, her laugh, more buoyant than it had been all night, pushed through the surrounding noise.

Who could have taken her away but a lover she'd kept secret? He tried not to let his imagination get the better of him.

As the sole foreigner among a dozen people at a midnight food stall, he felt conspicuous. Only in her absence did he notice the attention they were paying him. At one point he heard someone mutter that any girl with pink hair and a foreigner at her side must be a whore. He shifted uncomfortably in his seat and tried to hear what Le was saying. But she was too far away. When a waitress passed by, he paid her.

When he looked back at Le, her profile reminded him of the painting she had shown him. Her gift as a painter, he thought, might take her somewhere. But he thought she'd go farther as an artist here than in America.

Twenty minutes later she returned, fingering the pad of her phone. "I'm sorry. I have to go home."

"I figured as much."

They walked to the parking area. She was smiling, lost in thought.

"Where do you live?" he said.

He thought she might live in a back room of her gallery, or somewhere on the building's upper two floors. Many people who came from the countryside couldn't afford a room in Saigon. For five dollars a month the owner of one of his favorite restaurants let several guards and waiters sleep on the floor, or atop tables pushed together after closing.

"I rent an apartment in Thanh Binh district." She added almost boastfully: "I can see airplanes come and go from the top of my building. Sometimes I climb the stairs at night and try to imagine where the airplanes are coming from, where they're going. What languages the passengers speak, why they're coming to Vietnam. Have you ever watched a plane land from the top of a far-away building?"

Nathan shook his head.

"At first they're specks in the darkness, tiny as stars. But as they approach they become great balls of light. And when a plane lifts off, the light in the passenger windows makes the plane look like a bar of fire. It's beautiful before it flies too far away."

He exchanged his parking ticket for his motorbike and rolled it into the street.

"Maybe we can do this again sometime," he said, despite the evident futility of pursuing a relationship with her.

"Of course. That's what we agreed on."

"But I'd want to even without an agreement."

"Why?"

Her question hammered the point home, but he couldn't give up this quickly.

"Because I want to see you again. Not as part of an agreement, either. I'll help you regardless."

Her eyes widened. "But I'm going to leave in a few months."

He didn't reply. Her skepticism made him think she was being cold or was testing him. Or maybe she only wanted a little fun.

"It's complicated," she said, climbing onto his motorbike.

"No more than anything else."

"Sometimes you're strange, Nathan."

It was the last thing he wanted to hear. He thought they'd had a good time together, but this made him re-evaluate the entire evening, starting from the gallery. This, after the call she took, made him want to say something that would hurt her just a little.

He pulled into the street. Feeling her arms around him was a painful pleasure. He guessed it was the last time she'd do this.

"You're strange to me, too," he said over his shoulder. "It's strange to take a call this late when you're already out with me." He felt her arms loosen, and in the mirror above his accelerator he watched her grin fade. "Or should I say it's strange that you're out with me when you expect other men to call?"

She laughed, as if his words, harshly spoken, were a joke. When she saw he was serious she smacked him on the shoulder.

"You don't know what you're talking about."

"Then enlighten me."

"The call was from my uncle."

"Does he always call you this late?" he said, unable to keep the pettiness from creeping into his voice.

"No, but he often forgets what time it is here."

"It's after midnight."

She let her arms slip from him. "He knows I keep odd hours."

"So why'd he call?"

"To tell me he'd met an art professor from a local university. The man promised to help me."

Like a moment ago, when she dropped her embrace, he felt something vital – not just to his happiness, but to the meaningfulness of his life here – fall away.

"If you go," he said, "will you stay there?"

"Yes."

"And that's what you want? Or is that what your uncle wants?"

"We both want it. We're all we have left of each other – of our family." As if she was afraid of talking more about her family or herself, she shifted the conversation back to him. "And how long will you be in Vietnam?"

"I don't even know how long I'll be in Saigon. A friend in Hanoi offered me a job." He paused to let a kicking petulance die inside him. When he spoke, he found he still wanted to hurt her for taking her uncle's call. "I may have to leave Saigon in six weeks. Sooner if possible."

In his mirror he saw her shrug as if to say you've got your life and I've got mine, and the commitments we make are worth little. He knew she must wonder why he hadn't told her this before.

He dropped her off at the gallery and waited on the sidewalk for her to retrieve her motorbike and lock up again.

"I hope you stay in Saigon," she said.

"Why?" His staying only made sense in the context of her doing the same.

"Because our agreement is pointless if you're going to leave in a month or two."

As soon as the words left her mouth, he regretted what he'd said. Perhaps she was right that entering into anything now was pointless. More than ever before, Hanoi seemed a distant prospect now, and the job he'd nearly begged for had begun to lose its luster. She would be the only reason to stay in Saigon. He knew that the only more distant prospect than being happy in Saigon was being in love. Lust was nothing special. It was easy and it was everywhere.

"I haven't decided to do anything yet," he said.

"But I can't ask you to change your plans or give up a good opportunity."

"You can. I'm more accommodating than you realize." He stopped himself from going on. Inside him, he felt a clawing of something desperate to get out.

"Don't say that," she said, pressing the starter to her Future.

"Why not?"

"Because of the betrayal you'll feel when I leave. I know what that's like, and I don't want you blaming me."

He stayed there long after she'd driven away, wondering if it was the bluntness of her statement or its undressed honesty that pained him so much.

5

Nathan cleared his bedroom floor and laid down a map of Dong Nai province. He found Buu Long ward, bisected by Route 768 and dotted with lakes and ponds. Many were in an area with "Tourist Spot" stamped in red.

Three days ago, a local magazine editor asked him for an article on Buu Long Mountain. Only twenty-five miles northeast of Saigon, the trip would be easy, and six hundred words was little work for a commission that would cover half his final month of rent.

The telephone on his desk rang. Assuming it was Le, he wondered why she wouldn't try to reach him on his cell.

No one responded when he picked up and said hello, though he heard voices in the background and papers shuffling.

"Hello?" he said again.

"Nate? It's Anthony."

It was mid-April, near the end of the dry season, and Nathan had managed not to speak with him since leaving Hanoi. Le had become his priority over the last two weeks, and his preparations for moving north had stalled. With the extra writing work he'd been assigned, he had little extra time. The work was more profitable than usual, which he thought, ironically, might herald a change of fortune.

"I've been trying to get hold of you for two weeks. Where the hell have you been?"

"I've been out a lot. Why didn't you call my other number?"

"Because someone at work stole my cell phone and I never recorded your number anywhere else. Did you get the ticket I sent? It went out by overnight express four days ago."

"Yes." The ticket protruded from beneath a copy of the *Saigon Times* and a Styrofoam container of old takeaway. Nathan had tossed the ticket there after seeing the flight was one-way. The only relief he'd felt was that the ticket didn't even cost one hundred dollars. If he never used it, the money would hardly be worth worrying about. "I was going to let you know, but I've been swamped."

"It would've taken you two minutes to tell me. You call, say you got it, explain you can't talk. I accept it without question and I'm grateful. But don't leave me hanging. I deserve better than that."

"I should have called."

This seemed to appease Anthony, for when he spoke again he sounded calmer.

"In the note I attached I mentioned that you can change your departure date, but I need you here by the end of the month."

"I may need a few more weeks. I can't just up and leave right now."

"Up and leave? This isn't some surprise. We had an agreement."

"I hate to say it but I'm halfway out the door. Can I call you back?"

"What do I have to do to talk with you?"

"I'll call you later, I promise."

"What's your promise worth?" Anthony cleared his throat, and Nathan knew what he was working up to. "I sent you three e-mails in the last few days and you never replied to any of them. I was worried that something had happened to you. Like a motorbike accident, or that you'd fallen ill."

"No, nothing like that."

"Don't tell me you took another job."

There was no reason to tell him about the travel piece he was doing – at least not yet.

"I started seeing someone," he said.

There was a pause on the other end, and very faintly, somewhere in the background, Nathan thought he heard someone being strangled.

"What?"

"I said I'm seeing someone."

Anthony's laughter sounded less scornful than disbelieving, and Nathan waited for him to stop before asking what was funny.

"Nothing," Anthony said, sober again. "Who is she?"

"You don't know her."

"Is it that pink-haired girl?" he snapped.

"Yes."

"After Huong, I thought you gave up on locals."

Out his window Nathan saw a motorbike pull onto the sidewalk. Le got off and, in the side mirror, fixed her windblown hair.

"I just never found anyone I could be happy with."

"And when did you fall in love?" His tone had turned nasty, and 'love' came out sounding like a dirty word.

"I never said I did."

"You're going to stay in Saigon now, aren't you? That's why you've been avoiding me."

"She plans to go to California. She says her paperwork is..."

"Every Vietnamese has a plan to leave, Nate. All our students back in the day used to spout off about going to America. The cyclo drivers under the tree by our school said the same thing when we got coffee outside before classes: they'd put in applications at the consulate or had some obscure relation twice removed who promised to fly them to America. Huong had the same plan. Marrying me was the first step, but I never took her away." A moment passed as Anthony refocused on his original concern. "Don't tell me you're backing out. Not after all the trouble I've gone through to help you."

"I know what you've gone through." Nathan couldn't find the right words, and hoped he didn't sound insincere. "But I can't walk away from her, not now."

"What do you mean 'not now'? Did you get her pregnant?"

"No. But it's been a long time since I found anyone worth getting to know."

"Nate," he almost shouted, "she's hardly the only great girl in this country. Get up here, man. You can't afford to pass on what I'm offering. You owe me, remember." He seemed to think he knew what Nathan was going to say, because without prompting he touched on the subject of fate. It made him sound the more desperate. "Nothing's ever meant to be. Fate's just a kind of propaganda that humanity's been leaning on for thousands of years – and the Vietnamese more than anyone."

Nathan heard Le climbing the stairs to his room.

"Like I said, this is a bad time. We're about to go to Dong Nai."

"Dong Nai?"

"I'll tell you later. I need to go."

"Tell me now. I don't want to wait another two weeks."

Le was at his door, knocking and calling his name.

"Hold on." He set the phone down and jumped over his bag to let her in. "I'm on the phone," he told her as she walked to his bed and fell backward onto the mattress.

"Who is it?"

"Anthony."

She glanced at her watch. "The later we leave, the hotter it'll be."

Frowning, Nathan picked up the phone. "Sorry, I had to let Le in." On the other end Anthony was quiet. "Can I call you tonight? We'll hash things out then, I swear."

There was no telling what Anthony was thinking in his silence.

"Anthony? Hello?"

A series of shrill beeps made him flinch. The line had been disconnected.

"What did he want?" Le asked, sitting up.

Nathan didn't answer.

"Does he want you to come to Hanoi earlier?"

"He just wanted to talk." He sat next to her. She had paint on her chin, and he wiped it off with his thumb.

"What did you tell him?"

"I told him I'd met you. And that you meant more to me than his job offer."

He thought he saw disappointment in her face. Or maybe she thought his answer was stupid.

"But a job's important, and the salary's good."

"Money's not everything."

She began collecting bottled water from the refrigerator and sun cream for their trip. "Don't you owe him a lot of money?"

"Yes, but he said I could pay him back any time. I didn't even want to borrow it, but he was so overbearing that I..." The holes in his argument had begun to breathe; he heard them whistling as he tried to justify what he was doing. He shook his head, disgusted by the situation.

"You're giving up the job?"

Her questions were sharp, as if she were accusing him of a crime. But what did she want him to do – leave her to repay a loan one or two years earlier than if he stayed in Saigon and took on extra work? Since leaving Hanoi, his desperation had given way to a hopefulness that centered on Le. With her he felt closer to a future he'd always wanted. As long as he had a plan to repay Anthony, he felt that things would be okay. The problem was that he had no plan.

"I don't know," he said, shouldering his bag. "Let's go. I'll deal with Anthony later."

Buu Long Mountain's temple priest agreed to meet Nathan and answer his questions. The man was generous with his time and Nathan donated to the temple's upkeep before leaving.

Le stayed outside for the hour Nathan was gone. Sometimes he'd glimpse her through the temple door, sitting on a low wall beside the giant Bodhisattva statue and sketching in a small pad she kept in her purse.

The Bodhisattva was the temple's most impressive aspect. Although seated in a lotus position, it was still so large that it resembled a windblown cloud rising from the mountaintop. A bottle of rice wine had been placed in the circle of its fingers and it hung there upside-down.

It was two o'clock when Nathan left the temple to look for Le. He found her squatting at the edge of an overlook. Squatting made her more Vietnamese in his eyes and he imagined how she'd look doing that in America; at a bus shelter, say, or in a crowded mall, or beside the entrance to a trendy café.

A lush vista came into view as he approached her. The valley below was a palette of monsoon colors: a deep green of banana, acacia, and fan-shaped palm trees; of rice fields and wild grasses and clay-red roads; and brown rivers and streams winding through it all like the veins of some tropical fern magnified a thousand times. Over distant treetops rose a yellow-white spire. The priest had told him that Tan Trieu church, the oldest church in southern Vietnam, could be seen from here.

A plastic bag flew across his vision. After watching it pass between the mountaintop and street, his eyes settled on Long An Lake, a short walk away. The lake's edge was black from the shadows of surrounding trees, but its center reflected the sky. On the far side were what appeared to be the jagged remains of a former mountain, and young lovers pedaled around them in swan-shaped boats.

Nathan came up beside Le.

"Do you ever think it's strange that you live in Vietnam?" she said, leaning against his leg.

"This is where I want to be now. My life here's interesting." He stopped talking when he sensed she was asking something else. "If you're talking about the war, that was a long time ago. It had nothing to do with me."

"Do you want to be Vietnamese?"

He shook his head. "I'm American. That won't change no matter where I live."

"You sound so sure of yourself."

"I am sure."

He sat down and she hugged his arm. "So if I live the rest of my life in America, I'll still be Vietnamese?"

Never in all his years living abroad did he question himself in this way, and it wasn't anything he had much interest in. But her eyes showed earnestness, and he couldn't say what he thought. Who she was when they were together meant more to him than that she was Vietnamese.

"Part of you always will be."

"And if I become an American citizen, it's only a piece of paper. A person's blood doesn't change when they leave where they were born, does it?"

He shrugged, even less interested in such talk. He leaned forward, peering down at the valley below them.

"It's the same with you," she went on. "You're not Vietnamese, even if you do speak the language."

"I don't want to be Vietnamese."

"Of course you don't," she said. "And I don't want to be American."

She leaned her head on his shoulder, and the soft pink hair on his cheek was warm from the sun and redolent with a perfume that never seemed to leave her.

"There's nothing wrong with that," he said. "Lots of Vietnamese who left after the war have come back. They did well for themselves overseas and now they're helping Vietnam do better."

"My country has many problems."

"Every country does."

She reached behind them to her bag. "Aren't you hungry?"

"I'm starving," he said, granting her the change of subject.

As she removed a rolled-up mat and spread it between them, he realized no one was around them. The only sign of other people was the miscellany of narrow, tile-roofed houses between the jungle and river below. But even down there no people were visible. The rolling heat meant it was the hour of siesta. He imagined entire families sleeping on the floors of their homes, their warm limbs overlapping.

She shook out a plastic bag and scattered its contents on the mat: baguettes filled with grilled meat, pickled vegetables, and seasoned pâté; hard boiled eggs and steamed buns; and two custard apples, their bumpy green rinds blackening from the heat.

Biting into his sandwich, Nathan shared with her what the priest had told him about Tan Trieu. "I forgot to ask him what Tan Trieu means."

"It's Chinese," she said, passing a water bottle to him. "It means New Dynasty."

He couldn't recall which dynasty the name referred to. "There was a kingdom here?"

"No. But it was once home to exiled kings. Since we're so close, I'd like to visit."

"What's your interest in it?"

Handing him a hardboiled egg she said: "The idea of exile."

As he peeled the eggshell, his mind turned over what she said. He shouldn't be surprised she knew Tan Trieu as a place of exile, but her interest suggested that she identified with it. He still wasn't convinced she'd soon leave but felt that she often let her dreams take over and run rampant.

Even so, what she said made him wonder what it meant to be exiled. To live away from one's native country, of course, for whatever reasons. But how difficult was the journey, and where did it end? What did exile do to a person, and what sort of person would choose to exile herself from the place her identity had been formed? What was he, and what had contributed to his becoming that way? Most people he grew up with had rarely left Ohio, much less American shores, and yet here he was, halfway around the world, in a country that had defeated America in war, where his skin, hair, and eyes marked him as foreign, and where his view of the world was so different from everyone else's.

If he was an exile, he'd become one by choice. There would come a time when returning to America would no longer be possible. He knew this and thought about it often.

He tried to imagine what Le envisioned of the years ahead but couldn't come up with an answer.

"I've decided something," she said as if voicing the conclusion to a problem she'd been mulling over. "If my visa application gets rejected, I want you to stay in Saigon. I don't want you leaving me behind."

Strangely, her words seemed to embarrass her. She stared at the ground, not even brushing away her hair when it slipped from behind her ears and swept her eyes. Her shrouded face gave the impression that her hair was blushing.

And then he realized that she could mean anything by what she'd said. She could be admitting that she loved him just as she could be suggesting that she viewed him as her ticket to America. This sort of muddle was emblematic of his experiences with Vietnamese women.

"Do you want to go to Tan Trieu?" she said.

There was excitement in her voice, and he interpreted it as the feeling she had being with him. Still, her enigmatic statement had left him hesitant.

"I'm willing if you are."

They climbed down the mountain's steps, avoiding the outstretched cups of several crouching, deformed beggars. From the road he looked up at the Bodhisattva.

Le waited in the street while he retrieved his motorbike. When he came up to her, he asked if she knew the way.

"We can ask for directions at a roadside stand."

"They'll want us to buy something."

"Then I'll buy something, you cheapskate."

He had a hard time starting his motorbike, but finally managed to and pulled onto the dusty road. The air was hot, fragrant with citrus, and pomelo stands dotted both shoulders. What looked like old fishing nets hung from them, weighted with the green, gumdrop-shaped fruit. They approached a stand, purchased a pomelo, and got directions.

The sky was a marbled blue now, and sunshine brightened the phoenix tree canopies along the road. Gated mansions – weekend getaways of Saigon's newly rich – were set one hundred feet down driveways that had been hacked through the surrounding canebrake. A long dirt road wound between two enormous houses; above it hung a placard that read: Dang's Pomelo Orchard and Riverside Café. Nathan slowed down at Le's insistence.

"What about here?" she said.

Passing through the bamboo gate, he questioned again what she'd said at Buu Long. If he were willing to stay in Saigon for her, what more was he willing to do? And if he went to Hanoi, what then? He'd have the upper hand if her visa application were rejected. But this was only to his advantage if she loved him.

Sunlight pierced the treetops. Driving through alternating sun and shade, what lay before them unfurled in blinding flashes. At the bottom of a slope stretched a narrow brown river. Thatch huts strewed the near bank.

He parked under a grove of trees, then followed Le into the largest hut.

Inside, a woman in a threadbare yellow shirt and gray pants lay in a hammock with a newspaper over her face. Hearing them enter she stood and brought them a laminated drinks list. They sat at a table and ordered tea. Nathan looked out the window.

At one end of the river four evenly-spaced bamboo poles jutted from the water. Attached to each was the corner of a net, the large middle of which remained submerged. Two boatmen were raising the net with a hand-crank.

A crane in the treetops spread its wings and launched toward the river's edge. Three more followed from the jungle's green shade. The birds eyed the fishermen as they reeled in the net and picked their catch.

Nathan leaned forward, mesmerized by the scene, when an earthen vase on the sill caught his attention. He was taken by the antiquated pottery, which held a spray of star-shaped flowers. Despite the increasing number of upscale antique shops around Saigon, the vase was unlike anything he'd seen. There was something impressive about the pocked clay sides and serpentine etchings, something authentic and rare. He was surprised to come across a vase like this in the middle of Dong Nai. He took it in his hands to examine it.

"Careful with that…"

Nathan turned to see the tea seller hurrying over.

"It's several hundred years old."

Nathan's grip tightened. Shocked at the casualness with which he'd been handling the vase, he carefully handed it to her.

She grabbed the wilted flowers and tossed them out the window. The woman dried the vase with the bottom of her shirt and offered to let Nathan inspect it again.

He took it again carefully. "Why are you using this if it's so old?"

"What would I do with it if I didn't?"

"But where did you get it?" he said. "And how do you know it's old?"

Le clicked her tongue as if his questions were impolite.

"We were digging a well by our house," the woman said, pointing to another thatch dwelling downriver. Next to it was a meter-high circle of cement with a slatted board across the top. Beside the well was a plastic bucket attached to a rope. "We had to dig two days to reach water. Around the third meter we came upon ten pieces like this."

Turning it in his hands Nathan felt moved by this evidence that not everything connected to the past had been destroyed but was preserved deep in the guts of the land, as if the earth itself knew the value of these objects and didn't trust humans to care for them. The thought that other pieces would remain undiscovered for hundreds, maybe thousands of years longer also reassured him.

"They must be Khmer," he said.

The woman smiled, evidently pleased that he knew something of the local history. In fact he knew little, only that this region of Vietnam had once been Khmer, part of what was now Cambodia, and that in the fourteenth and fifteenth centuries the Vietnamese forced the Khmer south and west beyond the Mekong River. The brutal Khmer Rouge incursions of 1978 had been inspired by this ancient land grab.

"There were enough pieces for everyone digging the well," the woman said.

Le leaned forward with newfound interest and fingered the whorls ringing the vase's mouth. "If you found these just digging a well, there must be more buried."

When the woman didn't respond, Nathan asked if she had dug anywhere else.

"There's no need to. Besides, who has the time or energy to dig for what might not even be there?"

All three of them looked toward the woman's home. A little boy stood naked on the porch, crying for his mother. The woman rose and walked into the sunshine, calling out to see what he wanted.

Nathan watched Le inspect the vase again. "Don't you find it strange there's not more interest in these artifacts?" he asked her.

"Why is it strange for something time has protected this long to stay protected? Why must the past be dug up?"

"You don't think it's worth learning what's down there?"

"I only think it's lovely," she said. "It reminds me of Song Be pottery. Besides, who am I to say what's worth learning?"

Nathan couldn't get the Khmer pottery out of his mind. By what process had it been buried? And if such a perfect specimen could be dug up, what else was down there? Why was there no greater attempt to excavate these artifacts and learn about the past?

This land had originally been Khmer, not Vietnamese, and artifacts like this dated Tan Trieu far beyond first churches and exiled kings. Perhaps it was enough to have this vase, and to know that the past wasn't dead, only buried. Or maybe the woman made the past alive again simply by placing flowers in it every day.

He was reminded of a Saigonese man who'd told him about being imprisoned after the war. Despite having served in the southern regime as a doctor, he was sentenced to five years hard labor when the new government took over. One day, while digging trenches near a former American barracks, he unearthed a heap of books. When the Americans fled, he explained, they abandoned their military equipment and personal effects. Discovering old American magazines, comic books, or novels was no surprise. They were probably tossed outside by ransacking North Vietnamese soldiers and pushed into the soil by rain. The surprise was that he'd found one book in perfect condition, as if it had been placed there just before he unearthed it: a leather-bound Bible. When the day ended, he tucked it in his pants and brought it to his cell. Every night, at the risk of being caught and punished, he and a prisoner named Lam studied the Bible by moonlight. "That was a difficult time in my life," he said, "but that book saved me. It was all I had. I was a Christian – and still am – but the communists said that Christianity was an imperialist religion and whomever they suspected of being a follower was forced to renounce his faith. The greatest gift I ever received was that Bible. I felt like God had buried it in the midst of our privation and wanted me to dig it out." He rolled up his sleeve, exposing a faded tattoo: *For the Lord heareth the poor, and despiseth not his prisoners*. "Shortly after my release, Lam died. On his first death anniversary I got drunk and made my younger brother tattoo me."

The woman had gone to fetch the boy a towel. On her way back she chased her chickens from a flat basket of cashews drying in the sun.

When she entered the hut and sat on her hammock, Nathan asked if anyone in her family had fought with the Americans during the war. "My father and two of my older brothers. My other brother was too young to fight, but he died, anyway, after 1975."

Nathan was silent a moment. "Have you lived here all your life?"

She picked up her newspaper and started fanning herself with it. "My husband and I lived in Saigon until the war ended. He was just a translator, but still they put him in a re-education camp. That's him by all those rubber trees, bleeding them for sap."

Nathan was reminded of "the law of three-generations" – the former official policy of punishing "supporters of the imperial aggressors." Running a café out of a thatched hut on the outskirts of Bien Hoa was probably the only business this family had been allowed to engage in.

The sawing of the man's blade became audible only after the woman pointed it out. Nathan watched the man, shirtless and thin, cut diagonally at the bark with a scythe.

The woman offered to call her husband over.

"That's okay," Nathan said. "I was just trying to understand this place better."

The man was far enough away that when he stopped cutting, the sound continued another second.

"Why did you ask her so many questions?" Le said to him in English.

"She's an exile, too."

She shook her head, apparently annoyed by his way of looking at things. In Vietnamese she mumbled, "She's not an exile. For all you know, her ancestors are from here."

"What does that matter? Politics can be localized within one's own family."

"I don't care if your Vietnamese is perfect, Nathan: you'll never understand family politics in Vietnam. But if you insist on defining exile so broadly, go ahead. Call it exile if you want."

He couldn't understand her tone. If she disagreed with him that was fine, but her remonstrance, with a subtext of cultural conceit, took him aback. This was a land of exile. Not only had Vietnamese kings been made to live here after dethronement but the remnants of an ancient Khmer civilization, forced to stay unearthed, would never rejoin their homeland.

The more he considered this, the more he thought there was something to it. After all, here he was, an exile by choice – an expatriate – and here she was, soon to be an exile as well. Perhaps this was at the heart of her frustration with him.

The church bell chimed in the distance four times. Before the sound faded away the woman stepped outside again.

"We should think about going home," he said.

Le appeared not to hear. She was eyeing the vase again. "Do you think it's valuable?"

"I'm sure it's worth more than the woman realizes. Or maybe she knows but doesn't care."

"If you think it's valuable, we should come back at night and dig for more."

He assumed she was joking. "If we dig far enough, we might reach Angkor Wat. Think of the treasure we'd find there."

She looked at him. "Why did you say that?"

The hurt in her voice surprised him. "Were you serious?"

"It's obvious there are more vases waiting to be dug up. These people are too lazy to do it, so why don't we?"

"Because it's not our land, for one."

"That's why we do it at night."

"And because you'd have to do it by yourself. This is her property and what's on it – or beneath it – is hers. Anyway, I'm not that desperate for money."

"You don't have to be desperate," she said bitterly. "People make a living digging up old pottery, don't they?"

"They're called archaeologists," he said in disgust. "And they do it without wanting to enrich themselves."

His harsh tone had no impact on her. "Do you think she'd sell this to me? Would it be foolish to offer as much as three hundred thousand *dong* for it?"

The thought of giving the woman twenty dollars for this ancient, beautifully preserved vase repulsed him. "I'm sure it's worth more than that."

"But do you think she knows?"

"Ask her," he said.

"I'm going to take this. I bet she won't even notice it's gone."

"What?"

"You heard her say more could be dug up. What does she do all day but nap in a dirty hammock, hoping for a few customers? If she wanted, she could dig up dozens of these." She paused when Nathan laughed unkindly. "It's nothing for her to let one go. She only appreciates it as something to stick flowers in."

"You can't just take it," he said, hurling the words at her.

But Le was already stuffing it into her bag. "Leave some money on your chair. She'll be happier with that than this vase."

He yanked her bag away, spilling her cell phone, sketchbook and pencils, and a number of other articles. For good measure he tossed her bag onto what had fallen out. "Give me the vase." He rose from his chair and lifted it from her lap. When he had it, he walked outside to the woman and handed it to her. "What do I owe you?"

As he paid, the woman commented that he and Le made a good couple.

Nathan forced himself to smile.

"We don't get a lot of pink hair here," she went on in a friendly way. "There's an albino fellow who sells half-hatched eggs near Buu Long Mountain, though. His eyes and skin are pink; his hair has no real color. It's like the fiber on a coconut husk."

Nathan stepped away, commenting: "Pink's not her natural color."

The woman looked back at her hut and seemed to consider this.

He returned to where Le sulked in her chair. He picked up her bag and gathered its contents. He was in a hurry to leave.

Only when he started back to his motorbike did she get up. But rather than follow him she headed for the woman. Blinded by the sun, Nathan shielded his eyes to watch. The woman lifted the vase while Le pointed something out. He was too far away to hear them, but he knew what Le was doing. A moment later she fished her wallet from her bag. Not wanting to see the woman succumb to Le's pressure, which was surely nothing compared to the pressure of being poor, Nathan walked the rest of the way to his motorbike.

But when he tried the ignition, nothing happened. After ten tries he realized his battery was dead.

A few minutes later the crunch of shoes on the road told him Le had finished her transaction. He didn't know what he'd do if, entering his view, she was carrying the Khmer artifact. She hugged him from behind, forgetting the old indignation. He could tell she hadn't obtained it.

"She wouldn't sell it. But if I'd tripled my offer, I'm sure she would have."

Nathan wasn't sure if she'd given up or was hoping he'd lend her money. "My motorbike's dead. I have to push it into town and find a mechanic."

They started down the path, keeping in whatever shade the trees offered.

At the main road she stopped and looked at the darkening sky. "It's getting late."

"We're not far from Saigon. Even if it takes a few hours to get fixed, we can still return home at a decent hour."

"They won't work late."

"They work late everywhere when there's business."

"If it takes long," she said, "we'll have to spend the night."

He turned to her, hoping she'd conveyed an invitation. But her face, peering soberly down the street, indicated only practical concern.

No local mechanics had what he needed. Unless he wanted to take a bus back to Saigon and return the next day, they'd have to wait until morning.

Finding a place to stay was easy, as the area, popular with tourists, had several rundown hotels. No one hassled him about not having his passport, nor was sharing a room with Le a problem.

No sooner had he entered the room than he collapsed onto the bed. His face and arms were sunburned; even a shower felt like too much effort.

Le climbed on top of him and started rubbing his shoulders. Lying on his stomach with Le's knees below his armpits, he could see a portion of the room: an orange plastic chair pocked with cigarette burns, a worn green carpet, and a chipped wooden dressing table with a disposable comb on one side. In the corner was a bathroom with a frosted glass door. He closed his eyes, newly aware of a karaoke parlor next door. The faint, off-key singing disappeared as Le chopped at his back with the edges of both hands.

"What should we do tonight?" she said.

"I haven't thought about it," he mumbled into a moldy pillow.

She straightened up, still straddling his back. "Maybe we could have an exciting adventure."

"What do you have in mind?"

She didn't answer right away, and he raised himself slightly on the bed. With his fingertips he pulled at her chin so that her lips nearly touched his. She turned away.

Nathan leaned back onto the mattress. If he refused to acknowledge her rejection then he could believe it never happened. But when he looked at her face, resentment coursed inside him. "How do you really feel about me?" he said.

She started prodding at a cigarette burn in the bedsheet. He could see her fumbling for something to say.

"Are we simply two people helping each other? Or are we more? I need to know what you think about me. What you feel when we're together like this."

"I'm happy. I wouldn't be here with you if I weren't."

"That's all?"

"Isn't it enough to feel happy?"

"Do you like me, Le?"

"Sometimes."

He abruptly rolled from the bed to his feet. As his vantage changed, their hotel room struck him as smaller and dirtier than he'd first realized.

"What does 'sometimes' mean?" he said.

The vagueness of her replies passed into her expression. "I mean when I don't let myself think about the future."

What was she talking about? Everything she did was meant to get her that much closer to America, including being with him. She always thought about the future, so when she said 'sometimes' was she really telling him 'never'?

"I have a plan," she went on. "If it doesn't work out, I'll have to gamble more on my future."

They were each a gamble for the other, he thought. Of course, in Vietnam the risk was greater for a Vietnamese than an American, particularly when the former was a woman and the latter a man, which was nearly always the case. She'd be branded a whore by her own people and a gold-digger by foreigners, and if their relationship didn't end in marriage she'd have to move forward in life as one who'd taken a chance and lost. They both knew that foreign men were afforded any number of chances with women. He was expected to roam, and his passport meant he could always start over elsewhere.

"I know you have a plan," he said. "It just seems there might be a place for me in all your big, faraway dreams."

"You already have a place."

He crawled back on the bed and closed his eyes. The room turned quiet for a long moment. Finally he said, "What's this adventure you have in mind?" She didn't answer immediately, and her reticence made him open his eyes. The hint of a smile played on her lips.

"I was thinking that if we went back to that café at around midnight, we could dig up more vases."

He groaned loudly and sat up again. He felt like there was nothing he could say that he hadn't already.

"It would be easy to get a shovel," she went on, "and in two or three hours, with both of us digging–"

"What's your obsession with these vases?" Her behavior struck him as utterly out of character, and he couldn't help feeling repelled by her greed.

"You said yourself they're valuable."

"I have no idea, Le. We don't have any idea what that vase is worth. Or if she was even telling the truth." By the way Le crumpled the blanket in her fists he knew she was angry. "And so what if they're valuable? I'm not involving myself in any black market for antiquities. What if we're caught? People get executed by firing squad in your country for political corruption and selling drugs. Can you imagine what would happen to me as a foreigner?"

"You worry too much. If anyone catches us, once we explain what we're doing they'll want to help. They'll want in if they stand to gain something."

Nathan would never be convinced to do what she proposed. Yet he was certain she was right: she could pull this off because there was some demon driving her on, and because in Vietnam schemes like this were commonplace. The more elaborate they were, the more attractive they seemed to people.

Once when he was in Hue he met a cyclo driver who asked what he knew about Mexican freighters. Nathan had laughed at the question, admitting that he knew nothing. Deadly earnest, the man explained that he was planning to sneak aboard one. He'd hide in the hold, carrying nothing but a few gold bars, a loaded gun, and bags of dried fruit. When the ship docked in Mexico he'd find someone to exchange his gold for a U.S. passport.

"I know about the coyotes," he said. "I pay them three thousand dollars and they take me over the border in a fruit truck."

Nathan asked if he had that much in gold, but the man waved off the question.

In his fifties, a look of poor health draped his lank, leathery face, and a milky cataract trickled down one eye.

He said that because of his association with the losing side of the war he'd suffered intolerably the last thirty years. In a show of aggressive, overplayed bravado he claimed he'd kill to get to America. Getting caught, he said, wasn't an option.

"I'm ready to die. It's better than suffering the rest of my life here."

He grew agitated and, with his good eye gleaming feverishly, asked if Nathan thought he could succeed.

But Nathan wouldn't encourage him. "Not a chance. You'll end up in one of four places: a Vietnamese jail, a Mexican jail, or an American jail...or six feet underground."

As if Nathan had committed an injustice by speaking honestly, the man glared at him and then started pedaling down the street.

"*Đụ má*," he called over his shoulder, not realizing Nathan understood the profanity hovering in the hot air.

The memory aggravated Nathan's resentment toward Le, and he tried to dissuade her again. "What about the woman? Won't you be stealing from her?"

"I asked her if she owned the land around her café and she said no, but that she'd been living there for years. She has no claim to anything."

"You know what will happen if you get caught, don't you?"

"What?" The tone of her voice was challenging.

"The consulate will find out." He watched a hateful half-grin twist her beautiful mouth. "Even if you're merely accused," he went on, making this part up, "they'll rip up your application. No country will give you a visa if you have a criminal record. You'll never be allowed to leave Vietnam." He could see she hadn't considered the repercussions if her scheme went awry. "It's a stupid risk."

She sank down on the bed with her back to him. When she spoke, it was to the wall. "I could pay you if I had money."

"Pay me for what?"

"For the help you've given me."

Nathan shook his head, not wanting to be reminded of their agreement. "I don't want your money. I've helped you because I like you."

"I like you, too. But being able to pay you would make things less complicated."

"Complicated how?"

"You wouldn't understand."

"Le..."

She got up and went into the bathroom. Through the door he heard the bathtub fill with water.

She was still bathing when he drifted to sleep.

When he woke up the next morning the room smelled of garlic and fish sauce. He saw on the dressing table two Styrofoam boxes in a plastic bag. She'd apparently gone out to get dinner and brought him back something to eat.

Across the room, she was sleeping in a chair.

6

S pring had come, and with it butterflies in the early mornings; clear and cloudless skies; children flying kites at dusk; yellow and red *so ri* fruit sold on busy street corners; and intense, scorching heat – followed quickly by summer; not the end of sunshine (it never ended) but the start of rain, storms, two-hour squalls and flooded streets; children on school holiday; deeply green foliage; the wide flat tops of phoenix trees bursting with red flowers; more people on the streets enjoying the cooler, pleasanter nights; corncob stands turning the chemical air farm-y and sweet.

Opportunity, too, accompanied the change of season. July had snuck up, and Le's visa application had progressed. The consulate had summoned her for a final interview. Never had he seen her so excited, yet he remained convinced she had little chance at getting what she'd banked her future on. He felt that she'd built up her expectations like a house of cards: one without a safety net to catch her when they collapsed. He'd waited long for this eventuality, and his wait was nearly over. If he didn't catch her – for her fall might be that swift – he'd be there to help her to her feet.

Adjusting her black wig in a mirror, she'd become a perfect likeness of the long-necked girl in her paintings. He asked why she was wearing it.

With a barrette between her teeth she said: "For my final interview I want to be conservative." She turned to look at him. "You're making me nervous."

He lingered in the doorway, taking her in. He was amazed that an entire season had passed since they'd met. While he knew her much better now, and considered her his closest friend in Saigon, their lack of intimacy frustrated him.

Only the previous week he thought this had changed. As was often the case, however, her behavior one moment hardly predicted her behavior the next. Their recent outing to a bowling alley was a perfect example.

She'd beaten him on the last frame and, because they'd wagered dinner on the game, he had to take her wherever she said. They'd gone to a Chinese restaurant and ordered her favorite fried rice and dumplings. Afterward they'd ventured to an upscale lounge. While sitting in a dark corner she'd lifted his arm across her shoulder and placed his hand beneath her shirt collar, then slowly straightened up so his hand slid down the warm swell of her breast until her nipple pressed his fingers. She'd let him touch her for several minutes, but as soon as she pulled his hand away it was like nothing had ever happened.

He felt that their closeness in the lounge would lead to something deeper. He had been hoping for this for a long time, and wanted more.

When he shut the door to the back room, Thao, the girl Le had hired to manage the gallery today, put down the Korean fashion magazine she was flipping through and motioned him over.

"Are you excited?" she said. "She's going to your country. And when you move back you can see each other there."

"Talk like that's a little premature..."

Thao smiled uneasily. "You don't think she'll get a visa?"

"Few people do."

She stared at him disbelievingly.

Her blindness to the odds Le faced surprised him. She had apparently never considered that Le might fail.

He walked to the lacquer painting Le had shown him three months before: a woman in a white *áo dài*, her neck impossibly long, her face turned toward a burned forest behind her. In a corner was a small sticker. Leaning forward Nathan saw written there: Sold to Mr. Yamashita.

"Are you a painter, too, Thao?"

"No," she said, almost sheepishly. "I'm hopeless with a paintbrush. I can't even use chopsticks properly."

"The face looks just like hers, don't you think?" he said, pointing at the painting. "From a distance it could be a photograph."

"She's beautiful. But I don't like the way her face looks there."

"What do you mean?"

She shrugged. "She has a bright future, so she should look happier. If a professional artist painted me, I'd make sure I was smiling. I'd do everything possible to appear sexy."

A moment passed before Nathan realized this was a joke. "Has she ever talked to you about her uncle?"

She shook her head. "I didn't know she had one. I'm just here because I'm good at selling things and Le trusts me."

"You know her well?"

"I've known her a long time, but not well. To be honest, I was surprised when she asked me to work here."

A few minutes later Le emerged from the back room.

"Come here," Nathan said. "Since this is the first time I've seen you with black hair, I want to see you beside the woman in your painting."

"There's no time," she protested. "I should try to be at the consulate early." She hurried out of the gallery before he could stop her.

The consulate guards didn't inspect Nathan's passport. Just seeing a white face seemed to satisfy them. Nathan placed his passport and cell phone on a plastic tray, watched them tie these together with a rubber band, and took a numbered card. Le, however, was stopped and peppered with questions: What's your business here? With whom do you have an appointment? When were you issued this passport? Is this your first visit here?

Nathan was ushered through the security detector into a large waiting room. Looking around, he saw various forms on metal shelving units up and down the white walls; posters of U.S. landmarks and advertisements for university business degrees; rows of seated visitors;

and a counter where low-level consular staff sat indifferently as Vietnamese people jostled with each other to submit their applications.

Behind him, Le stepped onto a platform so a guard could brush her with a metal wand.

A minute later she hurried over, giggling nervously. "I thought they might arrest me."

"You do look suspicious."

Her giggling ceased. "Do I?"

He pointed at her gray-and-black striped suit. She even had a black sunhat, though she now clutched it beneath one arm. "You look like a gangster's moll."

Ignoring him, she pulled out a crisp blue folder. "Are you sure you filled this out right?"

"Of course."

She laughed again, straightening her jacket. "It's just a thirty-minute interview. Why am I nervous?"

Nathan waited for her to sign in. Behind the counter window a paunchy American man walked past. Immediately Nathan recognized him – Andrew, he recalled – as one of Anthony's old friends. Nathan had been introduced to him shortly after arriving in Vietnam. At that time Andrew had just passed his civil service examination and was preparing to fly to the U.S. for training. Nathan thought he should say hello, if only to give Le more confidence in him and in what she was over-worrying.

Without looking up, the woman behind the window pointed at a door to the side of the room. Le thanked her and came back to Nathan.

"I have to go. I don't think you can accompany me."

"I'll wait across the street." Squeezing her hand, he wished her good luck.

When she disappeared, an unpleasant thought hit him: if her interview went badly, the closeness they'd achieved, if not yet the intimacy, might be irrevocably lost.

He started toward the exit.

"Nathan."

Nathan turned to see Andrew rapping on the counter window, then waving him over enthusiastically.

"What are you doing here, Nate? I haven't seen you in two years, I bet. Not since I started here."

"You haven't changed. Except it's hard to tell with that thick glass you're standing behind."

"If I look heavier and balder, it's definitely the glass. Anything I can help you with?"

"Actually, I'm with a friend. She just went in for an interview."

"Shopping for a visa?"

Nathan nodded. "Immigration."

"Wife or girlfriend?"

"Girlfriend, I think. It's hard to tell sometimes."

Andrew's smile flickered. "I see."

Andrew and Anthony had known each other since before Nathan arrived in Vietnam, but their friendship had always been spotty. Anthony used to say that Andrew tried too hard with him, as if he had a crush, but it seemed to Nathan that he'd calmed down since entering the diplomatic corps.

"I guess there's no point telling you her name," Nathan said.

Andrew looked at him strangely, then glanced at the Vietnamese employee sitting beneath him. "No," he said, frowning. "That's not how we work."

Nathan smiled. "Just wanted to make sure you're on the up and up."

"That I am. By the way, Anthony wrote me the other day. He said he'd finally lured you into his empire."

"I'm thinking about it. But it's a little complicated now."

"Oh, right." Andrew threw a look at the door Le had passed through. "His e-mail made it sound like a done deal."

"He's a good talker."

"I was going to call him tonight." He looked at Nathan skeptically. "Should I tell him I saw you?"

"I can tell him."

"He'll want to talk about you. And he'll think I kept this a secret from him if you tell him after I call."

Nathan laughed, although he knew Andrew wasn't kidding.

"He told me you accepted his offer," Andrew went on. "He said he notified several candidates that his search was over because he'd found you."

"Like I said, it's more complicated than that."

"You should call him, then." His voice had taken on an urgency, as if he was speaking of a moral imperative. "I've got a meeting to go to now. Let's get together sometime."

For a moment Nathan couldn't move. The encounter was unexpected, and the shock of their conversation hit him after Andrew left. People in the waiting room were watching him, and only when the woman behind the counter looked up, lowering her glasses to see him better, did he head through the exit to reclaim his passport and cell phone.

He crossed Le Duan Street and ordered tea at a café. As he sat there, with one eye on the consulate, he wondered what had kept him in Saigon for more than half a decade. Certainly the city had changed since he'd arrived, but could those changes have outpaced the changes that had occurred in him?

Fifteen minutes ago he'd felt happy, but now his happiness was tinged with the fear that he'd have to let go of something dear.

It was a strange contradiction that happiness had to be balanced by loneliness. In America, country of wide-open spaces and inspiring nature, it was acceptable to feel lonely, for loneliness was almost inescapable in such a landscape. But in Vietnam it was different. Saigon was so crowded, so lacking in space and nature to get lost in, he felt that loneliness had no place there. Yet he did feel lonely: loneliness more profound than he'd known in America. In Saigon, where humanity had taken to places that Americans would never dare inhabit, loneliness seemed a kind of failure. He dreamed sometimes of being alone in a great expanse, but unable to move, rooted like a tree.

The pattern had been established long ago: starting out happy, loneliness slowly catching up. If happiness were a rock, loneliness was the moss that slowly crept over it.

He wondered what Le would do if faced with this pattern in America. Would it change her? Would she recognize it? Or would her twenty-four years here protect her? He turned the question inward, asking himself what aspects of Vietnamese life he might never be able to recognize or understand. He was assailed by countless notions borne out of the chasm between privilege on one side and privation on the other.

By the time Le emerged from the consulate, dark clouds filled the sky and the sun had disappeared like a pill dissolved in water. She must have only just removed her wig, for she was shaking out and fingering her pink hair. She stopped on the sidewalk, peering up and down the street. Nathan didn't get up right away. He enjoyed watching her like this: from afar, knowing she wanted to see him.

When she started for the corner he went after her, threading his way through traffic, calling her name when he was near.

"How'd it go?" He touched her hand, her arm, her cheek. "You're still alive, and your body's intact – all good signs."

"It went okay," she said. "It's hard to tell with Americans. They're serious but also friendly. I don't know what's real. The worst part was dealing with the Vietnamese staff. They look down on people like me."

She described how she'd complimented a woman at the immigration counter on a pendant she wore only to be told to save her flattery and pretty smile for someone who could help her. "I guess it was just her way of trying to make me fail."

"You should have told someone what she did."

"And jeopardize my chance of getting a visa?"

He retrieved his motorbike and pulled onto the sidewalk, waiting for her to climb on. When he turned in the direction of her gallery, she leaned into him.

"I don't want to go back."

If he didn't know her so well he might have mistaken the urgency in her voice for anger and guessed she'd fared poorly in her interview. In his handlebar mirror, however, he saw her faintly smiling.

"Where, then?"

She pointed down the street. Only a few hundred meters away, Le Duan ended at the zoo and botanical gardens. "Let's go there. It's quiet and we can walk around."

As they got close enough that he could make out the words Thao Cam Vien on a weathered signboard above the entrance, he realized three years had passed since he'd last visited. He didn't like zoos, but it would be as good a place as any to hear about her interview.

Aside from a few parking lot and ticket booth employees, and someone in a hammock strung between both groups, the zoo seemed empty.

She was right in her prediction of quietness. The loudest noise was the rustle of leaves overhead, and the occasional cry of a monkey or bird. Honking cars and motorbikes were muffled both by distance and the density of surrounding trees.

They drifted past an island of blonde and black-haired monkeys. Several people were throwing apple chunks across the scummed-over moat. Monkeys beyond throwing range gave angry, low-throated hoots.

Soon they were standing before a pen of goats, which crowded in front of them bleating for food. Behind the pen was a French-colonial building, its yellow paint faded, its roof tiles dirtied with bird droppings and fallen tamarind pods. The blue shutters on the second-story windows were thrown open and Nathan saw two women staring down at them, smiling as if something were funny.

Le reached over the fence to let a goat lick her hand.

"I like goats," she said. "They're curious. A goat's more of a thinking animal than a sheep."

"I've never thought about that."

"The goats should know me. I visit them whenever I come here."

"Le."

"Yes?"

"Aren't you going to tell me about the interview?"

She waited until the goat lost interest in her and wandered off. "They said my application looked fine, but they told me – they were only being honest, they said – that I wasn't the strongest candidate. But since I have proof of support, they suggested I not give up."

Her words lent force to his belief that she'd never stood a chance. Yet she still clung to this last thread of hope – the consulate's parting words had put a gleam in her eyes – and he felt badly for her. Not knowing what else to say, he told her she'd done well.

"I was heading for the exit when someone called my name. He said he met you in the lobby, that you're old friends. Why didn't you tell me you knew him?" There was accusation in her voice.

"What would I have told you? I didn't know he'd approach you." Nathan wondered how Andrew had recognized her.

"I don't like him," she said flatly.

"Yes, well, I don't much either."

"He asked if we were planning to get married."

Nathan was stunned. "What did you tell him?"

"I asked why he was asking. 'An informal inquiry,' was all he said. He made me more nervous than I was before my interview."

"I wonder what that was about."

"Did you talk to him about me?"

"I didn't tell him your name and he didn't ask. Mostly we talked about Anthony."

"I hope I never see him again."

Nathan couldn't imagine what Andrew had wanted. The first possibility seemed altruistic: he meant to expedite the process for her, as a favor to Nathan. The second, however, seemed hostile: he wanted to catch her in a lie. Enormous implications lay between the possibilities, and Nathan had no way to know which was correct. Andrew had no reason to demonstrate loyalty toward Nathan, which is why Nathan's hunch aligned with the latter scenario. To Andrew, maybe this was a way to be loyal instead to Anthony.

"Have you ever eaten hippo?" Le asked, venturing toward the adjoining pen.

A cat with no ears slinked around the dead grass behind the pool where a hippo, immersed to the top of its head, stared at them both.

"Where would I have possibly eaten hippo?"

"I don't know. Africa?"

"What makes you think I've eaten hippo in Africa?"

Laughing, she grabbed his arm and seemed to perk up. They watched the earless cat skulk around a pile of vegetation put out for the hippo to eat, then scamper off when the hippo blasted air from its nose.

"I can smell its breath," she cried, covering her mouth and nose.

She hurried down the path, leaving him behind.

He caught up to her in front of the elephant pen, where four small elephants shared a patch of dirt less than half a football field in size. Swinging their heads from side to side, they gazed across a dirty channel opposite the zoo boundary. Two new buildings were being constructed, and red and yellow cranes could be seen transporting concrete blocks in their pivoted arms. A heavy chain around the elephants' hind feet kept them from moving more than one step in any direction. There was little shade, and they continually tossed dust on themselves with their trunks.

"I come here sometimes," she said. "You wouldn't know by looking at them, but they're intelligent animals. They're said to have excellent memories."

"I guess that doesn't do them much good here. All cooped up like that, they probably lost their minds long ago."

Behind them a woman on a mat with straw baskets before her started calling: "Sugarcane for the elephants! Two sticks, two thousand *dong*!" Her baskets bulged with stacks of purple, fibrous sticks.

Le bought a dozen pieces and handed half to Nathan.

The elephants, having observed the transaction, extended their trunks in anticipation of being fed. Le launched a stick towards the smallest one. It bounced to a rest in an orange dust-cloud at its feet.

The wind's coolness foretold rain. A violent gust showered brown leaves down from the enormous trees around them.

A girl of perhaps two, in pigtails and a flowered dress, tottered toward them from the side. An old woman followed, pushing a carriage. "*Voi!*" the girl said, pointing at the elephants and looking back at her grandmother. "*Con voi!*" She came up to Nathan and Le, grabbing Le's leg for balance and gaping up at her.

When the girl noticed her sugarcane, Le gave her a stick, and the girl looked again at her grandmother.

"Say thank you," the grandmother said. "This is her first trip to the zoo. She really liked Monkey Island. Didn't you, Lan?"

Tugging at the cane, the girl nodded shyly.

"The elephants like to eat that," Le told her. "Want to see?"

Le tossed another stick of sugarcane into the pen. An elephant lifted it with its trunk and pushed it into its curved, whiskered maw.

The sound of it chewing made the girl laugh and stamp her feet. Nathan glanced at the grandmother. She was straining her eyes at Le.

"Excuse me," the old woman said.

Le took a half-step back, appearing alarmed by the woman's scrutiny. "Yes?"

"I'm sorry, but..." She placed a hand over her mouth, as if she couldn't believe what she was about to say. "Don't I know you?"

Le shook her head. She seemed upset by the woman's suggestion. "I've never seen you before."

The woman pointed at her. "I think I knew your mother."

Le's face hardened as the woman bent down to pick up her granddaughter. "I don't think so."

"You speak with a northern accent. Are you from Hanoi?"

Le glanced warily at Nathan. "Yes, but I've lived in Saigon for eight years."

"My name's Van." She paused, apparently to give Le a chance to remember. "And yes, it would have been a long time ago that I last saw your mother. I must be getting old; I can't recall her name..."

"My mother's been dead fifteen years."

Nathan stared at Le. She had told him that her mother had run away when she was a girl.

A pained expression flashed across Van's face. "May I ask your name?"

"I really don't think there's any possibility..." Le laughed uneasily. "I'm sorry, you've mistaken me for someone else."

Van lightly bounced her granddaughter in her arms. "Your mother was a nurse, wasn't she? Married to a soldier? Or was it a doctor? Wasn't she widowed during the war?"

"She ran a flower shop. And yes, my father died during the war. But he was hardly the only one."

There was a lag between Van's questions and Le's replies. Van looked at Nathan as if to see if he noticed, too.

"What do you do?"

Le paused so long Nathan thought she wouldn't answer. "I'm a saleswoman."

Nathan stared at her in surprise. He thought she might have told

Van that she owned a gallery and painted. He supposed she'd been truthful – she did sell paintings, after all – but he couldn't help wonder why she was purposely being vague.

"Excuse me, but what's your name?"

Le sighed. "I'm not who you think. There are thousands of girls like me in the city – girls from Hanoi who came south. Surely you're remembering one of them."

A smile flickered across Van's face, and she raised a finger as if an important memory had come to her. "There was something about a marriage offer. Could it have been for one of your sisters?"

"I'm an only child. Please don't ask me more questions."

Nathan felt awkward caught in the middle, but the encounter interested him. Le's rejection of the woman's claim to know her touched on a theme he could never get her to open up about: her past. He continued to observe their interaction, but with his eye now on Le. If indeed she'd never met Van, why would she get so worked up over these harmless questions?

"I remember something about a famous doctor's son. But he went to America to study and never came back." She smiled at Nathan. Apparently giving him the benefit of the doubt about his Vietnamese ability, she said to him: "Oh, it's terrible getting old. One's memories seem to float in muddy water."

Nathan smiled politely back at her while Le remained silent. She seemed paralyzed, unable to walk away.

"I'm sorry to have bothered you," Van said. "I must be remembering someone else after all." She hugged her granddaughter to her shoulder. Grabbing the carriage handle, she headed off.

When the woman was out of earshot Nathan said: "Why didn't you tell her your name? She asked twice."

"Why should I tell a stranger my name? She was crazy."

"You could have told her your first name. She thought she recognized you."

"I was a little girl back then. And with black hair, not pink. How could she recognize me after so long?" She laughed at what she evidently considered the absurdity of it. "Anyone who knew me back then, if they saw me now, would think I'm wearing a disguise."

"But was she wrong about everything?" Nathan persisted, wondering what might have transpired if Le hadn't removed her wig. "Did she really mistake you for someone else?"

"What do you think?"

"I don't know what to think. You even told her that your mother died fifteen years ago."

"Well, I lied. I didn't want to talk to her about my family."

"But I can't understand why any of this would upset you."

"You can't understand, no."

"But you could help me."

"I don't want to help you."

He glared at her. To not want to help him was selfish beyond comprehension. If she didn't want to help him, what did that mean?

Raindrops began to fall, splattering in the dust. In no time it fell in torrents. They ran inside a Chinese-style pavilion, where they brushed the water off each other's clothes and faces.

Cement benches lined each wall, and Nathan sat on one the rain hadn't drenched. The red walls looked like they hadn't been repainted since the war. Lovers' names and the dates they'd trysted covered half the open interior. Scratched in lopsided hearts were the names of lovers; or, in some cases, wished-for lovers:

Phương love Bắc 14/02/04
Biển love Sương 8-8-03
Nhượng và Trung (Tây Ninh và Tiền Giang) 8-11-04
Trần + Beckham 20.3.03
Khanh ai shiteru Tomoko 14/02/02

He too might once have scratched his name beside Le's on this wall. But it felt childish now; a foolish exercise in declaring something that might disappear before the last letter was written. He wondered if any of these people remained together.

Rain ran off the peaked roof in silver rivulets. Le sat on his lap and he pulled her close, wanting to put his arms around her and breathe in what was like a gentle rubbing of frangipani on her skin. He noticed her reading the names on the wall.

"I have to go back to work," she said.

Nathan didn't know if she meant now or if she was simply reminding herself of the fact. "But it's raining."

She slid off his lap. "Would you ever marry a Vietnamese woman?"

At first he couldn't answer. "If I loved her. And if I knew she loved me."

"But for you, happiness means staying here?"

"To me happiness means many things. It isn't specific to one place."

"What's it specific to?"

The answer came quickly enough. "To whomever I love. And to whatever I make of my life."

Her lips curled doubtfully. "You don't want to be rich?"

"Rich would be fine. But I'd prefer just not to be poor."

"You're not ambitious."

"Maybe I'm a little left of center, but being rich isn't as important to me as how I live. If I don't have the freedom to make my own decisions, I'll never be happy."

"Life's easier for you than for me – you were born into privilege." She paused as if to let him respond, but he wouldn't deny what she'd said. "I wonder if I'll talk like you after living in America a long time. Or if I have children there, if they will."

"Maybe your uncle already does."

Rain leaked from the roof, and she kicked idly at where it fell. "I want to be with him. He has no one to care for him."

"What about his family?"

She took a moment to answer. "He never married."

"It's letting up," he said.

"Does it rain much in Los Angeles?"

"It's between a desert and the ocean. It hardly rains there at all."

"Then I'll miss the rain."

She walked out of the pavilion. Cupping her hands, she tried to catch the water that dripped from the trees.

"What will you do if the embassy doesn't give you a visa?" he said when he was next to her.

"I'll have to find another way."

He started to ask something more, but she pressed her fingers to his lips and stopped him.

"No more questions. I've been answering questions all morning."

For the first time he saw the weariness in her eyes. Probably last night she'd hardly slept. Respecting her wishes, he still wondered over her reluctance to talk about this uncle who wanted to give her a new future. He couldn't help but think this was a strategy of hers. But a strategy for what? Could she use him more easily if he didn't ask about her past and future?

They retraced their way across the zoo. Puddles on the asphalt reflected the sun shining through the clouds, and from somewhere they heard water flowing from a catchment area. The air, cleaner after the rain, smelled of trees.

"Tonight," she said, "I want to do something special for you."

"Special in what way?"

"You'll see."

They came upon a small monkey outside its barred cage. Soaked to the skin, it sat beside a trash receptacle, eating a discarded sandwich.

"Look, it has no tail," Le said.

Nathan saw that the monkey indeed lacked a tail, while the ones in the cage where it belonged all had one.

"It has no tail, just like me."

He looked at her, wondering what she was talking about. "Like you?"

"In Vietnam, a person with nobody depending on them is called a monkey without a tail."

She waved the monkey over, but her movement scared it. It clambered over the wall in front of its cage and slipped through the bars.

Le lingered for a moment, watching something in the distance. Her eyes were fixed on the exit. Van was there, walking with her granddaughter.

When they were out of sight Nathan suggested they continue.

7

Out his window, Nathan saw her waiting for him beside her motorbike. Watching her remove a cigarette from her handbag and approach a sidewalk barber for a light, he realized he hadn't seen her smoke since their journey on the train.

He was hurrying on a shirt when his cell phone vibrated. The words 'Anthony calling' flashed on the screen. Nathan guessed that he'd just received his e-mail in which he explained why he'd been out of touch. He'd concluded: "If you haven't already, please forget about me working for you and hire someone else. As for the money I owe you, I'll pay it soon. That's a promise I'm staking our friendship on." He pocketed his phone and went downstairs. By the time he handed his room key to the guesthouse manager, the vibrating had stopped. Le gave her cigarette to the barber as Nathan crossed the street to her. She wore a shapeless combination of black trousers and a long black shirt, sleeveless and shiny beneath a streetlight. "I'll drive," she said.

He climbed on behind her as she started her motorbike.

She turned right on Ton Duc Thang and soon passed the western edge of Boson Port. When they hit Nguyen Hue and were heading toward the People's Committee Building, the street became packed as if some huge, chaotic demonstration was underway. Young people on motorbikes, bumper-to-bumper in paralyzed traffic, waved Vietnamese flags and banged together whatever made noise: bamboo shafts, metal soup ladles and trash can tops, plastic grilles torn from fans, steel hubcaps unscrewed from parked cars.

"What's this?" he said. "A national holiday I forgot about?"

"A soccer match against Cambodia."

"Then the whole city's going to be like this." When she didn't answer, he suggested they return to his guesthouse. "It'll be quieter there."

"Where we're going is quiet."

She turned off of Le Loi onto Nguyen Thai Hoc. Soon they were crossing Ong Lanh Bridge into District Four.

Her nearness was intoxicating. She'd clung to him the first few months they'd seen each other, for he always drove them. But tonight she controlled the motorbike. When the clogged streets thinned out and she hit fourth gear, and it seemed like they'd lift off the street if he held out his arms like wings, he leaned into her and locked his hands over her stomach. With his thumbs against her ribcage, he thought of how close they were to her breasts, and how easily he might slip a finger beneath her waistband.

He asked where they were going, but an oncoming truck blared its horn and drowned out his question. A blast of wind from its passing shook them violently, cutting down their speed. He didn't ask again.

They crossed the Te Canal and drove on until District Four became District Seven, and then District Seven became Nha Be.

Suddenly it was rural, and the intermittent marshland, with its canals and rivers, reminded him of the Mekong Delta. They passed over another bridge, its surface a patchwork of rotting boards. Although barely wide enough for a car, it was full of other motorbikes, pedestrians, vendors pushing food-carts, and lovers by the rails.

It was then that the activity around them fell away, and the night became a passage they were fated to travel – it didn't matter where, for this was already a destination he could be happy with. It was a piece of the puzzle to his life in Vietnam, and being able to connect it to other experiences enlarged his sense that he belonged here.

Eventually, the road became bordered with small eateries and shops and neon *nhà nghi* signs. The words literally meant 'rest house,' but were, in most cases, love hotels. Anthony once described what they were like: the rooms unclean, the lobbies and halls dark and dank, and the walls so thin you could not only hear couples fucking but you could even hear them breathe.

They passed three *nhà nghi* in the space of a block, and he was surprised to see Le look in their direction.

When the last one was behind them and the road had grown dark with walls of nipa palms along both shoulders, she pulled over and stopped.

"Are you lost?" he said. When he touched her, she was trembling. Without answering, she made a U-turn and returned to the gaudy brightness. She chose a small, crowded eatery, which from the street had little recommending it.

They sat by the window. Cigarette smoke hovered around them, and Vietnamese pop music, too loud for conversation, blared on the stereo. Across the street, the Nha Nghi Tinh Xa glowed with strings of red lights streaming down its façade.

Le called to a waiter for two beers.

"I've never seen you drink," he said.

She rested her head on his shoulder. "I want to get drunk with you. Hopelessly, stupidly drunk."

He knew now that he'd make love to her in one of these hourly hotels. He still couldn't imagine what kept her from spending the night at his guesthouse, where they'd have all the privacy they needed. And if she weren't to stay the night, it should be even less of a dilemma. No one would say anything to her or otherwise pose a problem. In the end it didn't matter where they went as long as they were together.

When the beer arrived, they touched glasses. The cold trickled down Nathan's throat like an electrical charge.

Her face reddened after a few swallows, and for the first time that night she looked into his eyes. He felt her searching – not for an answer to some mystery he embodied, but for a clue, maybe, as to what she'd find if she took him apart and studied him. He looked steadily back, but there was nothing he hoped to find that wasn't already before him.

He ordered another beer and filled half her glass. Whatever would come next involved all his imagination, so the silence they shared was only silence perceived from the outside.

When the waitress removed their bottles and Nathan gestured for another round, Le nodded her approval. But to him the heavy movement revealed sadness.

"What's wrong?" he said, worried she was having second thoughts about being here.

"I was just thinking...I'd like to go to Phu Quoc before I leave." Phu Quoc was an island south of Vietnam. It, too, had once been Cambodian, and the French and Americans had both used it as a penal colony. "I'm sure it's nothing special to you. You've been almost everywhere."

"I've never been to Phu Quoc. Why do you want to go?"

"My uncle escaped Vietnam from there. He gave away all his money for a seat on a fishing vessel crammed with people – so many that there wasn't room for food or water. Pirates attacked them once, and several people drowned. They were at sea for days. A Japanese cargo ship finally ran across them and took them aboard. He ended up at a Malaysian refugee camp, and after ten months there he was allowed to go to the United States."

"He fled, even though he was from the north?"

She nodded, but didn't say anything more.

"I'd like to go there with you."

She glanced around them. "Wait here. I'm going to drive down the street, then come back and park behind that *nhà nghi* over there. In five minutes I'll message you to meet me."

"Why make it complicated?"

"I'm in control tonight."

She grabbed her purse and left him. He watched her drive down the dark road. With alarming suddenness, she disappeared.

Her discreetness annoyed him. Surely this happened all the time on this road. What did it matter if a foreigner trysted with a Vietnamese? Besides, the distance from downtown protected them from familiar eyes and those who'd gossip about them. While it was nothing for him to bring her to his guesthouse – he'd suggested it numerous times – she rejected the idea. Her refusal confused and frustrated him; other foreigners in the guesthouse had Vietnamese lovers spend the night. The time when police raided hotels and guesthouses in the middle of the night to break up a foreigner and a Vietnamese belonged to the past, at least in the cities. Again, he felt that for her this was simply making good on a promise.

A minute later she emerged from the dark road and pulled up to the Nha Nghi Tinh Xa. A parking attendant pushed her motorbike behind the building and she followed him.

Nathan's phone vibrated, and for an instant he worried it was Anthony. The message read: *In rm 5. Pls hurry.*

He passed two young men at a check-in table, ignoring their stunned silence. Room five was at the end of a dim hall, unlocked. The hall light slipped inside the dark room, showing Le on a bed with her back against the headstand. She was naked.

He froze, taking in the sight of her: her body blending in the darkness with the color of the sheets; her legs stretched out; her nipples gazing back at him like the eyes of a creature wishing to remain hidden. He shut the door behind him. The light disappeared, and with it the illumination of her nakedness.

Finding her like this vaguely disappointed him, for he'd relished the idea of a slow progression toward intimacy, toward a shared vulnerability that would make sex feel like love.

He undressed at the edge of the bed. When he lifted off his shirt she wrapped her arms around him and pushed her warm breasts into his back.

He didn't like this darkness. He wanted to see her. He wanted to see them together.

"Let me turn on a light."

"No." She pulled him down on the bed, easily breaking his resistance. "This is me paying you back."

"Don't say that." He strained to see her face.

"But that's what I'm doing. I've said it all along."

If she insisted on thinking of this moment as an obligation, he wanted to know what she thought she owed him. But her mouth on his prevented him from asking. Given her repeated emphasis that this was a practical arrangement, her passion surprised him.

She climbed onto him, rubbing his chest with her hands. His eyes had begun to adjust to the darkness, and she was visible now on top of him. In the dresser mirror behind her, he saw that in passion, too, her grace didn't fail. She straddled him, and the slow, undulant motion of her body as she rocked back and forth was like something blown by the wind, or buffeted from behind by waves.

With her hand she guided him into her, and his thoughts, which so often clashed when they were together, evanesced.

At one point his hand brushed the pillow. It was wet. The worry that she'd been crying interrupted his pleasure. But it wasn't worth asking about now; sadness had no place in this moment.

After trading her parking ticket for her Future, she asked Nathan to drive.

"Tired of being in control?" he asked.

"I'm just tired."

On the way home he remembered the damp pillow. "Were you crying in the *nhà nghỉ*?" he said over his shoulder.

But she either didn't hear him or didn't want to answer. Fearing some unpleasant truth, or worse, that he'd forfeit the intimacy they finally found, he didn't repeat himself. Why should he? If she wanted him to know anything, he was confident she'd tell him. Even stranger than her silence, however, was that she didn't touch him on the ride home. Perhaps what they'd shared made things more complicated for her. If so, he was happy for that.

At the next red light he leaned back into her. In his handlebar mirror he saw her smile unevenly.

She pointed ahead of them. "It turned green."

He twisted the throttle and moved through the intersection. "Where are we going?"

"My gallery. I have something from the consulate I need you to explain. They gave it to me after my interview."

Rather than mope over this reminder of their predictable, prearranged script, he took a longer way than necessary and drove slowly. For despite his misgivings, what had happened tonight meant progress and he was too happy to let anything spoil the rest of their night.

8

The scene through the gallery window was itself like a painting of expatriate extravagance. Nathan walked inside only to find he knew no one.

If he hadn't been held up at the magazine office, editing several pieces they were in a rush to publish, he'd have returned home to change into what Anthony called his "missionary ensemble": white shirt, navy tie and slacks, and black shoes. They were the only decent clothes he owned. Tonight he should have known better than to show up wearing faded jeans and a striped oxford with coffee-stained sleeves.

For the first time since meeting Le, three days had passed without his seeing her. He'd thought nothing of it the first day, when she said an old girlfriend wanted to spend the evening with her. He'd thought nothing of it the second day, either, when she claimed that being out late the night before had left her too tired to see him after work. But on the third day he suspected that their tryst at the *nhà nghỉ* two weeks ago was behind the distance she'd put between them. All they'd done since then was study English at Bac-Nam and share one quick, quiet meal.

The last three days, however, worried him. She didn't answer his calls or respond to the messages he sent. He messaged her in the morning that he'd visit her at work, but when he arrived she wasn't there. Thao, filling in for her again, knew nothing of her whereabouts. As he was leaving, she remembered to give him two invitations for the gallery opening that weekend. "Le asked me to give these to you," she said.

Suits and dresses sparkled in the intense gallery light. Conversations about business, high-end serviced apartments, and weekend jaunts to coastal resorts, excluded him. Who were these people, he asked himself, and why had they been invited here? The guests were all part of the same faceless animal. Without each other, they'd be nothing. His smile faded as he told himself: No, Nathan, without each other they'd be just like you.

The awkwardness of standing by himself compelled him to send Le a message: *I'm at gallery. Where are you?*

A Vietnamese woman in a short red dress was circling around with a tray of fluted champagne glasses. When she passed Nathan, he lifted two from it.

A jeweled hand fell on his arm. The hand belonged to another Vietnamese woman in a black crepe dress. "Do you have an invitation?" she said.

Nathan set both glasses down and reached into his pocket. He removed his invitation, unfolded it, and showed it to her. "I'm with the owner of Bac-Nam Gallery."

The woman looked at him in surprise. "Are you the writer?"

"I guess so. Unless she's seeing more than one writer."

The woman smiled uncomprehendingly.

"I'm him," he explained in Vietnamese.

"You speak Vietnamese?" she asked, blinking rapidly.

"Only inasmuch as you understand me."

"I heard that you spoke Vietnamese, but I can't believe you speak it so well."

He picked up the champagne glasses he'd set down a moment earlier. "Sorry I'm underdressed."

"It doesn't matter." Her attitude toward him had warmed considerably upon hearing him speak Vietnamese. "Where's Le?"

"I don't know."

"She's just being fashionable, I suppose." She glanced at her thin black watch. Just below her elbow was a vague tan line, as if she wore long gloves to protect her skin from browning. Her eyes moved to the glasses he was holding.

"One's for Le," he said. He realized then that he'd already drunk from both.

"When Le gets here, tell her to find me." She squeezed his arm and held it.

"What's your name?"

She pointed to a name on the invitation she'd collected. "Thanh," she said. "That's me. And this is my gallery. Stop by any time."

"Thank you."

"It's nice to speak with a foreigner in Vietnamese for a change." She squeezed his arm again. "I'd like to talk to you more. What will you do when Le leaves for America? Will you be here by yourself?"

"Her leaving isn't exactly a given."

She looked at him oddly, as if his comment had sprung from neither Vietnamese nor English and defied explanation. "Come by sometime. I'm almost always here..." She let go of him and stepped back into the party.

He drifted around the crowd's perimeter, taking in the paintings. They were mostly oils in muted colors, of women in cream *áo dài* under butter-yellow trees, and water buffaloes pieced together from varicolored shapes. He wandered into an alcove and found on each wall a nude painted in a completely different style.

The morning before he and Le had slept together, she'd shown him a recently finished self-portrait. Like the one he came across in Hanoi, she was nude, floating on the air, with city ruins, smoke, and fire in the background. The grotesqueness of the neck, the unnatural distance between the head and shoulders, had detracted from the erotic impression the painting might otherwise have given. But because he'd seen that body, had felt its warm flesh with his own fingers, it now transformed in his memory to more than just an image: it had become both memory and wish.

He heard someone enter the alcove behind him. Expecting the person to be a stranger, he continued to look upon the paintings.

"I'll be damned. Nathan?"

Nathan turned and saw Andrew. In a dark gray suit and tie, he stood holding a half-full wine glass.

"Andrew," he said, startled.

"What are you doing here? Hanging out by yourself is a bit antisocial, isn't it?"

Nathan detected a tinge of sarcasm in Andrew's voice. "Maybe a little," he said.

Andrew surveyed the room's paintings. Waving dismissively at the walls he said, "You're not really interested in these, are you?"

"More than the party," Nathan said. "I didn't know you were the gallery type."

"I come to network, I suppose." He smiled, revealing faintly wine-stained teeth. Taking a gulp of wine, he said, "By the way, I spoke to Anthony after I saw you at the consulate. He said you left him high and dry. He sounded pretty upset."

Nathan cleared his throat, but it didn't help loosen an explanation for the problems he knew he'd caused Anthony. "I didn't know you and Anthony were such good friends anymore," Nathan answered.

"We're normal friends." He glanced at a painting and, in what struck Nathan as an artificially casual tone said: "Anthony has rubbed plenty of people the wrong way, it's true, but he must have done something terrible to make you abandon him like that."

Nathan had no idea how his action had affected Anthony's company. Until now, he'd been able not to think about it. "Like I told you before, it was complicated. It was complicated to begin with, and it got more complicated after I met someone."

"Met someone? Oh, yes. I remember now. I saw her after her interview."

"And?" The word came out too quickly.

Andrew's lips lifted over his teeth. "And it's funny," he said. "I used to know a girl who looked a lot like her. In fact, their similarities would take your breath away."

His speech became slurred saying this – and goading – and Nathan saw now that Andrew was drunk. He didn't reply.

"I see you don't believe me. But if I introduced you to the girl I once knew, I wonder if you'd see the resemblance."

Nathan turned toward the gallery to see if Le had arrived. He didn't want her subjected to Andrew's scrutiny.

"Does she know what you did to Anthony?"

"I didn't do anything to Anthony," Nathan said with false calm.

Andrew snorted and took another drink. "He's in pretty bad shape, did you know? He had to step away from his company for two weeks – doctor's orders. Did you know about that?"

"No."

"Naturally a few deals collapsed while he was gone. Five of his staff absconded with some contracts he'd nearly finalized, then quit and started their own agency. He lost a lot of money from that, and now he's short-staffed. Did you know about that?"

"Those things aren't a direct result of anything I did."

"Or didn't do," Andrew put in.

"You can stop with the lecture. I formed my own opinions a long time ago."

Andrew gulped again at his wine. "Anyway, he's a better person now than when he lived here. Of course he drinks too much, but in this country who doesn't?" As if to prove this, he raised his glass and drained the last inch of dark liquid.

Nathan wanted to end the conversation: people had gathered nearby and it would be awkward if they overheard. Andrew seemed to pick up on this and, to Nathan's surprise, relented.

"The least you could do is e-mail him. It'd do him good to hear from you."

"I'll do that."

"You owe him a lot of money, don't you?"

"He loaned me some a while back, but I'm on top of it."

Andrew paused, as if hoping Nathan would divulge the amount. "By the way, where's that girl you're seeing?"

"She's not here."

"I hope it's not because of anything I did."

The comment set Nathan on edge. "What did you do?"

"Nothing," he said. "Then is she out celebrating without you?"

"What are you talking about?"

"I'm talking about how the visa god came through for her. Do you intend to marry her now, or will you let her slip away?"

Nathan shivered violently.

"Mind you, just because her visa's been approved doesn't mean it'll be issued."

"What do you mean?"

"After her interview, I took it upon myself to review her file. Granted it's a little late, but when I went over her application I noticed a discrepancy between her support documents and what she said in her interviews. I can't help wonder if she lied about her uncle in the U.S."

"What sort of discrepancy?"

"That I can't say. But has she said or done anything to arouse your suspicions?"

Nathan was paralyzed by a dark, alien feeling. He was in a position, after she'd hurt him, to hurt her back. With or without knowing it, Andrew was offering him a chance to destroy Le's dream.

If he were to speak, he couldn't be sure of what he'd say. He slowly shook his head.

"As far as you're concerned, I suppose, there's more where she came from. Perhaps I'll go mingle with some of them now." He turned to the doorway. Halfway out the room, he saluted Nathan with his empty glass and stumbled back to the party.

Stunned by the news about Le's visa, Nathan stood there unmoving. After the difficulties of the last several days it was hard not to let suspicion get the better of him. He was in the habit of trusting Le, perhaps because he was desperate for her to be honest with him. But at the same time he felt she'd hammered him with lies – or had hidden from him truths on which his happiness with her depended. Never before had he felt this way, and he began to blame her for it, and resent her, for she knew this would hurt him – she must have known, if she'd thought about it even for a moment.

He forced himself through the crowd and slipped out to the street. Little girls in loose, dirty clothes wandered around the sidewalk selling roses, and one skipped up to him. "You buy rose for wife," she said, smacking his arm with a flower wrapped in plastic. "I sell you cheap."

Another girl ran up with a bucket of roses on her hip. "Hello, Joe. You buy?"

"Not tonight."

With the arrival of a third girl, they stopped pushing their roses on him and began chatting with each other. He overheard one of them ask if the rich people in the gallery were leaving.

The parking attendant had rolled Nathan's motorbike into the street. As Nathan climbed onto his Dream, a street sweeper hit his leg with her broom and continued toward her orange trash cart. An old oil lamp hung from the cart, burning weakly. Nathan stared at it, half-expecting it to go out. But it clung to whatever force kept it alive, even in the battering breeze.

He sat on his motorbike fingering the starter. Before long the scratchy sweep of the woman's broom grated on him and he pulled into traffic, wondering where to find Le.

A hard, needling rain was falling when he left the *bia hoi*. The cheap watery beer had relaxed him, but the endless invitations to join neighboring parties of drunken men put him off. To them he was merely an amusement, a diversion from their boisterous talk about massage girls and gambling, and he was experienced enough to spurn them decisively.

Traffic along Pasteur Street was heavy, and mud from spinning motorbike wheels soon splattered the cheap, single-use raincoat he'd over-worn. By the time he reached Bac-Nam, rain had soaked his shirt collar, where it had collected from his face and neck.

He pulled onto the sidewalk, which the downpour had cleared of vendors and pedestrians. A scrap of paper hung from the door. Protected from the rain by an overhang, it flapped in the wind.

A message had been written in thick black pen, and although the rain had smeared the large letters, they were legible:

> Now hiring: Experienced full-time gallery manager.
> Qualified applicants please contact Mr. Hung.

A phone number appeared beneath.

Who the hell is Mr. Hung, Nathan fumed, tearing down the sign and stuffing it in his pocket.

He looked inside. The only person who appeared to be working was Thao, who was poring over a magazine as usual. Nathan was hardly surprised not to find Le there, but even so he approached Thao to ask where she was.

"Didn't she tell you?" Thao offered him a paper towel to wipe his face but he refused it.

When he asked her to explain, she said that Le had closed her gallery.

"Who's Mr. Hung?" He pulled from his pocket the paper he'd torn from the door.

"He's the new owner. I'm working for him now." She smiled at him. "It's all because Le got a visa to your country."

Nathan paused. "How did you know?"

"She sent me a phone message three days ago." She gave him a strange look, and he guessed she wanted to know why he was asking her these questions.

From the corner of his eye he noticed that the storage room door was closed. He wondered if Le's paintings were still there, but it wasn't important to him now.

"I need to talk to her," he said. "But she doesn't pick up when I call and doesn't return my messages. I don't know how to get hold of her."

"That's strange," she said, looking confused. "Why don't you visit her at home?"

He tensed with embarrassment. "I don't know where she lives."

Her lips fluttered wordlessly, he knew, with questions she couldn't bring herself to ask.

There was no obvious path to reach Le. All was guesswork now, and the way, if Nathan could find it, would have to be traveled in a blind, hurried spin.

"I'll have to try somewhere else." He turned toward the street, but when he got to the door he stopped. Although he couldn't stand being in the gallery longer, the dark street and sky, and the silver-coin splashes of rain on the sidewalk, now felt like a bigger threat to him.

Not knowing where to go or what to do, his thoughts returned to the party he'd recently left. He thought he might go back to look once more for Le when he remembered his conversation with Andrew. He felt a powerful urge to convince him to revoke Le's visa. He was about to step into the rain when Thao called out.

"Wait a minute," she said. "Mr. Hung left a folder here today. Maybe it has information you could use."

She bent down behind the desk where she'd been sitting and Nathan could hear her open and close several drawers. In a minute she stood up with a black folder in her hand and began flipping through a number of papers inside.

"Here's something," she finally said, walking over to him. "Does this look right?"

Nathan took the paper she held out and tried to decipher the penciled address beneath Le's name. It was an unfamiliar street that, in all his years in Saigon, he'd never visited. But it was in Thanh Binh, the same district where Le had told him she lived. Nathan entered the address in his phone.

He almost asked Thao to call him if Le returned to the gallery, but now there was no need. "If she comes here," he said instead, "don't tell her you gave me her address. Or that I'm looking for her."

"I won't."

Nathan thanked her and left.

Thinking of what he'd say to Le once he finally saw her again, he found that the coldness within him and the rain weren't so easy to disregard. Against every impulse he had, he decided to wait until tomorrow to drive to Thanh Binh. By then, he hoped, his yearning to requite the pain she'd inflicted on him would be gone.

He hoped, too, that by tomorrow his inclination to urge Andrew to revoke Le's visa would give way to some more forgiving part of himself.

But he wasn't sure he could forgive her. He wanted her to know how it felt to have a dream crushed by someone she trusted.

9

No one answered the door when he rang the bell. He stepped back to look around the gated entrance. To one side, hidden behind a potted sago palm, was a sign he'd overlooked: *Doorbell broken. Please knock.*

When he knocked and no one answered, he stepped back again, inspecting the second- and third-floor windows. For a moment he pictured Le sitting on the rooftop's edge, watching planes come and go from Tan Son Nhat.

The building was like an old animal halfway through its molting; the building's gray skin, shaded by trees along the sidewalk, showed beneath a once-yellow coat. Mildew streaked the worn façade. It was the sort of place he admired: beaten up but not defeated. He doubted Le felt like this about her home, if in fact she lived here. Glancing at his feet, where ants swarmed over a crushed gecko, he guessed that pride had prevented her from inviting him here.

A curtain fluttered at an open window. He cupped his hands and yelled through them: "Le! Come down and open the door!"

The next thing he knew, two padlocks slid away from hooks above the inside door handle. The tinted glass made it hard to see whoever was staring out. What he could see, though, was that the person never expected to find a Westerner at the door.

He'd been in situations like this numerous times. His white face often threw people into a panic, for perhaps they knew no English and never suspected him of speaking Vietnamese (though they'd just heard him shouting it). It was a game that began with a stalemate, over before it had started.

The door cracked open, revealing the sliver of a woman's face. She called behind her. Another young woman hastened to the door, draping herself over the first woman's back. They talked about him openly.

"He must be from the consulate."

"Wouldn't he dress better?" She looked past him toward the street. "And where's his car? He'd have a black Mercedes with an American flag on the door if he worked there."

"What do you think he wants?"

"Wasn't he calling for Le?"

He glanced over their heads and saw a room with a low table and three chairs. He heard a TV and the sound of running water. Magazines, newspapers, and wadded-up clothes littered the floor. Beyond this mess was a small bedroom.

The door opened wider so the two women could stand side by side.

"Hello," they said in English, laughing and slapping each other's arms for having spoken simultaneously.

"Is Le here?" he said in Vietnamese.

"Ui! I've never heard a foreigner speak Vietnamese so well!"

"Where is she?" His seriousness swept away their smiles.

"I don't know. Maybe she went to the American consulate." They didn't explain, but he didn't need them to.

"When is she coming back?"

The woman shrugged. "She left before we woke up."

"Excuse me," the other woman said, making another pointless attempt at English. "What your name?"

"Nathan." He waited for recognition to cross their faces, but it never did. It was hard to dismiss the hurt he felt that after four months Le must never have told her roommates about him. "What are your names?"

"I'm Phuong."

"And I'm Khanh."

"Can I wait for her here?" He saw his request made them uncomfortable. After all, they had no idea who he was, and he surely hadn't impressed them with his friendliness.

"You want to wait?"

"I won't stay long." At this point it didn't matter if he saw Le this afternoon. Now that he knew she lived here, he could return any time.

"Why do you speak Vietnamese?"

"For the same reason you do," he said. He regretted that he'd revealed his ability to understand them. Perhaps now they'd be more guarded and not speak freely before him. "I'll wait inside if that's okay."

"It's okay. But we're embarrassed by the mess. Le had friends over last night and they didn't clean up."

They led him through the clutter to a torn vinyl couch. Broken shrimp chips were wedged between the cushions. Across from him, a small metal sink overflowed with unwashed bowls and glasses.

"Would you like tea?"

"No," he said, sitting down.

As he tried to decide what to do, they told him they'd been Le's roommates for over a year. They enjoyed living with her because she, like them, was from the north. They were sad to see her go.

"Did you know her in Hanoi?"

"No. We met here."

"Does she ever talk about her life in Hanoi? Maybe her family?"

They shook their heads. "She's nice to us, but we haven't gotten to know her well. We tried, but..."

Nathan heard a noise beyond the front door and sat up. Someone walked past, but they were tall and thin, carrying themselves like a man.

"It must be crowded here with the three of you," he said.

"It's okay because we get along. Anyway, in two weeks when Le leaves, we won't look for another housemate. We both just got raises."

Her words stopped him. "Two weeks?"

They hesitated before answering, as if his question was strange. He realized later that they must have thought he already knew – otherwise why would he be here?

The news was a stronger blow than the first.

"Have you ever been to Los Angeles?" one of them asked.

He cleared his throat, trying to regain his composure. "Once."

His answer excited them. "What's it like?"

He stared vacantly at them, hearing their question but not understanding he was expected to answer it.

"We hope to visit her. We're sure she can introduce us to many rich, eligible men." Their laughter bounced off him like the first drops of a downpour.

They asked again what Los Angeles was like.

"I was there once a long time ago," he said, gripping the arm of the couch. Strangely, at that moment he could remember nothing of his visit but a couple he'd run into while walking along Santa Monica Beach one night. It was near midnight, and they were caressing each other beneath a pier where the tide had receded. He could recall not only their faces but also their surprised, then angry voices as they yelled at him to go back from where he'd come. They'd thought he was a tourist, and of course they'd been right. That had happened seven years ago, and now he could hardly remember why he'd gone. "You start to forget about a place after you've been away a long time."

"Surely it's different when you leave at her age. How could she forget about her motherland?"

"Her forgetting has already started."

"What makes you say that?"

"Because I've seen it with my own eyes."

"What have you seen?"

Tiredness blanketed him as he wondered how to make them understand. But to be convinced they needed to experience that kind of pain, not simply be told about it. "It doesn't matter what I've seen."

They sat with him a while longer before heading off to their room.

He slumped back on the couch, thinking how odd it was to be in Le's apartment. It hardly seemed possible that this was where she came after they'd gone out at night; that this was where she slept; and that Khanh and Phuong were the people she saw after saying goodnight to him. Not once had she mentioned them.

His decision to come here suddenly felt ridiculous. Catching her in a lie gave him no advantage, even if it was true that she'd been dishonest about her visa application. Her dishonesty would only confirm a suspicion and make him hate himself for having trusted her.

He'd put himself in a position to be hurt – and for what? For a Vietnamese girl with pink hair whose life dreams were rooted in misguided hopes? True, a visa offered her a chance, but happiness wasn't assured. Not once had he heard her talk about the struggles she expected to face. Not once had she made him think she was prepared for the hardships awaiting her.

He tried to recall exactly when mere affection had transformed into ardor. Unable to remember, he thought that maybe he'd never started simply with liking, but that in him, from the start, there had been love.

It was too precious a thought, though, and too conceited. He'd been foolish to fall in love and that was all. But he hadn't been cozened for the usual reason. Rather than his lack of money, her plan to go to America seemed at the heart of her abrupt coldness.

An old French song drifted from a tinny stereo in their room. Le's roommates had just turned it on, probably to fill the silence.

There was only one bed for the three of them. (Apparently, the window he'd yelled up at wasn't theirs.) In one corner was a small desk and chair. There were no paintings, only knickknacks on twin shelves. A poster of two Western children dressed like groom and bride faced a photocopied advertisement of *Titanic*. Khanh and Phuong periodically peered through their door at him. Finally, one of them said: "Do you have a girlfriend?"

At first he thought they recognized who he was, but their expressions indicated otherwise.

"No," he said, almost choking on the word. The realization struck with an anger he was unprepared for.

"Since you speak Vietnamese, it must be easy for you to find a girlfriend."

There was no easy reply he could make. "Does Le have a boyfriend?" The question would probably sound innocent to them, but to him it was a poisoned arrow. Not knowing where it might land, there was no way to defend himself.

"She has too many," the girls tittered.

If this was how they were going to be, why bother digging deeper? Suspicion exploded inside him – what had Andrew meant when he said he questioned her visa support; did he learn something about her uncle? – and he realized that if he wanted answers he'd have to look for them closer to the life that Le led here.

He stood and kicked through the clutter to their room. Frozen in their seats at his uninvited entrance, they could do nothing more than watch him barge in. Even when he began picking through various items, they merely sat there wide-eyed.

He raised the bottom of their bedsheet and spotted two suitcases under the bed. Only when he bent down and pulled one out did Khanh or Phuong – he no longer remembered who was who – stand up and protest.

"What are you doing?"

The suitcase was heavy – the weight of a new life. He tried to open it, but it was locked. Slamming it against the floor did nothing, either. He ran his hands over its surface and came across a raised black square containing a blank address card. He wedged his fingers beneath the square and ripped it off.

The girl bent down to push the suitcase back under the bed.

Nathan didn't prevent her.

"Get out! Get out before I call the police!"

He went to the doorway and stopped. "Don't forget to tell Le I dropped by. I'd leave her a note, but in all this disgusting trash I'm afraid it would get lost."

"Who do you think you are? Just because you're a foreigner doesn't mean you can abuse us. Get out!"

"It has nothing to do with my being a foreigner." He felt he needed to hammer that home, but he didn't know how. "It has to do with people being decent to one another."

"Is this what you call being decent?"

"With Le the rules don't strictly apply."

"What are you talking about? She's not even here."

He looked one last time around the apartment. "It's not supposed to end like this," he said in English.

She clearly hadn't understood his last statement. She seemed to think he'd cursed her. She punched him in the arm.

"I said get out!"

He reached for the door handle, then stopped and turned around. What had come over him? Le's roommates were huddled together, watching him closely. "I'm sorry if I frightened you," he said quietly, unsure if they could hear him. "I'm angry at Le, not at either of you." Alarmed by his own behavior, he apologized again and stepped outside.

Storm clouds were rolling in as he walked toward the sidewalk. A caged bird sang from a neighbor's window. The bird fell silent, though, when the door behind him slammed shut.

He got on his motorbike and noticed various neighbors milling about. He felt their eyes on him as he kicked his motorbike into gear and raced off.

At the first stoplight he came to, his eyes flitted to a long white scratch in the sky. The lower portion was broad, for it had begun to dissipate, but higher up it was narrow and concentrated. He could just make out the airplane at the tip of the trail. He could see it inching higher.

10

Not far from Le's apartment he spotted a Vietnam Airlines office, and without a second thought he decided to buy a ticket to Phu Quoc. If she were going to leave without saying goodbye, he'd make it easy. In fact, he'd beat her to it. If she tried to make contact, he wanted her to find him away on his own adventure, having left her before she could leave him.

"How many people?" the woman behind the desk asked indifferently. A female colleague stood behind her, separating her hair into braids.

"One."

She took a long time to find him a seat, as the phone rang and she answered it rather than the woman braiding her hair. The delay, combined with the women's indolence, angered him beyond reason.

"How many days?"

The question triggered something inside him, and he wondered if he was about to commit a grave mistake. "Two days."

The woman lifted her finger to the screen and scanned a list of flights. "You're in luck. There's a flight leaving in three hours."

As he resumed his drive home, the clouds opened up. By the time he arrived he was soaking wet, and his ticket had gotten damp where he'd stuffed it beneath his shirt.

The rain had stopped when he went to flag down a taxi to the airport. He hurried past children playing badminton in his alley and ignored construction workers who shouted nonsense at him. As he passed by, he feared that these people, and this dank, dirty alley, were the only moorages to which he'd ever secure his life.

He sensed an emptiness to his surroundings now, as if some element, or some color, or something else he always took for granted, had been carried away by the brief but powerful shower.

This alley had seemed normal to him yesterday, even picturesque in its vivid, cramped way, but such perceptions already belonged to the past.

He found a taxi parked beside the curb. In the back seat he asked himself what it would mean to leave Saigon. But he knew the answer lay in action, not in wonder – it would take leaving to find out.

Out his window the city blurred past.

By the time he entered the airport, regret had stolen over him. What the hell was he doing here?

The travelers around him, the airport staff, the x-ray machines – standing in an actual airport – brought home the fact that he would never see Le again. Moving slowly, he came across a traveler's kiosk. Exchange rates and hotel discounts framed the service window. A woman inside saw him looking at the destinations they advertised and greeted him.

"I want to change my flight," he said, showing her his ticket. "Can I fly tomorrow instead?"

She turned to a computer on the counter and started typing. "Yes, sir. There are seats left on the seven a.m. flight. Shall I book it for you?"

"Yes. And I want to buy another ticket for the same flight."

From his wallet he pulled out a piece of paper with Le's name and address scribbled on it. "Her name's written there."

She asked if he had a hotel. When he said he didn't, she reached beneath the counter and sorted through a stack of brochures, tossing out ones for Phu Quoc.

He made a quick determination based on the listed prices. "This one. Make it one room. And leave our departure open."

He paid for Le's ticket and, feeling like he'd shucked off a heavy weight from his shoulders, went to find the taxi stand.

He had the taxi drop him off at the head of Le's alley. The dimming light and clatter of kids playing outdoors were to his advantage, he thought, as he passed her door. But it was still too light out for him to tell if anyone was home.

He spotted a noodle-stand in a small courtyard and sat at a table facing the alley. No one bothered him or obstructed his view of her door as he whiled away the time over a bowl of *bún thịt nướng* and three bottles of Saigon Beer. In case he needed to leave right away, he paid whenever he ordered.

As far as he could tell, Le had been gone since early morning. He supposed her roommates had contacted her after he'd left, complaining about what he'd done. But she couldn't be angry with him. If anything, she'd be scared. Aware that he knew her address, perhaps she was avoiding coming back. Unless she'd persuaded her roommates to bring her belongings to her, though, she'd have to return sometime.

He'd just ordered another beer when a motorbike pulled up to her door. As it rolled to a stop the headlight dimmed and he saw her seated behind a Vietnamese man – a *xê ôm* driver, apparently, seeing her hand him money and wait for change. Had she already sold her Honda Future? Or was there some other reason for her to use a motorbike taxi?

He realized he lacked a plan to get her attention. If he called out she might run away. And if he rushed into the alley, he'd have to deal with the man who'd dropped her off, not to mention other people in the street who took it upon themselves to interfere.

As soon as the man drove off, Nathan hurried into the alley. Le was already halfway to her door.

To his surprise, she didn't enter her apartment. He stopped and watched her disappear around the corner. He gave her a head start and then followed her.

Behind the apartment was a small door he hadn't been aware of.

It clicked shut – and locked – before he could reach it. With his ear against the door, he heard her ascending the stairs. When the stairs became quiet, he kicked the toe of his shoe into a wooden square at the bottom. The square fell in cleanly, and he knelt down to look through it. Craning his neck, he saw a stairwell rising into darkness. Uncertain what he was getting into, he crawled through the opening with barely any room to spare.

Littered with trash, the stairs rose four floors. There were no doors at the landings, only steps continuing upward. At the top was a wood panel where a door should have been. He slipped past it onto the rooftop.

In the surrounding buildings people were visible through barred windows and balconies filled with plants and hanging laundry, but the side facing the street was unobstructed. Like an actress on-stage, Le sat at a table in the middle of the rooftop, looking toward the airport.

Each step he took made him feel like the roof would collapse beneath his weight. Le whipped around, gaping at him as he grinned at her. He'd hoped his presence would shock her.

She pushed herself out of her chair. "Oh my god," she said, covering her mouth with both hands.

Instinctively he continued toward her.

Without looking away she positioned herself behind the table, nearly tripping over a second chair. He heard her mumble something, but the words, like a prayer, were indistinct.

As she stared at him, the wind rippled her black dress. Her outfit was unfamiliar, and he assumed that she'd bought it for her life in California. He'd never seen her so beautiful.

The distant sounds of children playing, families watching TV, and traffic swirled about them.

"What are you doing here?" she stammered.

Near enough that he could grab her if he wanted, he finally saw her as she was at this moment: her eyes were red and swollen, and tears streaked her makeup. The tears surprised him; he hadn't taken her for the sentimental type.

"You're scaring me," she said, backing away.

"That's because you can't run away from me here."

She dropped her face into her hands, but he didn't console her. Her crying angered him, and he resented this show of fragility. Was her emotion real? Or just a trick to elicit the sensitivity he'd always shown her?

Five years before, when he returned to Vietnam, Huong's reaction had been similar. He'd found her alone at her apartment and surprised her. At least then he'd been able to blame himself for what happened during his absence: after his mother died, he'd given neither her nor Anthony any indication he was coming back – he'd simply shown up three months later, choosing to visit her first, and expecting that nothing had changed. Who could fault them for getting together when he'd left them in the dark? Back then Anthony had been crazy about her. He'd been crazy about her, in fact, before Nathan had.

"Crying doesn't help," he said flatly.

She spoke through her fingers and the pink hair that swept over them, but he couldn't understand her. He came up and pulled her hands apart.

"Why have you been avoiding me?"

She didn't answer.

"Did I do something wrong?"

She backed up a few more feet, until she was an arm's length from the roof's edge.

"Be careful, Le. You don't know where you are."

She turned around and gasped.

He hurried to her and looked down into the street, where shirtless children, miniaturized by distance, played soccer and ran about recklessly, unconcerned by traffic speeding past. His anger, his confusion at what had happened the last few days, kept him from touching her again. She made no move toward him, either.

"Come back to the table and let's talk. I'm not going to hurt you."

"There's nothing to talk about."

For a moment anger made everything around him burn white – the small table and chairs; the tangle of phone wires over the street; the high walls of neighboring apartments; the electricity-tinted sky. His anger was with himself, and he began to imagine she'd been cruel to him because he'd left her no alternative.

"It would've been easier if you'd asked me to come over," he said. "I never wanted to stake you out."

Her eyes seemed larger than usual as she wiped her tears. "Please, Nathan, just go away."

"Do you really expect me to leave now?"

Sniffling, she shook her head.

What was she crying for? Didn't she finally have everything she wanted?

When he asked her what had happened, and why she hadn't told him that she'd been issued a visa, she said: "I was afraid, Nathan. I don't know why. It was easier not to deal with you. And besides," she added, crying again, "I don't have a visa anymore."

"What?"

She managed to calm down long enough to explain. The embassy had called her that morning, half an hour after she'd sold her motorbike, and asked her to bring her visa with her. When she met with embassy officials, she handed it to them, and then it was given to an employee with instructions to destroy it. "They said that I'd lied about my application and they had no choice but to do this. It didn't matter that I'd already bought my ticket to America."

Andrew's words from the party shot into Nathan's mind. That he might have gone out of his way to get Le's visa revoked seemed unlikely. If he had followed through, he must have had good reason – what did he have to gain from that but hours of extra work? Although Nathan was curious, he had no desire to learn what Andrew's role had been, if any, in revoking it. The only thing that interested him was that Le could no longer leave for America.

Between sobs she claimed to have nothing left. She'd lost her gallery and couldn't bear to face all the people whom she'd told she was leaving. "It's not that I care what they think. It's that I don't want to be reminded every moment of what I've lost."

Nathan couldn't bring himself to say he was sorry – he wouldn't say it, even though it pained him to see her so anguished.

"I need to know something, Le. When they gave you the visa, why didn't you tell me?"

She took a moment to compose herself. "I said I'd be your girl-friend so you'd help me. From the beginning I was honest about that."

"You never had feelings for me?"

"I didn't know how else to get you to help me."

"So sleeping with me was just part of the deal?"

She paused before nodding.

"I don't believe you."

"You expected it. That's how life is, right?"

He supposed that in Vietnam it was. "Love's not a transaction."

"Love?" she said angrily.

Her tone stung him. "Maybe not love. But something close."

"No," she said. "You don't understand me."

He had no idea how to argue against such a charge. "How am I supposed to understand you when you've been lying to me all along?"

She didn't reply immediately. When she answered, her voice was gentler. "I only wanted your help to get a visa. I didn't have money to pay you."

"I don't believe you. You were always affectionate with me."

"But that was our agreement."

He hadn't wanted to become involved with her in the first place, he told himself. Yet against his every intention to fall for her, and every indication that a relationship must be short-lived, he'd poured every ounce of hope into being with her. He'd given himself to her, stripped of protection.

"What are you going to do?"

"I'm leaving Saigon," she said. "I'm never coming back."

"But where would you go? In Saigon you know people, you have friends, a place to live. You still have a good life here." He stopped, waiting for her reply, but also wondering if she really meant what she said.

She shook her head, saying nothing.

"And what about us? In a few days, a week or two, maybe you'll feel differently."

"It doesn't matter anymore," she said, wincing. "Nothing I feel tomorrow or in a few weeks will compare with this. Anyway, you deserve better than me."

"Let me decide that."

"You can decide whatever you want. But I have to make my own decisions now. My life, I have to start it over."

The old question – why trade success for failure – crept onto his lips but he didn't ask it. He knew that success and failure were different to her than to him.

A circle of light, hardly bigger than a star, had emerged on the horizon. The longer they watched it the bigger it grew. Soon the outline of an airplane was visible. Every few seconds a red light blinked on its tail.

"Come to Phu Quoc with me," he said. "You said you wanted to go there before leaving."

"Nathan," she said, taking his hand. "Please forget about me."

"I already have the tickets."

She gave him a surprised look.

"I bought them this afternoon. I thought you and I…"

She put her fingers on his lips and cut him off. "The truth is, Nathan, I don't ever want to see you again."

As if the wind were pushing him, he backed away from her, until he could see the entire length of the roof's edge, until the table and chairs came into view and then the bright apartments on either side, and until she was very small standing there with her face buried again in her hands, sobbing.

He yanked the panel from the stairwell door and hurried down the dark stairs.

Through his bedroom window, the moon rose slowly, perfectly full. He wondered why the higher it climbed the smaller it became. Was it hurtling into the far unknown? Or was it a trick of angles, an effect of the earth's rotation?

Trying to understand how he'd misjudged Le so badly, he couldn't sleep. He threw on some clothes and went downstairs. The guard lay snoring on a table. Nathan inched the door open and slipped out onto the street.

The city felt unfamiliar at three in the morning. For the first time he could remember, there were no sounds of human activity. It was cool and quiet, and he focused on the silence without moving. After a moment he realized that he could hear the Saigon River.

Turning right on Ton Duc Thang and following it past the Legends Hotel, the river came into view. Across the street was a small park where old French cannons pointed over a wall. The park was popular with young lovers, and he was surprised to have it all to himself.

He sat on the wall dangling his legs over the water. Occasionally a barge chugged past, and in the light cast by billboards on the opposite shore he could see inky silhouettes of people on board.

America rolled into his consciousness like waves of heat: images of people and places he knew there wavered on their edges. In dreams these old friends sometimes beckoned to him to return, his dead parents begging him, though for the last year or two those dreams had stopped. But the more he thought about it, the more he realized he couldn't go back: he had no money to return and start over. Combined with what he owed Anthony, this chained him to where he was. He looked into his hand and saw he was holding his cell phone.

Not caring what time it was, he dialed a number and put the receiver to his ear.

"Hello?"

Anthony sounded like he'd just uttered his final breath.

"Sorry to call this late." In the background he heard Huong ask who it was.

"Nathan?"

"Yeah..."

For several seconds Anthony said nothing. "Are you drunk?"

"No."

"Then why the hell are you calling?"

Anthony's anger was unmistakable. Over two months had passed since they'd last communicated – a marked lapse for their friendship, if he could still consider it that.

"I'm not sure."

Anthony laughed witheringly. "It's three in the fucking morning. What do you want?"

"I needed to call you."

On the other end he thought he heard a door open. He could almost imagine the balcony, the rattan furniture, the moonlight reflecting off of West Lake. The thought of being in Hanoi made him regret chasing love over career opportunity.

"If it's money you want, I'm not giving you any more."

"It's not money."

"Is it that girl?"

Nathan looked behind him. A motorbike had stopped at the curb, and the man and woman on it were watching him. Apparently uncomfortable with Nathan's presence, they drove away.

"I bought a ticket to Phu Quoc today. I was supposed to go this afternoon, but I couldn't do it. I couldn't leave her." He didn't know how to explain. Where was he to begin? "I'm in a bad way right now."

"Are you going to make me guess what happened or are you going to tell me?"

"I don't know if I want to talk about it."

"Fuck off, Nathan. You drop out of my life for almost three months, you break a promise to join my company and screw me in the process, and now you tell me you don't know if you want to talk? It's three in the goddamn morning. Spit it out."

"Le's leaving Saigon tomorrow."

"Leaving for good?"

"She wasn't even going to tell me. She threw everything we had in my face like it was shit."

Anthony said nothing, and Nathan wondered if he felt that he'd done the same to him.

"I staked out her place tonight," Nathan went on. "I waited three hours to see her, but I should have just gone to Phu Quoc. She said she never wants to see me again."

"Why are you calling me?"

The question came out so forcefully that Nathan couldn't immediately answer. "Because we're friends."

He laughed. "You sure have a fucked-up notion of friendship."

"I know I do." The chastisement felt good. He was ready for it and wanted as much as Anthony could dole out.

Anthiny enumerated the ways he had let him down. Nathan listened to every word.

"Everything you say is true," Nathan said. "I don't have excuses. But..." He tried to fight down the tremor in his voice. "But I found something I wanted in Le. As soon as I met her everything that used to be important changed."

"You still haven't told me why you're calling."

"I did tell you. I'm calling because I value you as a friend. And I'm sorry."

"Is that all?"

"What do you mean?"

"Nathan." Anthony paused. "If you turn me down again, I'll never forgive you."

A moment passed before Nathan realized what he meant. "Are you talking about the job?"

"It's the whole point of this call, isn't it?"

Nathan asked himself if the reason behind his call was not to rekindle their friendship but to ask Anthony to help him change his life.

"I'm tired," Anthony said after the quiet moment grew long. "Just tell me yes and I'll FedEx you a ticket in the morning. A week should be enough to cut your ties and leave Saigon. I put off hiring anyone in the hope you'd come around."

"You'd do that for me?"

"I never liked Le, you know – never liked the idea of her – but I'm thankful she ended your relationship. I know you think she was cruel to end things like she did, but it's better this way. Soon you'll see you have small mercies to be grateful for. This job's only one."

"You never met her."

"I didn't need to. She was after your money, like Huong was after mine, like every Vietnamese woman's after every..."

"She didn't need money. Her uncle in Los Angeles was supporting her."

"It's all the same thing, Nate. If it's not money, it's a visa. If it's not a visa, then it's something else. Never the heart, though. In those cloying love songs you hear in cafés and on state-run TV, maybe. But in reality, in the life that's lived around you, no one's ever after the heart. Remember this the next time you think you're falling in love."

Nathan's chest clenched. The feeling was so painful he had to massage it with his fingers. "Anyway," he said, "it's over…"

"Nathan."

"Yes?"

"Say you'll take the job."

In his head, Nathan realized, he'd been readying to leave since getting the news about Le. "I will," he said. "That's what I want."

"You said the same thing before, but this time I believe you. It'll be good having you around again. Huong feels the same way." Anthony's voice turned more subdued. "My health's been bad, you know. I've had to take it easy the last few weeks."

"You? I didn't know." He suddenly remembered what Andrew had told him.

"That's because you never answered your phone or e-mails when I tried to contact you." He stopped to drink something. "Like I said, it'll be good having you here. I might not be my old self for a while, but I'll come around."

"What's the matter with you?"

"I don't know…Life gets stressful."

The wind picked up off the river, and Nathan bent his head to hear Anthony better.

"Huong just shut the bedroom door. If I don't return soon, she'll lock it."

"Sorry to call so late."

"Don't sweat it."

"I didn't realize you were so sick. If I'd known…"

"Don't sweat it, Nate. I'm not dying or anything."

"And the job…"

"You don't know how to end a conversation."

Nathan laughed uneasily. "I guess I feel like a lot still needs to be said."

"Then call me again tomorrow and let's talk."

Nathan took his time returning to his guesthouse. Back in his room, he opened his balcony door and gazed over the flame trees below.

Dawn would soon spread over Saigon, draining the lonely night into a blue abyss.

When a street sweeper made her slow approach Nathan went inside to find his tickets to Phu Quoc. Returning to the balcony he tossed them onto the street. The sweeper stopped and looked up at him. Neither of them said a word, and when she continued with her work Nathan turned around and went to bed.

11

"Who's it from?" Nathan looked at a clock on his wall and saw it was nearly noon. He pushed at his hair, which was matted from excess sleep.

The deliveryman only pulled impatiently at his sweaty uniform, saying nothing.

Had Anthony sent him something after he'd accepted the job at his company? It would be like him to bulldoze him with gifts, with pressure tactics he could conveniently call kindness. But to send something now didn't make sense.

"Where was it posted?"

The man flipped through a pad of crinkled papers. "Saigon," he said.

The cardboard at each corner of the package was frayed, and the ribbon-made handles had left grooves where the weight of the thing had rested while being carried. There was nothing on the package but Nathan's name and address. The man handed him the pad to sign.

It was a confirmation of receipt. The sender's information was in a small box – a looping script blown to the right. There was no name other than a florid signature at the bottom he couldn't read. When he saw the address, however, one mystery, apparently solved, became a bigger one.

Immediately he knew it was a painting. But what did Le mean by sending him a painting he'd neither bought nor asked for? Surely it was worth several hundred dollars – a large sum in Vietnam.

When the deliveryman left, Nathan dragged the package to a chair and ran his hand over the cardboard, looking for an opening. His eyes stopped on the handwriting in the center of the package, each letter thickly drawn, pregnant with deliberation. His name appeared darkest of all, as if she'd traced it over and over.

The painting materialized in slashes as he tore the wrapping. Soon the picture emerged: a night dappled with stars; moonlight reflecting off the wings of bats in the sky; a silvery, snaking river flanked on both sides by rioting foliage; a nude woman floating on her back, her grotesquely long neck jutting up as if for a last glimpse of whatever the current was carrying her away from.

It was a morbid tableau and he couldn't understand why she wanted him to have it. The strange neck sprouted from her shoulders like a flower stem. As in the other paintings, her profile was as faultless as a photograph.

Wedged between the painting and frame was a small envelope. A hollowness descended on him, and all he could do was gaze at the envelope's barber-striped border and the words *Air Mail – Par Avion* stamped in an upper corner.

Taking a deep breath, he shook the letter out and began to read.

Dear Nathan,

I remember how much you admired my gallery's lacquer paintings and how encouraging you were about my art. It's because of you that I'm leaving Saigon to find myself again. I won't tell you where I'm going, but my decision to leave is the only choice I feel I have. I told you the truth when I said I'd give anything to be an artist. And it's even truer that you gave me strength through your own example, turning away a good job for something you hoped would give you more happiness.

You must find it ironic that I'd write about truthfulness when you think I lied to you all along. If in fact I told you lies it was only to protect secrets I couldn't have you know. I was afraid I'd expose them, and my fear pressed so hard on me I thought it would overwhelm me and I'd tell you everything. In the end, that's why I left like I did.

I hate myself for hurting you, but it's nothing compared to how I feel for putting so many walls between us. I can't blame you if you don't believe me, and I'm sorry if that's the case. Perhaps you've decided I was cruel and selfish, but I was trying to spare you. You deserved more than I could give. Only now can I admit this.

I hope to see you again. But what does a hope like that mean now? I'd rather wrap my hopes in silence, to preserve them, and I want you to know that if you don't hear from me again it's because I think it's better for us both. Silence, you know, doesn't necessarily mean the end of something.

Love,
Le

He opened his desk drawer. Letters and postcards from the U.S. were crammed into a folder. For a moment he wanted to look through them, to review the months and years lived by friends so far away he was sure that time and distance had dislodged him from their hearts. But the thought terrified him and he shut the drawer. He stuffed Le's letter in an empty coffee cup, then took a lighter from his windowsill and pressed his thumb on the metal edge. A flame shot out and danced in the wind from his fan. He touched it to the letter.

Smoke rose and grew thick. Pieces of ash swirled around him, drifting onto his desk. An odd thought made him smile: During his seven years in Saigon, in all the squalid and depressing places he'd lived, not once had he had a smoke alarm. Some of his landlords had asked if he cooked or smoked. When he said he did neither, they assured him he was safe.

In Hanoi, he'd have to make sure he had one. It was better to be safe than sorry.

12

Saigon was easier to leave than Nathan expected. There was no telling when he'd be back, and part of him thought he never would. The ambiguity surrounding his departure left him curiously empty, as if the sum-total of his experience here had amounted to nothing.

A dull, spitting rain fell ceaselessly during his final week in Saigon. The sky was continually bloated and gray. The city looked like it had absorbed all that was unclean, and rain was the only means to wash it away.

On his last day, staff at the magazine he'd worked for sent him off with a less than rousing cheer, and at night an acquaintance he bumped into insisted on buying him a beer, then half-heartedly tried to drag him to a massage parlor.

"I forgot you don't go in for that kind of thing," his friend said petulantly after he'd given up trying to persuade him.

"Go ahead," Nathan said, not wanting to end his last night on a bad note. "Don't let me ruin your fun."

"It's not fun. It's something to pass the time."

They shook hands awkwardly and wished each other good luck.

"I reckon it's only a matter of time before I see you again down here," the man said. "Everyone knows Hanoi can't hold a candle to Saigon."

On his way to the airport the next morning Nathan realized he was leaving no "footprint" of his time in Saigon. He didn't know if he should feel depressed or liberated by the idea that were he to come back one day no evidence would exist of the life he once led here. Aside from a few friends, he'd be treated like a stranger in a city he knew better than any other in the world.

These days the only traces most foreigners left were underused belongings, humdrum gossip, and old lovers. In a way, he tried to tell himself, leaving no trace here was a sign of success. There was purity to the notion, as if he'd succeeded against the odds to avoid something regretful.

The flight's brevity surprised him. Given so many historical and cultural differences between the north and south, he'd forgotten only a thousand miles separated Saigon from the capital.

Standing at Noi Bai's baggage carousel, he recalled the vast grid of farmland that had grown larger out his window as the plane descended. It was Red River country – rice paddies stretching to unfamiliar mountains and small, tile-roofed houses spotting the flooded green – the cradle, as the north saw it, of the country's civilization. The Saigonese often conceded this to Hanoi, though they staunchly claimed for themselves a southern culture, untrammeled by northern influence. Northerners, his Saigonese friends liked to tell him, were different from them: colder, stricter, less trustworthy, worse at business but more rapacious, unfunny, cruel, uncharitable, arrogant, firm in their rejection of modern ideas and practices. But he never put much stock in these pronouncements. The one northerner he'd known well was Le, and she hardly fit such a profile.

Anthony met him at the exit holding a white balloon. Filled with helium, it bobbed above his head.

"Some woman was selling these on the highway. They were cheap, so I bought her entire inventory for my kids. They're in my Land Rover, probably losing air."

"It's like you're picking me up for a date," Nathan said, reaching for the balloon.

"Think of it as a gesture: what's mine is yours. Have I ever been less than generous with you?"

Nathan felt uncomfortable at the reminder that Anthony had given him so much already.

Once they'd pushed past a pack of waiting taxi drivers, Nathan noticed, as he had on his previous visit, that the air was different than in Saigon. It was like drinking a glass of water only to find that afterward he was still just as thirsty.

The smell of rain hung in the air. The clouds the airplane had descended through appeared to have fallen and grown thicker. The weather wasn't merely warm, like he expected, but humid. By the time he reached Anthony's Land Rover he was blotting his forehead with his sleeve and tugging the back of his shirt where sweat made it cling to his skin. When he got inside he asked the driver to turn on the air-conditioner. The man was someone different than when Nathan last visited.

"One day Huong found him in a guestroom with one of the maids," Anthony explained. "We got rid of her, too. Unfortunately, her sister also worked for us. She complained so much about the dismissal that we threw her out as well. Last I heard, the girls' father sent them both to Taiwan to be housemaids."

Vietnam was exporting more workers overseas, many of them contracted as maids in Korea, Taiwan, and Hong Kong. It was hard to imagine women from the Vietnamese countryside becoming maids in foreign countries. Of course, these women didn't make the decisions themselves, but were following their parents' directives. It was also how scores of them ended up in Cambodian brothels.

"How's the family?" Nathan hadn't heard Anthony complain about his home life since they'd resumed communication. That, along with the balloons in the back seat, made him guess that things had improved. Anthony seemed to be making a fatherly effort.

"We're like different species with overlapping territory. We're still learning how to co-exist."

On both sides of the highway, beer and cell phone billboards rose from the rice fields, blighting the ubiquitous green. The landscape took hold of Nathan's imagination, and he didn't have much to say. He only realized he was thinking about Le when Anthony broke the silence with a proffered thought about her.

"What happened with Le was a blessing in disguise."

"It didn't happen like I wanted it to. I feel like it ended poorly when it didn't have to."

The driver punched the brakes, jerking them forward in their seats. He turned and apologized, but Anthony had his eye on Nathan and didn't respond.

"What did you expect?"

"I didn't think it would get to me so much, that's all."

"It was just a matter of time. Better for it to happen now than later down the road."

The words made his loss feel more irretrievable. But there was truth in what Anthony said. And he sensed that truth, if he believed in it, could shield him against pain.

"Just forget about her and move on. You made a good decision by coming here."

"I hope I don't regret it."

Anthony slapped him on the knee. "I have a new rule I try to follow. I won't let myself speak or even think certain words. One is *forever*. Another is *unhappiness*. So is *trapped...helpless...*and the most important one to avoid is the word you just mentioned."

"You forgot *suicide*."

"I didn't forget," Anthony said. "We all need last resorts." His serious face slackened a bit. "That's one of those sacred words. You need a certain amount of courage just to get it off your tongue."

"It's an extreme rule, isn't it?"

"What's the matter with it? I thought it would resonate with you."

Nathan paused to consider the advice. In the end, he disagreed. To live like that was no good. If he ever started to, he'd know it was time to leave Vietnam.

"Some ideas seem innocuous on the surface. But they'll bore into you if you let them. Think about it. It's the only way you'll survive here."

It wasn't any way to survive, Nathan thought, turning back to the window.

They were approaching a wide river. A sign before the bridge passing over it read Sống Hồng: the Red River. Factories in the distance spewed white smoke over the otherwise agrarian countryside. Across the river, the transformation from countryside to city began in earnest.

"Tell me again what I'll be doing here," Nathan said, wiping away the fog his breath made on the window. He was tired of talking about the past.

13

The house was on an island on Truc Bach Lake. Two stories tall and shaded by trees, both sides were wreathed with bougainvillea. The road in front was dusty from construction, but it too was shady and made doubly cool by zephyrs off the water. There was noise here, but the overall feeling of quiet impressed Nathan.

"Not too hard on the eyes, is it?" Anthony said.

Nathan laughed. The house was better than Anthony had described.

"I tried to get you a place near me, but at the last minute the deal fell through." Anthony unlocked the door and held it open for Nathan. "It's the best I could do. I had to sign a long-term lease and pay for it two years in advance."

Nathan stood on the step, peering inside. "Two years?"

"You better not run back to Saigon next week. Not after this."

Nathan couldn't think what to say. He hadn't made a two-year commitment.

"Two thousand a month, twenty-four months paid in advance." Anthony handed him the keys.

Nathan cringed at the figure. "That's insane money."

Anthony laughed. "Don't you like it?"

"I love it. But..."

"If I were single like you," he said, not letting Nathan finish his thought, "I wouldn't want to live anywhere else."

The first floor alone was bigger than anywhere he'd lived in Vietnam. Furnishings were standard in rented homes, and here was no different. In addition to a sofa, two chairs, a dining table, and a roll-top desk, there was a TV, DVD player, and stereo. Slipping off his sandals to avoid tracking dirt onto the polished floors, he wandered to a narrow spiral staircase. The black metal rail was cool to the touch. Turning his hand over, he half-expected to find it smeared with fresh paint.

"Where are the rats and cockroaches? I'm not sure I can live in a place that doesn't come with pets."

Anthony's expression told him not to joke about it. "You're going to make a better life for yourself. When you live in a cave for seven years it does things to you. A decent place to live can make all the difference. People respect you more when you live in a nice home in a nice neighborhood. I want you to know what that's like."

Nathan climbed to the second floor. After glancing into an office equipped with a scanner, printer, and antique escritoire, he stepped into the bedroom. A mosquito net descended from the ceiling to a queen-sized bed. Beside the entrance to a marble-walled bathroom were another TV and DVD player.

"I don't deserve this."

From the bathroom came the sound of Anthony urinating.

Truc Bach Lake was visible through the balcony door. Nathan could only see a sliver, roofed by gray sky, but it was enough. A view of water felt like a luxury that belonged to someone else. The small lake ended at a narrow, well-traveled road. Beyond it spread the much larger waters of West Lake. He went out onto the balcony.

The view from his guesthouse in Saigon had been of a dirty road and a sidewalk filled with barbers. That the changes in his life could be so immediate and comprehensive was hard to believe.

Anthony glanced at his watch. "I'll let you get settled. You've got a big day ahead of you, so rest up. Check out your neighborhood. See what you think of the girls on your block."

"What are you doing tonight?"

"I have a family commitment. I'd invite you, but it wouldn't be fun."

"I'll see you tomorrow, then."

"I'll come by at seven-thirty and take you to work."

Nathan stayed outside, watching motorbikes pass on the small road below. Where the road curved around the lake were cafés and shops. The island's quietude provoked in him a moment of anxiety until he realized that in Saigon quietude was what he'd always sought.

Above the trees in the distance, an airplane had begun its descent to Noi Bai Airport. Watching it high over the water he wondered where Le was now, what she was doing, and with whom; wondered if she was filled with regret or had found some new hope to dedicate herself to; wondered which was the greater struggle for her: the past, present, or future.

Unable to answer these questions, he felt like he'd never really known her. As he considered this, the incipient loneliness he felt in this house, in this city he didn't know, evolved into an unsupportable weight inside him. He couldn't help but dwell on the possibility that she'd already forgotten him. He stepped back into his bedroom as a light rain began to fall.

The house felt too big for him, and whichever room he occupied, the others were loudly empty. He told himself that his loneliness had less to do with Le than because life in a new place was always hard at first.

A minute later the skies opened, and the thrumming of rain on the roof echoed throughout the house.

At six in the morning, he wandered onto his balcony to watch the sun rise over both lakes. To his left, neon Nokia and Tiger Beer advertisements blinked pink and blue on the water, and lights started to flicker on in neighboring windows.

The sky slowly gradated to a soft, powdery blue, dusted with broken clouds. From nearby roe tree canopies, birdsong drifted to his ears, growing louder as the morning brightened.

The prospect of his first day at Anthony's company exhilarated him. The feeling lodged in his stomach like a vague sickness.

Anthony arrived in his Land Rover at exactly seven-thirty.

"How was your first night?" he said as Nathan climbed in.

"Like being in a nice hotel."

They approached the island's small bridge. Food vendors congregated here, huddling over their goods.

"Have you eaten?" Nathan said.

"I never eat breakfast."

"Can we stop so I can grab something?"

"Here? Why don't we go someplace civilized?"

"There's no point if I'm the only one having breakfast. Anyway, I don't like eating with an audience."

Anthony told the driver to stop. Nathan stepped out and bought a baguette filled with fried egg, paté, and vegetables. He felt Anthony's eyes on him as he bantered with local customers.

"Mind if I eat in here?" Nathan said as he got back in the car. But Anthony was already on the phone.

When Anthony hung up Nathan asked if he always got calls that early.

"The first calls come at around seven. You'll get them, too, pretty soon."

"Not if I keep my phone off."

Anthony ignored the remark. "I hope you're ready to work. I'm guessing real estate requires more time and energy than writing."

"That's because you don't write."

"I don't write because I don't have the time or energy after work."

Nathan knew that Anthony would only try writing if everyone else was doing it and making gobs of money. "I'll have to pencil in some writing time, even if it means sacrificing sleep."

"Things are happening at the agency," Anthony said with a tone of friendly warning. "You're going to be busy. Busy and tired."

Ten minutes later the driver pulled through a gold metal gate and parked beneath several areca trees. The villa was a deep rich yellow, though mildew spilled from the clay tiles of the sloping roof, streaking the stucco above the topmost windows. The dark green shutters on all three floors were open, and inside Nathan saw ceiling fans spinning.

"This villa's nicer than many embassies around town. But maybe I feel that way because it's mine." Anthony draped an arm around Nathan's shoulder. "If you tell me you're disappointed, I'll make the guardhouse by the gate your office."

By rights, Nathan thought, Anthony should be proud. His friend's transformation from struggling teacher to successful businessman was almost impossible to comprehend.

"How'd you swing this place?"

"It's my job."

Anthony clapped him on the back and led him inside.

The first thing Nathan saw were people at a meeting table, looking uncertainly from him to Anthony. A phone rang somewhere, and a young woman ducked away to answer it.

"I've arranged your official welcome for this afternoon," Anthony said, leading him along. "You can introduce yourself then." Another half dozen employees were milling between their cubicles and the binder-filled shelves against the wall. Nathan was surprised Anthony had so many employees, even if he couldn't have been paying them very much.

A few days before, Anthony had divulged that his highest-paid employee only made two thousand dollars per month. Now that Nathan worked here, he'd placed a moratorium on salary increases. Year-end bonuses, too, would be smaller. Nathan had told him he was uncomfortable being the reason for the staff's decreased pay, but Anthony insisted that he not worry.

"Let me show you your office."

Nathan followed him up a marble stairs.

"You and I are up here," Anthony said when they reached the second floor. "Above the fray, so to speak."

He continued toward a closed door. Anthony's name stretched across a gold plate in the middle of it.

The office was spacious, and light streamed through its thinly draped windows. As in many Vietnamese homes and offices, the ceilings were twelve feet high. Air pushed down from rotating fans and a

Japanese air-conditioner was mounted above the door like the head of hunted game. Anthony's office was large enough for a dozen people to work in.

Anthony pointed to a door across the room. "That's the bathroom. It's got a shower and a bathtub fitted with jets."

"I could live here," Nathan said, stunned again by the outward signs of Anthony's success.

"We could be flatmates if you did. I've been known to spend the night here myself."

"Why? Your house is down the street."

"It's a necessary escape sometimes."

When they left Anthony's office and entered another large room, Nathan was seized with trepidation. He had no relevant experience for this job. To go from travel writing to real estate management felt like a sideways jump that would leave him sprawled on his back.

Anthony pulled the curtains open. Sunlight streamed in, awakening the room from slumber. Before him was a wide desk, a bookshelf-lined wall, a table and small refrigerator, and a sofa for receiving guests. Two oil paintings leaned against a wall, waiting to be hung.

"Think you can work here?"

Nathan nervously laughed. "I just hope I don't screw up." His eye caught four thick binders of company literature on his desk.

"I'm the one who keeps this company afloat, not you or anyone else. If you remember the pressure's all on me, you'll be fine."

"There'll be pressure, I'm sure."

"Look, I started this from nothing. The pressure for me to succeed was much worse back then. The fact is I learned by making mistakes. You have the good fortune to follow the path I already cleared."

"You've got a stronger constitution for business than me. I worry I don't have what it takes."

"You're just jittery because it's new," Anthony said, waving his hand impatiently. "All this job requires is commitment. There's nothing special about that. Anyone with half a brain can do well here."

Anthony was right, Nathan guessed. But it wasn't his intelligence he was concerned with.

"Seen enough?"

"I don't know what else I should want to see."

Anthony smiled. For a moment he seemed to be asking himself if Nathan indeed had what it took to succeed.

As they walked back to Anthony's office Nathan said, "I'm impressed."

Anthony shrugged. "I'm stuck in Vietnam, so I might as well work in a comfortable environment."

"What I mean is you've done well for yourself."

"My company's only been around for four years, but yes, we've done well. Real estate's still a relatively untapped industry here. People don't know what they're sitting on. Plus, the tax laws are full of loopholes. It's a goldmine, Nate. I got here at the perfect time."

"You dropped off the map for a while, then the next thing I knew you had a real estate business going. For a while I thought you were like Robert Johnson and had met the devil at the Crossroads."

Anthony laughed, and it reminded Nathan of late March when Anthony could barely manage a smile.

"You think I sold my soul to the devil to run a real estate company in a developing communist country?"

"I have no idea how it happened. Whenever I asked, you gave me some cryptic, dismissive answer."

"There's really not much to it. I called a friend in Malaysia who wanted to set up a real estate business in Vietnam. He flew here and I told him that no matter what happened I wanted in."

Anthony sat heavily in his chair and went on. He said he'd been worried that his Malaysian friend might not come through, but after several weeks he called to offer Anthony three hundred dollars a month to start.

"That must have been hard for you and Huong."

Anthony shook his head. "It didn't last long."

"What changed?"

"Our luck. And everything else."

Despite the business getting a few breaks in the beginning, he said, the mother company's board of directors made a connection between losing money and the overt corruption in Vietnam and after six months they dropped the country from their investments. By the end of the first year all the foreign real estate investors had withdrawn their overseas managers and thrown in the towel.

"That was all the opening we needed. My friend and I picked apart their businesses, and developers whose contracts had turned worthless soon asked us to take over their properties. Occasionally we served as a joint agent with a company set to crumble. When that happened we were already positioned to take over. We were like vultures watching them die."

In just a few months, he continued, they had become Hanoi's veteran real estate company. A large London firm eventually approached them; their backing made business pick up as never before. "I became a legally certified agent through them and now I'm a member of the Royal Institution of Chartered Surveyors. Along with a fifteen-year operating license from the Ministry of Property and Investment, that makes me legit."

"What happened to your friend?"

"He came into money. He did the wise thing and dropped out. Then, wise or unwise, he handed everything over to me."

Nathan had more questions, but he couldn't find his voice. Already he felt overwhelmed, but there was something else he was getting lost in.

"Stop thinking about her."

Anthony was right. Without realizing it, Nathan had been wondering what Le might think if she could see him now.

14

On Sunday, after lunch, Nathan drove downtown. He found himself in the vicinity of the gallery where, several months earlier, he'd spotted a portrait Le had painted. Curiosity propelled him there again.

Working in the gallery were the same two girls as before. They were helping other people, however, and though they greeted him warmly they didn't seem to recognize him.

As he inspected the paintings, he began hoping to find another self-portrait of Le. He shook his head at this awareness, yet his eyes jumped from one painting to the next. None were of Le.

As before, numerous paintings had not been hung, for the walls lacked space. Dozens stood in vertical rows of four and five along the floor. It was in the third row, the second painting back, that he experienced a shock almost as great as the first time he visited the gallery – here was another portrait of Le, emerging from a lotus pond, hovering between two faceless women collecting and bundling the flowers in short canoes.

When he realized that neither girl working there would soon help him, he removed his cell phone and bent down to photograph the painter's name in the corner of the picture. With an idea firmly in mind, he looked out the window. Not finding what he wanted on the sidewalk, he decided to walk across the street and wait in a narrow alley. From a café there he could sit and observe the gallery at his leisure.

He ordered coffee and, over the next fifteen minutes, watched the odd motorbike pull onto the sidewalk across the street. None, however, were delivering paintings, and none belonged to the man he was looking for.

The café was apparently not a place where foreigners often came, and he soon became the center of attention. Even now, after so many times, it wore him down.

He had e-mailed Le his new cell phone number several weeks ago, but when she didn't respond he called Thao at Bac-Nam to ask if she knew how to get in touch with her. But she had no idea. Coming across another of Le's paintings, then, was perhaps his only chance to find her.

Overhead a sheet of blue plastic protected the alley from rain when it began to fall. Soon it came down in torrents.

Nathan paid for his drink and, when he turned back to the street, sheltered by his umbrella, he saw the deliveryman he'd been waiting for drive up to the gallery. Rain had drenched his shirt and the front of his pants and flattened his hair to his scalp. Luckily no paintings were tied down behind him. Getting caught in the rain, Nathan mused, seemed to be this man's talent.

Before Nathan could intercept him, the man disappeared inside the gallery. But a few seconds later the girls working there forced him outside again. From across the street, over the downpour, Nathan heard them berate him for tracking so much rain inside.

There was nothing for the man to do but peel off his shirt and wring it out. Afterward he wrestled it back on and lit a cigarette.

Nathan crossed the street, dodging the sparse traffic. "Excuse me," he said.

The man looked up wide-eyed. At the sight of Nathan he started coughing, and smoke briefly obscured his face. "Hello," he managed to say.

"Can I ask your name?"

The man touched his chest and said, "Lam."

"Do you remember me, Lam?"

"Yes," he said. "You came here a long time ago."

"Those girls inside constantly abuse you."

Laughing uneasily, Lam glanced toward the gallery.

"You didn't deliver any paintings."

"No. Maybe on Monday or Tuesday."

"Do you earn much here?"

Again Lam laughed. "I'm very poor," he said, making a sour face. "I have a wife and two babies at home, but the gallery pays me next to nothing."

"Are you working for them today?"

"Sometimes they ask me to bring things here, but since the weather's turned bad they probably won't ask me to do anything. I only get paid when they have something for me to do."

"Do you want to get paid today?"

Lam pulled on his cigarette, then flicked it into a small current racing past the curb. "What kind of question is that?"

"It's an offer. I'll pay you ten dollars for something easy."

Lam leaned back against the building. "What is it?"

Nathan reminded him of his conversation with the girls in the gallery back in March. To Nathan's surprise, Lam nodded.

"They thought you wanted to cheat our boss."

"Right. But I never intended to buy anything. I only wanted to meet the painter."

Lam glanced back at the gallery. "How do I earn the money?"

On his cell phone, Nathan showed Lam the photo of the painter's name. "There's another painting of hers inside, a new one. I want you to take me to wherever you go to collect her work." Nathan knew it was a strange request, and that a strange request might seem to Lam more trouble than it was worth. He was ready to pay as much as Lam asked for, even if only for directions. Despite the crudeness of the gesture, he took a ten-dollar bill from his wallet to show Lam he was serious.

Lam nodded.

"My motorbike's beside the post office," Nathan said. "I'll follow you."

On the way to his motorbike, Nathan bought a pair of disposable raincoats. When he pulled up beside Lam, he tossed one into the metal basket beneath his headlight. Lam shook it from the bag and tugged it over his head and shoulders. In a flapping of thin plastic they were off.

Nathan trailed Lam through the city. Few streets were yet familiar to him, and he was struck by how different Hanoi looked to Saigon. In Hanoi the French presence could still be felt, preserved in the architecture and layout, whereas in Saigon the atmosphere still harked back thirty or forty years to the American era, the notion of aesthetics crowded out by practicalities of war. The scale, too, was different. Hanoi was a smaller, more manageable city, yet it was hard to imagine ever knowing it as well as he'd known Saigon.

In a few minutes they were skirting West Lake, on the side opposite from where Anthony lived. Here it was dirty and cramped, a far cry from what he'd seen of Hanoi up to now. The road soon gave onto stubby vegetable fields to the left and a littered shoreline to the right. They came upon a broken-down mule-cart beneath a tree, and at the next muddy turnoff they veered into an area of small, colorful houses and chickens pecking at stones. Perhaps because it was Sunday, and raining, few people were out. They'd been driving only fifteen minutes, but Nathan felt like he'd entered a quaint country village. The rain soon stopped.

Lam pulled up to a woman at a road-stand for a pack of 555s. After ripping the pack open, he discovered his lighter was waterlogged. The woman sold him this as well.

"The painter lives here?" Nathan asked.

Lam nodded at a house across the street. "That's where I've picked up the paintings the last month or so."

"What's the painter's name?"

Lam thought for a moment. "I forget."

Nathan handed him the ten dollars and watched him drive off.

The painter's house was a beat-up blue, its façade streaked with water stains. A frangipani tree bloomed in the yard, and a few spindly trees leaned toward the street. Small pots of flowering cacti dressed up the doorway.

Le was from Hanoi, though he didn't know in what part of the city she'd grown up. She'd never described living near West Lake, and the omission reminded him how much she'd kept him in the dark about her past.

No one answered when he rang the doorbell, and his calls echoed in the darkness of the front room. Glancing behind him, he saw the cigarette vendor wander across the street to the gate.

"No one's inside," he told her.

She pointed to a path that led behind the house. "Walk toward the lake. She always paints under the banyan tree."

As he stepped toward the path the woman asked if he was a painter.

"No," he said. "But I admire her work." He left her smiling at him, clinging to the gatepost.

An admixture of certainty and uncertainty, of excitement and dread, whipped through him. If Le were truly here, might this mark the resumption of an old journey or would it finally bring closure to it? There was no telling what she would do if she saw him again. His expectations were low, but even if his presence upset her, he still had a right to see her. Rationalizing his feelings, however, got him no closer to what he wanted from her. Acceptance would be enough, then perhaps they could take things from there.

Potted plants and trees lined the path; the shade was cool and wet, trilling with cicadas. In the middle of the path lay a cracked palette, a farrago of bright and dark colors. Behind this were overturned jars.

As he stepped over them he saw Le at the end of the path. Her back was to him, draped with untied hair. A strip of plastic tarp, bluer than the sky, stretched above her, and she stood on a tawny circle of reed mats speckled with paint. Beyond this spread West Lake, its dark waters rippling. An easel stood before her, and she was gazing at it, not painting.

He was struck by something different about her, and he waited tensely for the feeling to clarify. But he wasn't about to stand there forever thinking about it. The longer he waited, the more nervous he got.

Halfway to her he realized she'd changed her hair from pink to black. For a moment he thought the woman might not be Le at all. But her profile, and her height and figure, made him certain that it was – and, with black hair, she was also the woman in her paintings.

The sense of familiarity grew stronger the closer he got. He wanted her to turn around, but her canvas held her gaze. When he was twenty feet away, he stopped.

"*Em ơi*," he called out.

Le turned as if her shoulder had spoken, and it was then that her familiarity resolved itself in profile. She turned all the way around and froze. Her mouth dropped and stayed open, as if at any moment she might shriek. She stared at him, one hand over her heart.

"Nathan," she said, barely able to get his name off her tongue. "What are you..."

Intensely conscious of himself, he could only gawk at her. He waited for bitterness to assert itself in his heart, but all he felt was a pleasant numbness.

She was looking around, he thought, for someone to help her. He saw that she was scared.

"I've been hating you for a long time," he finally said. "But hate's not why I'm here."

"How did you find me?"

He stepped toward her again but stopped. "At least, I don't think I hate you. I should, but right now I feel pretty in control of myself. I think I might actually be happy to see you."

Had their time apart healed him? Or was it having found her like this that made him happy?

She set her paintbrush and palette on a table, and then, eyeing him suspiciously, walked toward him.

"What is this place?" he said as she came close enough they could have touched.

She raised a hand to wipe her forehead, leaving a smear of paint behind. He reached to clean it off her, but she drew away.

"I said, how did you find me?"

Her shirt, which fell past her knees, was splotched with paint, with swirls of bright colors covering her breasts and stomach. He had never seen her wear such a thing. She looked completely different from the Le he'd known in Saigon.

"I met someone who knew your address."

She seemed to become a bit more relaxed. "But why are you here? Did you come to Hanoi to find me?"

"No. I moved here for that job at my friend's real estate company."

The sound of a fish breaching the lake's surface made them turn toward the water. Nathan's eyes swept over the canvas she'd been painting, but he couldn't see it well.

Le's eyes filled with tears. "I don't know what to say to you. Why are you here? What do you want from me?"

A long moment passed before he said, "Well, some tea would be nice. And maybe a chair to sit in and drink it."

"Tea?"

"Iced tea, if you don't mind. As you can see, I'm sweating."

She turned to the house but didn't move toward it. He heard her release a lungful of air.

"And a chair."

Two chairs stood beside the door to the house, and she hurriedly brought them over. "Iced tea…"

As she disappeared inside her house, he walked to where she'd been working. Her canvas was half-sketch, half-painting. When he looked for a girl with a stem-like neck, he found none – only a small boat along the shore with unrecognizable objects around it. Lifting his gaze from the canvas, the tableau was filled in before him.

The tree shade where he stood smelled of her, and he felt he could stay here for hours watching her, or sleeping at her feet, or creating something beside her. Recognizing the feeling, which was more powerful than anything he'd felt in many weeks, he drew back into himself as much as he could.

He scanned the far shore trying to locate Anthony's home. The general area was not hard to find, for the Sheraton, rising above the trees and the multi-story lakefront homes, was less than a five-minute drive from where he lived. But the distance made the houses look small and indistinguishable from each other. With the big banyan tree here, he wondered if he could identify Le's home from where Anthony lived.

He turned around and decided that this was indeed a good place. Le's painting space, the old house and overgrown path, the breeze off the lake, the copious shade of trees, the air loud with cicadas, the fading blue of the house, the roof tiles full of fallen flowers and leaves – all these things somehow made it so.

She returned carrying a tray. As she poured tea, he noticed that her slender fingers, too, were stained with paint.

They sipped their tea in silence.

Needing a starting point Nathan said: "What made you change your hair? I almost didn't recognize you."

"I didn't like how it looked."

"But you never complained about it before."

"It gives me a different kind of confidence."

"Confidence in what?"

"Starting over."

He sensed that she wasn't in the mood for small talk, but he'd only started the conversation he wanted to have with her.

"I'm surprised you're living in a place like this."

"You say it like it's a beautiful house."

"I can tell it was beautiful once."

"It's a simple place. Simple is what I need right now."

"I see," he said, falling silent.

She sat there, not saying a word, either. Her hands, trembling slightly, peeled away from her teacup. "I lied to you."

He waited for her to explain.

She looked toward the lake. "I never had an uncle in California."

A burst of heat flashed behind Nathan's eyes.

"The man I called my uncle is named Quan. I've known him for many years."

He didn't need her to tell him that this lie, too, had been a means to an end, but he couldn't help wonder how different things would be now if she'd been honest from the start. Maybe he wouldn't have grown so close to her in Saigon, and by this point she'd be gone from his life forever. In a twisted way, he felt almost grateful for how things had turned out. After all, he was with her again now.

"If Quan isn't your uncle, who is he?" Nathan forced himself to ask.

Until she'd lost her visa, she said, he was her fiancé. He was also a painting prodigy and the youngest son in a rich, powerful family. But he was spoiled, too wild, and when he had run into trouble three years ago – she was vague about this, but he wanted no details – his parents sent him abroad. He had enrolled in a prestigious art school in California and now made his living there as a painter. He hardly needed to work, partly because his parents supported him, but also because his paintings sold well. Because he couldn't return to Vietnam for fear of reprisals, he had convinced Le that if he posed as her uncle she might obtain a visa to America and join him.

Listening to her, Nathan wondered if all of this were a lie, too, rehearsed for his benefit on the small chance he'd force her hand. He marveled at his own calmness. Perhaps he'd expected this all along.

"And the house?" he said.

"It's Quan's father's. He says I can stay here as long as I like."

He looked coldly toward the lake as she explained how Quan's father owned the property and others like it in the neighborhood. When her visa was revoked, he'd offered to help her. "Fulfill your promise as a painter," he'd urged her. The house was to be Le's home and studio. He'd put no conditions on her staying here.

Nathan stared at the residue at the bottom of his tea. For a moment, he thought that he still hated her after all. "You're still seeing him?"

"No. But after my visa was revoked his father offered to help me."

"Maybe he hopes you and Quan will work things out."

"His hopes for us don't matter."

Watching her for a reaction, he wondered if she were deceiving him again. There was nothing for her to gain by it, though, and he dismissed the thought. It was hard to believe she would have given up her life in Saigon for a run-down house and an easel beneath a banyan tree, even if living here were free. While he recognized her talent, he never thought she had an artist's single-mindedness and temperament. The thought reinforced the idea that he never really knew her.

"Tell me why you're here, Nathan."

He didn't know what else to say. "I don't know why. I didn't plan it. I guess you were on my mind."

"I don't believe you. Thinking about me and going out of your way to find me are different."

"Are you upset I'm here? Because I sort of thought you'd be glad to see me and know that I wanted some kind of fresh start for us."

"So that's what you want? A fresh start?"

Nathan wasn't sure what he was saying. "I don't know what I want."

"Well, I do. I came here to change my life."

"And does your new life have to exclude everyone from your past?"

"It's simpler that way."

Nathan wondered where the anger in her voice came from. And then he found himself feeling angry with her.

She offered him more tea, but he covered his glass with a hand. "I don't know why I'm here. Call it impulse, or call it whatever you want. But I'm ready to be friends with you. No arrangements, either. Just friends."

"I don't know if I'm ready."

"That's fine. Do whatever is best for you. We both know you're capable of looking out for yourself. Anyway, you know how to reach me if you decide you want me around."

She was looking off to the side when he said goodbye. She still hadn't moved when he turned down the path toward the gate. He watched her a moment longer, then headed for the street, where the road-side vendor gave him directions to return home.

15

His days at the office revolved around combing through agency e-mails, answering client inquiries, and submitting draft proposals for formal contracts. Twice a day he did an office walk-through, speaking with each employee and asking about whatever problems he or she had. Some work he delegated, but most of what appeared on his desk he dealt with himself. There were valuations and reports to write, and investors inquiring about the local market constantly coming and going. It was essential that he keep on top of all the properties they were developing for purchase, renovation, and lease. During lulls, Anthony asked him to take a few high-level employees aside to help them improve their English. Normally he attended two meetings a day, which was in addition to general office administration. After a few weeks he felt his work squeezing him on all sides.

The money was even better than Anthony had promised and would be enough to settle his debt with Anthony in slightly more than a year. But money wasn't what he was after, and soon he was waking up each morning overwhelmed with malaise. It took several weeks to unlock that feeling and understand that it came from not writing. Behind it was a kind of warning: you'll regret most the things you haven't done with your life, and in the end it will tear you apart. Time wasted, a voice told him, was time forever lost.

When he returned home at night, time for himself was scant. If it wasn't too late, he'd drive to a café near Le's house and, from a lakeside seat, try to glimpse her painting beneath the banyan. Like his writing, however, little resulted from the investment of time. Sitting, of course, got him nowhere.

Making friends in Hanoi was hard, particularly since he spent so much time at the office. As with other things, it was simpler to rely on Anthony. But he found he had little in common with Anthony's friends, who for all practical purposes were business contacts anyway.

Late one morning Anthony called him into his office. Sitting at his desk, he was grinning into a local magazine.

"Well, I did it," he announced as Nathan came in.

"Did what?"

"Helped you where you were unable to help yourself."

Nathan couldn't guess what he was talking about. He hadn't come to Anthony with work problems, nor had he asked for any favors.

Anthony pointed at a page of photos in the magazine. "There she is. One of the hottest properties in Hanoi. Beautiful, successful, well-connected, rich. And thanks to me you've got a date with her."

Nathan's first thought was to protest, but something stopped him. He stood there dumbly, smiling uncertainly.

"I understand your surprise," Anthony said. "I couldn't believe it myself when she said she was free tonight after work. A woman like her, not only single but free on a moment's notice..."

Nathan looked at the magazine. The woman's photograph was slightly blurry, but her image was clear enough to see she was beautiful.

"Damn right she is," Anthony said. "Her name's Hoa."

Hoa's photo was in a section entitled "Voyeur." Other photos included the state visit of Norwegian royalty; the New World Hotel's ten-year anniversary; the launch of a Vietnamese gas company; a group of foreign lawyers waiting before the Opera House for a cyclo tour of Hanoi; and an organized walk to raise funds for Agent Orange victims from the war. Hoa was photographed at the opening of a new bar. She was slender and elegant in a thin-strapped evening dress, her hair ran halfway to her waist, and her face was tinged red, evidently from the champagne in her hand.

Her appearance was faultless, yet Nathan felt no excitement being set up with her. Still, he had no reason to decline.

"I know it's short notice, but after work tonight the two of you are going to join me and Huong for dinner. Afterward we'll turn you loose on each other."

"Does she know about me?"

"Huong and I told her all about you."

"What did you tell her?"

"Good things, of course. Huong laid it on thick. You'd think it was my wife who was excited to go out with you."

Nathan's stomach stirred nervously as he handed back the magazine. Anthony tilted it under the light to study Hoa's photo, shaking his head appreciatively.

Nathan thought he heard his office phone ring. Anthony didn't seem to have anything serious to talk about, and Nathan was busy. "I'd better get back to work. I have a marketing meeting soon."

"Hold on a second," Anthony said. "This is probably going to sound silly, but Huong asked about you last night and I didn't know how to answer her."

Startled, and suspicious that Anthony was baiting him for a particular end, Nathan waited for him to go on.

"After we discussed you and Hoa, she asked if you plan to marry and have a family. She made me promise to interrogate you."

Nathan pretended to caress a crystal ball and channel his future. "Divorced a few times, but never married."

"Too bad. I was going to suggest we swap wives after you're hitched."

"No offense, but Huong's not my type. I once thought she was, but that was before I knew what I wanted."

"What?" Anthony said, sounding incredulous. "You two were serious for a while. She says that if she hadn't married me she'd have married you when you came back."

That Huong would have said this surprised Nathan. He suspected Anthony made this up to get a reaction. "We wouldn't have lasted. We're not each other's type."

"Why quibble over 'type' when it's only a matter of swapping?"

"This isn't a conversation I'm prepared to have."

"Anyway," Anthony said, laughing, "she likes you. Whenever she gets mad at something I've inadvertently said or done, she says she should leave me and run to you. It's a great joke to her."

"She says what?"

"It's partly to make me jealous, but also because, unlike me, you were born for domestic life."

Uncertain why Anthony or Huong would think this, Nathan didn't know how to respond.

"If something happened to me," Anthony went on, his laughter gone, "I'm sure she wouldn't waste a second before calling you."

His effort to make a joke of his predicament at home had started off innocuously, but something now corrupted it. Nathan worried that his name came up when they argued, and that Huong used him to get under Anthony's skin. He wondered what Anthony said about him to convince her she was wrong.

Nathan forced a laugh, thinking he was ridiculous to care what Huong thought of him, but it failed to dispel the awkwardness. Anthony seemed to be waiting for his response, but after a moment he gave up.

"Seriously, what do you think your future holds?"

"I have no idea. That's something I need to figure out while I'm up here."

"'While I'm up here,'" Anthony repeated. "You don't sound like you're planning to stick around."

"I probably will. But I've been thinking of moving back to the States once my time here's up."

For a few seconds Anthony glared at him. "I'm not your warden, you know."

"I'm just saying that my future's on my mind."

"You really think you can go back?"

"What do you mean?"

"You and I, we've missed the boat. We're stranded here now. If you go back, you'll only find yourself in Vietnam again – maybe three or four years later, but with lots of time and money wasted."

"Why are we stranded?"

"Nate," Anthony said, looking at him sternly, "who the hell would hire us? They'll look at our CVs and laugh in our faces. Even with my real estate experience, it would never translate into a comparable position in the U.S. Even with my credentials I'd have to start at the lowest rung. Besides, getting a good job back home mostly depends on who you know. Who do you know who'll help you over there? You don't even have any family now."

The mention of his family took him aback. "There's always graduate school."

"Sure. If the prospect of being a hundred thousand dollars in debt afterward doesn't bother you."

"Not a hundred thousand dollars. Tuition at a state school's not that much."

"Nathan," Anthony said brusquely. "It's not only tuition that will put you in debt. It's living."

"I've got time to figure it out."

"Do you? You're nearly thirty. And you're committed to me for at least a few years."

Nathan bristled at the arrogance behind Anthony's prognostications. Rather than argue, though, he reminded himself that they'd never discussed how long he'd work here. Anthony had merely extended him an opportunity, which mostly had to do with paying him back several thousand dollars. But it wasn't as one-sided as that: Nathan's agreement to come here benefited Anthony, too. In any case, he'd signed no contract. And if Anthony asked him to, he'd refuse.

"Where would you go? Back to Ohio?"

Nathan saw the confidence of an easily won argument in Anthony's face.

"I haven't thought about it much."

"No one in Ohio would know what to make of someone who spent seven years in Vietnam. They'd think you were a communist.

Besides, you have too much Vietnamese in you now to go back to what you had there."

"I don't want what I had. I just want to be able to choose what to do with my life. Maybe I'll go to California. I like the sun."

"You sound like that girl in Saigon who broke your heart."

Nathan bit his tongue. "She never made it to California. Now, if it's all right with you, I've got a meeting…"

"Where is she now?"

"Still in Vietnam."

"In Saigon? Looking for someone to marry and take her away?"

"Why don't you ask Andrew? He always has his nose in other people's business."

"Maybe I will."

"If you don't mind, I need to get going."

When Nathan made to leave, Anthony said: "Maybe California's the right place for you, then. Sometimes I think hell's not as bad as advertised, either. I mean, look at me: Not long ago I was convinced that Vietnam was right for me."

"I hope I answered Huong's questions satisfactorily," Nathan said. He walked out of Anthony's office – quickly, before Anthony could call him back.

Back in his office Nathan remembered that Le had invited him that night to an exhibition of century-old German drawings. Although her invitation had been casually offered – "Come if you have time," she suggested in an e-mail – he was irritated at having forgotten it. He viewed her invitation as an opening for the two of them.

After work he followed Anthony to his villa. Huong was in the living room, smoothing down her short, frilly dress before a mirror.

"We should have left by now," she said in greeting to them both.

"Good to see you, too," Anthony said.

Nathan sat on a chair by the window. On the floor, Anh and Hao lay on their stomachs. Their grandparents sat behind them. All four were riveted to a *Tom and Jerry* cartoon dubbed in Vietnamese and didn't look at Nathan or Anthony when they entered.

Anthony returned with two drinks. After handing one to Nathan he stared blankly at his children. Nathan sipped the clear liquid in his glass and winced. Anthony had poured him three fingers of straight gin.

"Huong," Anthony said after gulping his drink. "Take Nathan upstairs and pick out something for him to wear. He seems to think he'll impress Hoa with what he has on."

"He looks fine," she said, sighing for Anthony's benefit. Turning to Nathan with the imprint of impatience Anthony's dallying had left on her, she said in Vietnamese: "Hoa's excited to meet you. If you make a good impression, and I know you will, she won't notice if you show up wearing a dress."

"But if the point is to make a good impression, wearing a dress doesn't seem like the way to do it."

"Did Anthony show you her picture?"

"Yes." She was clearly eager for him to say what he thought of her, but he didn't want to give her something to share with Hoa later, even if it would benefit him. In English he said: "Where are we going tonight?"

Hao rolled onto her side and shushed them. But when she saw the angry look Huong flashed her, she smiled innocently and rolled back onto her stomach. Anthony's mother-in-law raised the TV volume with the remote control.

"A place called Au Co, off Xuan Dieu," Anthony answered. "It's romantic at night."

Nathan had driven by it before. While it looked nice from what he'd seen down its sloping drive, he was surprised they hadn't chosen some place more exclusive. "Maybe we should've just had dinner here."

"No," Huong snapped. "I want to get out sometimes, too." As if embarrassed by her outburst, she left the room.

It was too late to back out now, Nathan thought, but he'd try to create an excuse to leave dinner early. Even though he and Le weren't together anymore, he couldn't get past the feeling that it was too early, or just wrong, for him to see someone else. The only woman he felt capable of being close to – the only woman he wanted to be close to – was Le.

On the TV, Tom howled in pain after Jerry smashed him over the head with a frying pan. The kids and their grandparents burst out laughing.

"It numbs the mind just being here," Anthony said. "Let's wait outside for Huong."

Nathan followed him across the room and through the door.

16

When they arrived, Hoa was on the open second floor, gazing at a pond behind the restaurant. The pond's existence surprised Nathan, though he supposed it shouldn't. Water was everywhere in Vietnam: no coincidence that in Vietnamese the word *nước* denoted 'water' as well as 'country.'

When she stood to greet them, he saw she was taller than her photo had indicated. Her striped blazer and trousers reminded him of the outfit Le wore to her final interview at the consulate.

Hoa exchanged a kiss on each cheek with Anthony and Huong and, when his turn came, he nearly choked on her perfume. He withdrew from her cheek, which was so warm he thought it must be blood rather than rouge that gave her such healthy color, and sat beside her.

"You didn't bring her a gift," Anthony said. Then, looking at Hoa: "I instructed him clearly to bring you something nice."

"I was in the office all day," Nathan protested. Everyone laughed at his defensiveness.

"That's okay," Hoa said. "But next time I won't forgive you."

"Hear that, Nate? She let you off the hook. Don't let a woman like that slip through your fingers."

Hoa's perfume clung to him. Grabbing the wet face towel from the bamboo tray before him, he tried discreetly to wipe his face.

He'd been so conscious of meeting Hoa, and of being observed by Anthony and Huong, that he'd only given their environs a passing glance. As Anthony ordered for everyone, Nathan looked around. On the far side of the pond, bathed in moonlight, several men squatted with bamboo fishing poles between their knees. They appeared to be watching the restaurant. Trees that might have been weeds a thousand years ago swayed behind them. The men looked like cats that had emerged from a forest, intent on the strange civilization across the water.

A small boat bumped against a floating hut in the pond's dark middle, and someone hovered in the doorway, watching them like the fishermen were.

"How do you and Nathan know each other?" Hoa asked Anthony, disturbing Nathan's observations.

Nathan watched Anthony rewind through time, to when they'd exchanged their first hello. "We lived in the same Saigon guesthouse. He rented a room above mine and annoyed me with his noise. I went upstairs to make him shut up, and to appease me he invited me out for a beer. A week later I got him a job at my school. Come to think of it, I'm always helping you land a job."

"Not the writing job."

"That was more like volunteer work."

Hoa turned to Nathan. "What did you write?"

"Short articles no one read," Anthony answered.

"She was asking Nathan, not you," Huong scolded him.

"He's basically right," Nathan said. "Although I surprised myself a year ago by getting a travel article in the *San Francisco Chronicle* and another in the *San Jose Mercury News*."

"Those were the only things that paid decently, I bet. Why didn't you send them more articles?"

"I did. But they weren't interested. And then, for some reason, I stopped trying."

"What was your last article?" Hoa asked.

"Something on Buu Long Mountain, but I'm not sure it got published. The last thing I saw in print was a piece about Friendship Village."

"Friendship Village – for Agent Orange victims?"

"Yes."

"You should keep writing," she said.

Anthony chuckled into his drink. "Nate's an expert on many things, you know."

The wariness in Hoa's eyes showed that she knew Anthony was capable of saying anything.

"Take lacquer painting, for instance. His knowledge on the subject is unmatched."

"That's very interesting."

"It *is* interesting." Anthony was smiling, having a good time with this. "I like lacquer painting, too – I have expensive pieces in my home and office – but I only know a fraction of what Nate knows. Can you believe that when he was in Saigon he actually fell in love with a painting?"

Before moving to Hanoi Nathan had shipped his belongings to Anthony's address. One item had been the lacquer painting Le had sent him. Anthony claimed that his children had opened it when it arrived, and that he couldn't help having seen it. When he'd guessed that the subject was Le, Nathan affirmed with surprise that it was. Anthony laughed in equal surprise, saying he'd only been joking.

Hoa clapped in amusement, then touched Nathan's hand on the table. "Maybe you should write about lacquer painting. If you learned about it in Saigon, take advantage of it. A newspaper that rejected you might want something like that. And Anthony says they pay well."

"I don't have time," Nathan answered.

"That's true," Anthony said. "If you published something now, I'd think you were shirking your duties to my company."

"I like lacquer painting," Hoa said. "But I don't know much about it."

"Nate has a beautiful piece hanging in his bedroom. A beautiful painting of a beautiful girl. In Saigon he was best friends with a gallery owner. If he wasn't at home, you knew he was at that gallery losing himself in all the beauty there."

Nathan's gaze lingered on Anthony, wondering what had triggered this bit of viciousness.

"I know some galleries in Saigon," Hoa said. "Which gallery did your friend own?"

He considered making something up, but he didn't care what Hoa learned about his relationship with Le. Le wasn't a source of embarrassment to him the way she seemed to be for Anthony. That Anthony would mock him like this, deliberately putting him in an awkward situation, angered him. Not knowing how to stop him, he sank further into the helplessness he'd felt since Anthony showed him Hoa's photo.

"Bac-Nam," he answered.

"I think I know it. Is it on Nam Ky Khoi Nghia Street, in District Three?"

"Yes."

"Then I do know it. But only vaguely. I forget if I met the owner." She shut her eyes and rapped her forehead with her knuckles. "What's her name?"

But Nathan didn't answer. He was staring at Anthony, messily smiling at him.

"All that's in the past," Huong said. "Nathan lives here now. And he works so hard I'm sure he doesn't have time to go to galleries anymore."

"Aren't you burned out on those places?" Anthony said, leaning in. "Such pretentious people there..."

"I've been to a few in Hanoi already. They're not bad."

Hoa spoke encouragingly. "Like Anthony said, you must know a lot about Vietnam. As a foreigner, that knowledge puts you in a unique position. It makes me wonder why you work in real estate. It seems like a waste of your skills."

Anthony laughed. "His problem is he has skills few Americans value: fluent in Vietnamese, eats dog meat, drinks snake wine. All of it gets his pecker up. Vietnam's in his blood."

Huong broke the awkward silence that followed. "Nathan was the only one we trusted to work for us. I had to pressure Anthony to hire him."

"That's right," Anthony said, as if he'd forgotten. "Hiring him was your idea, wasn't it?"

Nathan turned to Hoa. "I never heard this before."

"He's too modest," Anthony said. "Aren't you, Nate? Modest like Ho Chi Minh."

Sensing the potential for Anthony to segue into more embarrassing areas, Nathan asked Hoa how she and Huong knew each other.

"We've always known each other," Hoa answered.

"Since childhood," Huong said. "Both our parents helped secure supplies along the Ho Chi Minh Trail during the war. Afterward, the government rewarded our families with a small room to live in and a bathroom to share with twenty other families. Hoa was my neighbor. We grew up together. I'm sure I told you about Hoa when we dated."

Nathan listened to them share anecdotes from their past. Soon they were speaking in Vietnamese, laughing at old times. Their switch to Vietnamese induced a weariness to settle over Anthony.

The evening wore on. Anthony drank more than Nathan was used to, giving rise to a crimson glow on his face and neck, while the heat and humidity covered it all in a clammy sheen. He constantly wiped his forehead with a wet face towel, then began using Huong's, which she hadn't touched.

On a TV at one end of the restaurant the BBC ran a story about the Iraq War. There was no sound to the broadcast, only images of American soldiers patrolling a debris-filled street in Mosul.

Nathan saw that Anthony's attention had strayed from the table; he, too, was watching the TV.

"Those insurgents are tough little bastards, aren't they?" Anthony said.

"They blew up sixty people in a Baghdad market yesterday."

Anthony's eyes drifted to Hoa. When she noticed him looking at her she stopped talking.

"I bet you didn't know that Hoa's fired artillery from American tanks," Anthony told Nathan.

Hoa smiled, dabbing her lips with her napkin.

"What are you talking about?" Nathan said.

"Tell him, Hoa."

"I was in Houston last month, pushing business deals, and a company I was working with invited me on a retreat. I had no idea the retreat would be full of tanks and artillery. Our instructors were veterans from Vietnam and the first Iraq war, and they trained us on GPS devices, military gear, navigation tactics, everything. We learned things as a team. And I have to say, I've never had so much fun."

"It didn't bother you?" Nathan said. "Going to America and seeing adults and company leaders playing war?"

"No," she said. "I made many friends."

"To me," Nathan said, wanting to make a point while avoiding provocation, "turning America's war machine into personal recreation is a little sick. As if you can't get enough of it on TV or in history books, and have to destroy some beautiful area for kicks."

"Get off your soapbox already." Anthony's eyes were narrow with a malevolence Nathan wasn't prepared for. "It's not sick or destructive. It's classic teambuilding – not war games or whatever phrase you want to disparage it with. What's sick about it? Are people dying? Is the environment getting napalmed? No." Anthony answered his own questions quickly, not allowing Nathan a word in edgewise. "And guess what? I like the idea so much I'm thinking of bringing the concept here. A kind of paradigm shift – keep the real estate thing going but branch out. No one's doing company retreats here. The market's untapped."

"I just thought Vietnam had enough of that sort of thing last century."

"I'm sure they did. But we're not talking about war. It's about making people work better. It's about making Vietnam more productive." He seemed to find in his words a catchphrase: "It's productive, not destructive. And I think it's brilliant."

"It's not as bad as you think," Hoa said, as if Nathan needed placating.

Anthony drained what was left in his glass and told a waitress to get him another. "He's new to business," he said, wiping his mouth with his hand. "Green about the whole game and how it's played."

Nathan didn't say anything. He'd become interested in Huong's silence – from the corner of his eye he saw her watching him.

Anthony leaned forward, intent on saying more. "Like I said, I'm thinking of importing the concept here. You can fire AK-47s at Cu Chi, so why not build a command station and let people drive tanks on the mountains around Ba Be Lake? Investors were going to build a golf course there five or six years ago but never did. So we take the land off their hands and give them something for their lost investment. It'll be a steal for us, and good for them, too. Hoa and I've been talking about working together on it. I'm thinking of putting you on this, Nate, give you your first big project."

Nathan tried to move the conversation somewhere safer. "You can get government approval on imported tanks and a military retreat? And what about customs? Aren't tariffs on imported vehicles over one hundred percent?"

"They're around two hundred percent. But anyone well connected can avoid that. I'm sure the same goes for tanks. Just get the government to oversee the whole enterprise, promise some officials a cut of revenue, and voilà. The only problem is that decommissioning makes it nearly impossible to get American tanks. British tanks are much easier. Old British FV4201 Chieftains are the way to go."

There wasn't much Nathan could say. Anthony had obviously done a lot of research already. "To me it's a waste of money."

"That's the greenness again," Anthony said to Hoa. Then to Nathan he said: "It takes money to make money. And the Vietnamese would love this. Hoa said so herself, and Huong thinks it sounds fun, too."

Nathan excused himself to the bathroom. To his surprise, Huong did the same. They walked down the back steps, and when they crossed the courtyard to an outbuilding with paired doors, Nathan looked at Huong, pointed at a sign with a man's figure on it, and reached for the doorknob.

"Nathan," she said, waving him back. He followed her to the side where they couldn't be seen. "Tell me what you think. She's nice, isn't she?"

"She's all right."

"All right? That's it?"

Something in her smile made him uncomfortable.

"You've become quite the commodity," she went on. "Good job, high salary, fluent in Vietnamese. You don't seem to understand that you can have anyone you want."

Her reasoning didn't appeal to him, however true it might be. "I tried once," he said.

"That didn't count. She was only using you for a visa."

"It counted." His awkwardness with Hoa was proof.

Anthony had referred to Hoa as a hot property, and now here Huong was calling him a commodity. For those who made their lives buying and selling, perhaps it was natural for their relationships, too, to develop like businesses. There was a bottom-line involved with whoever they dealt with, and friendships were either profitable or not. He didn't want to be considered an investment, asset, resource, or any other dehumanizing term they bandied around.

Maybe he was only being petty, he thought. But where did such pettiness come from?

Huong touched his arm, smiling almost pruriently. "What you're looking for might be right under your nose."

For a moment he thought she was referring to herself. But the thought was self-indulgent, and he flushed with shame at the idea. The intentness of her stare, however, kept the thought alive. His only escape from it was to look away.

The pond was visible from where they stood. An oil lamp burned inside the floating hut, and the flame flickered as if it might be snuffed out. Focusing on the unsteady glimmer, he realized that the flicker was only bats feeding around the light's nimbus. The man he'd seen in the doorway was gone – but not gone, for his head now emerged from the pond and began to circle slowly around the hut.

It was loneliness Nathan felt, seemingly out of nowhere, and he had to fight an urge to confide in Huong about Le. If Huong really wanted him to be happy, she might even tell him to leave dinner early. But he didn't feel she had his best interests in mind. He sensed that, like Anthony, she had her own plans for him.

In the bathroom, his cell phone vibrated. His first thought was that Huong had sent a message from the other side of the wall, giving up the indirect approach to tell him what she hadn't been able to say to his face. Instead, he saw a number on his screen he didn't recognize. The message was in Vietnamese: *It's Le. I wanted to remind you about the exhibition at the Fine Arts University. Or are old drawings of the German countryside boring to you? Tonight's the last night.*

Nathan messaged her back: *Not boring. At dinner with friends now. Trying to get away. I'll be there.*

Huong was waiting for him when he got out and, as they returned to the table, he asked what was eating at Anthony.

"What makes you think something's eating at him?"

"He's turned extra nasty is all. But maybe it's my imagination."

"There are problems," she said, but they were approaching the table and she couldn't say more.

Hoa was by herself. Nathan looked toward the bar, around the corner from the outbuilding. Anthony was there, fingering an empty shot glass. Nathan wondered if he'd heard them talking.

"What were you two gabbing about back there?" Hoa said when they sat down.

"Just the weather," Huong said. "Nathan says all this rain we've had depresses him."

"Why don't you take a trip? One of my friends just came back from Phu Quoc and raved about it."

Hoa's mention of the island shot into his ears like cold water. "I don't think I'd like it," he said.

"Really? I hear it's a perfect escape. No noise or pollution, and beautiful, romantic sunsets..."

"There's no such thing as a perfect escape." Saying this, he realized he was extinguishing an attempt to draw him out. He promised himself not to speak if there was any question about sounding affable. He soon forgot, though, as Huong asked Hoa about a new salon, leaving him alone with his half-drunk beer.

When Anthony returned, he was on the phone. He'd brought back two whiskey shots. He pushed one across the table toward Nathan, but Nathan pushed it back. Anthony stopped talking and without cupping his hand over the phone barked out: "Drink it, goddamnit. I got that for you."

"I don't like whiskey."

"Drink it anyway."

Nathan threw back the shot and chased it with beer. When he'd quenched the burn in his throat he glanced at Huong and saw her smiling at him – the same lurid smile as when she told him he could have any woman he wanted.

Anthony hung up and started texting a message. Without looking up he said: "I'm serious about developing company retreats. It's a big niche that needs to be filled. I'm putting you in charge of it."

"I don't know anything about it."

"That's the whole point. You get experience. Learn on the job. Grow some thicker skin. Feel the thrill of making money. You can be Vietnam's 'corporate retreat guy.'"

"I'll think about it."

Anthony dropped his phone on the table and turned to him. "What are you talking about? If I tell you to do something, you do it. Are you my boss? Are you paying my rent? Did you bring me here from Saigon and save me from a hopeless situation?"

"Yes on the first two, no on the last one. Corporate retreats are no problem, but playing with tanks doesn't appeal to me."

"I'm counting on that changing."

Nathan didn't want to talk about work anymore, nor did he wish to argue over obligations. But it was hard to keep silent. He resented being forced to do whatever Anthony said, even if it was a simple matter of carrying out his job. Wishing he could make his own choices, he realized that there was something he *could* do on his own – always there was that. The consequences of going through with it, however, were uncomfortable to consider.

Hoa's arm touched his, and he saw that even she was part of something Anthony had forced on him. If there was a distinction between what Nathan owed Anthony and what Anthony had imposed on him, he couldn't determine what it was.

Anthony gestured to a waiter for the check. "I have to stop at the office and then hit the sack early." Clapping his hands, he tried to corral everyone into calling it a night.

"Now?" Hoa said. "I was going to suggest we go to the Sofitel Plaza. They're hosting a charity event that's getting good media attention."

"We'd like to," Huong put in. "But my parents are expecting us back."

"Just half an hour?" Hoa said. "It never hurts being on TV and in the papers."

"If the cameramen have a choice between you and me," Anthony said, "they'll focus on you every time. I could wear a gorilla costume with our company logo on the chest, but I wouldn't get a bit of attention with you there."

Hoa laughed at the compliment.

"As long as Nathan's there, that's fine." Anthony turned to him. "Just stand next to her. That way you're bound to get equal exposure."

"Come with us," Hoa implored Huong in Vietnamese. "It'll be more fun with four people."

Aware that Nathan understood what Hoa said, Huong glanced at him. "We're both tired," she said in English, "and my parents won't want us out late. They're watching the kids."

"It's only eight-thirty."

"They go to bed early, unfortunately."

"They also wake up before five," Anthony said, "to commence their routine of slamming doors and calling to each other from all over the house."

"I'm sure we don't have the energy you two have," Huong said.

The bill came and Anthony paid, adding a generous tip. Nathan hung back as they left, following Huong and Hoa. Anthony walked at the head of their group, phoning his driver to pick them up.

When they got to the sidewalk, Nathan stepped into the street to flag a taxi. When one pulled up, he climbed in back and told the driver to wait for Hoa.

"Where you go?" the driver asked, pressing the meter on his dashboard. Nathan snapped at him to reset it and wait until he started driving.

"When my friend gets in," Nathan said, "take us to the Fine Arts University."

A moment later the Land Rover pulled up. Anthony opened the back door for Huong. She waved at Nathan, but Hoa entered the taxi then and blocked his view of her.

Hoa began powdering her nose as the taxi did a U-turn.

"Where are we going?" she said when they drove past the road that would take them to Sofitel Plaza.

"I have someplace in mind."

"But I promised to attend the event."

"Meeting businesspeople after work is like meeting businesspeople to do more work. I don't want to network when I don't have to."

"But I'm expected to go."

Nathan had no intention of attending a get-together with her associates and competing for media exposure. "I can drop you off if you'd like."

She frowned. "I can go somewhere else first, I guess. Just as long as I show up before the event ends."

As the taxi wended through traffic Nathan noticed the gap between their legs. It had grown larger after he told her he had a plan of his own.

She didn't protect her cell phone from view, and he watched her type in Vietnamese: *Do you know where's he taking me? He's cute but super-serious.*

Assuming she was communicating with Huong, he took out his own cell phone and composed a message to her as well: *Remind me not to let Anthony set me up on more dates. Hoa's beautiful but one-dimensional.*

The Fine Arts University had come into view when he received Huong's reply: *Be open to possibilities.*

Hoa took his arm and walked with him through the university gate. He wondered if Huong had sent her the same message.

As they reached the entrance she hesitated. From her expression he guessed that she hadn't counted on visiting an exhibition of nine-teenth-century German drawings. She peered around as if hoping to find someone she knew, someone she could talk to rather than waste her time on these old sketches of the German countryside. Apparently not recognizing anyone, she followed him to a signboard that elabo-rated on the artist's life.

Nathan spotted Le among young, arty-looking people along a wall of the exhibition. Rather than take part in their conversation, she was studying a drawing of two girls cycling down a country road. She picked at the buttons of her white shirt, which was too broad in the shoulders and fell halfway down the thighs of her pants; a plain, unflattering outfit that seemed to emphasize the simplicity she now sought.

It took her a moment to see him. She smiled and made as if to come greet him but stopped mid-stride when she saw he'd brought someone. She stared at them, frozen like a statue.

Hoa pulled Nathan to the first drawing.

17

By the time Nathan finished seeing the exhibition it was after 9:30. Although he hadn't intended to stay long, more than an hour had come and gone. Hoa was sitting on a chair, playing with her phone's ringtones.

Outside, night had settled among the courtyard's flowering trees, statues on plinths, and French-style buildings. At first he thought the courtyard was empty, but a movement at the base of a tree caught his attention. Le sat with her back against the trunk, picking fallen leaves.

He was about to approach her when Hoa came up and pressed against him.

"That girl outside is watching you," she said.

"I hadn't noticed."

He felt the firmness of her breasts on his arm, and to his side he saw the vee-shaped space, the silken shadow, of her cleavage. Strangely, this didn't excite him. He wanted to be with Le, to be with her as he'd been with her in Saigon, but without the falseness of an arrangement. The old resentments, however, refused to die.

"Sorry you didn't like the exhibition," he said. "We can go if you want."

He waited for her to step outside, but she hesitated.

"You're not like most men I meet."

Nathan smiled inwardly. "What are most men you meet like?"

She paused before answering. "They try harder to impress me."

Nathan was silent. He didn't want to tell her that what he desired had nothing to do with her.

"Anyway," she said, "I think it's fascinating that you and Huong once dated for half a year. It must be strange to see her married to your best friend."

"At first it was. Now, I just want them both to be happy."

"You don't think they're happy?"

"I'm sure you know better than I do."

Hooking his arm with hers she said: "Anthony used to call me all the time."

"What, to talk?"

"Well, I guess it started with talking. It was back when I was struggling a bit, and he went out of his way to help me."

He looked at her, then quickly looked away when he realized he didn't want to know what their talking might have led to. "I guess most things start with talking."

"Sort of like what we're doing," she said and laughed awkwardly.

"I wouldn't know. I have no idea what you and Anthony used to talk about."

"Come to think of it," she said, letting go of his arm, "neither do I."

Several people left the exhibit, forcing Nathan and Hoa to step aside. They were Vietnamese, and they stared at the two of them as they passed.

Looking at her watch, Hoa noted that it was getting late. "Let's go?"

Her event would be in full swing now, and it was clear without her saying that she had it on her mind. He pulled out his cell phone. "I'll call you a taxi."

She didn't protest. They walked down the steps and passed the tree where Le sat looking toward the street.

He waited with Hoa on the sidewalk. When the taxi rolled up, the driver popped open the back door and yellow light spilled from the cab to their feet.

"Are you staying here?"

"For a bit," he said.

Her hopeful expression disappeared as she looked from him to the taxi. "It's okay. I'll tell Huong and Anthony I had a good time anyway."

Nathan estimated what the ride would cost, added half to the total, and attempted to pay it in advance. But the driver, unused to dealing in Vietnamese with a white face, kept trying to pull Hoa into the transaction. She wouldn't join in.

The taxi pulled away, and he was aware of himself standing alone. But he didn't want to move until he felt confident he could speak with Le.

She'd moved from the tree to the statue of a national hero he didn't recognize. The taxi would have been visible from there, and if the wind had been right, she'd have heard their conversation.

"Who was she?" Her voice was small and neutral.

"My boss's friend."

"That was a strange way to accept my invitation. Some artists I know were here. They asked if you were the foreigner I'd invited. I pretended I didn't know you."

Nathan leaned against the statue. As far as he was concerned, she had no right to be jealous over who he'd come with. Still, he was hardly unhappy to discover she had these feelings. Even more than that another woman found him attractive, he was pleased that she had noticed. But the feeling left quickly. He knew it did him no good.

"Maybe it was just my way of being with you," he said. "You saw I sent her away."

She looked at him a long time before replying. "Your friend Andrew e-mailed me this morning. From the embassy."

The abrupt mention of Andrew stopped him cold. "What for?"

"He asked me about Quan. He said I'd have to provide a statement if they decide to deport him. I told him that I'd be happier if they found something to put him in jail for."

Nathan didn't want to talk about Quan, but she seemed intent on informing him about his situation. Or was it her situation she wished to tell him about?

"Is that all Andrew wanted?"

"He told me you were in Hanoi. I replied that I didn't know."

"Good idea."

She looked down at the lawn, where the shadows of people inside the exhibition hall moved back and forth. "I'm glad you're here, Nathan. I'm not sure I realized it until I saw you with that woman."

She stopped herself from saying more. He encouraged her, though, and she grabbed his hand.

"Is there any reason you would want me back in your life?"

Feeling his pulse race he said, "Let's walk."

They meandered down the sidewalk, passing people huddled beside buildings, eating and talking. His giddiness around her was little different from what he'd felt around her in the beginning. Despite the upheaval she'd put him through, being with her felt right.

They crossed the street in front of the Soviet Friendship Palace and soon found themselves at Quan Su Pagoda. Small fires burned in the stone altars on each side of the entrance, their flames reflecting off the pagoda and the tall trees before it. With every lull in traffic, Nathan could hear the remains of spirit offerings crackling in the fires.

"Have you been here before?" Le said.

"No."

"It's been years since I have. When Quan's mother died, I came here with his family to have a send-off ceremony for her soul. I was only a teenager then, but I remember everything. It was spring, raining off and on all day, and I cried because I felt like I'd lost my own mother. She was nice to me, so generous, and always encouraged me in my painting. She was a good influence on Quan, too, and when she died I was left to watch his life unravel slowly. His father was rarely around, and his older brothers and sisters were too busy with their own lives to pay any attention to him. At that point, I was probably the closest thing to his mother that he had.

"I think I risked so much to be with him out of respect for his mother. She wanted us to be together. I'm sure she wanted us to marry. And even though he went to America, I'm sure she would have wanted me to join him. But now, if she were alive, I think she'd see I'm better off without him. What happened between us would have saddened her, but she'd be even sadder about the person Quan's become."

Nathan was satisfied hearing this. But just the sound of Quan's name set him on edge and reminded him again of what he'd been through with Le.

"What if he returns?"

"To Hanoi? He won't. This place holds nothing but bad memories for him. He'd end up in Saigon before here. And he'd go to Canada or Australia before that."

"Do you still love him?"

She shook her head and smiled sadly. "His father entertains distant hopes for us, but our fates are decided. I've changed my life. I'm changing it every day. All that matters now is that I paint. Growing up, that was all I ever wanted, but somewhere along the way I got pulled in the wrong direction."

"It's hard for me to understand. I feel like there were a thousand things you didn't tell me back in Saigon. That you could have but chose not to."

"I'll tell you whatever you want to know," she said in a voice he had to lean toward her to hear.

"Your background is still a big mystery. You made me think you only had an uncle, and the stories you told me were convincing. The more I learn about you, the more I feel like you're a stranger to me."

Le lowered her eyes to the ashy ground.

An old frustration hit him. "Why didn't you trust me with the truth?"

"I have no good answer, Nathan. I've asked myself this a million times – or you have, in the conversations I often imagined us having – but I've never been able to answer it. And don't think that I'm a stranger to you. You know me better than anyone. Tell me what you want to know."

He hesitated, trying to sort through all the questions he had. He felt like a direct channel led from his head to his heart, and what had filled the former quickly emptied into the latter. Now his heart felt heavy and his mind seemed to float like an upturned fish inside his head.

"Will you try to leave again?" he said.

"No. I'm happy here."

A breeze rustled the leaves overhead and blew more ash from the altars onto the ground. Thinking about what she'd said, he watched the gray dust scatter in all directions.

"Do you still love me?" she said.

No, he wanted to say. I've stopped loving you. But forming the words and speaking them convincingly were different. "I don't know. I remember loving you. But now..."

"Because I–"

"No, stop," he said. "I don't think we should talk about that now. It's enough just to talk. And to be here. But not about that."

Spotting a package of discarded incense on the ground, Le bent down to pick it up. She shook out the few sticks inside and, after lighting them in an altar's flame, planted them in a porcelain urn. Smoke wisped upward, adding more perfume to the muggy air.

She closed her eyes, her lips trembling in mute prayer. Then she clapped her hands together, raised and lowered them three times, and opened her eyes again.

They wandered back to the sidewalk.

Le offered him a ride home, but he declined, explaining that he had to retrieve his motorbike from work. His office, on the opposite side of West Lake from where she lived, was too far for her to take him. They stood waiting for a taxi to drive by.

"I'd like to watch you work sometime," he said.

"I'm afraid it won't be exciting."

"All the same, I'd like to watch."

She considered this for a moment. "I'll let you come, but on two conditions."

He couldn't imagine what conditions she'd place on his visiting. He guessed that her conditions would be more like favors, but then felt bad for doubting her. "What are they?"

"Write an article about it. And try to get it published in America." When she saw he didn't understand, she said: "You're a writer, not a businessman. You're only working in real estate because you owe people money. A publication will bring in more, and you'll be using your writing skills, doing something you believe in."

"It's been a long time since anyone imposed conditions on me."

She smiled. "I start painting at five-thirty."

"That's early. But I'll be there."

"If you bring that girl from tonight I'll lock the gate and not let you in."

"No girl. I promise."

A taxi appeared. As he got inside she told him, "In the prayer I just made, I apologized to Quan's mother and said I was done with him forever." When Nathan didn't respond she added: "You and I aren't the same people we were in Saigon, but I'm not a stranger to you, Nathan. Even if you think I am, that's no reason to avoid each other, is it?"

Her words surprised him. Hearing her say this made him question if they were hovering at the threshold of an old, proven, deeply felt mistake.

"It probably is," he said. "But that won't stop me coming over."

She stood at the gate as the taxi drove away, the light from the altar fires flickering behind her.

Light slanted from the shuttered windows of Anthony's office. Guessing that a janitor was working, or that Anthony had forgotten to turn off the light, he didn't bother checking on it. He started his motorbike and shifted into gear.

He hadn't gone far when he decided to pass by Anthony's house to see if he was up. In a mood to talk, he hoped they could sort out their differences.

He flipped off his headlight and coasted to a stop behind a tree on the edge of Anthony's yard. The croaking of frogs was deafening and, in the thick branches above him, fireflies flashed.

On the balcony, Huong stood on a short stepladder, tying a string of red lanterns to the eaves. Her white pajamas fluttered in the breeze, appearing to pull at her from the side.

Whenever she finished tying one lantern she moved the stepladder forward, climbed it again, and tied the next. When the lanterns hung from one end of the balcony to the other, in a curving line like an eerie red grin, she went inside and got a string of white lights. These she wrapped around the balcony railing. The mid-autumn festival was a week away and many people were decorating their houses. Behind her the living room was dimly lit, the walls changing color with whatever was on TV. He wondered who was watching it – or if no one was and Huong had left it on to keep herself company.

Nathan messaged Anthony on his phone: *Thanks for tonight. It didn't go anywhere, though. Nice girl, but I guess I'm not ready yet. What are you doing?*

Down the front of Huong's pajamas, silver coin-shaped patterns shimmered in the moonlight. For an instant she appeared as a strange, hovering reflection of the lake. Though he was observing her from afar, he thought he'd never seen her so enticing.

She'd been nicer to him tonight than she had for some time. Perhaps it was only a matter of seeing her away from home, where she could set aside the struggles of marriage and family. Or maybe the pressures of a public outing had made her kinder. Or maybe he'd been wrong about her all along. Everything he heard about her, after all, came from Anthony.

After waiting several minutes for Anthony's reply, he sent another message: *Where are you? If you're home, look outside. Huong's on the balcony and I'm parked by the water watching her. If there's a goddess of red lanterns, I think you're married to her. Care to join me in my admiration?*

But that message, too, went unanswered.

He waited behind the tree until Huong returned inside and one by one the lights of the house went out. The string of lanterns swayed in the wind. For a few moments longer he watched the dark house, then started his motorbike and headed home.

18

At 5:45 a.m., the patio behind Le's house appeared to have just been swept, and newly washed clothes already dripped from a line. The lake was placid beneath the clear, paling sky. Beyond the shore, ducklings followed their mother past the formless lip of water.

A door opened behind him. Le came forward holding two cups.

"I made us tea," she said, offering him one. "Though I wasn't sure you'd come."

"Why wouldn't I? You invited me."

She sipped her tea, and over the cup's rim her eyes smiled.

She led him into her studio and pointed him toward a small desk and chair like a child might use in school. The broken canvases, empty paint jars, and dried brushes on the floor were a veritable obstacle course, but he solved it and settled into the paint-splotched seat.

In his notebook he sketched the room's layout, then wrote a caption below it.

Her studio is surprisingly spacious. Lacquer paintings are propped against the walls and canvases everywhere are filled with images: people working in rice fields, tending ducks in a stream, burning incense in temples. In the background of many paintings West Lake spreads like a somber mood.

He glanced again around the room. He felt like he wasn't just sitting in a corner of her studio, but in a corner of her mind. A breeze leapt through the window, touching him like the breath of someone intimately close.

"Let's start at the beginning," she said.

She walked to a pile of boards on a shelf and selected a rectangular piece of wood, neatly cut to scale. "Lacquer painting always starts with *vóc*." She spelled the word for him. "It's the foundation on which everything stands. For a lacquer artist, choosing *vóc* is like adopting someone into your family."

He jotted down everything she said, stopping her whenever she used an unfamiliar word.

"After selecting the *vóc*, there are traditions you must follow to make it conform to your vision and turn out how you want." She lifted the *vóc* for him to see. "A craftsman cuts it, then covers it with a mixture of sawdust, clay, and lacquer. This strengthens and protects it against warping. *Vóc* is an important element, and you have to choose it with great care."

She went to a worktable overflowing with sketchpads, paint-stained strainers, and porcelain urns containing paintbrushes, knives, and scrapers. Beside the table stood a metal cart full of labeled jars.

"These are my materials."

She wheeled the cart toward him, showing him what the jars held: black and reddish-brown lacquers; four kinds of red pigment; gold and silver leaf; mother-of-pearl; varicolored snail shells, and the hollowed-out eggs of different birds.

"These materials are basic, but producing them is complicated. Some are so expensive that even one painting, if it turns out badly, could bankrupt me." She waited until he finished recording her explanation. "Have you been to Vinh Phuc province?"

"Not yet."

She nodded at his notebook, and he realized this meant he was to write down what she said.

She spoke slowly, pausing to allow him not only to transcribe her words, but also to structure the material coherently, which proved helpful when later he revised it.

Vinh Phuc is eighty miles northwest of Hanoi. For Le, traveling there is a pilgrimage. Without Vinh Phuc's unique rocks and trees, Vietnam's lacquer tradition would be entirely different from what it has become, and inferior to the lacquer traditions of China, Japan, and Korea.

Vinh Phuc possesses a unique type of cây sơn *tree, the source of lacquer used in her paintings. The tree is tapped midway through the sun's rise, a window of no more than an hour. Once dry, the sap is processed into a black lacquer called* sơn then *and a reddish-brown lacquer known as* sơn cánh gián *(named for the wings of a cockroach).*

When she told him that Vinh Phuc is renowned for having Vietnam's best secret-keepers, he looked up and asked what she meant.

"Do you have many secrets?"

"Probably no more than anyone else," he said. Given their past together, the question set him slightly on edge. "Why?"

"In Vietnam, secrets are important. Maybe you think that's strange, but if we didn't keep secrets our lacquer traditions wouldn't exist. Even now, while I can show you the techniques I use and explain the process generally, secrets are still important. Lacquer artists have to understand this, and protect what they do, otherwise they'll fail." She looked at him hard. "It's true in life, too."

"One of the most interesting things about lacquer," she says, "is that the production of certain materials is shrouded in mystery."

In the mountains around Vinh Phuc two kinds of special stone exist: thần sa *and* chu sa. *In artisans' homes these stones are ground into powder and poured into a small container. This container is placed in a larger container and heated. When the contents of the outer one begin to boil, the container inside reaches a temperature that separates the powder into four distinct layers of red pigment:* sơn trai, sơn tươi, sơn thắm, *and* sơn nhì. *According to an image's demands, any of these pigments can be mixed and used to paint the* vóc.

She unscrewed a jar. After showing him its red powder, she opened several other jars so he could see their rich colors. "I could paint a hundred years, but still I'd never know the secret to making the right pigment."

It takes an entire week to make enough pigment to fill a small teacup. Only one family in Vietnam knows the secret to making these pigments, which are more valuable than gold, and they have risked their lives to protect it. When French colonialists tried to force them to divulge their methods, the family refused. They remain steadfast even today and will not sell their pigments overseas. The pigments are made exclusively for Vietnamese lacquer paintings made in the traditional style.

Only one village in Vietnam produces the gossamer-thin gold and silver leaf essential to Vietnamese lacquer painting. This village, too, is tight-lipped about its methods.

"Secrets are important in Vietnam," she says. "One slip of the tongue can mean betrayal, and then the whole universe may crash down. History offers many examples. Countries, families, relationships, art – they're all vulnerable."

From where she stood, he could see a dark splotch of paint on her cheek, like a birthmark she'd hidden from him until now. He imagined that if he could peel it from her face he'd find a window to her soul that revealed everything about her – and perhaps learn the truth about her feelings for him.

She dusts a thin paper with chalk and uses it to trace an image of everyday life to the vóc. Next she mixes the sơn nhì and paints it over the tracing: a figure of Ông Táo, the Chinese Kitchen God. Gold and silver flakes are then sprinkled over it. As she spreads them with her brush, they become embedded in the tracing lines (now filled with the wet sơn nhì), helping preserve the image and make it brighter.

It is the layering of lacquer, a process rooted in an age-old tradition that younger artists have mostly abandoned, which brings the vóc to life.

Weather permitting, she will dry the vóc overnight on a rack. Ironically, only in humid conditions will lacquer from the Vietnamese cây sơn tree dry.

"In no other country will Vietnamese lacquer respond the same to the air and weather," she said, not without pride. "In no other country will it perfectly dry. No one knows why, and so this is a secret, too."

She removed a *vóc* hanging beside the one she just finished and brought it to her worktable. "This one's ready for a second layer of lacquer."

She applies the second layer, sprinkles it with gold and silver leaf, and, prior to drying, fits the vóc *with cheesecloth to protect it and prevent it from expanding. The* vóc *can be polished only when dry.*

When done, she hung it to dry, and returned with another painting she'd been drying the last few days. Vaguely, he could make out a woman's face in the *vóc*.

She repeated the process a third time, carrying out the final polish with a stone that was soft yet rough.

"Like the intestine of a chicken," she said, rubbing it against his arm. "Painting means applying one thing onto another, but polishing is an act of removal."

She pushed the black stone back and forth across the painting. After a few minutes the polishing had taken away some of the sprinkled gold and silver leaf, but it had also pushed the leaf irrevocably into the *vóc*, making it brighter while deepening its hues.

"One can polish too little or too much. Good artists develop an instinct for when they've produced the right colors. Only when the colors appear sufficiently rich does a painter know to stop."

She polished until the colors had indeed grown deeper. The face in the painting began to emerge.

Polishing requires more time and patience than painting. A single vóc *often takes two months to complete.*

If things don't go as planned – for example, if a lack of humidity prevents the vóc's *paint from drying and the whole layer must be scraped off and done again – often they can be fixed. Most times you're given a second chance.*

These rough methods, which produced such delicate work, fascinated him. The layering and constant polish required patience and muscle. Doing this every day, he saw, had made her strong. Her arms and shoulders were toned and, when she pressed down on the *vóc*, her thin muscles stood out against her skin.

On the far end of the cart were six jars of shells. She removed one labeled *vịt* and poured from it enough to fill half her palm.

"Shells are another unique aspect of Vietnamese lacquer painting. When using shells you have to take into account their thickness."

To keep the vóc's plane clean and smooth, she digs a few millimeters of space with a flat knife. Then she presses and glues down the eggshell. With a hammer she taps the pressed-and-glued shell until it breaks into fine pieces. After this she applies another thin coat of lacquer.

The hammered shell must be small enough for the artist to proceed to the polishing stage. Polishing requires not only delicacy, but also calmness and a willingness to spend the time needed to get it right. A work of art cannot be forced.

Le said that when she was just starting out she lacked the necessary patience. She either rushed or skipped important steps. Or she gave up, losing confidence when the images didn't come out how she wanted. It took years for her to get to this point.

She lifted a green petrol bottle from her cart. "This is for *toát* – the final application." She poured the petrol in a bowl and mixed it with *cánh gián* lacquer.

When satisfied with her mixture she brushes a thin layer of it over the painting. The layers protect the wooden board so it does not shrink, expand, or otherwise warp. The layers act like armor against moisture, insects, and viruses. Thus, the vóc is durable, and can outlast its creator by three or four hundred years.

Like every other step, layering ends with the vóc *hung on a rack and dried overnight.*

In the corner of the room was a tap and basin, and Le went there to scrub her hands with lye. The room filled with the sound of running water, and Nathan returned his attention to his notebook, continuing where he'd left off.

Anyone familiar with the state of lacquer painting in Vietnam will recognize that Le is an artist balanced on the edge of the 'old days,' when the sway of tradition could put off the chase for riches.

Traditional lacquer painting, a laborious process often lasting several months, is giving way to cheaper, faster methods of production. The idea, of course, is basic to modern life: the more paintings you churn out, the more money you can earn.

But there is a danger in this, for as one contributor to this process falters or disappears – the craftsman who cuts the board, the family that produces the pigments, or the village that makes the thin gold and silver leaf – traditional Vietnamese lacquer painting will weaken and die. Although Le would never admit it, she is a living storehouse of her own culture.

Nathan admired Le's determination to create traditional lacquer art; no doubt her move to Hanoi paved the way for her to succeed in this. Perhaps she had come to realize that her talent was singular and might one day provide her with something more life-affirming than she had found in Saigon.

He couldn't dwell on this idea for long; still scrubbing her hands, Le began speaking about her training at Dai Hoc Nghe Thuat.

At the Fine Arts University, where she trained for four years, students came from all over Vietnam to study lacquer painting. But come graduation, all that her peers had learned was how to produce cheap, imitative paintings as quickly as possible. Le, however, was different. Her teachers noticed her dedication to traditional methods and praised her. She was

*an old soul, they said, and predicted that in the long run she would come
out ahead of the rest.*

When Nathan asked what she thought had made her a successful
artist, she denied her success.

*"Success comes not only from what you produce," she says. "Even more, it
depends on how true you are in following the traditions to which your
paintings owe their uniqueness, their very life. In some places, pictures
painted by elephants fetch a high price, but does that make the elephant
successful? Does that make the elephant an artist?"*

*Even the most casual visitor to Vietnam will notice the abundance of
lacquer paintings in galleries around Hoan Kiem Lake and the Old
Quarter – tourist areas, almost exclusively, just like in Saigon. Dozens of
similar landscapes and scenes, done in the same uniform style, hang on
their peeling walls. Scores more are piled in corridors and spill forth
from backroom offices. While some are beautiful, Le would never wish to
stamp her name on them.*

"For some of my friends," she went on, drying her hands on her
shirt, "painting is a way to become rich and have high status. While
money and fame can be nice – and I, too, wanted both at one time – in
the end they're only trappings. Since moving back to Hanoi I've
learned that art is a way of being. It's a kind of freedom."

Had she told him this before, he would have doubted her sincerity.
But he believed what she said, and it made him happy that he could.
One didn't often come across this attitude in Vietnam, particularly
since – twelve years after the U.S. embargo had been lifted and with the
country pushing hard to accede to the World Trade Organization –
Vietnamese society now valued earning over nearly everything else.
Hanoi and Saigon were becoming affluent enough, quickly enough,
that it was easy to buy something new to replace and banish the old.
Society was wearing thin at its seams, though that didn't mean it was
falling apart.

When asked what her relationship is to her painting, she looks through the window at the lake.

"It's less a relationship than a sameness, like my reflection in the window of a moving train." She stops to reconsider the analogy. "But it's more accurate to say I'm a passenger on a train that is my painting. And the train is nothing but a figment of my imagination. In other words, my painting and I are one and the same. One exists within the other and carries it along."

At the end of a day, when she steps back from her work, she cannot account for the passage of time, cannot remember what has transpired between her brush and canvas.

"It's like giving life to something. And having given something life, part of me lives within it."

Nathan didn't know how to explain the feeling, but indeed there was something of her in all her paintings. Did it lie in the harmony of color, perspective, and imagery? Or was it more prosaic, evidenced by how life flowed from the center, by how the commonplace was inspirited by her vision and skill?

"Tell me," he said. "How do you give a painting life?"

"It's a secret even to me. I know there's life in a painting only when I've finished it."

Sometimes before she paints she sees the image in her mind; other times not. But one is always there within her.

"I've known much loss and sadness. But painting is a constant, and no matter what happens in my life I'll always be able to create. I believe that strongly and it puts me at ease."

They took a tea break hovering over her work. Nathan blew steam from his cup and drew a circle around what she'd just said.

Although his understanding of Vietnamese lacquer painting would never be complete, she made a special effort to help him learn. After he wrote everything down she had him repeat it to her, making sure nothing was missing, nothing wrong, nothing overlooked.

Perhaps she thought that as a writer he could introduce to the world something beautiful from her country. She knew that if foreign interest was strong enough it could help preserve a dying tradition that she, on her own, could never keep alive.

He came every morning after that, even after he'd submitted the article to several newspapers, and even two weeks later when the *Los Angeles Times* had accepted it. It wasn't much later that she asked him to come over after work, too.

19

The lake was calm and black beneath low-lying fog. Though it wasn't raining, the Land Rover's windshield accumulated so much moisture from the air that the driver had to use his wipers. The midmorning felt like dawn.

"Will you roll up that window?" Mrs. Thompson said. "It's cold back here and all that wind's blowing my hair."

In the five minutes they'd been driving around West Lake Nathan hadn't noticed that his window was open. Now that she mentioned it, he was surprised he hadn't; the wind streaming through the small gap between the window and frame was loud. After lifting his fingers to the space, they came away cool and damp.

"Of course. Sorry." He reached for the handle but the window wouldn't roll up. The driver fiddled with the console but that didn't work either. "That's as far as it goes, I'm afraid."

"Well, for heaven's sake. I hope the house you're showing us has windows that close."

"It's cold," complained the older of the Thompson's two sons. "And why does the driver keep crossing the center line?"

"Because it's Vietnam," Mr. Thompson said gruffly. "That's why."

"What's that have to do with anything?" the boy said.

"Traffic laws are new here and nobody knows what they're doing," Mrs. Thompson said.

"I could drive better than any of them," put in the younger son, who couldn't have been more than ten.

Nathan wondered if he should mention that the house was purported to be haunted. None of the agency's salespeople would have anything to do with it, which was why he had to show it. They'd been spooked by stories from the previous tenants, a married couple from Taiwan. Because Nathan had only heard a few of the stories himself, he could form but a limited picture of what had chased them away.

After the landlord's mother died in the house two years ago, her ghost was said to wander about. The staff suggested Nathan fabricate an excuse to keep the Thompsons from entering an altar-room that contained photos of the old woman and her late husband. When he asked why, they explained that the deceased's expressions often changed. If the photos showed them smiling, then their son had appeased them with prayers, burned incense, and offerings. If they were scowling, however, it meant he'd neglected his duties and whoever was living there would suffer.

The four-story villa was fully furnished, and, if the previous tenants were to be believed, the furniture sometimes shifted around late at night. There were stories of glasses jumping off the table during meals, and knickknacks flying off shelves. On separate occasions light bulbs throughout the house had shattered simultaneously. Once, the front door of their house creaked open; when they went to shut it they found a frog and bat on their front step, both flopping about in their death-throes. Two months before, their alarm clock went off early, and when they checked it the time-hands were spinning backwards. That day was the death anniversary of the landlord's mother, who died early one morning in July.

The old woman's ghost was said to be angry because her son, who rented out the home for over two thousand dollars a month, had never removed the altar from a room on the top floor, and had never introduced his dead parents to the strangers in their house.

Before the Taiwanese couple broke their lease, they came to speak with Anthony about the situation, which they claimed had become unbearable. They said they'd consulted with a lawyer and would bring him in if the agency and landlord wished to litigate the matter. None of their bluster had been necessary. Anthony had emerged from his office looking like he'd just awakened from a twenty-year sleep.

"That's the biggest crock I've ever heard," he said, interrupting the couple's account.

The husband puffed out his chest. "You try sleeping there some time."

"I'd love to," Anthony said. "But I'm committed elsewhere."

The man tried to explain again what they'd suffered, but Anthony told him to shut up.

"Have you removed all your shit?"

There was a collective tittering among the staff.

"Excuse me?" the man said.

"Are your things still in the house or have you already moved out?"

"We left last week," the woman said. "We couldn't stay another night, believe us."

Anthony turned to the gathered staff. "Binh, Quang, take these two…" He hesitated, as if seeking a word to put them down, but then seemed to reconsider. "Take them to the house and make sure they haven't destroyed or stolen anything. Then collect their keys and change the locks." He turned back to the couple. "Your lease is in all ways binding, but I don't care. As a businessman I believe in doing the right thing. We'll keep your deposit, of course, but we'll reimburse you for the advance rent you paid." He told the accountant to tally up what the couple was due. Waiting for the figure, he slumped into the receptionist's chair. Everyone watched him, not daring to speak. When the accountant announced what was owed, Anthony said: "Go ahead, get it ready in cash." When she had, he handed the money to the couple. "I'm a fair man, see?" He slapped the man on his shoulder humorlessly. "Now get the fuck out of my office."

Nathan was surprised by how rarely Anthony's staff left the company for another. Loyalty wasn't the reason, he decided. Anthony paid them well enough, but sometimes Nathan overheard them grumbling. Still, for many of them, who were old enough to remember going hungry as children, the most important thing was "to have rice in the bowl." Stability was important – they needed to know their future would be better than their past.

The only thing that kept Nathan there was the debt he owed Anthony. His sense of loyalty was strong, but he'd leave if the right opportunity came along. Such an opportunity was hard to imagine – it would have to bring him back, however circuitously, to writing.

The Land Rover pulled up to the villa. Nathan felt a faint chill seeing a light on through the open attic windows. While the shutters creaked in the wind, the rest of the house was lifeless. He watched Mr. Thompson lead his family away to inspect the grounds.

"Coming inside?" Nathan asked the driver.

Leaning against his vehicle the man pulled out a cigarette. "I'm not particularly superstitious. Still, I'll stay out here."

"You're not superstitious. But you're a little afraid of ghosts?"

The man coughed as though embarrassed. "Why take a risk?"

"And if it rains?"

They looked at the sky: the low clouds had sunk lower, and a milky mist swirled atop the villa's sloped roof.

"Then I'll wait in the car."

Nathan walked to the front door, opened it, and followed the Thompsons inside. Having decided not to accompany them through the house, he settled into a chair and removed from his briefcase the stack of mail he'd taken on his way out of the office. The first item he looked at was also the biggest: a thick manila envelope with Reuters News Agency printed across an address sticker in a corner. "Priority Mail" was stamped on the front and back.

Nathan's heart skipped a beat. He wasn't expecting a letter from Reuters. If anything, he would have expected something from the *Los Angeles Times*, with which he'd recently had a working relationship.

The envelope's thickness increased his wonder. He couldn't imagine how they got his address unless a Reuters correspondent he vaguely knew had provided it. He'd bumped into the correspondent some time ago at the only English-language bookstore in Hanoi and given her his new business card.

He tore the envelope open and shook out a letter and folder. The letter was printed on Reuters' letterhead.

Dear Mr. Monroe,

I've read your travel pieces in the *SF Chronicle* and *SJ Mercury News*, as well as your latest article in the *LA Times* on Vietnamese lacquer painting. I've also received good word about you personally from Kate Stein, Reuters' Vietnam reporter until last month. It's hard to find good people who know Vietnam and have the ability to report a story. Not insignificantly, we're having difficulty securing work visas for our journalists, which is the main reason I'm contacting you: you're a good writer, and you're already there.

I'd like to offer you the chance to report for Reuters, at least until we can sort out our visa problems with the Ministry of Foreign Affairs. Perhaps you're not interested, or maybe you're committed to other work. However, at this juncture we want you to consider working for Reuters on a freelance basis. I'll give you details if and when you indicate interest in such an arrangement.

I took the liberty of enclosing a topic we want you to report on: Tu Du Hospital in Saigon and their efforts to help children allegedly born with Agent Orange-related diseases. Having lived in Vietnam as long as you have, I'm sure you're aware that Vietnamese citizens are suing the U.S. military for damaging the environment and poisoning human populations with toxic chemicals used during the war. They allege a high incidence of congenital birth defects, leukemia, and other untreatable conditions directly linked to Agent Orange. We need this piece by November 15th, before a U.S. Federal Appeals Court makes a ruling. Will you accept our offer?

Regards,
Dennis Jasper,
Senior Editor, Asia Bureau
Reuters News Agency

Nathan ran his finger over the majestic blue letterhead, savoring the rush of excitement. The offer was in all respects a great opportunity; a step up from the mindless work he'd been doing at Anthony's firm. Although the money would be worse, and the work temporary, at least with writing he might do some good. He could live with that.

He picked up the folder. It was thick, crammed with copied articles from *Time, The Economist, The South China Sea Morning Post*; various articles pulled off the Internet; and several pages of statistics. Also included were Xeroxed photographs: grotesque images of deformed children and livestock, and of a hospital with the words *Bệnh Viện* above its entranceway. He soon came across another – this of shirtless pilots mugging before a military tanker plane on which someone had scrawled: "Only we can prevent forests."

He skimmed the material to get a sense of recent developments. Families and their livestock continued to suffer more than thirty years after the end of the war. In and of itself this was nothing new; rather than the physical devastation that resulted from fighting, there was emotional devastation wrought by exodus, separation, and loss. But the photos were different, for they gave suffering a face – if the reports he'd been given were accurate, the face of suffering belonged to millions.

Groups had organized to lobby for attention. They'd filed a class action lawsuit against the U.S. government, which was blocking attempts to make it share what it knew about the effects of Agent Orange, the non-soluble defoliant that had laid waste to Vietnam's populous countryside. Nearly five percent of the entire country had been affected by Agent Orange's prolonged use, one article said. Another reported that almost twenty million gallons had been sprayed to destroy the vegetation hiding Viet Cong transportation routes. Vietnamese groups and individuals were taking up the cause hoping to pressure the U.S. to admit culpability and compensate those who continued to suffer from the toxin's ravages.

Agent Orange was increasingly in the news. Almost every day the media carried a story on it. Local fundraising like he'd never seen before was bringing attention to those said to be suffering from exposure to the chemical defoliant. Just the other day he came across an article reporting that those who'd fought for the resistance and had children born with defects caused by Agent Orange would receive more monetary support (up to $19 per month) for their medical needs. There was no avoiding the topic, so much publicity was it getting. Several foreign organizations had started fund-drives to help families struggling to raise children with deformities they claimed were a result of Agent Orange exposure. A recent photo exhibition on Agent Orange victims had also gotten a lot of press.

Several months before, Nathan's secretary, Xuan, had asked him what the American news reported about Agent Orange. She'd been dismayed to hear that the American public was likely receiving no information. He reminded her that the U.S. was fighting a war in Iraq, midterm elections were around the corner, and domestic terror alerts were constantly rising and falling. Somehow there was no room in the media spotlight for the case against America. Still she couldn't understand. When by government decree, he said, Iraqi casualty figures weren't allowed to be published, how could one expect anything more than the most peripheral attention to be given to alleged war atrocities committed thirty and forty years ago in Vietnam? He'd offered the explanation to her gently, but no degree of gentleness could soften the impact. She hadn't heard of the government's decree and knew little about the war in Iraq other than what friends had told her. For several days afterward she was cold to him, as if she thought he'd lied to her, or as if he was somehow complicit in the suffering of Agent Orange victims.

Though it frustrated him, he knew he was the closest thing to a culpable figure she could find. That determination was all his; she'd never deliver such a strong statement to him directly.

Without hesitation he decided to accept the offer. Immediately he felt what could only be described as relief: there were still things that were important to him here, and his complacency wasn't a permanent condition.

He wondered what Anthony would do if he were to quit. He felt no pleasure showing these people exorbitantly priced villas. It was true he had a responsibility to pay off his debts, but an equally important concern loomed over him: how long would he last living for a salary rather than a dream?

A door slammed upstairs. A moment later Mr. Thompson appeared on the stairs. Nathan invited him to sit down and didn't stop him from lighting a cigar, though it was company policy not to let clients smoke inside properties they were shown. Mr. Thompson lifted a vase from the coffee table and used its flat base as an ashtray. Noises of exploring continued above them. From beyond the near window, raindrops tapped on the eave.

Mr. Thompson removed his cigar from his mouth and fastened a look of confused wonder on Nathan.

"How the hell did you get involved in Vietnamese real estate?"

"I'm friends with the company president. He's the brains and energy of the business. I've only been on board a few months."

"I was sixteen when the war here ended," he said. "I'd never have guessed that the price of land here could ever match what you'd pay in Tokyo or New York City. I suppose that makes it a good business to be in."

Nathan shrugged.

"Obviously there's huge corruption behind the scenes. I mean, do you think it makes sense?"

Nathan was going to explain that land was the only real investment option available to the Vietnamese, for gold didn't appreciate, the stock market was too new and limited, and the enforcement of property taxes was virtually nonexistent, but he didn't feel like getting into an involved conversation.

"Not really," he said.

"You probably don't care. Just as long as you get your commission."

"I couldn't care less about a commission."

Mr. Thompson laughed. "There's nothing wrong with wanting to make money, but it's important to do it the right way."

"What do you do?" Nathan asked, the barb in his voice intended.

"I help develop Vietnam's timber industry. There's a huge market for everything from teak to cajuput to balsa. They've got more trees than they know what to do with."

"So there's a right way and a wrong way?"

"Of course there is." He thoughtfully inspected his cigar. "Some people just call it growing pains. My advice is to get out before the business changes you."

"I've thought about it. I have a bit of journalism experience."

Mr. Thompson fished in his pocket for something but came up empty. "That's nice," he muttered, chomping down once more on his cigar. "Reading the Sunday comics over a stack of pancakes is what I like."

Mrs. Thompson descended the stairs halfway and stared at her husband.

"What's the matter?" he said, fumbling to stub out his cigar. Then, defensively: "Hey, these things relax me."

"Where are the children?"

"They're probably just exploring upstairs." Mr. Thompson turned to Nathan. "What's up there, an attic?"

"The owner keeps his family altar up there."

"A family altar?" Mrs. Thompson said. "Surely he won't want us to keep it for him."

"I don't think so."

"The last thing we need is for the kids to break someone's family altar," Mr. Thompson mumbled. "I'm sure there'd be hell to pay for something like that."

Mrs. Thompson called her sons' names. When they didn't answer, she started back upstairs.

By the time she returned, the disturbing images of deformed children were thoroughly emblazoned on Nathan's mind.

20

The next day Nathan found Anthony sitting with his head in his hands, trembling. Every window shade was drawn, but sunlight still penetrated his office.

Nathan knocked on the open door, his gaze traveling between Anthony and two paintings of the sea on his walls.

"What is it?" Anthony rasped.

"I was hoping we could talk. But you look like hell, so maybe I'll come back later."

"No, no. It's okay. Unplug my phone, will you? I don't want to move."

"Why don't you lie down?" Nathan said, removing the plug from Anthony's phone.

"It doesn't help."

"If you want, I'll call your driver and have him take you home."

"Home? Where my kids run around screaming all day? It's an eternity of zoo feeding times there. Besides, my wife and her parents don't understand these things."

"Then use my place."

"My head feels like it'll split in half if I budge."

Nathan didn't push it. Anthony had been having migraines for over a month. Before that, he said he'd never had so much as a headache. Pressuring him to slow down was pointless. Ever since Nathan had known him, Anthony considered suffering a concomitant to life in Vietnam. "Suffering cleanses me of my sins," he joked when they lived in Saigon. Nathan was surprised to see a bottle of aspirin on his desk. Next to it was a small calendar and a framed photo of his wife and children.

"If you insist on staying and being miserable, I'm going back to work. Like I said, we can talk another time."

He headed for the door but Anthony weakly called him back.

"I said we'll talk, so let's talk."

He waved vaguely to the chair in front of his desk and Nathan sat down.

"I need a vacation from this hell," Anthony muttered.

"What hell are you talking about?"

"Work...Vietnam...my family." Anthony closed his eyes and told him to shut the door. "That's better," he said when Nathan came back.

"Shutting the door means something, right?"

Anthony nodded. "Listen, I don't ask much of you, I give you lots of freedom, so return the favor now, will you?"

Nathan smiled inwardly at the skill with which Anthony usurped his request to talk. "I'm all ears."

Anthony gritted his teeth and rubbed his temples with such force Nathan thought he'd penetrate the skin. "You ever get like this? Like your head's being tightened in a vise?"

"Until you decide to take care of yourself, you don't get any pity from me."

Anthony stared at him through a plaster mask. "I make a point never to miss work. Even now, when I feel like I'm dying, it's not enough to chase me away."

"Maybe you should rethink that. What's the point of persevering if it makes you feel like you'll die?"

Anthony raised his hand to stop him from going on. "You've missed several days lately, haven't you? Late coming to work. Long lunches. Leaving at five, even four o'clock sometimes. You do it when I'm gone or occupied. You think I don't know, but I know everything that goes on here."

"I wouldn't say it's happened a lot."

Anthony's laughter was flat and lifeless, like a car thumping along on punctured tires. "Why am I so patient with you?"

"I'm not sure," Nathan admitted.

"I even caught you sleeping in your office when you didn't show up for a meeting. Remember? It was the week before last. If you'd been another employee, I would've given you serious heat. You're putting me in an awkward position."

Anthony reached into his desk and shakily removed a staff photo. "Eighteen people are in this picture. In the last year I've hired six more, not including you. I swear, I feel like everyone sees me as an enemy. I'm not sure if it's because I'm their boss or because I'm a foreigner. But no one respects me. No one sees me as quite human."

He dropped the framed photo onto his desk, wincing at the clatter.

Nathan didn't take Anthony's disapproval seriously. Two days earlier Anthony had heaped praise on him for his work with the Thompsons. Nathan had helped them secure a lower rent, the removal of the owner's family altar, and a higher fence in the back yard to keep neighbors from peeking over and picking fruit from their trees (both of which happened on the Thompsons' second visit). He had even put in overtime to find a trustworthy housekeeper who could cook Western dishes how they liked. "You did well with that family," Anthony had said. "You went further than I would have gone to make them happy. You keep impressing me, Nate." But Anthony's praise didn't stick. Nathan was merely conscientious; he didn't think twice about helping the Thompsons. Yet helping them didn't satisfy him. He took no pride in being skilled at this line of work.

Xuan came into the office holding a tray. She placed two coasters on Anthony's desk, followed by glasses of iced tea.

"I think maybe you're thirsty," she said, smiling at them.

Nathan smiled back, but Anthony told her to take his away. "I didn't ask for this. And I've told you hundreds of times to knock before entering." When she tried to remove his glass and coaster he shook his head, which made him moan. "Just leave it!"

Xuan recoiled at Anthony's anger.

"Don't let his mood scare you," Nathan told her in Vietnamese. "I'm trying to persuade him to go home."

She apologized and hurried from the office. On her way out she forgot to shut the door. Nathan got up and did it for her.

"What did you tell her?"

"I told her your bark's worse than your bite. And that you're going home to rest."

Anthony pressed his iced tea to his forehead. "You've turned into one of them."

"One of whom?"

"One of the people who sees me as someone to take advantage of after I've gone out of my way to help them."

Anthony's words burned in Nathan's ears. "When you help someone, you shouldn't do it with the expectation there'll be a return in it for you."

"You're so fucking naïve. You're like a child who gets a taste of something he likes, then thinks he should be able to have it whenever he wants."

"Is that what you think of me or of the Vietnamese?"

"How I think of the Vietnamese is complicated," Anthony said. "I trust and respect you."

"What about them?"

Anthony glanced at the door as if to make sure it was closed. Squinting his eyes shut, he rubbed at his temples again. "They've suffered more than either of us could comprehend. And while that's easy to respect, wouldn't you say that on the very opposite end they're just as difficult to love?"

"I prefer to go through life without judging everyone so reflexively."

Anthony smiled weakly. "You're right. I wish I weren't like this. As far as I know I've become this way only recently – since marrying into the culture, or whatever I've done. It seems I can't get enough distance from my life to see where I've started to crack. And without knowing where I'm falling apart, how can I possibly keep myself together?"

His weak voice had grown bitter. Nathan didn't know if he was being serious or preparing to cut him down. Anthony sat in dark silence. He swallowed hard, wincing again as he did. "So what you said was good," he finally said, swallowing even harder. "I shouldn't be so judgmental."

"I wasn't criticizing you."

"Yes, you were. I needed it and like a friend you gave it to me."

"Anthony," Nathan said, "I'm telling you as a friend: Take some time off. Get away for a couple weeks. The firm won't collapse with you gone. But listen to yourself. The stress of this job – it's time to step back a little. You have to take care of yourself better."

"I'm glad you're here, Nate. We should go on vacation together. A long one, somewhere far away. Wouldn't Florida be great?"

Only when he started coughing did Nathan realize he'd been trying to laugh.

"When I was a kid, my family went to Florida every summer. We'd pile into my parents' car and spend three days driving south. Cooped up in the back seat, my brother and sister and I constantly fought. My parents would argue over where to eat, when to stop for a bathroom, how much to spend on motels." He closed his eyes again and took a shuddering breath. "For the last few weeks I've been dreaming about those vacations. That was thirty years ago, yet those memories have come back and are screwing with my head..."

"How do you mean?"

Anthony licked his lips and wiped his mouth. His mouth stayed open and he hovered a few seconds over what he wanted to say. "I mean I'll never have that again. Not with my family. Not with my life here. Not with–"

He began to gag. With his feet he pulled over the small trashcan beneath his desk, but he couldn't bend down to pick it up. Nathan hurried to give it to him. Anthony looked as pale as his office walls.

"Nothing ever comes up. It just stays inside, rotting my guts."

"You should go home."

"What I should do is sell this business, sell my house, cash in. I should go back to teaching or something. Move back to America. I could buy a place in the country, hole up and never see anyone again."

"If you do, will I have to give up my house?" Nathan said, trying to aim the conversation somewhere lighter.

"I negotiated hard for that place. I told myself: 'If I can get Nate this house, there's no way he won't take this job.' And I did, and I was right."

Nathan disliked being reminded of what Anthony had done for him, even if it was true he'd done a lot. "Still, your house is better than mine."

Anthony grimaced as he laughed. "Hey Nate," he said. "What was the name of that girl you were seeing in Saigon?"

"Le."

"She screwed you up more than you realize. You need to get over her. It wouldn't have worked out."

Nathan grew angry. Why did Anthony always bring her up? And what had triggered it now? For some reason the anger stayed with him. He was glad he hadn't told Anthony that she was back in Hanoi and he'd been seeing her again.

"We need reminding sometimes. I wish someone had shared the same wisdom with me before I'd gotten into the trouble I'm in now."

But to Nathan, what he was talking about had nothing to do with wisdom. Anthony was being condescending. Except for one night before Le left, Nathan hadn't come to Anthony about her. Maybe that was the problem. Even so, there were better ways to raise the subject than by making passing judgments.

"What did you want to talk to me about, anyway?" Anthony said.

They'd been focusing on Anthony so much that Nathan had almost forgotten. "Reuters contacted me..."

Over the last minute, Anthony had been cradling his head in his hands again. But at the mention of the news agency he lifted his head and peered at Nathan through the red slits of his eyes. "What do they have to do with anything?" he whispered.

"They want me to write some articles. Freelance stuff. About Agent Orange. The deadline for the first piece is three weeks away. I don't want it getting in the way of my responsibilities here, but it's not like I'm critical to the agency's functioning." Nathan laughed self-mockingly. "I'd like to cut out early for the next three weeks to write the articles. You can dock my pay."

Even more than the news that he wanted to write on company

time, Nathan's suggestion that his pay be docked seemed to infuriate Anthony. He struggled to sit up in his chair, as if it were a position from which his authority naturally flowed.

"In other words, you're bailing on me."

"I'm not bailing on anything. I just need some time to do a couple articles. How can I if I'm putting in eighty hours a week here?"

"You don't put in eighty hours a week."

"I used to."

"Have you heard of Sunday?"

"It's not enough."

"It's enough for my other twenty-four employees."

"I'm more efficient than them, and I hardly know what I'm doing."

Anthony's face twisted into something beyond a scowl. "What are you saying?"

"I'm saying these articles mean a lot to me."

"Maybe they mean more than they should. I feel like I mean nothing to you, and I should mean the most. I pulled you up when you couldn't do it yourself. I was there for you."

"You gave me a job, and I've done my work well. Like I said, I'm not even asking for pay, although I'll come to the office whenever I'm needed. I just have to...I need to write."

"It sounds like you've already decided. So why are we talking about it? Do you want my approval, my forgiveness, or both?"

"I don't need your forgiveness."

The dim light in Anthony's eyes grew dimmer. "But you need my approval."

"I don't need that either. Real estate means nothing to me."

Anthony fell back in his chair like he'd been shoved. "What makes you think Agent Orange is worth reporting on? From what I've heard, the evidence can't be corroborated. There's no direct link between Agent Orange and all the birth defects Vietnam reports. That's true, right?"

"It's more complicated than that. Politics got in the way of science after the war, and the two sides couldn't cooperate."

"Couldn't cooperate? Didn't the Vietnamese say 'we don't need you' when they needed us badly?"

"They had every reason to turn us away. It hurt them, but so did the embargo we put on them for twenty years. We killed more than three million people here, most of them civilians. And for a war we now admit we started on false pretenses. Why should they have wanted us back?"

"What are you now, some kind of saint? What do you hope to accomplish? Are you going to save all these sufferers? Convince Bush and his cronies that war's wrong, un-Christian, and unjust? What's the point of writing an article few people will ever read anyway?"

"I only want people to think for a moment. That's all."

"Think? That's the dumbest thing I've ever heard."

"All right: I want people to reflect. If the Vietnamese were like most Americans, they'd never forgive us. Plenty of Americans haven't forgiven the Japanese for bombing Pearl Harbor. They see a twenty-year-old exchange student from Tokyo and make a nasty comment about something that happened forty years before that student was born. And look at you. You've made yourself a life here. You even told me once that you could never live this well in America. You'd never have had this success if the Vietnamese hadn't gotten past the hardships we forced on them. They forgave us, and you're lucky they did."

"Your preaching nearly made me want to vomit again. For a moment I thought I was actually going to fire you."

"Do what you have to do." Nathan couldn't keep the defiance out of his voice. "I know I will."

Pain contorted Anthony's face so he was barely recognizable. "I'll tell you what. I'll let you work half-time for two weeks. Let's assume your article gets published. If there's any sort of backlash, I'll have to let you go. This is a business. I help people find homes. It's hard enough without my employees publishing political editorials in major U.S. newspapers."

"I've thought about leaving anyway. If Reuters offers me more work, that's what I'll have to do."

The red eyes looking back at him seemed to retract. Nathan hadn't intended for his words to be judged a threat; he'd merely spoken from the heart. He wouldn't take back what he'd said.

"Can't you handle kindness?" Anthony said. "And friendship?"

"You've changed. And so have I."

"So what if we've changed?" He stopped talking as Nathan stood up. "Change isn't something to lash out at. I don't like change much myself, but that's how things are."

"It's not the act of change I'm talking about. It's the direction of change on those rare times we're given control over it."

"I don't follow you."

"Anthony," Nathan said, pushing his chair close to the desk so he couldn't sit back down. "We're complicit in how our lives have turned out. We're not riding on an electrical track. We've chosen for ourselves exactly what we have right now."

"All I know is that I've gone out of my way to be your friend, and you've made no effort to reciprocate."

Anthony's bent figure caused Nathan a pang of concern, but the feeling was nothing he hadn't given voice to. Anthony massaged the back of his neck, unable to look at Nathan. His eyes now were riveted to the picture of his family.

"I'd rather you quit than make me fire you."

"If it comes down to that," Nathan said, "I guess I will."

"That's nice. Now leave me alone to die, will you? And shut the door on your way out."

Back in his office, Nathan took out the manila envelope Reuters had sent him.

Among the letter and Agent Orange materials was Mr. Jasper's business card. Nathan decided to accept his offer before any guilt he might feel over his present job reared its head. After opening his e-mail program, he typed in Mr. Jasper's e-mail address and a subject heading that read *Re: Work Opportunity*.

Dear Mr. Jasper,

I recently received your offer to write about Agent Orange. I've heard quite a bit in the news about it and the case against the U.S. military, and I'm interested in writing the articles you proposed.

Although I have committed myself to other work, my obligations to that party have, for all practical purposes, been seen through. I hope to begin immediately, and eagerly await more details. Thank you for your confidence in me.

Sincerely,
Nathan Monroe

With his cursor hovering over the 'Send' button, he wondered if he was doing the right thing. But there was no longer a clear division between right and wrong. The real estate firm would get along fine without him whether he was working half-time or not. Never had he felt necessary to the firm's functioning, to its vision of success. And Anthony, he thought as he clicked 'Send,' was in no position to stop him from chasing his real ambition. If Anthony wanted him to be happy, he wouldn't get in the way of this opportunity.

Real estate had been both a diversion and a gift, and it had been good for Nathan. After Le had disappeared, it was the net that caught his fall.

He smiled at what now seemed a funny notion: he never wanted to help foreigners find homes in Vietnam, nor did he want anything to do with setting up corporate retreats. One needs distance from one's life, he thought, to see where one has arrived. He had been poorer in Saigon, but also happier. Working for Reuters, he foresaw, would be nearly ideal.

As soon as the "sent" confirmation appeared on his screen he left his office again.

"I'm taking the rest of today off," he told Xuan as he strode by. "Call me only if it's urgent."

"Where are you going?"

"I have no idea."

She lowered the nail file with which she was giving herself a manicure and turned a worried face to Anthony's door.

Once Nathan was on his motorbike he felt the overpowering sense of having regained control of his life, and he let that feeling carry him around the lake to where Le lived and would be painting.

21

Rain on the Land Rover's roof, like the feet of panicking birds, awakened Nathan. He hadn't meant to fall asleep, but it wasn't even six a.m. and veering and bouncing down the dark provincial roads had a soporific effect on him. Beside him, Hoa, too, was asleep. Anthony, however, had his eyes on the road as if he didn't trust the driver to find where they were going.

Nathan hadn't had time to check his e-mail that morning. Anthony had picked him up so early that all he'd been able to do was brush his teeth and throw some clothes on before leaving. He couldn't help imagining that Reuters had already responded to him and that all he needed to do was return home to see what bright future awaited him.

Another early-October storm rumbled out of the darkness, its thunder ushering in the dawn like a band of drummers.

Nathan hoped the rain would continue all morning, for then it would be impossible to inspect the land Anthony wanted to buy and turn into a corporate retreat. They'd have no choice but to reschedule the trip. If he was lucky, the roads would soon be washed out.

Delaying the inevitable was futile, but there was always the chance that complications would arise. Nathan decided to test Anthony's resolve.

"With rain like this we won't be able to inspect the property."

Anthony tried to turn in his seat and look at Nathan, but his size thwarted him. He unbuckled his seatbelt to make it easier.

"Well, they're not going to make us slog through fields or ford streams. The property has roads. And even if they're muddy, they're sure to have photographs. We'll at least be able to travel the perimeter by car."

"We could put the trip off if it gets worse."

"Not a chance. We're halfway there already. Besides, when it gets light out you'll see farmers laboring. If they can manage, so can we."

"Our hosts may not feel the same way."

"They will. There's a lot of money in it for them."

Resigned to the long, uncomfortable trip, Nathan assured himself that Reuters wouldn't have responded to him this soon, anyway.

The rain let up half an hour later as they came upon a row of road-side eateries. Anthony suggested stopping for *phở* and coffee. Hoa awoke when they pulled onto the pitted shoulder.

Nathan helped Anthony move a plastic table closer to the Land Rover, ten feet from the nearest customer. He heard someone tell a waitress: "A goldmine just dropped in. Better decide now what to charge them."

In Hanoi Nathan had learned to ask what something cost before ordering it. But today he chose not to. Anthony had lived here longer than he had and, when he didn't bother to inquire first, Nathan supposed he enjoyed paying more than everyone else. And he'd be able to complain later about being overcharged.

After everyone ordered, Anthony pointed up the road at a golf course billboard. Two square panels of a painted fairway had come unglued and hung like eyelids on a green face. An advertisement in English ran: World Class Golf Course. America, Europe, Japan Vote Bac Can Number One Golf Course in Vietnam. Seven Stars!

"Seven stars," Anthony said in mock amazement. "That's two more than St. Andrews."

"A few years ago," Hoa said, "I read that a famous American golfer designed the course. But they never printed his name. They must have referred to him ten times as 'a famous American golfer.' Maybe the reporter thought that was his name."

"These billboards have been up for years," Anthony remarked. "The only problem is that no one ever bothered to build the golf course."

"The investment was there initially," Hoa said. "But it fell apart when officials started fighting each other for kickbacks and protection money. The capital required for a development license kept increasing until the investors were chased away. But by then they already owned the land. They've been trying to unload it since then."

"They're eager to divest themselves of ownership. It's a steal."

"Corruption isn't always bad, see?" Hoa said. "Greed is like two dogs fighting over a stewpot. Sometimes the pot falls and breaks, and then even the ants get something to eat."

She and Anthony laughed.

"Then it becomes a food chain moment," Anthony said. "The ants fatten up only to be eaten by birds. Then the birds by cats. The cats by dogs. And then the Vietnamese come in and get fattened by them."

"Actually, we eat all those things."

Nathan glanced at her. The morning's gray light fell on her small teeth as she laughed.

Sitting near the road was a bad choice. Transport trucks roared past and cut down on conversation. Often, motorbikes were forced onto the shoulder, clouding the table with dust and exhaust. They ate their breakfast with one hand protecting their bowls, ready to cover them at a moment's notice.

"I guess we could've eaten in the car," Anthony said. "But then we'd have deprived the customers around us of entertainment."

Nathan finished eating before the others and headed back to the Land Rover. As he stood gazing disinterestedly at passing traffic, Anthony called him over. In his hand, which he waved like a schoolboy, lay his cell phone.

"It's Andrew," he hollered. "He wants to say hello."

It was the last thing Nathan expected.

"Tell him I'm busy."

"He knows you're not busy. Here," he said, waving his hand again. "A quick hello won't kill you. He's on his way to work."

Nathan came over and took the phone, intent on keeping the conversation brief. He put the phone to his ear and said hello.

"Nathan – I'm glad I caught you."

"What's to be glad about?" he said, stepping away from the table.

"I'm glad because I want to apologize for my behavior the last time we met. I had a lot to drink, and things had been really stressful for me. Like you, I'd begun a relationship with a Vietnamese woman, and it had ended badly. I was frustrated, but I had no idea you were going through the same thing."

"What makes you think I was?"

"Anthony told me. Anyway, I want to say I'm impressed you followed through on your promise to work for him."

"I had nothing else."

"I'm sure it's different from what you were used to in Saigon."

A syrupy quality inflected Andrew's voice – a sound like sincerity – and Nathan didn't trust it. "I should probably be going."

"Wait a sec. I have a question I want to ask. A personal question. It's about Le."

For some reason Nathan gave him the benefit of the doubt. "What about her?"

"I knew her, Nathan. I knew her like you did, but for a much shorter period."

"Knew her how?"

"That club where she worked. Club Connection or whatever it's called. I met her there. Back then I was a consulate greenie and didn't know how to...handle myself properly. Going to a club's no problem, but dating one of their bar girls..."

Nathan smiled, recognizing the probability that Le had worked a different job there than what she told him.

"I told her I worked at the consulate because that always impresses girls, and she lit up when I said it. After that we went out a few times, until she realized I wouldn't help her get a visa. When I saw you two together, I thought: 'Oh, no. She's snagged someone I know.' But I decided to let fate run its course. Maybe I should've said something then, but coming from me I think you would've resented it."

Nathan didn't hear the second half of Andrew's explanation. "You dated Le?" He felt strangely calm asking the question. And the more he was told, the calmer he felt.

"Only until I realized what kind of arrangement she was after."

The word 'arrangement' gave Nathan pause. "And you slept with her?"

"On our second date. I think she was feeling me out on the first, making sure I wasn't lying about my job."

Another transport truck roared past and a cloud of dust from the loose pile of macadam in its bed enveloped Nathan. Covering his nose and mouth with his shirt collar, he turned away. Anthony, whose table had been spared, was casually watching him.

"So why'd you give her a visa only to take it away?"

"I didn't. That's not my department. But things get around the office, and since I knew Le from before, I was curious to learn more of her background. A buddy of mine in Immigration told me everything checked out; she had a family sponsor who could support her.

"Sometimes it's hard to know if a person's only very clever when they go through the application process, and manages by that cleverness to pass herself off as a strong candidate. If Le's candidacy had holes, she saw them in time to plug them up.

"The thing is, when I dated her she told me a different story from what I saw on her application. It was probably before she hatched her whole plan. Turns out, the uncle she claimed to have was an old boyfriend, a brilliant artist from Hanoi she was in love with. Apparently he was from a politically powerful family and, after taking part in a drag race in which the other racer slammed into a crowd and killed a few people, his parents sent him abroad. He got into an art institute in California and managed to stay in the U.S. He's loaded, and he tried to get Le to join him there. He was going to set her up with a painting studio and gallery, and he'd promised to marry her. It was everything she wanted. I have to admit, she's an amazing painter. I'm sure you've seen her work."

Nathan didn't answer. "But why revoke her visa?" he said. "What's it to you if one person gets through?"

"Because I knew she'd lied. All it took was a phone call to our consulate in Los Angeles, and a couple of officers went to investigate. They found someone different than who they'd interviewed a few weeks earlier. Apparently he'd hired an old man to play her uncle. This time they found Le's boyfriend. It seems he was living with a woman, an American no less, and he immediately pointed a finger at Le, saying she'd put him up to it. Obviously, he wanted to save his own visa and maybe his relationship with this other woman. He blew the whistle on Le.

"I always thought Le was smart. Smart and determined. Her only problem was that I knew her. If I hadn't seen you on the day she interviewed, she'd be in California now. Probably living with her boyfriend and his American lover. That would have made an interesting arrangement."

"But when you dated her, why did she admit she had a boyfriend in California?"

"Because she hadn't come up with the idea of an uncle yet. I doubt she'd thought things through back then. Most of what I just told you came out when the officers from the consulate threatened to deport him for fraud.

"Anyway, I'm not sure what happened to Le. I e-mailed her some time ago, but the last time our staff tried to get in touch with her they couldn't. It seems she changed her contact information and moved somewhere new. Do you know where she is?"

"I have no idea."

"I didn't think so. In any case–"

"Does Anthony know you went out with her?"

"Yes. I needed his advice, so I called and explained the situation. It was his idea that I tell you. He said you needed to hear it. He thought it was interfering with your work or something."

Again Nathan glanced at Anthony, who now leaned forward on the table. On either side of him Hoa and the driver were speaking, and Nathan wondered if he was smiling over something they'd said or if he had an inkling of what Nathan and Andrew were talking about.

"He told you to call me now?"

"Why, is this a bad time? I know it's early..."

"I'm looking at a property Anthony wants to turn into a retreat."

"Sorry. I didn't know you were busy. Maybe you can call me later. If you want to, I mean. I know this isn't the best news, but I think the truth is worth hearing."

A question tugged inside Nathan. "When you were seeing Le, what was her hair like?"

"Like? Nothing special. Long and black, like you'd expect. The same as at the consulate. Why?"

"She was wearing a wig then. Her real hair was dyed pink."

Andrew chuckled. "She wasn't exactly run-of-the-mill."

Nathan said goodbye and stood motionless for a minute, staring at Anthony. He felt certain that Anthony knew exactly what had been said. Nathan was convinced that he'd been the last to know something that concerned him so personally. He went up to Anthony and tossed his phone on the table.

"He's surprised you're working for me, isn't he?"

"We didn't talk about work."

"You two talked a long time, didn't you?"

"He had something to apologize for. Just like you do."

Anthony looked as if he couldn't tell whether or not Nathan was serious.

"You know what I'm talking about."

"I'm afraid I don't."

Hoa, lingering at the edge of their conversation, asked who Andrew was.

"He's a friend of ours," Anthony said. "Or of mine, anyway. He works for the U.S. consulate and may consult with us on this deal later. He thinks the idea's brilliant and wants us to be the first to get in on the corporate retreat industry."

The irony was too much for Nathan. "He wants to invest in it?"

"Depends on how we do things."

"But it's a conflict of interest for him, isn't it?"

"It's Vietnam. The lines are intrinsically blurry."

They climbed back into the Land Rover and drove off. What

Andrew had said stuck in Nathan's mind. He told himself it didn't matter what relationships Le might have had, with Andrew or anyone else, and that he'd known for a long time that she'd deceived him. But the news hit close to home and he was uncomfortable that Anthony knew about Andrew and Le – and had known before himself.

As if sensing Nathan's feelings, Anthony tried to draw him out with a joke, then by talking seriously about the importance of today's meeting.

"This is make-or-break time. If you have last-minute questions, ask them now. We need to go in there prepared and impress the hell out of them."

Hoa asked about bringing in a Taiwanese work crew to clear the land and build on it. Before Nathan knew what was happening, she'd pressed blueprints and three-dimensional retreat designs into his hands. He glanced at the long, checkered sheets, but lost interest when Hoa and Anthony began delving into the plan's minutiae.

Anthony asked about the timeframe to develop the retreat and Hoa suggested half a year once the Taiwanese crew was in place. Anthony hooted over the miracle of cheap, plentiful labor. Nathan felt Anthony turn to him while laughing, felt Hoa turn to him, too, and heard their laughter recede when he wouldn't join in.

"He's destroying the binding I did," Hoa said.

Anthony yanked the report from Nathan's fingers and smacked him in the chest with it. "Stop fooling around. I need you with us on this."

"I am with you."

Tossing the report in Nathan's lap Anthony said: "Why do I feel like you just said that to get me off your ass?"

Hoa's mouth had been drawn down in disgust, but now she smiled scornfully. Looking from her to Anthony, Nathan almost voiced the thought that he was somehow fundamentally different from them.

"Because I did," he said. "There's nothing I can contribute to this discussion."

"You can contribute by paying attention," Hoa said, surprising Nathan and pleasing Anthony with her criticism.

"She's right. You can also contribute by not moping like a little girl."

That was where the fundamental difference lay: what had value to them was what could be converted into money. What Nathan valued they could negate without a thought. Belittled first, and then negated, just like Anthony had done with Huong, with Nathan's writing, and with Le.

"Ah, forget him," Anthony said, answering some murmur from Hoa. "He'll be with us when it counts. There's too much at stake and he knows it."

As they discussed the retreat, Nathan glanced at the heavy clouds atop the forested mountains. They gave the sense of claiming ownership of them, as a head stakes its claim to a body. Further up the road, however, blue sky parted the gray.

Parked in front of a renovated French villa were two shiny BMWs. Anthony's driver pulled into the lot and around a large fountain, whose centerpiece was a limestone slab decorated with miniature temples and water buffaloes.

"Let's get tea and small talk out of the way," Anthony said as they stepped out of the Land Rover. "Nate, all you need to do is show these guys you're fluent in Vietnamese and pay attention to how we conduct business with them. Remember, I'm putting this project in your hands, so your responsibilities start now."

A dark pudgy man met them in the doorway. He led them into a room and seated them in low wooden chairs. Three men in baggy suits entered and extended their flaccid hands.

Hoa took care of the small talk. Whenever the men smiled or laughed, Anthony parroted them, showing he was on their side.

He leaned over to Nathan. "What are they saying?"

"They're talking about how much they look forward to working with us. The little fat guy said that even though some of them fought for the North in the war, no one harbors animosity toward Americans and he hopes we can be good friends and successful business partners."

"I've heard that speech a hundred times. Tell them what I tell everyone we work with: We're committed to making the future brighter for their province, and with their experience and kind help we'll do everything in our power to make this project a shining example of good business and local development in Vietnam."

"Why don't you have Hoa do it?"

"The point is to have a foreigner deliver the message. You're doing it for effect."

Nathan took a moment to figure out what to say, then relayed it in Vietnamese. The men stared at him. Without commenting on what he'd said, they praised him for his Vietnamese. After he answered questions about his background, a younger man named Phong stepped forward to usher Anthony, Hoa, and Nathan outside. Phong would lead them on a tour of the property in one of the BMWs they'd seen.

Anthony patted Nathan on the back as they left. "That's exactly what I hoped would happen. You probably just paid them the greatest compliment a foreigner's ever given them. They'll talk about you until the day they die."

Following them outside, Nathan sensed he lacked courage. He'd played directly into Anthony's plan. Once he realized it, he felt vaguely sick.

The road they took soon became a fissured, muddy track. When Phong suggested a schedule to clear the ground and pour foundations for the villas to be built, Anthony instructed Nathan to take notes. Nathan removed a notepad from his briefcase. Although he flipped to a blank page and set his pen against it, he merely scratched down the words "Retreat Schedule."

The area was mostly rice fields and vegetable plots. Thatched homes scattered the land, and every now and then they spotted cows grazing and children leading water buffalo along the road. Long dikes ran beside the fields, and rail-thin men draped in plastic sheets attacked the land with hoes.

Encircling the valley were low mountains close enough that individual trees on the slopes could be distinguished. Here and there the shadows of clouds turned the green mountains black.

"What will happen to the people who live and work on the land?" Nathan said.

Phong smiled casually, as if this was a needless worry. "Wherever you build, they'll have to move."

"They've been informed," Anthony said. "There's really no other option. The trails we build will be no problem – what's the harm in people walking around? But do you think they'll want military machinery tearing up their fields? Maybe some of them could stay, just for atmosphere. But the last thing we need is for some poor farmer napping in a field to get crushed by a tank."

Phong nodded his agreement. "There aren't many people here. None of the farmers you see own the land. If they're told to move they will. They have no choice."

But just because they were squatting didn't mean they hadn't lived here for generations, Nathan thought. "What does 'not many' mean? One hundred people?"

"The last we checked there were around fifty families, which means about three hundred people."

"Will they be compensated?"

"For what? None of this is theirs."

"And how much of this gets torn up?"

"What are you worried about?" Anthony said. "You think Vietnam lacks agricultural capacity? Virtually the entire country is farmland. And people from the countryside are flocking to the cities in droves. Yes, we'll build over some of the land, but we'll also create jobs and help Bac Can develop economically. It's called modernization and you can bet the vast majority in this province supports it."

Anthony's words reeked of self-justification, Nathan thought. Not everything he said was wrong, but it was one-sided – favoring his own interests. He seemed to forget that these people were powerless to fight for what they had. There was an awful irony in an American coming in with tanks and military equipment, forcing out the Vietnamese who survived hand to mouth off the land. No one seemed to recognize the irony. Or if they did, perhaps they didn't care.

"Don't think I haven't considered the downsides," Anthony

continued. "I want to be responsible, but I'm also determined to profit from the progress this area's set to make. I call the shots, you follow my lead – which means trusting me – and everyone goes home happy." He had his eyes on Nathan and was licking his lips as if they'd started to crack and bleed. "Do you trust me?"

"It's just that all of this is new to me. Seeing a plan on paper is one thing, but seeing firsthand the consequences of it is something else."

"But do you trust me?"

"I don't know. I don't like the idea of making life more difficult for these people than it already is. And for you to say it's no problem, I have a hard time trusting that logic."

Anthony sighed disgustedly. Nathan noticed that Hoa and Phong were watching them.

"You work for me, Nate. And you still owe me. Remember that? Disagree with this project if you want, but don't be disagreeable. There's a difference. And for as long as you represent my company, I expect you to contribute to this project and our relationship with these people."

"I thought you said I did well back there."

"You did. But do you have to ask Phong so many difficult questions? If you have questions, save them for me. I'll answer them later, as many as you have."

"I do have questions."

"Fine. And don't look so damn glum. Can't you at least pretend you're halfway interested in any of this?"

"I'm more appalled than anything else."

"See? That's exactly what I'm talking about. That's what I mean by disagreeable."

A river came into view, as brown as the mud along its shore. There were houses here and paved roads in need of repair. The ride smoothed out as they left the muddy track. A black Mercedes was parked in front of a dilapidated villa smaller than they'd been in before. Two women in conical hats squatted beside the car. Sweat dripped from their chins as they scrubbed dirt off the wheels with rags.

Phong pointed at the Mercedes and said that the investors had already arrived.

Entering the villa, which smelled of cigarettes and mold, Nathan made a silent pact to his friendship with Anthony that he'd do as he was asked. If this place was on the chopping block, destined to be developed, he'd rather be in charge of it than someone who didn't care what happened or how it was carried out.

22

"Two more whiskies," Anthony called to the waitress, who hovered near the restaurant kitchen. "And try not to play with your phone for five minutes before bringing them. My liver's still clenched with impatience from last time."

Without moving, the girl yelled to the bartender.

"She's just a kid," Nathan said. "Don't get on her so much."

Anthony laughed. "This country is overrun by kids. Eighty percent of the population's under twenty."

Nathan stirred the ice in his glass with a toothpick.

"Vietnam's wasting its boom years," Anthony went on. "One day all these young people are going to grow old and need taking care of. Where's the money going to come from? And the expertise?"

"There's nothing we can do about it. At least not this afternoon."

"I guess that's what we get for coming to a place like this."

Nathan had no qualms with the restaurant. He would have been just at home – more so, in fact – on a shaded sidewalk with watered-down beer and pressed sheets of dried fish skin. To him, that they were snacking on Jamon Iberico and Manchego cheese, and drinking from a $100 bottle of whiskey, made the place seem upscale. The service was neither better nor worse than anywhere else.

"I know I said it already," Anthony continued, "but I appreciated your about-face this morning. For a while you seemed bent on sabo-taging our deal."

"I wasn't going to sabotage anything. I just had...doubts."

With his thumb Anthony wiped the rim of his glass. "Are you doubting anything now?"

Nathan considered the question. "Just myself," he said, struggling not to say 'and you.' His fifth whiskey had dulled the censor in him.

Beyond the window where they sat, in the day's fading light, two women began wrapping decorative lights around a tree. An electrical outlet had been drilled into its base and, when they plugged the lights into it, the lower half of the tree flashed blue. The lights glittered in the darkening air – the kind of deep, glowing blue that had awed him as a child.

He was happy the trip to Bac Can was over and he and Anthony had decided to celebrate together. The trip had ended on a high note, with their Vietnamese counterparts agreeing to the terms Anthony proposed. On the ride home, Anthony promised to work with Nathan to minimize the impact of the retreat they developed. Given how the trip had ended, Nathan no longer felt the urgency to check for a reply from Reuters.

The waitress brought over two whiskeys, leaving their old glasses but removing their unused napkins. Anthony once-overed her body with his eyes.

"We've had disagreements from time to time," Anthony said after she'd gone, "but I still trust you more than anyone else. Even now, after all the changes we've been through, we're not as different as you prob-ably think."

Nathan didn't feel this, but he cozied up to Anthony's words none-theless. The alcohol in his body made this easier.

"Do you agree? That we've never been that different?"

"Sure," Nathan said. It was what Anthony needed to hear, and he was willing to play this game, whatever its rules and desired result, for both their sakes. "I wonder if we'd be friends like this in America."

Anthony paused before sipping his whiskey. "It always pisses me off when you say things like that."

"Why?"

"Because it suggests our friendship's only based on convenience, on circumstance."

"But that's partly true."

Anthony scoffed. "So for you, it's just a marriage of convenience..."

The word "marriage" struck Nathan as such an odd way to describe their friendship that he couldn't guess what Anthony meant by it.

"It might have been true at first," Anthony continued, "but we've known each other more than seven years now. If anything were to happen to me, I'd want you to be there for Huong and my kids. You're my best friend."

"Thanks." Although he felt Anthony expected him to say more, he couldn't find the words.

Anthony was quiet for a moment. "What I just said – does it mean anything to you?"

"Of course."

Anthony's mood darkened. "I talk too much. I tell you things I shouldn't."

"If it makes you feel better, I don't listen to you anyway."

Anthony overturned his glass with a bang. Dregs of liquid pooled on the table. He dipped a finger into the alcohol and drew a spiral whose lines bled together. "How about telling me something you shouldn't?"

Nathan hadn't been drunk for many months, and it had been even longer since drunkenness felt good to him. Now, however, he imagined spending all afternoon and evening drinking with Anthony. The warmth of the dimly lit room was like the pleasantness of a summer evening. Or a memory of many evenings in Saigon long ago. Feeling the revival of an old kinship with Anthony, he embraced it.

"I'm seeing someone again," Nathan said.

"What's that?"

"I said I'm seeing someone."

"And when did that happen?"

"A long time ago. Long enough for it to be meaningful by now."

Anthony chuckled.

"Do you want to meet her?"

"Right now?" Anthony looked into his whiskey glass as if he was only half-listening, but Nathan sensed his keenness.

"Why not."

"Who is she?"

Anthony turned to him, and his hard stare raked Nathan's face. Nathan's voice caught. "Remember the girl I was seeing in Saigon?"

"Like a bad dream. I hope you're not seeing her again."

Nathan winced and blamed himself for telling Anthony the bad about Le to the exclusion of the good. "She's in Hanoi and we're giving things another shot."

A sour look passed over Anthony as he moved his chair to face him. "Are you really such a masochist?"

"Things are different now," Nathan said.

"No, they're not. Don't succumb to the illusion that anything changes here. Jesus, Nathan, what are you doing?"

"I'm happy," he said. And then, with drunken petulance: "Let me live however I want."

"But Nate, I can find something better for you. Just give me a little time."

"You mean like Hoa? No, thanks."

"No, not Hoa. Something better."

Nathan shook his head.

Just as he was about to retract his offer to introduce Anthony to Le, Anthony changed his tune. "I hope you know what you're doing. As your friend, I'm just trying to look out for you."

"Yeah, thanks."

It was nearly five o'clock. He'd drunk enough whiskey, and their long day together had exhausted him. At this time of day Le wouldn't be painting. Maybe Anthony could have his driver drop him off at her home, then he could introduce him to her quickly and say goodbye. He would have to do it eventually, yet he remained wary of what Anthony might do when they finally met.

Anthony excused himself to the bathroom and staggered away.

Left alone, Nathan pressed his hand against the window. The cold glass foretold the difference in temperature that awaited them outside, and it reminded him of the drafty windows and doors in Le's house. Autumn was getting cooler.

Looking across the room to where Anthony had disappeared, he wondered what he was getting into. He worried that Anthony's mistrust of Le would seep out invisibly and poison their private world.

He called Le to see if she was home. She didn't pick up right away, but rather than hang up he let it ring. Finally she answered. "Sorry," she told him. "I left my phone in my studio and didn't hear it at first. I was painting when my cousins arrived."

The mention of family had a sobering effect on him. "Your cousins?"

"They're in town so my auntie can see a doctor. They say they'll be here for a few days. Where are you?"

Nathan failed to keep his disappointment out of his voice. "I'm out with Anthony. I want to come by and introduce him to you."

"Now's not a good time."

Women's voices drifted to his ear in the background. It was difficult, given the low volume at which he could hear them, to understand what they were saying.

"But I want to meet your family, however distant they are to you."

"Have you been drinking?"

The question surprised him. "We've been celebrating a bit, yes."

"Maybe another time, then. I'm sorry, Nathan, but I need to go. We were in the middle of a rather awkward discussion when you called. Have fun tonight."

Suddenly he didn't want to spend any more time with Anthony. "What were you talking about?"

"Nothing very interesting. They want me to give them money."

When he asked what had happened, she explained. That morning, three generations of distant family had piled onto a motorbike and driven to Hanoi. They'd shown up at Le's door two hours before, after calling her on the way to find out where she lived. The auntie had already asked Le to take in her daughter so she could find work in the city. When Le balked, using her landlord as an excuse, they asked for money. Le couldn't say no twice. Because the only things of value she owned were her paintings, she decided to sell them. Half an hour ago she arranged for a dealer to appraise all her work. He would come tomorrow morning. She hoped that her paintings, all together, would fetch what her relatives had asked for.

It sickened him to hear they were pressuring her like this. "How much do they want?"

"A few thousand dollars. My auntie asked for more, but her daughter said it was enough."

"What do they need it for?" He imagined it was because the old woman was sick, but he wanted to make sure.

"A new motorbike. New cell phones. Different things."

"You're not going to do it, are you?"

"That side of my family helped me when I was younger and had nothing."

He couldn't stop his voice from rising. "Have you thought this through? You'll end up selling your paintings for less than they're worth."

"If I can help them, that makes me happy. For as long as I can remember, I've been sending them small amounts of money whenever I had it. It's my duty to them."

"You never told me that."

"But all Vietnamese do this. I didn't know I needed to tell you."

Rather than appease him, her way of thinking frustrated him more. "Your paintings are good, Le. The money you could–"

"Stop it, Nathan. Talking about money like this doesn't suit you."

"Why not?"

She paused before speaking, as if to give him the chance to recognize an obvious truth. "Because you're a writer, not a salesman. Leave the money-making to Anthony."

Her words stopped him. As far as he could tell, he was nothing anymore. A quitter didn't seem to qualify for much.

But what pierced him was the realization of how much he had become like Anthony, and in such a short time. She was right, of course, but then he'd been right, too – she could make a better living if she went about it differently.

He envied her confidence in living as she now did. Perhaps his worry was misplaced after all; he should have been celebrating her renewal as an artist, encouraging whatever force spurred her on. That neither of them could get ahead financially, however, made it seem like they were perpetually mired.

On his way back Anthony detoured to the bar and asked to see another bottle of whiskey.

"I'll call you later," Nathan said into his phone. "Maybe I can visit tomorrow."

"I wish I could see you tonight. I miss you already."

A minute later Anthony came back. He told Nathan he'd just called Huong. "She thought I was already home."

"It's that big house you've got," Nathan said. "It must be hard to keep track of everyone there."

Anthony frowned and shook his head. "So is your girlfriend coming here or are we going somewhere to meet her?"

"Neither," Nathan said. "Her relatives stopped by unexpectedly."

Anthony swept his arm across the table, knocking their plate of ham and cheese to the floor. His eyes shot open wide – he seemed surprised by the sound of porcelain smashing on the tiled floor, and he looked at his hand as if it had acted independently of him. Their waitress hurried over to clean up the mess, and Nathan apologized to her.

Without commenting on what he'd just done, Anthony mumbled: "Just because I don't like her doesn't mean I'll cause trouble. You don't trust me. You don't trust me like I trust you."

Nathan asked himself why he wanted to introduce Anthony to Le in the first place. Would it make his life easier if he had Anthony's approval? Would Anthony respect him more for seeking it? In his drunkenness, his mind tumbled back to the conversation he'd had with Le.

"They asked her for money. But she's got nothing to give them, so she's selling her paintings for a pittance."

"She must have learned that from you when you were at that magazine in Saigon."

"You think it's funny?"

"Not really."

Anthony withdrew from his pocket a silver clip stuffed with cash. In its maw was the careful organization of two currencies. The moss green of American twenty-dollar bills was pressed against an assortment of blue, pink, and green Vietnamese *dong*.

"How much does she need?"

"Put it away."

Anthony unrolled his stash of money. "Choose her best painting and I'll pay whatever you say. Consider it a lesson in how to handle her family in the future. You can pay me back later from your salary."

"How is this a lesson?"

"Ever hear of a one-off? Give them more than they ask for – once. And tell them to enjoy it because they'll never get another penny from you again."

When he held out the money, Nathan pushed it away.

"Take it. Just don't tell Huong about it. If that's not enough, I'll give you the rest at the office." He slipped the empty clip into his pocket and once more held out the fist-sized wad of bills.

Nathan thought Anthony must be as drunk as he was. Was his own drunkenness why he didn't get mad at him now? Nathan again pushed the money away, more forcefully this time.

"Le has her own way of making money."

"I'm trying to help."

"No, you're making things harder, worse."

"I'm helping more than you are. You don't have the money." Anthony laughed. "Penury's chronic with you."

But at least I still have dreams, Nathan thought.

"Just consider it an advance on your salary," Anthony said. "Or would it help if I called it a bonus?"

"I haven't done anything to deserve a bonus, especially when you've put a moratorium on pay increases for everyone else. And if I need an advance, I'd rather come to you for it than have you offer it like this. Out of sympathy. Or to be some kind of hero."

Anthony's cell phone beeped and he smiled at the message he'd received.

"Happy Halloween, baby," Anthony said. "I wonder who sent this. I can't place the number, and the body doesn't ring a bell, either."

He passed his phone to Nathan. A grainy photo of a naked, undernourished-looking woman filled the small screen. The woman lay on a bed with Hello Kitty sheets. She wore a black mask and witch's hat, and an overhead light illuminated her small pointy breasts, sunken stomach, and sparse triangle of hair between her legs. It wasn't clear if she'd taken the picture herself or had someone do it for her. Nathan found himself slightly repulsed by her.

"Wrong number?" he said. "That could be an embarrassing mistake."

"I'm not sure. I usually know who it is."

Nathan wondered how many women sent Anthony nude photos. Were they sex workers? Women he met at bars? His own employees? Thinking of Huong, he decided he didn't want to know.

"What's written under the picture?" Anthony asked.

Nathan scrolled down and read the Vietnamese. "She's horny and wants to see you. But you probably guessed that from her picture." He handed back Anthony's phone.

"I wish I knew who she was."

"Better not let Huong see that."

Anthony laughed. "Huong was talking on my phone once when a photo like that came through. Like now, only a number showed on the screen. I said it must have been sent by mistake, and Huong messaged the girl back telling her never to contact me again. She didn't seem upset. She was kinder to the girl than I expected."

Nathan told Anthony he wanted to go home.

To his surprise, Anthony didn't object. When he finished typing something into his phone, he pushed himself out of his seat and lurched back toward the bar. He flipped through a drinks menu and pointed at something.

"Get me a bottle of this. And give me the bill while you're at it." Even before the bill came he leaned against the bar and totaled what he guessed he owed. He dropped a wad of cash on the counter.

The bartender reached behind him and took a bottle of whiskey off the shelf. In Vietnamese he said: "That's sixty-five dollars."

"What did he say?" he shouted at Nathan.

Nathan told him, but Anthony didn't listen. He pushed his cash toward the bartender. "Here. You figure it out."

When Anthony had his change, he lurched back toward the table.

"Are you sure you don't want to keep drinking? My driver doesn't go home until I'm ready for him to."

"I've had enough for one afternoon."

"If you leave now, where am I supposed to go?"

"Your home doesn't seem nearly as bad as you describe it." The settledness Anthony always rejected was hard for him to fathom. "I wish I had it myself."

"Be careful what you wish for. The way things look, the chance might come sooner than later. And what will you do if it does?"

"I don't know," Nathan admitted.

But somewhere inside him, not far from the surface of his life, he was confident he'd be ready.

Nathan walked home. As he steered his body through the Old Quarter toward Truc Bach, the periodic shouting of English words became more frequent, and he picked up his pace. But the more he walked, the more he tripped over the uneven sidewalks; the brighter the neon from the endless mom-and-pop stores shone in his eyes; and the louder the city's clamor buffeted him.

Crossing Phan Dinh Phung Street, he came upon a quiet expanse. Behind a tall, barred metal gate, Cua Bac Church towered over the surrounding trees and buildings. White light poured through the open entryway and the overlapping circles in the rose-patterned window above it.

Approaching the church he saw guests filling half the pews, while a white-robed priest at a podium spoke with outstretched arms. A couple in matching white stood on the stage between the priest and a singing choir. White flowers on the corner of each pew decorated the center aisle.

Nathan hovered in the entryway, mesmerized by the clean light inside and the pure sound of voice that made the chaos behind him disappear. The light and voices had a liquid quality, and he had a sense, merely standing there, of being bathed by both.

An old man in a striped tracksuit, kneeling to arrange flowers in plastic holders on the floor, waved him inside.

"Are you here for the wedding?" he said. "Or to worship?"

"I'm not sure why I'm here," Nathan answered.

"It doesn't matter. Please, come in."

Nathan wandered down one side of the nave. Paintings of Jesus on the cross hung on the church's blue-gray walls, and on the ceiling above the chancel spread the words *Regina Martyrum Ora Pro Nobis*. Several wedding guests turned and smiled at him as he settled into a pew near the back. They were young – men in jackets and jeans, women in *áo dài* or knee-length dresses and colored leggings.

The atmosphere was marked by a kind of seriousness he associated with America; a purposefulness he rarely found in Vietnam, a peacefulness warm and familiar.

Anthony and Huong had married in a restaurant one afternoon near her parents' home. Anthony had described the ceremony as "standard Vietnamese Buddhist ritual, which is to say a bunch of mumbo-jumbo." They'd invited Nathan, but he'd used a writing assignment as an excuse not to attend.

Nathan wondered if the man who'd invited him into the church had suspected him of drinking; if the guests five pews in front of him could smell his whiskey breath; and if the people who'd watched him proceed from the entryway to his seat noticed his drunken gait. He also wondered how Le would react being here with him; not long ago she told him that she'd never been inside a church.

He gazed at the bride's profile, whitened with makeup. A white shawl draped her shoulders, but on her exposed back the skin appeared darker, perhaps from a lack of powder or merely from shadow. From the shawl down, her arms, too, were bare. He found in her a vague resemblance to Le, but he couldn't put a finger on it.

The bareness made Nathan want to touch the woman's skin. It was this, he decided, that had made him think of Le.

As the priest lifted his arms, everyone in the wedding party stood. The priest spoke in a strange, formal Vietnamese that Nathan never had occasion to hear before; he was reading from the Bible.

Two nights before, when Nathan last slept at Le's, it had been colder than now, and in her bedroom she'd stuffed old paint rags in the cracks of her window to keep them warm. But her tactic failed and, as they lay in her bed reading, she'd risen and taken the blanket with her. "Where are you going?" he'd said, then realized she wanted him to follow her – she was leading him, fully in control, as on the first night they'd slept together. She brought him outside, beneath the banyan tree, beneath the plastic tarp which blocked a square of sky, erasing the stars and moon. This was her outdoor workspace, and it smelled of earth and paint. Her straw mat was rolled up and stuffed in a crevice between branches; she pulled it out, unrolled it, and started a small fire in a charcoal burner nearby. She lay down, pulling the blanket over her. Shivering, Nathan lay down, too, then peeled the blanket back and wrapped himself around her. She was warmth like he'd never known warmth, and she was wet like he'd never known her to be wet. He entered her and they folded into each other like creatures of the deep sea sharing the same shell. Afterward, as she stretched across his chest, tousling his hair, she wondered aloud what he'd be like when he got old. Would he be fat? Bald? Cranky? But her last question – how many people would love him? – made him ask what she meant. "Do you want children?" she'd said. And at the mention of children Nathan had thought of Anh and Hao. "Yes," he said. "When it's time." She was quiet for a while and then said: "Me, too. When it's time."

Nathan tuned in briefly again to the priest's speech – "Marriage should be honored by all, and the marriage bed kept pure, for God will judge the adulterer and all the sexually immoral. Keep your lives free from the love of money and be content with what you have" – and then he tuned right out again.

For a moment he considered contradicting Le's wish and going directly to her house. He wanted to observe her with her relatives, to hear what they talked about, and to see if she transformed into the Le whom Anthony warned him about. He was clear-headed enough to realize that he was, more than ever, afraid of losing her – not to a rival, or to ennui, but to a particular history in which he played no part. Despite Anthony's warnings, he was ready to sacrifice all he had for a future with her. But what was best for their future? The individual choices he was used to making now compelled him to question how they might affect her. This was a different way of living for him, and he knew it would take time to get used to. Inevitably he would make mistakes along the way.

"But if the unbeliever leaves," the priest continued, "let him do so. A believing man or woman is not bound in such circumstances; God has called us to live in peace. How do you know, wife, whether you will save your husband? Or, how do you know, husband, whether you will save your wife?"

Nathan wasn't here to listen to a Vietnamese priest read from the Bible. He was here because of the light and because a chorus of voices had sung beautifully in the lonely night.

He sat there until the priest brought the bride and groom together. He asked each in turn if they would be faithful to and respect each other. *Thua có*, each said, and the promises brought polite applause from the pews.

Nathan rose and walked down the aisle to the entryway. He heard a rustle of coats and jackets behind him as people turned to watch him leave.

The man in the tracksuit waved a basket of white roses at Nathan as he went by.

Stepping outside again into darkness and noise, Nathan felt vastly better. He hoped it wasn't merely the effect of alcohol.

23

Nathan slid his paddle into the water and, using his wrists and forearms, pulled back with it on the right. Lifting it out in the same motion, he slid the paddle into the water on the opposite side of the kayak and pulled it back as before. With momentum the twin motion became nearly effortless. The kayak moved forward, though it was Anthony who propelled them from the rear.

"That's the movement you want," Anthony said. "Pull down with your top hand to steer left."

A few feet to their right were the plastic buoys of a fishing net extending from the Hanoi Club's pool. Farther back was the asphalted shore from which they'd launched.

This wasn't Nathan's first time kayaking, but he hadn't done it since college. There was a newness to it, and being on the water at sunup, before much of the city was out of bed, was invigorating.

Setting his paddle across the kayak's nose, he dipped a hand into the lake and watched his fingers magnify. "It's cold. The bottom must be freezing."

"The whole lake's shallow. The temperature on the surface is the same as any place deeper."

Behind them, at the bottom of a sloping road, the Hanoi Club glittered in the dawn. The cramped, narrow houses along Yen Phu Street above, with cats lazing on the rooftops and yesterday's laundry billowing behind fenced-in balconies, seemed to exist on a different plane.

"Careful looking behind us. I don't want you dumping us into the water."

Earlier, Anthony had explained how he used to kayak on the lake every morning, back when he was trying to get a solid footing in real estate. "In the middle of the lake, with nothing to disturb me but the wind over the water, or the occasional fish jumping, and with the sky lightening gradually, I felt like I was the only person in the world." He said he hadn't enjoyed peace like that in what felt like forever. He wanted to kayak more, but his schedule wouldn't let him. "Having two kids and staying out late most nights means sacrificing simple pleasures like this. Or maybe I've just gotten old."

Anthony had hardly fit in the kayak when they pushed it into the water. He'd taken the seat in back not by choice but because he couldn't squeeze into the smaller one in front. The way he manipulated his paddle, however, showed he possessed a good deal of strength, even agility. But after a few minutes his breathing grew labored. Nathan asked how often he exercised.

"These days, never." Anthony paused for breath. "You know my schedule. I'm at the office from seven in the morning to eight at night. Beautiful is the day that ends in a swank, quiet bar. It's preferable to sweating on a treadmill."

"You should take better care of yourself."

"That's the tradeoff I've made. I want to change things. But it's not easy."

Nathan thought about what he'd recently sacrificed in his own life. In retrospect, he wasn't sure the sacrifices had been worth it, but he'd shaken up his life like he wanted, and his relationship with Le, though a work in progress, gave him hope. He felt he was inching closer to restoring the equilibrium in his life. He was also paying his debts back, a little at a time.

"Two months ago you suggested that I'd sold my soul to the devil. Now I wonder if it happened. In a previous life or something."

Nathan had forgotten his comment until Anthony reminded him.

He had a vague memory of the context in which he'd spoken, but for Anthony to recall it indicated it had struck a chord.

"I've sacrificed a lot for success. And now, maybe health and happiness will always be out of reach. Sometimes I feel like I can graze them with my fingertips. But having either one will take a special effort."

There was no question that Anthony's life here was a result of hard choices. But what exactly had he sacrificed? There was a difference between giving up something valuable and merely giving up.

As they paddled farther out, their view opened. To the left, where the land pushed sharply into the water, three turtles appeared to float amid an island of trash. As Nathan strained his eyes in the weak matutinal light, the turtles transformed into human heads – snail catchers.

"Tired already?" Anthony said, splashing water onto Nathan's arm. "You're making me do all the work."

Nathan resumed paddling, glancing occasionally at the snail catchers until they dissolved in the distance.

Out of the blue Anthony said: "It's gotten unbearable, Nate. I've had enough of this shit."

Nathan assumed he wanted to return to shore. Concerned again about his health he tried unsuccessfully to turn and see his face. Nathan could do nothing but sit where he was, facing the open water. "Enough of what shit?"

"My life here."

A fish breached the surface. Nathan gazed at the ripples it made, waiting for Anthony to explain.

"The good thing is I've learned what I want and know I'm capable of getting it. The bad thing is I've learned what I don't want and know I'm incapable of getting rid of it."

"What's the good thing?"

"Just being successful in the world. I know I stack up. And I know how to determine what's worth risking in my life. I can see the risk and I can see the payoff, and I can make my way between them. I feel like even if I lose for a while, in the end I'll come out on top. I've never had that confidence before."

Nathan sensed he was leading up to something, though he couldn't tell what. In any case, he couldn't see the relevance to Anthony's life now. "What are you getting at?"

"Maybe what I say today isn't what I'll say tomorrow, but lately I've become sensitive to how short life is. I can't get it out of my head. And when I think about it, late at night when I should be sleeping, when all I have for company is a bottle of Chivas and the croaking of frogs out my window, I realize that if I don't leave Vietnam soon I'll be destined to die here. My roots here are deep, but they're not so deep yet that I can't uproot them and plant them somewhere else."

Nathan wondered where Anthony's family fit into all of this. "Have you spoken with Huong about it?"

"She only thinks I'm complaining. And isn't that at the heart of everything?"

"I don't know."

"See, she's become a living metaphor for my life here. Our relationship's like a business, the sole aim of which is to put forth good face to the world. Who I am and what I need she's not concerned with. To her, my being a man means giving everything to make my family rich and respected. But I've done that. So what's left? I've tried branching out from our 'partnership' – it's only happened a few times – and I suspect she has, too. For a long time we've been running on fumes. But they're burned up now. Nothing's left."

Here on the lake there was no need for Anthony to control what he said. Nathan was grateful to be in the front of the kayak, unable to meet his eyes.

"The things that happen to me here fall almost exclusively into patterns of bad and bizarre. They make me feel like I'm getting messages."

"Messages? From who, God?"

"I'm delusional, right?" He burst out laughing but stopped when the kayak nearly tipped. "It's like some higher being's scripting what happens around me, giving meaning to every encounter I have and the bizarre things I witness every day. I've been trying to figure out what it all means, and the only explanation I can come up with is that I'm getting messages. And that all I've got to do is act."

Seeming to sense Nathan's disbelief, he continued.

"I'll give you an example. An overt one. Two days ago, Huong and I visited friends at the Melia Hotel. My Land Rover was being repaired, so we took my old Vespa. We were leaving the hotel when she remembered she wanted to buy something in the gift shop, so I said I'd wait for her on the sidewalk. When I pushed my bike in front of the hotel, five young men approached me with a deliberateness I'd seen before and knew meant trouble.

"All five were well dressed – I'm talking imported silk specially tailored – and spoke English like they'd been educated in the United States. Actually, one said he had been, but he wouldn't tell me where. They strutted up and made a tight circle around me. Then they started asking me harmless questions but soon got hung up on my Vespa. They called it 'a cheap-ass bike,' implying that I was poor. I didn't say anything; I've learned that in Vietnam ignoring insults is more effective than responding with my own. They wanted to take my Vespa for a spin and said they'd buy it if they liked it, as if they were doing me a favor. When they saw I wouldn't play along, the one who said he'd studied in America put his hand on my steering wheel and leaned toward me.

"He said if we'd met years earlier – twenty years; he didn't even know his own history – his immediate reaction would be to kill me. He said at their ages he and his friends would be soldiers, and of course they'd carry guns. He made a gun of his fingers and pressed it against my temple. Then he said this is what our encounter would have come to, and his patriotic duty would require him to pull the trigger. 'I'd do it happily, too,' he said. 'I'd blow your head off and be a hero.'

"I could've told him I had nothing to do with the war, that my parents had marched in Washington against it, and I could've told him I helped found an orphanage in Saigon but withdrew my support when the Vietnamese in charge were caught embezzling the funds. I could've told him any of those things and more. But he wouldn't have listened. Instead I told him he needed to study his history, that twenty years ago he'd be harassing a Soviet engineer, not an American soldier. He and his friends started talking angrily in Vietnamese and pressed even closer. Just then Huong came out of the Melia and hurried over. She put an end to everything right there. As we drove away they called her a whore and a traitor – not to her face, of course, but to her back."

Nathan had angled his body enough that he could now see Anthony as he spoke. His face twisted horribly as he recollected the encounter, and the strange shape of his mouth made him seem desperate.

"To me there's a message in an encounter like that. It's like someone inside my head is screaming for me to leave." He gaped at Nathan, as if searching his face for an explanation.

But it had happened to Nathan, too. In Saigon people had tried to run him off the road; had swung at him in traffic; had cursed him; stared at him menacingly and openly made fun of him in Vietnamese. In Hanoi he'd already been confronted twice by drunken soldiers sitting among friends – once outside the History Museum and once at a streetside snail restaurant. The difference was that he didn't let it get to him. There were no messages in these encounters.

He turned back to the front of the kayak. "But isn't that how it is wherever you're not like everyone else?"

Anthony was silent behind him, and Nathan could imagine his expression: one of hurt for Nathan's failure to sympathize more.

"Children have thrown rocks at me on the sidewalk, Nate. Women driving motorbikes with kids in their laps have tried to run me off the road. Only two weeks ago a group of boys no older than seven ran up to me screaming 'Fuck your mother!' – in English. There was nothing I could do. They're children, for god's sake, and dozens of people around were watching to see how I'd react. I've rarely felt so helpless."

"If you spoke Vietnamese..." Nathan stopped to make sure he put this right: "People respect you when you know their language. You become more human to them, more like themselves."

"I'd only get in more trouble if I was able to speak my mind. Think of the foreigners you know who've responded to one drunken, abusive Vietnamese guy, only for all the Vietnamese around, who'd been enter-tained by the whole spectacle until then, to suddenly band together to beat and rob him."

"I don't know anyone that's happened to."

"Well, I do. And that's what would happen to me if I knew Vietnamese."

Uncomfortable with the conversation, Nathan started paddling again. In a moment Anthony joined him.

Soon they came upon a bank of high, crumbling mud. A beard of weeds rose and fell at the water's edge, and ragged trees stood ten, sometimes twenty feet along the ridge. Trash scattered the slope like vestiges of winter snow.

They reached an opening with a view of the water park. A white Ferris wheel dominated the sky. The wheel's red middle was spiked like a cog, making the whole resemble the guts of an old watch. The Ferris wheel seemed to be asleep, and Nathan had the odd sensation that if they made too much noise it would awaken with a flashing of lights and a creaking of infuriated gears.

Anthony pointed his paddle to an area bordering the water park. It was light enough now to make out the lotuses there, thousands of them floating like an island.

"In the spring it's a sea of pink and white. When the flowers open at dawn, dozens of women in short boats sing together and collect dew from the petals. Restaurants buy the dew to make lotus tea. It's the most perfect thing I've ever tasted."

A dike ran behind it and Nathan realized that more lotuses grew in the water beyond that.

"It sounds like a scene from *Three Seasons*."

"What ever happened to the lotusland I once knew?" Anthony said. "Vietnam's changed forever."

"It's only a lotusland for foreigners."

"Not anymore. Plenty of Vietnamese have enough money and time to indulge in their country's pleasures. You've got money now, Nate. I'll turn you into a lotus-eater before I'm done with you."

Nathan found the comment strange, considering he still owed Anthony money.

Anthony's breathing had become more labored, but from the corner of his eye Nathan saw his paddle slice expertly through the water, propelling them ahead. It was hard keeping up with Anthony, and he wondered if he was trying to prove something.

The broken land became higher ground where vegetables grew in neat rows. A thatch hut stood where it ended, and people sat before it at miniature tables. An old woman was wiping a glass case in which cigarette cartons were stacked beside bottles of soybean milk and soft drinks.

Anthony told Nathan to stop paddling. "Can you smell that?"

Nathan inhaled the misty, still-cool air. "Coffee?"

"Let's get two and take them back out on the lake." As they approached the shore, a dozen children appeared and rushed up to them. Two bold little boys grabbed the kayak's side and made as if to push it under water. Anthony splashed them. They backed off, uncertain of his intentions.

Nathan caught the woman in the hut looking down at them. "Still want coffee?" he said over his shoulder.

"Yeah, but be quick."

Nathan cupped his hands around his mouth and yelled for two iced coffees.

"I take milk," Anthony reminded him.

"I thought you took brandy."

"I will if she has it."

Nathan relayed Anthony's request to a little girl nearby. Watching her run away, he was impressed by her attentiveness – until she ran past the hut and, starting to scream, toward the houses behind it.

He called to the woman again. When she nodded, he glanced at the other children. Amazement plastered their faces. He could almost hear questions forming in their minds: who was this white man in a kayak, and by what magic had he spoken Vietnamese? Just like that, they were as well behaved as lambs.

Above them the old woman called a boy over and told him to deliver the iced coffees she'd made. The boy hurried down the dirt hill.

"Hold the coffees while I paddle us away from here," Anthony said.

Nathan took the coffees and explained that they'd be back later to pay.

Anthony pushed his paddle against the shallow bottom, and they drifted backward. Nathan waved to the kids as the kayak retreated. His wave, combined with the prospect of them leaving, triggered mayhem on the shore.

"Here's fine," Nathan said when they were a hundred meters away.

"Not yet." Anthony was puffing hard, sending the kayak a full meter ahead with each thrust.

When Anthony finally laid his paddle across the kayak, the hut on the ridge looked like a cardboard box dumped there by one of the enormous houses behind it. The wind here was stronger than close to land, and small waves raced beneath them, sloshing the coffee in their glasses.

"There's no brandy in mine."

"We can go back if you want. I know how much you enjoyed being attacked by those kids."

"Ninety per cent of my life's devoted to not getting trapped. If you take things further with Le you'll know what I mean."

A cloud passed over Nathan's mind.

"Haven't you ever felt trapped here?"

"Not like you're talking about."

"Let me tell you, it's no way to live. Every part of my life's ensnared: my house, my business, even my children – Huong's name's attached to them all. If I leave her, she gets everything. If she leaves me, she'll take everything. I'm being bled at both ends."

Nathan grew cold.

"I'm thinking of leaving. Back to the States. Becoming a business consultant would be the easiest thing. I've got good contacts here and I know my way through a thousand legal loopholes. But part of me just wants to disappear, in some place big and empty where no one will ever bother me again."

"Are you being serious?"

"About leaving? I've been toying with it for a while, but recently I've put out feelers. I don't know how many chambers of commerce I've already contacted."

The kayak slowly turned, and Nathan found himself facing the city. Dark pastels streaked the sky over Hanoi. Teetering between night and day, the colors stretching between the two lines were strangely unbalanced. The entire sky looked like it needed a violent shake.

"What about your kids?"

Anthony didn't answer immediately. "They have to go through an early period of being Vietnamese. Later they'll realize they'd rather be American. I figure I've got a decade before my obligation as a father really hits. Maybe longer: they don't have to choose their citizenship until they're twenty-one."

Anthony had said the same kinds of things back in March, when Nathan first agreed to work for him. There was no question Anthony was serious.

"I want to leave everything I have and start over. In America, not here."

Nathan was at a loss for words. From his disordered feelings, what he felt most strongly was anger. Finally he said: "Don't do it. Think about your family."

"I know it sounds terrible. But consider it from my perspective. Huong doesn't love me. Her parents, who I never wanted to live with us, have taken over my house and don't even have the decency to acknowledge me when I say hello. And my children, my own flesh and blood, hate me. You've seen it – it's unnatural. I'd rather be dead than live like this."

Nathan listened carefully. Part of him fantasized about being in Anthony's shoes – not as the owner of a real estate firm, but with a house of his own, and having started a family. How had things become so bad between Anthony and Huong? Not long ago they were happy together and their lives much simpler.

"How many chances in life do we have to make a family?" Anthony said. "The odds were stacked against me from the start. If I'd known, I never would've let myself get to this point. But it's happened. So now what? To accept things is the same as throwing my life away. Do you see this, Nate? Can you understand it from my perspective?"

"It's complicated…"

"I'm telling you, I don't want to die here. I don't want to be buried here. I don't want to decompose in Vietnamese soil. I don't want to fertilize their rice fields or fruit trees or flower gardens. Or weeds in a ditch. I've given enough to this place already."

"What do you want from me?" Nathan spoke harshly, barely resisting the urge to chuck his glass into the lake in frustration.

"What do you mean?"

"I mean, why the fuck are you telling me this? How am I supposed to react to what you're saying?"

In the ensuing silence the sound of water smacking their kayak grew loud. "For a long time I've been afraid to bring it up. I just didn't know how. But since you asked..." Anthony's voice had become strangely pleading.

Another long moment passed.

"Actually, I've decided to leave," he said at last. "For California. And I'm not coming back."

Nathan couldn't grasp what he was saying. Today was the first time he'd heard Anthony talk about leaving.

"When I go, I need you to do something for me. But I don't want you to answer me right away. I don't even want you to look at me after I've said it."

"Jesus Christ, Anthony."

"Listen to me!"

The kayak rocked and Nathan thrust his hands to the sides to steady himself. "What is it?"

"I want you to take over for me. The company. All my peripheral business commitments. My whole life here: everything I have and everything I do. I want to give it to you so I can leave."

"What the hell are you—"

Anthony struck the water with his paddle and a sound like gunshot flattened out in Nathan's ear.

"Shut up and let me finish. I want you to take over the real estate company. In the beginning you'll fill in for me as I travel to California ostensibly for business. A few weeks should be enough to set myself up with an opportunity." He cursed himself before going on. This time when he spoke his voice was gentle, even contrite. "And I want you to take care of my family. Until things are back to normal for them, become the husband and father I couldn't be."

"Are you crazy? I can't do that."

"Yes, you can. Huong thinks you're a better person than me. My kids are nuts about you. Even Huong's parents talk to you when you're around. And I know the feeling's mutual. I know you're fond of them."

Nathan shook his head. "You can't do this. They're your family."

For the next few minutes he enumerated the reasons why Anthony couldn't go through with this. Getting divorced would be more responsible, at least, than just running out on his family. It was a cowardly choice, and Anthony was wrong to think Nathan could simply step into the void he'd create by leaving. Nathan wasn't ready to be a husband, much less a father. But Anthony, after listening to him with a strange calm, said he was wrong.

"I trust you, Nathan. You're a good person. You're not like the rest of the people I know here. If I hadn't thought you were staying in Ohio six years ago, I wouldn't have gone after Huong, and you might have married her when you got back. It's not a stretch to think that. And my kids could easily be yours. You'd be a better husband to Huong and a better father to Anh and Hao than me."

"I have no feelings for her anymore. And besides, I'm building a future with Le."

Anthony ignored this. "We all need second chances. I'm taking mine at the same time I'm giving you yours. It's perfect for us both."

Nathan was angered by Anthony's patronization, but not nearly as much as by his recklessness. The notion of second chances stuck in his mind. He dwelled on this, on the second chance Anthony had given him, and on the second chance he and Le now had, until a new thought pushed against it.

"You've been planning this all along, haven't you?" Nathan said. "This is why you wanted me to work for you. This is why you took me back so quickly after Le and I broke up. It was all a set-up."

"Not at first. The idea came to me over time, after I'd already tried getting you here."

Nathan turned just enough to look at him again. The position hurt his neck but there was something he needed to see. "I can't do this and you know it."

"Yes, you can. I told you, you'll take over the agency first. Do it for one or two months. That'll be long enough for me to register a new business and transfer some money. After that, maybe we can go into business together. I'll be your contact in America and you'll be mine here. If you don't like it, you can cash out and do your own thing. I'll even forgive what you owe me and pay off your other debts, too."

"There's no way I'm doing this. And you can't either. You'll ruin their lives."

"Listen to me. We'll work together. It won't be nearly as demanding as real estate."

"You're dropping a huge bomb on me."

"I'm doing it. I've already looked into it. My contacts here are solid and with Vietnam's entry into the World Trade Organization the sky's the limit." As if hypnotized by the sound of his dreams, his face had glazed over from the exertion of a sustained, forced enthusiasm.

Anthony's phone rang. He removed it from his jacket but didn't answer it.

"Was that Huong?" Nathan said when it was quiet again.

"Huong never calls me. That was about work." Anthony laughed bitterly. "I should be happy I get these calls every morning. But sometimes that sound is like a prison warden ringing his bell, demanding that I spend another day chipping away at what life I have left." He stared at his phone, then raised his head and looked across the water.

"But the early calls aren't so bad." Anthony laughed without heart. "It's better than the routine I had in Saigon, isn't it? Sometimes I'm not sure, but if I tell myself enough that it's true, I almost start to believe it." He slid his phone back in his jacket. "I have to get back now."

"But it's Sunday."

"It doesn't matter."

They dumped the ice from their glasses into the lake and started back for shore.

When they arrived, the crowd of children was gone. Anthony gestured for the old woman to hurry down.

As she descended the dirt slope, holding her pants at the knees, Anthony dug out his wallet.

"I don't have change. And I bet she can't break this." He held up a fifty-thousand note. "What do you have on you?"

But when Nathan tried to remove his wallet, the boat began to rock and this time it was Anthony who lurched for the sides to keep his balance.

"What do we owe you?" Nathan asked when the woman made it down.

"Six thousand."

Anthony tapped his arm. "Give her this. Ask if she can break it." The woman leaned forward and reached first for the two glasses, then for the crisp pink note Nathan held out. She looked at the money like she didn't want it.

"Don't you have something smaller?" she said.

Nathan spoke over his shoulder: "You're right, she doesn't have change." He tried again to pull out his wallet but Anthony stopped him.

"Just give it to her. We made her come all the way down."

Nathan waved away the money.

Before the woman could reply, Anthony placed the end of his paddle against the lake bottom and pushed them away from shore.

24

Anthony didn't show up at work on Monday and, on Tuesday, he messaged that he'd be late, only for Huong to call after lunch to say he wouldn't come in at all. His absence placed additional stress on the office, as an important meeting with the Ministry of Property and Investment was slated for early the following week. There had been disagreements between the Ministry and the Hanoi People's Committee over the granting of a sublease license. None of the staff knew clearly what the agency's role had been throughout the granting process, and Anthony was needed to provide information and smooth things out. The situation wasn't one that Nathan, or anyone else in the office, could handle.

On Wednesday Nathan broke his morning routine of visiting Le and arrived at work early. Xuan was already there, preparing tea beside her workstation.

"Good morning, Nathan. You're early."

"I don't have a choice. Did you call Anthony yesterday like I asked?" Nathan had called several times himself, but no one answered.

"Yes. His wife just said he was sick."

"Have you checked the messages?"

"Not yet. It's too early."

"Too early for what? The light's flashing, see?" He pressed the play button.

Unless the caller phoned at dawn, the message had been left late at night. As the tape rewound, he poured himself tea.

"Nathan..." The female voice was familiar. He was left to figure out it was Huong, for she went on without introducing herself. "I don't know where to begin."

Nathan set his cup down and turned toward the machine. "Anthony had a stroke last night, shortly after dinner."

Nathan felt something twist off inside him, and he leaned against Xuan's desk, his breath caught in his lungs.

"There was a lot of bleeding in his brain, and the doctors are uncertain about when he'll..." In the background, Anh and Hao were pleading for candy. She stopped speaking to shush them. "He's at a hospital near our house, but it's Vietnamese and they aren't equipped to deal with him. They'll transfer him to Bach Mai in the morning. After that the doctors will decide if and when he can have visitors.

"You can call me if you want, but I don't know anything more than what I've told you. The doctor says there's nothing I can do right now, and I should go about things normally until he tells me otherwise. Tomorrow I have errands to do, but I'll be back in the late afternoon. You can leave a message with our housekeeper if you need anything. Anyway, I thought you should know."

The last comment made Nathan laugh despite himself. But his laugh was abrupt. The gravity of Anthony's condition pushed hard at him. The message ended and the red light faded away.

"Why the hell did she take him to a local hospital?" he asked Xuan. "What's she doing, trying to keep him from getting good medical care?"

Xuan was in tears and didn't answer. The rest of the staff, as they trickled into the office, reacted similarly to the news.

Nathan didn't know what to do. Someone suggested starting a collection for Anthony's family. After everyone chipped in fifty thousand *dong*, Xuan presented Nathan a small brick of bills. She'd tied the money with rubber bands and put it in a plastic bag.

Several of the staff began conferring on what to do with the money, and Nathan, at a loss how to contribute to the discussion, retreated into his office.

For the next hour he tried to reach Huong but couldn't get through. He was going to call Anthony's number, but something didn't feel right about it and he decided to try to get hold of her later.

By 9:30 the office was a shambles. With little hope of getting any work done, Nathan sent everyone home.

He stood in the doorway of Anthony's office, rooted with worry and fear. Anthony's work now lay in his charge, and everything had suddenly become Nathan's to learn and wield like a leader. He stared at the bookshelves lined with files and notebooks; the full desk with papers piled atop his inbox; the computer to which Nathan had never been given a password. He tried to think of someone else among the staff who could take Anthony's place, but promoting someone above himself would be an admission of his own fraudulence. Whoever he chose would still receive only a fraction of his salary, and they could never replace the American face so important to the company's clients.

No matter how obligated he felt to Anthony, especially now that Anthony was incapacitated, the last thing Nathan wanted was to take over the company.

He walked behind Anthony's desk, his eye catching the photo of Huong and their children. He found it curious that Anthony wasn't in the photo, too, and wondered if Anthony had deliberately chosen one that excluded him. But it was a cynical thought, more so given the circumstances.

Their kayak outing a few days ago sparked in his memory, and he remembered Anthony confessing his dream of leaving Vietnam, abandoning everything and everyone. A sinking feeling spread through him at what else he'd said: Part of me just wants to disappear, in some place big and empty where no one will ever bother me again.

A vinyl scheduler lay on Anthony's desk. He scanned the meetings and deadlines penciled in. Anthony's writing was tiny and cramped and Nathan strained his eyes to read it. The fifteenth had been circled what seemed a hundred times, and beneath it, in the only red pen on the page – as if Anthony had written it before anything else – was the entry: *9 yrs in VN*. There was nothing beneath it, or elsewhere that week, showing he planned to celebrate.

Nathan set the scheduler atop Anthony's inbox and carried them into his office.

He'd given little thought to his trip to Saigon. With Anthony out of commission the trip became almost unsupportable. Had Anthony never suffered a stroke, taking a day or two off would have posed no problem. Unwilling at first though he'd been, Anthony had given Nathan his blessing.

He felt guilty leaving Hanoi when Anthony was in hospital and the company had no one to lead it. But it was only for one day, and he was going there to work, not holiday. Though concerned that problems would arise in his absence, he was confident he could deal with them when he returned.

He left Xuan a note, explaining he wouldn't be in tomorrow and to call him only in an emergency. "Work forced me to fly to Saigon tonight," he scribbled. "I'll be back in twenty-four hours."

Going outside to get his motorbike, a weight lifted off him like some monster that had been riding his shoulders. But the reprieve was fleeting, for the seriousness of Anthony's condition, and a realization of the struggles that lay before him, consumed Nathan as he drove past the guard and the black waters of West Lake came into view.

He pulled up to a tree in front of Anthony's yard and parked. No one answered the doorbell when he rang. And when he looked for Binh, the gardener, he was nowhere to be found. Had Huong sent her workers home? Or had they left on their own, aware that Huong wouldn't be around to manage them? Surely they didn't go with her to the hospital.

Nathan made his way back to his motorbike and stared up at the house. More than ever, it appeared too large for the small rise of land on which it stood. Four stories high, and taller than the surrounding trees, the house would have fit better in Beverly Hills. Nathan stood dumbfounded thinking of the transformation Anthony's life had undergone in Hanoi. With all his success, how had things gone so wrong?

He drove off looking over his shoulder for some sign of life that he'd missed.

Approaching Ngu Xa Street, he hesitated to turn onto Truc Bach Island. A tugging inside him urged him to travel around West Lake. He wanted to visit Le and tell her about Anthony's stroke. Was it that he needed to talk about it, or did he find such comfort in her that nothing else would do?

He found her in her front garden. White orchids in straw pots rested in furrows she'd dug with a spade. Dirt smeared her chin and covered her hands.

She lifted her conical hat as he squatted beside her. The soft, dug-up earth sank beneath his weight.

"Why aren't you at work?" she said, looking at him in surprise.

"I sent everyone home."

She searched his face, waiting for him to explain. When he did, she reached over and squeezed his arm. Dirt came off on his shirt-sleeve and she tried to brush it away. "What do you think will happen?"

"I don't know. And I have to go to Saigon tonight, which is harder to do now."

She turned to her unplanted flowers. "But he's your friend. What if something happens?"

"What if what happens? You mean if he dies?"

She scraped the dirt off her spade with her fingers. "Yes."

"There's nothing I can do." What he said sounded strange to him, but he didn't dwell on it. "I'll only be gone one day, and I've asked Xuan to call me if there's an emergency."

Deep in a furrow Le had dug, two worms jerked back and forth. Rather than having two rounded ends to their bodies they each only had one. Realizing that she'd sliced through the worm's body, he looked away uneasily.

"Let's go inside," she said, standing up. "I'll wash up and make you something to eat."

Nathan had no appetite, but still he followed behind her, already preparing in his head what to take on his trip.

25

Sunlight through the curtains woke him. A moment passed before he realized where he was.

November mornings were different in Saigon: neither frigid nor wet, and not as short as in Hanoi. In Saigon there was sun.

Boarding the plane the previous night, he'd carried in his veins the cold damp gray of Hanoi. There was no trace of that feeling here as he drew the curtains. At seven a.m., it was hard to believe in such blue autumnal skies. Down below, sunlight brightened every inch of the street.

He left the hotel to find something to eat. With Anthony heavy in his thoughts, he reverted back to when they breakfasted together on De Tham Street, filling their stomachs cheaply: a plain baguette and glass of black coffee. As he ate, he wondered if Anthony was having breakfast now, too. Was he conscious, and if so, what occupied his mind? Chasing his bread down with *cà phê đá*, Nathan knew his responsibility to Anthony would increase exponentially when he returned to Hanoi.

On his way to Tu Du Hospital, he was shocked by how much the city had been torn down and rebuilt. Although the day was cloudless, no view of sky was unobstructed: along every street he traveled, odd-angled arms of cranes extended hundreds of feet overhead.

At the hospital entrance, he threaded his way through a slow-moving crowd. Once in the maternity ward he followed a faded blue arrow to a corridor of offices. He stopped when a woman poked her head around a door.

"Are you Mr. Nathan?" She stepped forward and smoothed her medical smock.

"Ms. Loan?"

Shyly she shook his hand, then led him into an unadorned guestroom furnished with a chipped table with tea implements on it and two heavy wooden chairs on each side. Framed photos of a hospital ceremony hung unevenly on a wall.

"So," she said, pouring tea. "How exactly can I help you?"

She was generous with her time and, after an hour, he told her that was enough. She was a member of the Steering Board to Overcome Consequences of Toxic Chemicals and off the top of her head could recite statistics for whatever he wanted to know.

Vietnamese and American figures differed greatly in quantifying the damage caused by Agent Orange. He knew, for example, about the backlash in America against claims that 3,000,000 Vietnamese had been affected by the chemical defoliant; that 200,000 children born with disabilities related to Agent Orange direly needed medical care and rehabilitation; that in a survey of nearly 50,000 Vietnamese war veterans, more than 16 per cent claimed to have family members suffering from Agent Orange contamination. Not surprisingly, the U.S. government put all these figures much lower.

"We need money," Loan said as Nathan tucked away his notes. "The children have so little. It's why they're here. Their families are either too poor to pay for their care, or else they have no family." She handed him a sheet of paper with relevant NGOs' contact information. "In your article, please tell your readers how they can help."

"I'll do what I can." Nathan placed the sheet inside his briefcase. "May I see the children?"

"By all means. They're excited to meet you." Her expression changed as she checked her watch. "They're not finished with class, but the last few minutes are usually a lost cause, anyway."

They started for the second floor.

"What are they studying?" Nathan asked.

"Japanese."

"Why Japanese?"

As they climbed the stairs she explained that Japanese institutions had been very charitable with the hospital. Some children had been flown to Japan for surgical procedures unavailable in Vietnam. A Japanese teacher came three days a week with his wife, who helped the nurses care for children whose conditions required round-the-clock attention.

"Do any Americans volunteer here?" he asked.

"Every now and then we get curious visitors who donate money and supplies – but no, Americans don't come regularly. At least not to Tu Du."

He heard the children from the top of the stairs. When he stepped onto the second floor he wasn't prepared for what he saw.

Five children crowded the corridor. Of the five, one had no chin, one had teeth where her nose should have been, one was armless, another legless, and of those who did have arms and legs their limbs were either too short, or shriveled, or had an unusual number of digits.

Off the corridor were four rooms. In the doorway of the first, two nurses held infants. One infant's head was the size of a watermelon – bigger than the rest of his body – and covered with scabs; the skin had stretched until it split and bled. The other infant, wriggling in the nurse's arms, had skin plastering the sockets of her eyes. Both children, Loan told him, had only partial brains.

Behind them were a dozen cribs fitted with thin, discolored mattresses. The other babies were much like these two: heads swollen four times their normal size; armless, legless, or with atrophied appendages; eyeless; cleft-lipped; missing half of their brains; blind, deaf, mute. A television installed in a corner showed an American action film dubbed in Vietnamese – to entertain the nurses, he supposed. Most of the infants lay on their backs, their hands jerking at their sides, and a weak collective wailing swirled in the room.

Loan cooed at the children the nurses held, playing with their feet. She stopped when the older children down the hall called to her, asking who she was with.

"He's the reporter I told you about."

The children, some of whose disabilities affected how they spoke, crawled up to Nathan and tried to pull him into their class.

"If you have class, why aren't you in it?" Nathan said. He was surprised his Vietnamese didn't faze them.

"We're smarter than the other kids," one child said, and his friends agreed, laughing at their excuse.

"Their learning's not as structured as at a regular school," Loan said. "But they do pretty well for themselves."

Nathan followed her into the classroom. When they sat in the back, the students turned away from their teacher. Their commotion attracted the children in the corridor back to class.

Nathan apologized to the teacher, who introduced himself in English as Nakajima, and gestured for the kids to pay attention to their lesson. When their excitement died down and class resumed, Mr. Nakajima called a student to the board. He'd written a question there and wanted a boy of around twelve to answer it.

Nathan watched the boy twist out of his seat. His head looked rather too small, and his back was bunched at the neck, pushing one shoulder higher than the other. His shriveled legs required him to let himself down headfirst, guiding himself to the floor with his arms. He scooted backwards between rows of desks, dragging his legs, then clambered onto a bench beneath the chalkboard. Mr. Nakajima handed him chalk, and the boy reached up to write his answer.

Class lasted another five minutes. Before Mr. Nakajima dismissed the children, Nathan thought he felt his phone vibrate. He pulled it from his pocket but found the screen blank. He remembered then that he'd turned it off after walking through the hospital gate.

His thoughts strayed to the real estate agency and, with a profound sense of disloyalty settling over him, he wondered again about Anthony. He struggled to convince himself that there was nothing he could do to help him. He'd return to Hanoi tomorrow morning before work and determine what to do then.

But he couldn't rid Anthony from his thoughts, and the guilt he felt, despite the arguments he developed to counter it, intensified. He excused himself and went outside.

The corridor was empty now except for a nurse folding sheets and towels. Nathan stepped past her and headed for the end of the corridor. When he crossed the stairwell entrance he discovered another room.

A nurse inside was hanging paper dolls between two cribs. This room, too, was for infants, though they were even younger than the ones next door. A toe-less baby with fingers extending from the stump of his half-arm reached toward her through the slats of his crib. Nathan continued past before the nurse noticed him.

At the end of the corridor he called Xuan.

"New Century, may I help you?"

"Xuan, this is Nathan."

Xuan exclaimed in surprise. "You're in Saigon? Why?"

"Something came up. I'm just calling to see if anything needs my attention."

"No, not really."

The vagueness in her tone bothered him. "Any news about Anthony?"

"Not yet. As soon as we know it's okay, we're going to visit him in the hospital." Voices in the background grew loud, and Xuan paused as if to see what the matter was.

"What's wrong?"

"Just people downstairs shouting. I think they're joking around. If anything happens, I'll ask Tuan to deal with it." Tuan was the marketing director and had been working there almost from the beginning.

From the classroom door three students crawled outside to help the nurse with her folding.

"I have to go," Nathan said.

"You'll be back tomorrow morning?"

Nathan swallowed involuntarily; the prospect of returning to Hanoi paralyzed his voice. "The day after," he said.

"But your note says tomorrow morning."

"I have to be here one more day."

She didn't protest or inquire further, and he said goodbye.

Rather than return to the classroom he stepped inside the room where he'd seen the nurse hanging paper dolls. She now held a baby in her arms, bouncing it lightly and humming a song.

She shifted the baby in her arms, holding it firmly against her shoulder. Its large head swayed but she cupped the back of it, guiding its forehead to her lips.

The next thing Nathan knew he was moving toward her, reaching out to accept the baby's almost weightless substance. The baby's fingers grazed his cheek where he balanced it uncertainly. He wondered how he looked right then – like a father? Or an impostor of a father?

The nurse rearranged one of his hands to support the baby better. "She's smiling."

"She's probably laughing at me." Nathan peered into her face. The baby's eyes protruded, and wherever she looked her gaze never stuck. Once, however, he thought her eyes lingered on his.

When he approached her crib she began to squirm. He hesitated before returning her to the dirty mattress.

"What will happen to her?" he asked.

"I don't know. But I don't expect she'll live long."

For a long time Nathan stared at the baby. The idea that she wouldn't live – that this infant who'd just touched his cheek and struggled in his arms might soon die – seemed impossible. Even though her physical problems were in plain sight, he still felt there was an extraordinary amount of life in her body.

"Why not?"

"She needs special surgery. Unfortunately, we can't perform it in Vietnam. If she'd been born in a rich country she'd have had the procedure within the first week of birth. Even if she had it done now she'd be brain damaged all her life. But she won't live that long. The fluid in her head will build up until its cuts off the oxygen to her brain."

"How long are you talking about?"

"A few more months. Possibly another year."

Nathan couldn't take his eyes off the girl. When he did, he realized that most of the other babies in the room had the same condition.

Loan walked into the room and stood beside him. "If we could accommodate every parent who contacts us with the same needs, our hospital would become a city of disabled children. These are the lucky ones."

Her last words lodged uncomfortably in his head.

"How do you know Agent Orange caused their conditions?"

"Technically we don't. We can't afford medical tests for every child. But they're from areas where Agent Orange was heavily used. Some of their parents were tested before and high dioxin levels appeared in their blood." She motioned to the corridor. "The other children are waiting for you. They're excited to answer your questions."

Nathan didn't want to leave yet.

"You're welcome here anytime," she said, apparently sensing how he felt.

Back in the classroom, the children were eating yoghurt and fruit and singing a Japanese song. Nathan sat beside Mr. Nakajima, who was conducting wildly with a plastic spoon. With great mental effort Nathan joined in the children's clapping.

There was nothing haunting about the Debonair Hotel's airy bar, twenty-five floors above the city. Yet even here, young women in tight revealing dresses filtered in and out of the adjoining dance club – sex workers, he guessed, hired by the manager for a cut of what they made going home (or down a few floors) with a customer. Everything else looked bright and pristine.

Nathan flagged down a waitress for a glass of water. She brought him one and he drank it before she walked away.

For the last three hours he'd wandered ghost-like through the city. Passing from one street to another had made him nostalgic, and there were moments when it was easy to believe he'd never left.

When he'd reached as far as District Five, he encountered an old woman staggering from an alley, her face forced downward from the weight of what lay across her shoulders. At first glance her burden looked like a poorly rolled carpet. But as Nathan came nearer he realized what it was. He stopped walking, unable to look away from this old woman and the young man who hung across her like a human shawl.

The woman's face was deeply tanned, and so pitted that she seemed to wear a mask of dried orange rinds. She struggled with every step. When she got to a bus shelter she gently lowered the man. She sat down, laid him sideways across her thighs, then pulled his jerking head to her chest and held it still.

The man's head was oblong, and his mouth hung open, slavering. His arms were skeletal, and his hands turned inward with the fingers bunched tightly together. Like the air bubble in a water level, his eyes rolled from side to side. He couldn't have been more than fifty pounds, and the woman no more than eighty.

She began massaging the young man's legs. When she reached his feet, the soles of which looked freshly washed, Nathan saw that his toes were connected by folds of skin.

When he lived here, why had he never noticed such people? In his attempt to live simply and integrate into this place that had become his home, had he been blind to the struggles around him?

When the woman maneuvered the man back onto her shoulders and boarded a bus, Nathan kept going. The deeper he penetrated the city, the more struggle he saw: thumb-sucking children wandering alone through the night selling lottery tickets in cafés, sidewalk restaurants, and gas stations; construction workers hauling stacks of bricks by hand and pounding thick cables on the ground with hammers; teams of women breaking rocks with pickaxes; on the top step of a vacant building draped in dust-encased tarp, a woman sleeping with three children clutching at her from the step below; workers walking along steel girders thirty stories overhead, detectable less by the dim lights suspended near them than by their white hardhats bobbing in the moonless sky.

He and Anthony had grown close in neighborhoods like this. When the downtown bars and clubs got too predictable, they'd even sought these places out, driving to the outer districts and engaging with local people. That was the time of their "one-dollar nights": drinking and joking and having long conversations in which they tried to make sense of Saigon. That routine had ended when Anthony caved in to

Huong's demand – the same she'd previously made with Nathan – that he spend every night with her.

Sweaty and numb, Nathan had come to the Debonair to escape the gloom that had settled over him.

He ordered a Singapore Sling, not knowing what it was, only recalling that in Hanoi Anthony had once ordered it at the Metropole Bar. Later that night, thoroughly drunk, Anthony had commented that the drink had a sharpness to it, like a cleansing agent might.

The drink's seven-dollar price tag hardly registered with Nathan: for the first time he could remember, it felt good wasting his money on something he'd soon piss into the sewers. He laughed to himself, hating what he stood for anymore.

Across the room a Western couple with an infant triggered his memory of the hospital. He could still feel the weight in his arms of the baby girl who would die because the simple procedure that might save her wasn't available in Vietnam. Suddenly the emotional dam he'd hidden behind cracked, unleashing a tearless flood.

He regretted having taken a job at Anthony's company. He'd cashed in a dream, but for what? For the situation he now found himself in? For a slow, painful strangulation of his soul? Writing had always been the most important pursuit for him, and money alone seemed a poor reason to give it up. The idea that his opportunity with Reuters was a chance he might never have again beat on him mercilessly. But what was he supposed to do now?

Coming to Saigon when Anthony was hospitalized had been a bad decision. Yet if he'd stayed it wouldn't have helped. Anthony had agreed to let him come here; being in Saigon for a short time wouldn't leave Anthony worse off. The company could manage. There were other employees closer to Anthony's work than he was.

But the more excuses he made, the more he realized this wasn't the issue. He couldn't quite grasp it, but he knew all these things were symptomatic of a bigger problem. Somehow, at some point in time, their values had sharply diverged.

The question hanging over him now wasn't whether or not there would be repercussions for flying here, but what they would be. Of course he had an obligation to Anthony and his company, but what about his obligation to write about Agent Orange? He kept reminding himself that Anthony had approved the trip.

Nathan straightened in his chair, wondering at something new: was he jealous of Anthony's success where he himself had failed – and more so because Anthony didn't appreciate all he had?

A young Vietnamese man in a starched cream suit delivered his drink and, bowing while stepping backwards, thanked Nathan for nothing.

In all his years in Saigon, rarely had he come to such an upscale place. It wasn't for the money – he'd never been rich, but a seven-dollar drink was affordable on occasion – but for the feeling that he didn't belong. And he didn't belong because he didn't see the point in trying to fit in with these people who'd never see Vietnam except as some small, self-serving opportunity.

At least once a week Anthony stopped by the Sheraton on West Lake. The top-floor bar looked out over the water, and at night, with the surroundings plunged in darkness, he might have felt he was anywhere in the world. The opposite shore sparkled like Christmas lights, and even the giant Ferris wheel, on summer nights when the amusement park stayed open, looked magical turning under the stars.

"Quiet's why I come here," Anthony had told him more than once. "That, and to be reminded there's still mystery for me in Vietnam."

Anthony liked it during the rainy season when he often had the bar to himself, for the shelter it gave felt impregnable – "Like a fortress," he'd said. The only people who approached him then were bartenders and bored bar girls, and as far as Nathan could tell they were some of his favorite people.

Sometimes Nathan went with him when he needed the same thing, though he could find an equal feeling in less exclusive places, and was interested moreover in making his own discoveries.

Feeling that nowhere in Saigon could compete with West Lake's sweeping openness and quiet beauty, Nathan glanced around the bar. A Vietnamese girl in a short black dress and halter-top hovered nearby. He knew she had her eye on him because he was alone. He frowned and looked away, ending the hope she seemed to have that he'd gesture for her to join him.

He tried to imagine Le across the table from him. But it was an incongruous image, making him feel even more foolish being here. Le, if he'd brought her, wouldn't have ventured past the opulent lobby – not even to wander down hallways whose walls were mounted with paintings as big as cars.

In Hanoi several weeks before, Nathan had driven with her to the Sheraton. As they'd come upon the entrance, he saw her, in his handlebar mirror, staring at the enormous 'S' that capped the hotel. He'd driven down the sloping road, over a stone bridge, and toward an empty parking area. When she asked where he was going, he said there was a bar inside with a view over West Lake. She immediately voiced her opposition. At first he thought she was joking, or only needed persuading, but she refused to enter. He never learned what had been the matter – perhaps she felt underdressed; or disliked the idea of him spending so much money on them both; or thought she'd be intercepted at the door and, viewed as too poor to enter, told to leave. Without stopping, he'd continued past the lot and through an exit.

He imagined the painter's eye she'd bring to the people in the dance club – fat, ruddy-faced foreign men caressing the young sex workers who alternately clung to them and gyrated to the Filipino cover-band – and one revolting image after another flashed through his mind. But she'd never paint a scene like this: the nine levels of Hell were for Buddhist monks to paint inside their pagodas. An hour later the bar no longer felt like the escape he'd sought. He began to think there was filth around him he couldn't see, particles of corruption and decay settling on the surface of every table and person and in all the drinks they rapidly consumed.

Raucous laughter exploded around him. The bar grew louder with people talking over each other. Whenever he expected the noise to die down, it picked up again louder than before. He shouted to a waiter for his bill.

Nathan's lips cracked feebly upward at a thought: in a city as polluted as Saigon, oxygen was in short supply. Why compete for it twenty-five floors above the city where the air was thinner and people here needed so much of it?

Rain was falling when he walked past the lobby's doormen and outside.

He lifted his collar behind his neck and ran into the downpour. This would surely be the monsoon season's last storm, he thought.

When he returned to his hotel he phoned Huong.

"This is a bad time," she said, her voice cracking with emotion. "Can I call you tomorrow?"

"Call me anytime. But how is he? Is he conscious?"

"Nothing's changed. He's just this inert body with tubes running through him. I'm sorry, I have to go. I'll call you tomorrow or the day after."

The phone clicked and he stared at the wall, picturing Anthony as she'd described him.

He washed his face and called Le. They spoke for over an hour. "I should've brought you with me," he said before hanging up. Afterward he was kept awake by the easy imaginings of what that would have been like.

The next morning Nathan called the airline office. The woman who answered told him no seats were left on the flight he wanted to switch to. Not knowing what else to do, he inquired about the following day. She found him a seat on a midnight flight.

"If that's my only option," he said.

"It's not your only option, sir."

Until he realized she was referring to the flight he already had, he wondered if somehow she knew the problems he'd create by making this change.

"How many times can I change my ticket?"

"There's no limit, sir. But you may be stuck if you wait too long."

He confirmed the details, worried that by the time he returned to Hanoi he'd have missed three days of work.

26

On his midnight flight home, Nathan reviewed his notes from a meeting at the World Health Organization, interviews with two families in Cu Chi, and two more visits to Tu Du Hospital.

Soon he fell asleep. He dreamed he was back in America.

His dream's circumstances were unclear. All he knew with certainty was that he was wandering through a vast supermarket. Such a large, well-organized store contrasted strongly with Vietnam's overcrowded minimarts, and in his dream he was aware of being in a different country.

The other shoppers paid him no attention, which was another contrast to Vietnam. They were fantastically tall and overweight, and their plodding steps rattled the bottles lining the shelves of the aisle he was in. Fat enlarged their features to grotesque proportions, and everyone's noses, lips, and jowls, even the backs of their necks, swelled with excess flesh. Their eyes were slits encased in too much skin, and a purpling, as from ruptured blood vessels, peppered their puffy faces. Wherever he went, he heard them panting.

Eventually he came upon the store's meat section. Hordes of shoppers crowded around the cold storage bins, inspecting packaged meat. With everyone pushing at each other to grab what they wanted, he couldn't get close. Many customers had tucked their packages under their arms, concealing and protecting them as they hustled to the checkout lines. Near the exit, separate fights had broken out.

The furious push toward the bins prevented him from seeing the meat selection. The section took up a full half of the store, and a rancid stench filled the air.

A breach opened before him, and he squeezed between the pulsing mass. When someone pushed him aside, branding his shirtsleeve with their sweat, he found himself in someone else's way, and the longer he stood there the more he became an object of animosity. He wanted to ask if the meat was fresh, but there was no store employee around and no customer he dared approach.

A wave of impatient customers shoved him forward. Their collective force pressed him against the edge of the bin, where he could finally see the meat that people were rushing to buy.

In every package, smashed between yellow Styrofoam and plastic wrapping, were bloodless, hacked-off pieces of human body parts. But even in this revolting display there was something more shocking. Every body part was deformed: a three-fingered hand; a webbed foot; a fleshy cheek spotted with black warts; a chest with the heart and lungs outside the body; the folded, stick-thin legs of a paraplegic. Orange lights above the bins radiated downward, giving the body parts a sickening tint as if to emphasize they were raw.

Nathan tried to retreat but the crowds pushing against him were like a wall. As he shoved his way out, a strange noise rose from the bin. Glancing back he noticed that the packaged parts had begun to move. Like fish yanked from the sea they flipped about the bins until a store employee beat his way into the crowd, thrust a hand inside, and turned a knob. The orange light overhead changed into a dark, lurid red. The deformed body parts immediately settled again into lifelessness.

Nathan woke with a start. He knew at once he would quit Anthony's company.

Perhaps next week he'd draft his resignation. But to whom would he submit it? He supposed he could slip it into Anthony's office mailbox and let it sit there until Anthony was well enough to return to work. Or he could have it delivered to Anthony's house in care of Huong.

But no – he was trapped. Where Anthony's most strenuous efforts had failed to bring Nathan into the fold of his company, his stroke might manage it perfectly. All Nathan could do was hope Anthony quickly recovered.

He lifted the closed window beside him and looked at the plane's blinking wing. *Do Not Step Here* flashed into his vision and disappeared.

Briefly he wondered why Huong hadn't called like she promised.

Hesitating in the agency doorway, he savored a moment longer the scent of late autumn that blew off the lake. The scent carried hints of Ohio in November, and he breathed it in until his lungs hurt.

Standing there he became aware that people inside were watching him. Already it was half past ten.

Without a word to anyone he shut the door and started for the stairs. Passing his fellow workers, whose heads hung morosely over their desktops, the pleasure and excitement he once felt coming here was now severed, irrecoverable. The office atmosphere was cheerless and morgue-like. But the feeling more likely stemmed from the fact that these people resented him.

Halfway up the stairs he stopped to look over the handrail. A full third of the employees were missing. No desks had been cleared, which indicated no one had quit, but this absenteeism was obviously a coordinated effort.

Xuan didn't bother to acknowledge him when he approached. When he said hello she glared at him and wanted to know where he'd been.

Over the last two days, she told him, the company had fallen into disarray. Employees were feuding, and with no one at the helm, client meetings had been abandoned and Xuan was forced to cancel or postpone those that were scheduled on the following days. Two computers had disappeared, and an important client had backed out of a property he intended to purchase.

Nathan didn't have to ask about the absent employees. She volunteered that everyone had grown afraid that the firm would go under and didn't want to be trapped aboard a sinking ship.

"So they're not just skipping work..."

She looked at him in amazement. "They're interviewing for jobs."

"Do they think they can do whatever they like with impunity? Apparently they think there's no punishment for insubordination..."

She stared at him like she couldn't believe he thought they were guiltier than he. "They're concerned about their families." She spoke slowly, as if this was necessary for him to comprehend. "Most of them grew up poor and hungry. They want something stable."

"Are they coming back?"

But she wasn't interested in his question. She wanted him to understand something more.

"In Vietnam, when you have a job and career you think is stable, only to feel like it's been taken away overnight, you'll do things you wouldn't normally do to get that stability back." She paused to let him absorb this.

"Call them. Tell them that if they're not back before lunch they're no longer employees here."

"You can't make that decision," she said, struggling to contain her anger. "Only Anthony can."

"What can Anthony possibly do now? I said call them..."

He stared at her until she withdrew a list from her desk, picked up her phone, and started punching in a number. Satisfied that he'd reestablished his authority, he went into his office, closed the door, and tossed his briefcase on a chair.

Why, he wondered, was he expressing outrage over an act he'd normally support? He knew he was being unfair, but the situation confronting him wasn't fair, either.

He realized only now that they'd expected him to lead them. The problem was that in all his life he'd never wanted to be a leader.

Slumping in his chair, he shuffled through folders and binders that had been transferred here from Anthony's office. Half the pile was marked "Ministry of Property and Investment."

He called Xuan on his intercom. "Come in here, please."

"But I'm trying to reach the absent employees."

"I said come in here."

She entered a minute later and set a glass of tea on his desk – like a deferential wife trying to appease an angry husband.

"What is this stuff? And what am I supposed to do with it?"

"You're supposed to read it."

He dumped the files he was holding onto his desk and heaved a disgusted sigh. "But what for, Xuan? Is it urgent or just for my review?"

She glanced at the clock and, suddenly alert again, nodded at the stacks. "You better hurry."

She pointed behind her, where the whiteboard by her desk showed his and Anthony's schedule. Arrows drawn in black marker indicated what she'd transferred from Anthony's workload to Nathan's.

"You have a meeting in fifteen minutes with a group from MOPI," she went on. "I put it on your schedule three days ago."

"I wasn't here three days ago," Nathan snapped, pulling himself close to his desk. "Damn it, there's no time to prepare for this. What's the meeting about?"

"I think they heard complaints and are coming to investigate. It's also time to renew our license."

"But our license is good for fifteen years."

"The rules have changed. License holders must now apply for yearly stamps of approval."

Her words relieved him. A "stamp of approval" was likely nothing more than a payoff disguised as procedure.

The intercom at Xuan's desk crackled to life and one of the staff said her name.

She ran back to her desk. "Yes?" she said.

"MOPI's here. Should I tell them to wait?"

Xuan shot Nathan a look both helpless and vindictive, then hurried off to speak with the staff directly.

Nathan's tie felt tight around his neck. After wrestling with the knot, he yanked the tie from his collar and dumped it inside his desk. His time at Tu Du had been difficult, but at least there the struggles he'd encountered moved him. If he'd been torn over letting the company founder for a few days in order to write an article about

Agent Orange, he no longer felt conflicted. With a suddenness that was almost violent, an idea about what might come next in his life shattered inside his brain. If Mr. Jasper liked what he wrote, Nathan would e-mail him a special request. A saying Anthony sometimes used around the office came to mind: "Success breeds more success. If you do everything like your life depends on it, you'll never fail."

Full of a determination to succeed, he undid his shirt's top button and reached for his iced tea. Condensation had pooled on his desk and soaked into the stacked material. It occurred to him to push the stack from the water, but it didn't seem worth his effort.

27

Cloud shadows glided over West Lake then were lost in the leafy trees and newly built villas beyond the shore. Now and then a motorbike passed along the path to Nathan's back, or an electric drill whirred from a construction site, but mostly it was serene.

At the edge of the water, the snail shells he'd pushed with his foot into a pile already numbered twelve. None housed anything living. At some point the snails had either slipped away or been eaten.

The shells rattled when he added to them – adding not for any reason, only to put off doing what he came for. With his shoe he pushed them back in the lake. The scum of rotting leaves, broken tree branches, and trash here was so thick the shells didn't sink. He watched this strange island butt against the shore as he gathered courage to approach Anthony's house.

Following the flagstone path to the front gate he spotted Binh, the gardener who watered the plants and flowers in the enclosed courtyard every morning. Nathan called his name. When Binh dropped his hose and hurried over, Nathan asked him to unlock the gate. "I'm here to see Anthony."

Binh became talkative as he let Nathan in. "In my opinion, he was too fat. Those things happen when you're like he was."

"I'm sure it was a lot of things," Nathan said, slipping into the courtyard.

"If he dies, I hope his family doesn't let me go. None of them are very kind to me. Yesterday the kids let the air out of my bicycle tires. And if I complain, I'll be out of a job. Maybe you can put in a good word about me."

"I'll do that," Nathan said, anxious to get to the house. But before he left, he asked Binh about Anthony's condition.

"I just know he had that stroke. They've got a live-in nurse, but visitors have stopped coming. Anyhow he's rich, so I'm sure he'll get better. He's lucky to have all that money."

Sunlight streamed through a hole in the sky as Nathan made his way to the front door. He thought he saw Huong pass by a window, but the person was gone before he could identify who it was.

He'd called Huong three days ago to see if he might visit. When she said to come whenever he pleased, he asked what had caused the stroke. "It started with a heart attack," she said. "The stroke hit shortly after I found him on the floor and called an ambulance. I didn't know until later that he'd suffered both."

The doctors at Bach Mai told her that Anthony's heart was weak, and its weakness had induced a narrowed brain artery to close.

Nathan rapped the door's brass knocker against its base. He shielded his eyes from the sun while waiting for someone to come.

Hao opened the door. She grinned at him, exposing a gap in her front teeth. Huong came up and sent her off.

Huong wore a tight DKNY t-shirt and pleated skirt that ended two inches above her knees. He noticed her toenails were painted maroon and gold and studded down the middle with fake diamonds.

"I thought you'd be at the office. It's nearly ten already."

He wondered if she'd seen him standing along the shore this last half hour. "I can't stay long."

"We missed you when the company visited the hospital. I heard you were in Saigon."

He nodded. "Anthony approved the trip before, and it was too late to change my plans."

"I haven't been there for a long time. Would I even recognize it now?"

He smiled uncomfortably. "It's changed. Just like everything's changed."

"But I like change. My life's much better now than when I was growing up."

Nathan stepped inside, struck by her tactless optimism. Where did Anthony fit into the changes that had brought her happiness?

Hao had joined Anh in front of the TV. A uniformed nurse sat by the window sending phone messages.

"Can I see him?"

"If you want. He's in the fourth guest room."

Nathan glanced at the marble staircase. "I'm not sure where that is."

Huong kicked lightly at her children's feet. "Kids," she said, tsk-ing them when they didn't respond.

Anh and Hao looked over their shoulders at her.

"Show Uncle Nathan Daddy's room."

A sour look spread over Anh's face. He'd turned four a few weeks ago, just before Anthony was stricken. "I don't want to," he said.

"I said show Uncle Nathan where Daddy's sleeping. Hao, be a good girl and drag your brother with you."

Hao pointed glumly at the TV. "Can I do it after it's over?"

"Don't disobey me."

When they got to their feet, Hao leaned into Anh and whispered something.

"I'll find him," Nathan assured Huong. This time she didn't stop him. As he started for the stairs, Hao announced she was going outside to play. Anh, without a word, ran after her.

Huong asked the nurse to watch the children. The nurse followed them outside, hardly looking up from her phone.

When Huong closed the door, Nathan realized her hair was shorter than the last time he'd seen her. She looked younger somehow.

"It's been a long time since it was just us."

Tuned to her subtlety, Nathan remembered how she'd spoken to him the night he met Hoa. But she was right – they hadn't been alone together since before she had children.

"Not since we were in Saigon."

"It shouldn't be like that." She gestured for him to sit down. "You look good. You've obviously been taking care of yourself."

"Not really."

She took a deep breath and smiled at him, her eyes tearing up. "You're a good person, Nathan."

He shook his head. "I haven't been good for a long time."

"You've always been good to me."

"I let Anthony down. Both of you, really."

She struggled to keep smiling as she dabbed her eyes with her sleeve. "I know you tried to persuade him not to leave us."

Nathan's stomach dropped. She knew. She knew and yet here she was, trapped by a reckless plan Anthony couldn't carry out. What had Anthony told her, and where did Nathan fit into his confession? He wished his name had never come up.

Her brown eyes, in the sunlight through the window, had become lighter, as if stripped of a protective layer. Something in them warned him to be careful.

"I don't remember trying to persuade–"

"Nathan," she said, her voice trembling. "The last thing we talked about was his plan to abandon us. He had his heart attack in the storage room, going through our possessions. I was crying so hard in our bedroom that I didn't hear him fall. He told me about your conversation on the kayak and that you tried to change his mind."

He couldn't imagine how difficult it must be for her, caring for an invalid who'd made clear his intention to abandon her and their children. Such a scenario was too cruel for both of them.

Looking at Huong he wondered how she could be expected to deal with Anthony's stroke after an admission as shattering as that. What motivation would she have to see him back to health? Surely, though, she realized Anthony would never leave them now. Maybe she saw this as a chance to win him back.

She locked the door then went to the window. Nathan couldn't see outside from where he sat, but he heard Anh and Hao faintly laughing.

Seeing Huong lock her children and the nurse out of her house alarmed him.

"I'm selling the company," she said, coming back and sitting down. "I've had it valued and am cashing in."

"Why? Why would you do that?"

"Anthony was the heart and soul of New Century, and I know it's not in you to take his place. I don't want the agency to lose money from poor management. And it's bound to if I don't sell it immediately."

"You could hire someone."

"Only Anthony could make it successful."

"What will happen to all the staff?"

"You always think about others before yourself, don't you?"

He paused to see if she meant to be sarcastic, but he couldn't tell. A passing cloud had darkened her eyes again.

"No," he said. "Lately I only seem to think about myself."

"I don't think so." She leaned toward him with her cleavage visible down her shirt. "With the money I'll get, you and I could start something together."

Her words unnerved him, and the feeling mixed with his dread being here. "Like what?"

"We almost started something special back in Saigon. But for some reason I chose Anthony instead of you."

Nathan shook his head, unable to believe what he was hearing. "He's your husband. He's the father of your children."

A tear ran down her cheek and she wiped it away.

By the sound of it, she'd given up on Anthony. If he'd told her he was leaving them, he couldn't blame her. But to give up on him now seemed somehow too cruel.

"You haven't seen him," she added, almost like an afterthought.

"I don't expect to be thrilled by how he is." He watched her pull her shirt to her eyes and cry into it. "Where did you say he is?"

"The third floor."

Nathan stood up. He wanted to get away from her. When he was about to head for the stairs, he said: "Has he had many visitors?"

"None the last few days. They've stopped coming."

Nathan thought about this. "How many people know you're selling the company?"

"You, me, my lawyer, and, as of yesterday, the people who made the offer."

"No one at the agency?"

"Not yet. You can call a meeting next week to break the news."

Nathan stood frozen, unable to process what she'd said. After a moment he managed to turn away and went to find Anthony.

On the stairs he spotted a plastic water gun. He'd seen kids use toys like this and knew the water could be shot a great distance. The water pressure, when the mechanism was pumped several times, was strong enough on impact to make a child cry. Water glistened along the barrel, and as he picked it up he saw it was nearly empty. He set it back down, imagining the noise Anh and Hao had made chasing each other around the house with it.

When he reached the third floor, he could barely see the end of the hallway. The darkness gave the impression that Anthony was stashed away like an overused possession, broken finally and ready to be forgotten.

Toys were scattered here, too, with miniature cars lying overturned by a cracked-open door. He noticed a small puddle, and it took him a moment to make a connection between this and the water gun on the stairs.

Reluctance took shape in the hand he rested on the doorknob. Instinct told him to knock, but the polite custom seemed unnecessary.

The room was pitch dark. Before he could discern Anthony's figure beneath the bed sheets, the stench of something unclean, perhaps fecal, overpowered him. He lifted his shirt over his nose and opened the drapes and window.

Despite the breeze that entered, he switched on the overhead fan to assure the room of the circulation it desperately needed. He lowered his shirt and turned back to the bed.

In the morning sunlight Anthony's face was haggard. His thin, graying beard had patches matted like moss on a rock, and his facial muscles seemed to have been pulled out, like threads from a shirt, leaving his expression so slack he was barely recognizable. He looked like he'd aged ten years.

His sheet was oddly discolored. While white in most places, it was dark in spots, too. As Nathan got closer he realized that it was splattered with water from his waist to his neck. A hard lump formed in Nathan's throat.

He went back to the window. Outside, Anh and Hao played at the edge of the lake.

Nathan's hands began to ache, and he realized that he'd squeezed them into fists. Anger rose in him so powerfully it nearly blinded him. He left the room to retrieve the water gun from the stairs – for a moment the desire to hurl the thing down three floors and smash it overtook him. It was just as well Anh and Hao had gotten away. He didn't know what he'd have done had he caught them in the act – the very idea frightened him, such was his belief that he'd have hurt them – but he wanted to make them regret what they'd done.

Back in Anthony's room he set the gun lengthwise over his knee and pushed down on each end until it snapped in two. Water flew all over Nathan, and pieces of plastic shot across the floor.

"See what I did?" he said to Anthony. "They won't bother you with that anymore."

But Nathan knew that children, if resourceful, could replace a water gun with worse things to pick on someone weak. He began to think they'd resent what he'd done, and would take it out on Anthony when no one was around. Disgusted, he tossed the remains of the water gun into a trashcan.

His eye fell on a vase of dead lotuses on a nightstand beside the bed. The purple fist of blossoms had long ago unclenched, letting dangle a number of gray-streaked petals. He took the vase to the window and poured its murky water to the gravel below. He looked again for the children, but they were gone.

Where Anthony's sheet was wet, his skin showed through. Nathan grabbed a towel from the bathroom and blotted the water from Anthony's face. When he touched Anthony's unshaven cheek, he returned to the bathroom. He gathered a razor, shaving cream, and small porcelain bowl filled with hot water, and carried them back to the nightstand.

Sitting on the edge of the bed, he massaged shaving cream across Anthony's cheeks, neck, chin, and upper lip. With one hand he stretched Anthony's cheek taut and with the other carefully ran the razor through Anthony's beard, trying not to snag his hairs in the blade. A swathe of flesh appeared; not the pink he expected but a sallow gray, clammy beneath his fingers. He swirled the razor in the bowl until the cream dissolved, then tapped off on the bowl's edge the collected hairs between the blades.

Shaving an inert face was difficult, but eventually he finished.

"You look younger without the beard," Nathan remarked quietly. "Are you more comfortable now without it?"

There was no flicker of a response, though, and Nathan was left feeling that, no, Anthony wasn't any more comfortable now than he'd been before he came.

Nathan dumped the contents into the bathroom sink, rinsed the bowl, then brought it back into the room filled with water. He dabbed a corner of the towel into the bowl and wiped Anthony's forehead and the corners of his eyes. Except for the sluggish throb of a vein in his neck, Anthony showed no sign of life.

"Are they taking care of you?"

He didn't expect a reply. He didn't expect anything from the body lying before him. And he wondered if that was why he'd come.

Leaning over, he lifted Anthony's eyelids. The eyes that had been hidden stared vacantly upward.

"Huong's selling the company. Did she tell you?" The blue irises beneath him didn't seem to belong to a living person. "She's right that I could never manage it like you. She's doing it because she knows I'd fuck everything up on my own." He forced a weak laugh. "It'll be okay. And you'll return to your old self again in no time. But I'll tell you – you better get that stupid idea of leaving your family out of your head. You need them now like never before."

He straightened the sheet over Anthony's body and gazed down at him. He felt like he had when he toured Ho Chi Minh's mausoleum, gawking at an embalmed, discolored body displayed behind glass.

He opened the door and turned back a final time. He hadn't noticed until now that the floor tiles were streaked with grime. Dust blew along the sides of the walls, and long black hairs, presumably from Huong or the nurse, clumped around the bedposts.

"I'll come by again. And I'll make sure they take better care of you." He shut the door.

Cartoon music drifted upstairs, where he stood trembling from the shock of having seen Anthony in this condition.

From an open door down the hall someone started to speak. The voice was low and Nathan couldn't understand it. As he approached, he saw the shadow of a head against the wall, then, peering around the doorway, he spotted Huong's father. He sat stark naked in a straight-backed chair, with a low Chinese table before him. On one side of the table was a stack of folded laundry, while wadded clothes were strewn on the floor.

Huong's father had a t-shirt in his hands and was inspecting the picture on the front: a red sun with the outline of Florida inside it. The words Sunshine State sandwiched the picture. Huong's father slipped it on over his head. As small as he was, it tumbled to his knees when he stood.

"What about this one?" he said.

Only then did Nathan realize another person was there. An old woman with gray hair in a bun poked her head through a bathroom door. "Too big. They're all too big. And you're too old now to dress like a Westerner."

"It's good quality material," he said, tracing the Atlantic coastline of Florida with a finger. "If he dies, I'd like to have some of these."

"Huong will get mad if she sees you wearing that," she said.

He pulled the shirt off. "He won't need these anymore, anyway."

Nathan made his way quietly back downstairs. Huong was at the window when he reached the bottom step.

The TV cartoon grated on him immediately, and for a moment he thought he'd kick in the screen to kill the noise.

"How was he?" Huong said.

Nathan cleared his throat, trying to compose himself. When he didn't respond, she turned to study his face. She motioned for him to sit down but he stayed where he was, leaning against the banister.

"Is that how it is for him?" Nathan said.

"Is that how what is?"

"His room's like a morgue."

"What are you talking about? I've brought in nurses, doctors, whatever he's needed. He's getting good care."

Nathan forced himself to enter the living room, though the idea of getting near her repelled him. "It's like you're waiting for him to die. To die and leave you his money." He watched her mouth drop open and said accusingly: "That's what it is. Isn't it?"

She clamped her mouth shut with one hand as if she were going to cry out.

He went on, unable to stop himself. "He was right about you. You never loved him. You only wanted what he could give you."

"He was going to leave us. Had something happened to me, do you think he'd have stayed? Yes, he's unlucky about his health, but do you consider me bad for staying with him now? How can you blame me after what happened?"

Nathan looked out the window but saw nothing. What would Anthony have done, he wondered, if their situations were reversed? He didn't have an answer.

"And what about you, Nathan? What happened to the love you once felt for him? What did you give after taking so much?" She yanked open the door and waited for him to walk out. Resentment emanated like heat from her eyes. "It happens, Nathan. We're all guilty of the same things. Anthony was, too. The girls he went with, his drinking, my children..."

Nathan didn't know how he made it outside and to the road. Binh stopped feeding the caged parakeets Anthony kept and called out to him. But Nathan didn't answer. He hurried to the gate and down the walled lane until he reached his motorbike.

As he raced around the corner it hit him that there was no taking back what he'd said to Huong, and even if he was confident that she'd accept an apology, he wasn't ready to offer one. But without this, how was he to see Anthony again? Nathan started trembling so violently he had to pull to the side of the road.

He took his time getting to his office, where he dug through a closet for an old briefcase. Then he removed his personal effects from his desk and stuffed them into the fake leather interior.

When he left his office and walked outside, no one asked where he was going or what time he'd be back. He was sure Xuan would call him after finding his office keys on his desk, but two days later she still hadn't done so, and he realized then that he was free.

28

There weeks later Reuters e-mailed Nathan to say his article had been accepted and to expect another communication with minor editing suggestions. The e-mail also requested instructions on how he preferred to be paid.

In his reply he thanked them for the good news and provided the ABA code for his bank account in Hanoi.

As soon as he sent it the power shut off. Wanting to see if the outage had affected the whole neighborhood, he slid behind Le's easel and looked out the window. The world was plunged in darkness. He scrounged inside his bamboo drawers for a candle and matches. The mittens he'd just pulled on were too bulky to strike a flame, so he shook them off and did it with his hands.

His guestroom was cold and drafty. The window shutters rattled with every biting gust of December wind. He had moved here the day before Huong sold the agency.

He had expected to miss the house on Truç Bach Island, but when he moved here, cater-cornered from the Temple of Literature, the guestroom felt like home in a way the other place never did. The hardest thing to give up was the view of both lakes. But here, from his window over Van Mieu Street, he was compensated for his loss by the sight of the Poet's Balcony beyond the temple's wall.

Guessing that the outage would last a long time, he grabbed his coat and hat. He was about to go out for dinner when he heard someone climb the outer stairs and stop before his room. Because he lived on the top floor, whoever came this far up meant to see him. Opening the door, he found Xuan warming her hands with her breath.

"Am I intruding?"

"Not at all," he said, letting her inside. "Le just went home."

"Sorry I'm late. I had a lot to do."

Every Sunday she visited Anthony and updated Nathan on his condition. The first time she came here, Le was over, too, and they'd insisted that Xuan go down the street with them for dinner. At a small food-stall, Nathan gave her a copy of Thoreau's *Walden* and asked that she read it to Anthony, a little at a time. She'd agreed, thinking it would improve her English. The following Sunday Xuan told him that she hadn't understood what she'd read to Anthony, but she enjoyed it nevertheless.

Whenever Anthony regained consciousness, she'd tell Nathan. Only then would Nathan go back.

They sat at a small table. He relit two candles, then poured hot water from a thermos into a teapot. She was slightly winded from climbing the stairs; in the icy air her breath came out in clouds.

"How's he doing?"

"Better. The doctors hope he'll come out of his coma in the next few days. He's lost a lot of weight. And his beard makes him look old and frail."

"Are they taking good care of him?"

"Why do you always ask that?" She smiled oddly at him. "His room's clean and full of light and fresh air – the same whenever I've visited. A nurse was there, too. She turned him over once to stretch his arms and legs."

"Did you read to him?"

As she righted her purse in her lap and opened its clasp she said: "I got halfway through *The Pond in Winter* but couldn't finish."

"If you're that far, I'm sure you'll finish it next time."

She pulled the book from her purse and set it on the table. "That's something I need to talk to you about."

He felt a small sinking inside him. "What's on your mind?"

She tucked her hair behind her ears, though it hadn't been in the way. She seemed nervous when she spoke. "Do you remember I applied for work at three companies in Ho Chi Minh City? Well, one of them offered me a job. A real estate company in Phu My Hung wants me to start working for them right away."

"I see," he said. "Down to the big city, is it?"

"I have a train ticket for Wednesday morning. I spent all yesterday packing and celebrating with my family."

"You'll leave that soon?"

She nodded. "This is the last time I'll see you for a while. I want to wish you good luck and happiness in your life." They were quiet for a moment. "I asked Huong about you."

He tensed at the mention of Huong's name.

"She says you can come whenever you want. She knows you reacted before from your heart, but she insists you misinterpreted the situation."

Nathan didn't say anything.

Music began playing from her purse. She reached inside for her phone. "*A-lo*? Yes, mother, I'm on my way..."

While she spoke, Nathan opened *Walden* and glanced through the final pages. He was about to close the book when he came upon a passage that penetrated his dullness.

> . . . if one advances confidently in the direction of his
> dreams, and endeavors to live the life which he has imagined,
> he will meet with a success unexpected in common hours.
> He will put some things behind, will pass an invisible bound-
> ary; new, universal, and more liberal laws will begin to estab-
> lish themselves around and within him; or the old laws be
> expanded, and interpreted in his favor in a more liberal sense,
> and he will live with the license of a higher order of beings.
> In proportion as he simplifies his life, the laws of the
> universe will appear less complex, and solitude will not be
> solitude, nor poverty poverty, nor weakness weakness. If you
> have built castles in the air, your work need not be lost; that

is where they should be. Now put the foundations under them.

When Xuan hung up he dog-eared the page and replaced the book on the table.

He asked about her new job, but she didn't know much. She appeared to have taken the job for the salary, which was twice what Anthony had paid her. She asked if he thought she was doing the right thing, and he said that for her it sounded like she was. His words seemed to please her.

She turned to Le's easel. After studying the unfinished sketch, she asked about her. He said she was working hard these days on her painting.

"What are you doing for work? Are you still writing?"

"That's all I want to do. And I tutor English some evenings to cover my rent."

"But is it enough?"

"For me it is. I'm writing an article about the Temple of Literature. And I'm thinking of writing a book."

"About what?"

"About Agent Orange. About the people who've been affected. About the Vietnamese who are suing the U.S. military. And about the developments coming out of that movement."

"That sounds important."

"What's important is that it's worthwhile. Whatever I do, I need to care about it."

She blew into her hands again, and he regretted he couldn't make her more comfortable.

"You and Anthony are different," she said. "I didn't realize how much until now."

"But we're the same, too. Or once we were."

Finishing her tea, she said she had to go. He opened the door and walked her to the stairwell. A Vietnamese sitar was playing in the distance and they listened to it.

"You should marry a Vietnamese woman," Xuan said. "She'll take care of you and keep you company."

A surge of feeling toward her rose in him. For a moment he thought she understood him better than he understood himself. "I thought of doing that once."

"What about Le? Are you serious about her?"

"Yes. But we need more time to figure out what we want."

"I'm sure you will soon." She reached out to touch his arm. "Goodbye, Nathan."

"By the way," he called out when she'd descended a few steps. "Congratulations. Your news surprised me and I forgot to congratulate you."

"Thank you," she said. "I hope you see Anthony soon. I can't do it anymore."

At the bottom of the stairs she looked up and lingered for a moment. Then she waved and walked away.

He stood there afterward, staring at a part of the sky that glowed weirdly where the power hadn't gone out.

The news of Xuan's leaving made him feel she was taking Anthony away, too. She'd been his only connection to him.

She thought he didn't visit because he didn't want to see Huong. Apparently Xuan didn't know that he'd tried to go back but Huong wouldn't let him in. Binh had met him at the gate and told him she was thinking of hiring a guard. When Nathan asked if it was because of him, Binh just scratched his head. Nathan hadn't told Xuan this. He'd worried that if she knew, she'd back out of their arrangement.

29

Dang Thai Mai Road ended with a long stretch of temple stalls and lakeside restaurants, their clay-tiled rooftops littered with soot and dead leaves. Opposite the temple and across bulldozed land, imitation French-style villas had been thrown up like carelessly tossed dice.

The morning air was cold. Breathing it in Nathan imagined it must taste like the lake mist he could glimpse through the restaurants' hollow interiors.

He entered the compound. At the main temple dozens of women knelt on the ground praying. On the front altar above them stood the Court of Five Mandarins. From behind a gilded throne the Jade Emperor – a lacquered statue in a gold robe and tasseled red hat – gazed toward West Lake. Incense and the sounds of mumbled prayers filled the temple.

In the courtyard he passed people praying at twin altars. At the far end, votive offerings burned in a large furnace. Beyond the smoke – the medium through which prayers were transmitted to heaven – Le was sketching at the water's edge.

"That was fast," she said when he came up.

"I haven't visited him yet."

He leaned toward her easel. Her charcoal pencil showed faintly in the morning light, but the longer he gazed at her work the clearer the image became.

She'd drawn the temple's mother goddess, Lieu Hanh, like she'd drawn herself in other paintings: a crowned but otherwise nude woman hovering over the temple, her long neck craned as if searching for something not yet drawn.

"Are you done packing?" she said.

He nodded. Tomorrow was the first part of a journey he'd make down the Ho Chi Minh Trail, a long supply route North Vietnamese forces had used during the war. He'd received an advance from an Australian publisher to write a book about the wartime use of Agent Orange. The money would cover his travel costs and some of the time he'd need to write it.

She sketched a little of the far shore. "I'm happy for you. You deserve this chance."

"I'm lucky the chance came when it did. I'm not lost now like I was."

"Maybe it's true that good things happen when you least expect them."

"You could say that about bad things, too."

She laughed. "You're impossible sometimes."

A month away was a long time and he didn't know how they'd weather the separation. Worry accompanied the thought, but he was grateful finally to be doing what he needed for his life.

Need. For him work wasn't the only need. He needed Le, but he needed Anthony, too. He needed to commit himself more to the people in his life, for that was how he'd ever be happy. He realized that commitments accumulate, attaching to one another like links in a chain. Only then, when too strong to pull apart, would they become essential to his life. Only then would he have something worth caring for and protecting. That was one place happiness came from.

He looked around them. The temple had been built in 1573 to honor a celestial princess. And West Lake was said to have been created when a golden calf was lured by the tolling of a bell. The animal lost its way and circled around and around looking for its mother until its hooves created a basin that eventually filled with water.

Sometimes he wondered what West Lake had been like when the temple was constructed. Had life been so different then?

Anthony had introduced him to this temple shortly after he moved to Hanoi. Looking back, that seemed such a long time ago. Already it was March. In another week spring would officially arrive.

Back then they'd engaged each other in the kind of conversation they used to have in Saigon. It was the kind of mental exercise Nathan no longer had, and he missed it. Anthony had always been critical of Vietnam, but his was a thought-out criticism, and the things he said were usually well considered. Only after he moved to Hanoi and started his own business did this change.

Nathan imagined the maelstrom of thoughts that must be swirling in Anthony's head – with no way of being let out.

He heard Anthony speaking to him in an old conversation. "When I first got to Vietnam, people knew who they were and where they came from. They were good and Vietnam was good. Now the country's lost its identity in the stampede to make money."

"It's the type of people you go with. The people I know aren't like that."

"Maybe. But you can't tell me this place hasn't changed."

"We've all changed. You have. I have. People we know in the U.S. have changed, too."

Thinking back on that time emboldened Nathan and he told Le he was going to visit Anthony.

Driving down the road to Anthony's house, he was surprised to see so much construction. The skeleton of a new high rise towered twenty stories already, clothed by green netting. All around the site, wildflowers sprang from the dirt. Being amid so much newness made him aware that spring was finally here. He couldn't help feel that he and Anthony would brush aside their differences today. He twisted his motorbike's throttle and drank in the cool air that whipped his hair and made his eyes water.

The large villa looked freshly painted in the sunshine. Green buds lined tree branches while butterflies flitted around flowers fronting the house. He was struck by the lack of birdsong from the garden. His shock increased when he saw that Anthony's birdcages were empty. He couldn't imagine what had happened to the birds, which were a source of pride to Anthony and gave him more pleasure than Nathan thought possible.

Just then Anh charged from the house and into the front yard. He ran with reckless abandon, a red cape fluttering behind him, and Nathan thought he'd tumble at any moment and spill into the street below. His costume was that of a cartoon character Nathan vaguely knew. He clutched to his side a doll with Western features whose outstretched arms made it look like rigor mortis had set in. He squatted down to show his doll something on the ground.

Nathan called his name.

But Anh was holding a conversation with the figure and didn't hear him.

"Anh," he called again. This time the boy looked up. "Where are your parents?"

Anh shrugged, pushing the doll's head into the dirt. He was bigger than when Nathan had seen him four months ago. His hair was darker; his belly was rounder and peeked from beneath his shirt; except perhaps for his cheekbones, which were less angular than most Vietnamese, his face had lost some of its Western aspect.

"What's that doll you're playing with?"

"His name's Blue."

"Blue's a good name. It matches his eyes." He paused, watching Anh play. "Can you tell me where your dad is? I haven't seen him in a long time."

Anh pointed across the street. A gravel road stretched somewhere Nathan couldn't see for the pushed-together villas. "You can walk there. But you have to look both ways before crossing the street."

"What are you pointing at, Anh?"

Anh scrunched up his eyes like he was thinking. "I forget what it's called. But..."

"But what?"

He took a deep breath, letting it out as he finished speaking. "They put the dead people there."

A bright white curtain drew across Nathan's vision. Afterward he found it difficult to keep his feet beneath him.

The Vietnamese word for cemetery crept onto his lips. "*Nghĩa địa?*"

Anh nodded, looking back to the house. "Grandpa's watching."

Nathan turned. Huong's father stood at the window. On the chest of his yellow shirt was an outline of Florida. He seemed to be speaking to someone inside, but the reflection of sunlight on the glass prevented Nathan from seeing who.

"Where's your mom?"

Anh pointed toward the cemetery again. Fear tempered Nathan's urge to run there. From the yard it was hard to distinguish between a patch of dead grass and a gravestone – he didn't know what he was looking at.

How could Huong keep the news from him? He was sickened by the thought that maybe Anthony had wanted to see him, just once before dying, but Huong had refused to tell him.

More questions popped into his head; questions he couldn't answer. But one kept returning – larger, louder, and more urgent than the others. Only Huong had the answer to it. Not having been there for Anthony, he either had to accept what she said or accept nothing at all. Either way, he'd never know what Anthony had said about him at the end, or what he might have needed.

He ran across the street, leaving Anh to play with his doll.

The cemetery was on a slight rise enclosed by fir trees. At the back, a wire fence overtaken by weeds leaned forward nearly thirty degrees, and behind that was land in the initial stages of being cleared.

He walked up and set his hand on the cold pocked granite of a gravestone. He was the only one there. With pain flooding through him he began to search for Anthony's grave.

On the leftmost side of the cemetery he came upon a view of two narrow, parallel paths through the trees – flattened to the brown earth as if a skier had made them. West Lake was one hundred meters away.

An island of lotuses floated on the water.

Only the occasional motorbike passing by broke the quiet.

For a long time he stared at the lake. Through tears, the lotuses blurred and became a long, billowing ribbon of pinkish white.

Curious where the path led, he headed toward the lake's shore.

After a few steps he froze. At the water's edge a woman stood behind a man in a wheelchair. The man had light brown hair and was obviously tall despite being seated. Nathan could only see the woman from the back. She was dressed in a nurse's white uniform and hat. The man was visible from his shoulders to his head. Although Nathan's vantage was limited, the sight was a revelation.

"Nathan."

He whipped around. Huong stood behind him, looking over his shoulder to make sure Anthony and the nurse hadn't heard her. She motioned Nathan to follow her back into the cemetery.

"What are you doing here?" she said. In her eyes was a tiredness that might once have belonged to Anthony.

"That's him, isn't it?" he said, pointing through the trees to the lake.

She didn't answer, nor did she look toward the shore. Instead she waited, as if expecting an explanation for his presence.

"I heard he's doing better," he said. "I wanted to see for myself."

Finally she said: "We're leaving, you know."

"Leaving?"

"For California. As soon as he's cleared to go."

Nathan couldn't help remark that they must have worked out their differences. She laughed weakly and said that Anthony hadn't fully regained his speaking faculties. But he'd convinced her that he wanted a new chance. "His life won't be like before. He needs me. And I think that's good for us."

She didn't ask Nathan how he was, and he didn't offer the information. He knew she didn't want to involve herself with him more than she had to. It saddened him, but it was a necessary change.

"You probably don't want me seeing him," he said.

"As far as I'm concerned, that's for him to decide. I'm not sure he has any faith left in you, either."

Her words knocked off his face the smile that was trying to form.

He didn't blame her for saying this. She knew as well as he that ulterior motives had driven Anthony for a long time.

"I'm sure he doesn't," Nathan said. "But I'm willing to take my chances."

From his bag he pulled out an envelope. "I came to see you, too. Anthony loaned me this. I'm paying it back with interest."

She stared at the envelope. "It's not mine to take back."

He pushed it into her hand. "Anthony's too stubborn to take it, even though it's his." He wrapped his fingers around her hand until he felt her grip tighten. With his hand on hers he glanced into her eyes. The fire he was accustomed to seeing there was gone.

"He likes coming here," she said. "He'd sit by the lake all day if you let him. Sometimes I ask what he's thinking about, but he never answers me."

"Will he be upset if I say hello?"

"There's nothing he can do if he is. I guess that gives you the advantage."

He searched her face for encouragement but none was there. Without another word she turned and headed home.

In the cemetery's silence he heard the lake against the shore. He walked back to the parallel tracks cutting through the wood. As he made his way through the trees, Anthony and his nurse returned to view.

The island of lotuses shimmered on the water like a vision. They were close enough to shore that he might easily pull one out, but he didn't want to stir the mud where their roots ran deep. The water was clear, he could see small fish near the surface, and he didn't want to disturb this peace. In any case, now was not the time.

He turned toward Anthony, who was staring at something far away. West Lake spread beyond him – vast.

ABOUT THE AUTHOR

David Joiner was born and raised in Cincinnati, Ohio. He has lived off and on in Vietnam for many years, and now makes his home in Kanazawa, Japan. *Lotusland* was first published by Guernica Editions Inc. in 2015.

David's other novels are *Kanazawa* (Stone Bridge Press, 2022), a 2022 Foreword Indies Book of the Year Finalist for Best Multicultural Novel, and *The Heron Catchers* (Stone Bridge Press, 2023), winner of the 2024 International Rubery Book Award, a 2023 Foreword Indies Book of the Year Finalist for Best Multicultural Novel, a 2023 American Writing Awards Finalist, and a 2023 Next Generation Indie Book Awards Finalist.

AUTHOR'S NOTE

Thank you for reading *Lotusland*, a book that took me seven years to research and write. The version you just read is a newer version of what Guernica Editions Inc. published in 2015, re-issued to commemorate the 50th anniversary of the end of the war between the United States and Vietnam.

As a reader, your opinion, positive or negative, matters a lot to me. Readers sometimes ask how they can help promote my book. Word of mouth is one way, and ratings and reviews are another. If you have an Amazon and/or a Goodreads account, ratings are a simple but effective way to help, and they only take a few seconds of your time. Reviews may take a bit longer, but they greatly help other readers discover my work.

The more that people know about my books, the easier it will be for me to keep writing. Without reader support, an author's road to publication becomes more difficult. So please leave an honest rating or review – or both – on your favorite review sites. I appreciate your support more than you'll ever know.

ACKNOWLEDGMENTS

Many people helped me over the seven years (if you count the long breaks) it took me to write *Lotusland*. My gratitude goes out to:

The faculty and staff at the Vietnam University of Fine Arts for explaining to me the history and process of lacquer painting in Vietnam, and Saeko Ando for inviting me into her studio and letting me wander around like a bull in a china shop while I asked about lacquer painting in the Vietnamese tradition.

The staff at Friendship Village and Tu Du Hospital – and especially the children at the latter – who helped me understand better the continuing effects of Agent Orange on people's lives in Vietnam.

Lady Borton for taking the time to speak with me about the history of Agent Orange's use in Vietnam as well as contemporary issues relating to it, both in Vietnam and the United States.

Van Anh for helping me research various topics my novel explores, for translating when I needed it, and for her kindness and friendship.

Alastair Ewing for explaining the intricacies of Vietnamese real estate.

Ted and Linh for the use of their home in Mui Ne to write in (as well as their friendship and the friendship of their dogs).

Garry Powell, Jeff Gibbs, and Elka Ray for their close, careful readings of my novel and valuable feedback.

Lindsay Brown, Michael Mirolla, and Rosemary Ahern for their excellent editing.

Kathryn Guare for helping produce such wonderful paperback and e-book versions of my novel's re-issue, and Kimberly Glyder for creating a gorgeous cover for it.

Vietnam Today: An Interview with Novelist David Joiner
The following interview was first published in
Rain Taxi Online Edition Fall 2015.

by Garry Craig Powell

David Joiner is a U.S. novelist currently living in Kanazawa, Japan, although he has spent more than a decade in Vietnam since he initially visited the country in 1994, when he was the first American to live in Bien Hoa city since the end of the war. His debut novel, *Lotusland*, focuses on Nathan, a young American journalist living in Saigon. Nathan finds himself torn between love and duty, vocation and worldly success, when he simultaneously receives intriguing offers from Le, a poor but talented female lacquer painter, and Anthony, an old friend who wants him to help run a successful real estate business. With its complicated cast of characters and evocative settings, *Lotusland* is likely the most vivid novel set in post-colonial Southeast Asia that contemporary readers will encounter.

The following conversation with Joiner, whom I have known since we were in graduate school together at the University of Arizona in 1998, took place by electronic mail.

Garry Craig Powell: Although I know *Lotusland* quite well, having read a number of drafts of it, I don't remember its precise inception. Could you tell us a bit about how you got the idea for the novel, and what aspects of it seized your attention?

David Joiner: I don't know that a specific idea led to the inception of *Lotusland*, but I do remember wanting to fill a niche in U.S. literature about Vietnam. I wanted to set my novel in contemporary Vietnam, during the time that I was writing it, and have it turn the page on the war we fought there. I find it regrettable that America's focus on Vietnam remains squarely on the war. Even though the war ended in 1975, virtually every U.S. novel, movie, and play that deals with Vietnam does so by resurrecting the war. In many ways that makes sense because the event had such a huge impact on the U.S. -

and in fact on the world - and much of the literature that came out of the war has been incredible. But forty years on I feel like we should look for a different perspective on Vietnam.

GCP: That's certainly one of the most refreshing things about the novel. Rereading the published version, it struck me that although there are two ostensibly very different plots in the book - and I think they are of equal importance, unlike the typical novel's plot and subplot - both are thematically similar. In both Nathan's romantic relationship with Le and his blurred friendship/business relationship with Anthony, the conflicts come about because there are serious issues of trust. Was that deliberate and planned?

DJ: Yes, it was. I think issues of trust mark all relationships, no matter where one lives. But in Vietnam, where it can be difficult for people to meet on equal levels - economically, socially, historically, culturally, etc. - I think these issues are especially salient. One needs to be rather careful there both in business relationships (as with Anthony) and romantic ones (as with Le and Huong). After all, legal protections in Vietnam hardly exist. Also, Vietnamese people in general distrust their government, the police, and others in positions of power. That distrust often filters through to everyday relationships, which play out dramatically in the novel.

GCP: Another fascinating aspect of the novel is the complexity and ambivalence of the main characters. You aren't afraid to show them as inconsistent. Le's reticence and dishonesty causes Nathan a great deal of suffering, which makes us sympathise with him, yet he withholds his true intentions from Anthony too, and while he doesn't downright lie to him, he certainly misleads him. And Anthony, in spite of his apparent generosity towards Nathan, has ulterior motives. So there's an intricate pattern of deception or at least lack of frankness, which may be symptomatic of relationships in a developing country like Vietnam, where money corrupts everything. Am I on the right track here? You could take it a step further and say that material interests have made liars and cheats of people everywhere.

DJ: I wouldn't go so far as to say that money corrupts everything, but it certainly is corrupting. One often hears stories of people getting in trouble for something, fairly or unfairly, but managing to evade punishment by paying off people in high places. And people there know the power of money just as they do anywhere, but it's particularly insidious in Vietnam because no obvious model of upstanding behaviour really exists for people to follow. The government is corrupt at every level, and the police force essentially exists only to enrich itself. Why should society be any different from those who wield power and grow rich through no honest efforts of their own? And to get ahead in life, as Anthony and Huong have been able to do after marrying, one often has to do things that others might consider unethical. I wouldn't say they are liars and cheats, nor would I characterize most Vietnamese as such. Most Vietnamese I know, in fact, are lovely. People do find themselves in unfamiliar and difficult circumstances sometimes, and poverty often suggests a reason why people do things they likely wouldn't do if they were better off. Poverty in Vietnam is not uncommon, though it's usually not of such a desperate kind like you find for example in India.

GCP: As a State-of-Vietnam novel, *Lotusland* is a rich and textured portrait of the country that reveals both the worst things about it - the corruption, the poverty, and the tawdriness - and the best: the beauty, not only of its landscape and art, but often glimpses of transcendent beauty in quite ordinary scenes, as well as the humanity of the people, their present sufferings and their brave attempts to overcome the trauma of "The American War." I was particularly moved by the descriptions of the Agent Orange victims, and fascinated by the detailed depictions of traditional lacquer painting. Not many writers can plunge the reader so deeply and intensely into a foreign environment. How do you do that?

DJ: If it's a State-of-Vietnam novel, then by necessity it's one seen through the eyes of foreigners. That's the perspective I know, and I can write from it authentically. As for plunging the reader into a foreign environment, I'm not sure how much I've actually done this with *Lotusland*. Setting is important to my aesthetic, though, and I've always been fascinated by, even moved by, both the natural and urban landscapes of Vietnam. It's kind of a *wabi-sabi* ethic, where one finds beauty in the potential of things, in their imperfections. To me, no other country possesses the kind of beauty Vietnam is endowed with, and because that beauty, that aesthetic, really can't be replicated in the West, I need to paint scenes with a certain type of brushstroke to ensconce readers in the place itself. Vietnam is also eminently observable. So much happens in the streets and sidewalks of the cities, especially, that the life lived there is a gift to anyone drawn to writing. One's senses are overwhelmed at every moment, one feels enormously alive there, and I don't know how that could be kept out of any writing about Vietnam. I have a tendency to write imagistically, and to using setting like drapery - not to obfuscate the reader's vision, but to hang it as close as possible before their mind's eye so they not only see it but feel surrounded by it. That's the hope, anyway.

GCP: You succeed in your aim of "surrounding" the reader with the setting. I think you do that by using all your senses, not just visual images, but sounds, smells, tastes and sensations too. It's a heightened reality, a more intense one than we normally experience. As in much of the best writing, in Conrad for instance, the setting becomes a character. It's not merely backdrop: it plays a vital role in determining the fates of the human characters. I think you also immerse the reader in your lyrical prose. You must have an excellent ear for the music of English to be able to write so beautifully, so euphonically. Is that something you consciously developed?

DJ: I'm not sure...I think most writers of literary fiction possess a love of language, otherwise they wouldn't write. If I've succeeded in developing an interesting voice, it probably has much to do with what I've read. I started *Lotusland* in the middle of an intensive re-reading of Yasunari Kawabata's oeuvre. I remember using multicolored highlighters to mark up old copies of *Snow Country* and *Thousand Cranes*, to study and learn from them, and later typing out all of the former on my laptop. I was interested in how he did what he did in those novels—their indirectness, the power of silence, their pacing, the rhythms and deceptive simplicity of his prose (or the translation of his prose). In fact, the first scene of *Lotusland* is my homage to *Snow Country*. My novel, too, starts with a scene on a train, though his is more beautiful than mine, and more successful.

GCP: You're very modest: allow me to disagree, although I'm with you on the brilliance of Kawabata. But let's go back to setting. The novel is set mainly in Hanoi and Saigon, the two biggest cities in the country, in the early twenty-first century. Why did you choose to set it then and there? Since two of the main characters are Americans, why didn't you set it during or right after the war?

DJ: First and foremost, I wanted to write about places in Vietnam that I knew well, and I know Saigon and Hanoi pretty well - I've spent nearly ten years in those two cities. Also, both cities have changed dramatically since I first encountered them twenty-one years ago, and I'm sure my subconscious found both places fertile ground. There are other reasons, too. I wanted to veer far from typical wartime portrayals of Saigon and Hanoi - both novelistic and journalistic - and I wanted to present Hanoi, especially, in a way that managed to express its beauty. Hanoi is richer than Saigon with respect to the arts, and Vietnam's lacquer painting tradition was developed in the north. In terms of its temporal setting, *Lotusland* only works as a contemporary story, and so that choice was deliberate. I also wanted to share with readers how Agent Orange continues to affect people in Vietnam three generations since the war's end. Agent Orange is frequently in the news in Vietnam, yet how many people in the West realize the extent to which it continues to ravage people's lives? Finally, as I mentioned before, I didn't want to write another Vietnam War story. I was more interested in finding a different narrative about Vietnam, in inviting readers to step outside of that well-trod literary landscape.

GCP: And yet, even though the war has long been over, one feels its shadowy presence throughout the book, sometimes in completely unexpected ways - for instance, in the apparent lack of bitterness the Vietnamese feel towards these men from a recently enemy country. What makes this interesting, for me, is wondering how genuine it is. To what extent have the Vietnamese really forgiven the Americans (and the French who preceded them) and to what extent are they forced to be agreeable, because they, the Americans, are richer, and may be able to offer them jobs and visas?

DJ: That's a good question. I assume it's genuine. Vietnamese, friends and strangers both, assure me that they have forgiven but not forgotten what the U.S. did in Vietnam, and aside from a few drunks I've run into in Hanoi, no one has made me feel uncomfortable for being an American or blamed me for what happened forty and fifty years ago. Further, young Vietnamese people often don't show interest in the war. The war bores them, it's something they're forced to read about in school, to tune out when their parents and grandparents start talking about it, and it's part of many state-run programs that offer no appeal to the young. I've met college-aged students in Vietnam who thought their country had fought against Australia rather than the U.S. And yes, I do think that people make a distinction between "America the War Machine" and "America the Land of Opportunity." Getting to America is still viewed as a way to better one's life. And, by association, to better family members' lives. That's the story of quite a few Vietnamese people who came to the U.S. after the war, and who continue to come. Everyone remembers the success stories, which are often endlessly circulated, and people tend to see themselves in those who've done well. The Vietnamese, if I may generalize, are some of the most hopeful and forward-looking people I've ever met.

GCP: Another thing that I find engaging is the complexity and unpredictability of the characters' motivations. For instance, the young Vietnamese women who interact with Nathan and Anthony are all materialistic, but Anthony is just as crass in his own pursuit of wealth, and Le's apparent manipulativeness turns out to be more complex than it appears, and is arguably balanced by her genuine devotion to her art. I also admired the way the various conflicts - over whether Nathan should dedicate himself to writing or simply accept the very comfortable lifestyle Anthony offers him, and whether he should keep his promises to his friend, to whom he owes money and a job, or be true to his heart and pursue Le - are tangled together. Although Nathan is in his late twenties, *Lotusland* is a sort of bildungsroman, isn't it? Nathan is forced to work out for himself what is really important in life, perhaps a little belatedly - though maybe nowadays, since people mature later, the bildungsroman has to be about people in their late twenties or even older.

DJ: I think that's right. In *Lotusland*, Nathan struggles to learn what's most important in life, and unfortunately he makes mistakes, some of which hurt people along the way. But this is true of most foreigners I've met in Vietnam. The country offers many a chance to leave behind their own countries and the messes they've made of their lives there. Many people travel to Vietnam on a whim and decide to stay to reinvent themselves. Many foreigners I've met in Vietnam have only learned in their sixties and even their seventies what's really important in life. Or some have known all along, but for various reasons they've been prevented from living how they want to, from being the kind of person they dream of being. As a writer, I find the idea of "reinventing oneself" interesting. It's a theme that's passed through the lives of many older Vietnamese people I know, too - leaving Vietnam for the U.S., for example, and reinventing themselves there; and maybe later returning to Vietnam and reinventing themselves yet again. One also sees it among U.S. vets who come back to Vietnam and settle there. They often have demons they must grapple with in both countries, but the ones in Vietnam are frequently gentler, more welcoming, and - to go back to something we spoke about before - more forgiving.

As for materialism in Vietnam, I don't think it's as deep-seated as it is in the U.S. or many other developed countries. At least not yet. Vietnam may become as materialistic over time. I have a number of Japanese friends in their sixties and seventies who tell me that they recognize post-WWII Japan in Vietnam's fervor to rebuild the country.

GCP: So to some extent we can see the novel as an indictment of capitalism in developing countries, but it's also about the rootlessness of many westerners: Neither Nathan nor Anthony really belongs in the States any more. Why is that? Have they simply been lured by the exotic to Asia - are they what Edward Said has pejoratively called "orientalists" - or is there more to them than that? Are they adventurers or just misfits?

DJ: There's probably some or all of that in both characters. You find many expats unsure of their futures. For most, living in Vietnam is an adventure, and the quality of life there is often better than it is in the U.S. - unless you're extremely wealthy and well-connected back home. The weather in the south of Vietnam is great, you don't have to work all that hard, the food and coffee remain cheap and some of the world's best, people are friendly, travel opportunities are plentiful, it's easy to make friends, and the women are beautiful. A man, particularly, can live like a prince there - and be treated as an important personage. The lure to stay can be far stronger than the lure to return to one's own country. And while Nathan and Anthony have both encountered this in Vietnam, Anthony is the one whose identity has formed around near-overnight success and wealth. And it changes him. Just like it changes so many of us. I don't think that either of them are misfits, and I'm not interested in writing about misfits, anyway. I think both are quite earnest about their lives - about finding ways to become more happily rooted.

GCP: Much great fiction dwells on that theme. In Robert Musil's opinion, the only question worth the attention of intelligent people is how to live happily, and naturally place and way of life play a part in that. Good fiction is always about a specific place and time, and yet *Lotusland* also manages to be universal. How is that achieved? What would you say to someone who told you that he or she wasn't interested in Vietnam?

DJ: I don't think that life in Vietnam is so foreign that people anywhere couldn't relate to what happens in *Lotusland*. People could learn much about the country by reading my novel - or at least about the way one person sees Vietnam, as an American. If someone told me they weren't interested in Vietnam, then they're not likely to be interested in any place other than where they are. I do think *Lotusland* develops certain universal themes - love is one, finding one's place in the world is another, learning to do what is morally right is one more. I'm not sure how that's achieved in literature. But I think that writers as well as readers should have a wide range of experiences, and be curious about them afterwards, and care about them deeply, in order to deal with such themes successfully. Sometimes, though, I think it's a crapshoot. What writer can say with certainty that his or her novel will be viewed as universal?

GCP: You're right, you can never be sure. I'm not sure it's a crapshoot, though. That implies luck and I think it has more to do with skill. Isn't it a matter of writing so convincingly about characters from a specific time and place that no matter where you're from, you feel you know them and can learn from them? And to take that point further, do you worry that readers won't find your characters likeable or will be unable to identify with them? All of the main ones have serious flaws. Even Nathan is not only less than transparent with his friend Anthony, but also, in spite of some misgivings, accepts an "arrangement" with Le whereby in return for his help in getting her a visa, she becomes his girlfriend, which may strike some as sordid. Why didn't you make him purer and nobler?

DJ: Characters need flaws to be interesting, to seem more human, and for readers to feel they can connect to them. I was interested in developing Nathan's character in such a way that readers would root for him, while probably rooting against Anthony and even Le. And then I wanted to turn things on their head near the end to show that Nathan was flawed too, and that Anthony, for all his faults, was understandable. People are complicated - their intentions, good or bad, are often not well understood - and I wanted to show that. Hopefully on the final pages we see the characters on the threshold of becoming better people, of becoming less selfish, of figuring out their relationships and also their dreams. Nathan and Anthony are recognizably American, as American as any characters in fiction, and I never really worried that readers wouldn't identify with them. I didn't make Nathan purer and nobler because that doesn't particularly interest me in fiction, and I don't think he would come across as believable that way. But he's also not terribly sordid. He tries to be pure and noble.

GCP: And what about the female characters? Some readers, familiar with the stereotypes about Asian women, may be surprised by how strong and aggressive they are. Would you agree?

DJ: Absolutely. Vietnamese society is changing at lightning speed, and stereotypes like these are subject to change, if they were ever even all that true. Of course Vietnam is still a Confucian - that is, male-dominated - society, but one sees Vietnamese women everywhere who are stronger in mind and body than their male counterparts.

GCP: Your next novel, *Burning Green Sun*, is also set in Vietnam. Would you tell us what it's about and why the country fascinates you so much? Do you see yourself following in the footsteps of writers like Graham Greene and Marguerite Duras, or even ones from the colonial era like George Orwell, Joseph Conrad, and Somerset Maugham? Are you writing about "The White Man's Burden," and is that still relevant?

DJ: It's a near-total rewrite of the first novel I ever wrote. It's set in the early 1990s in the Mekong Delta of Vietnam and in Phnom Penh and the northern stretches of the Mekong River in northeast Cambodia. The characters are mostly river researchers - a French hydrographer; two American cetologists; a Cambodian ichthyologist; an American drifter who has left the U.S. for good, married a local Delta woman, and taught himself about life in the Mekong Delta; and an American traveller. Both countries fascinate me. In the case of the Mekong River in Vietnam and Cambodia, the natural settings are mesmerizing. I'm also fascinated by, and admire, how people live in such seemingly wild and untameable environments. There's a kind of genius in how people have learned to make lives for themselves on the river, and there's often a sense of seeing the world as it used to be hundreds of years ago. A great whirlwind of change is passing through the cities of Vietnam and Cambodia, but in the countryside there's a feeling of ancientness, of an ancient slowness, of something we've long lost sight of and fail to appreciate now.

And no, I don't see myself consciously following in the footsteps of the great writers you named. It may be useful to do so - to keep the bar raised as high as possible while writing - but I never thought like that. It would be crazy for me to. As for your question about "The White Man's Burden," I'll let others decide if I'm writing about that, or if such a thing is still relevant, but personally I've never considered it. Perhaps I should have, but I simply wanted to set an authentic story in contemporary Vietnam that might lead readers on a different path than the one that inevitably arrives at another war story. Perhaps that is a white man's burden after all.

2025: A Q&A with David Joiner

Following are some questions I've been asked since *Lotusland* was originally published in 2015. The questions came mostly through email exchanges with various people, but also in person with readers of the novel, or in interactions with those interested in the life I built for myself in Vietnam over the years. I've rephrased some questions slightly to frame them against the backdrop of *Lotusland*'s re-issue in 2025. I hope these questions will offer a useful perspective to understand the novel, and my writing in general, beside the interview I gave to the writer Garry Craig Powell in *Rain Taxi* ten years ago.

1. You've moved between Japan and Vietnam several times since 2011 and are now based in Kanazawa and Yamanaka Onsen. What is your relationship to Vietnam now?

What I can say is that I'm as fascinated by Vietnam and Vietnamese culture as I've ever been, and probably its literature more so than ever, and I continually look for opportunities to spend time there. Unfortunately, such opportunities have been distressingly few lately. Between 1994 and 2015, I lived in Vietnam for over eleven years, and when I wasn't living there I never let more than two years pass without returning. However, since 2015 I've visited only three times for half a year, and I haven't been back since 2018 – a gap of over six years that I regret.

I should add that I've been reading a lot of Vietnamese fiction in translation, and this has served as a substitute for returning to Vietnam, though nothing beats actually being in the country. I'm planning to return to Vietnam in late 2024 or early 2025 for a short visit, but I hope to return more frequently and spend up to half a year there annually. I used to speak Vietnamese conversationally, and I'd like to regain those language skills if I can, which is hard to do in Kanazawa as I have few chances to speak it. I still have friends in Vietnam and I'm keen to maintain those relationships. Social media allows this superficially, but it's not the same as spending time together in person. This is all to say that I miss Vietnam and look forward to going back on a regular basis, making it a significant part of my life again.

2. What is your relationship to Vietnamese literature and literature about Vietnam now? Has it changed since *Lotusland* first came out?

I'd like to think that this relationship has deepened. If it has, it's largely thanks to the number of literary works that have either been translated from Vietnamese into English, or that have been written in English by people of Vietnamese descent. My own library of Vietnam-themed fiction and poetry, for example, has certainly expanded over the last decade, though much of this was published before 2015 and I've simply found it, or was only able to read it, belatedly. I'm always on the lookout for literature set in Vietnam or about the Vietnamese experience generally, so my eagerness to encounter more of it hasn't lessened. In fact, because I haven't been able to return to Vietnam for several years, my interest in reading about the country has increased; it gives me a vicarious feeling of being back there, which I crave. I'd like very much to write another novel set there, partly as a way to connect more deeply with Vietnam and the literature associated with the country. I'd also like to interact with more Vietnamese writers as well as non-Vietnamese who write about Vietnam, which is more likely to happen the more I'm able to write and publish novels set there.

3. *Lotusland* originally came out with Guernica Editions in March 2015. How is the reissue of *Lotusland* different from the original publication?

While plot-wise it's much the same, I've shortened it by around twenty pages. I've softened the edges to some characters and scenes, eliminated parts that no longer resonate in the present social and political climate, and altered word choices here and there. For the reissue, I wanted to shorten the first half of the novel more than I was able to, and I also wanted to stretch out the time between Nathan's becoming separated from Le in Saigon and reconnecting with her in Hanoi, but for the reissue I wasn't able to do either one in a way that satisfied me.

In any case, I think it's a tighter story than it was, and more readable, too.

4. One often hears about novels published by small presses facing difficulties that Big Four novels rarely if ever encounter. What hurdles did *Lotusland* face in its original release, and what hurdles do you expect it to face with its reissue ten years later?

Most of all, it faced the hurdle of a lack of exposure. In 2015 it hardly got promoted, which isn't unusual for literary novels published through small and independent presses. But even without that, it faced the additional difficulty of not being submitted to the normal round of trade journals, which made it even harder for readers, bookstores, and libraries to discover – to simply know that my novel existed. Add to this the phenomenal and deserved success of Viet Thanh Nguyen's *The Sympathizer*, which came out at the same time as *Lotusland* and won the 2016 Pulitzer Prize for Fiction, and there wasn't much space in the press or general book media for my novel, I suppose. If a major publisher had taken it – and once or twice that nearly happened – I might now be relating a different story.

The reissue will definitely face the same difficulties. But with what I learned from my previous experience with *Lotusland*, I've started early to drum up interest in my novel. In the last ten years, the number of traditional reviewers has declined in favor of social media influencers, most of whom have profitable connections with major publishers and don't often read the books they're asked to promote. In a way, I'm fortunate to be better positioned now with three novels to my name and an international award for my latest work. One never knows who might find the novel, read and enjoy it, and pass it on to others who will do the same. This is generally how momentum builds for novels published to a limited audience. Famous writers selling hundreds of thousands of books don't really have to deal with this, but writers without massive followings and marketing budgets do.

5. You were able to promote *Lotusland* mostly on your own in 2015 in ways that writers in similar positions to you – having published with small presses – couldn't do. I'm thinking of your

reading at the US Embassy, your meeting with Vietnamese writers at the Vietnam Institute of Literature, your keynote presentation at the 7th Annual Engaging with Vietnam conference, and your interview on VTC10 TV. That suggests a certain level of success with *Lotusland*. What prompted the novel's reissue?

Again, when *Lotusland* first came out in 2015 it received very little press, and my publisher either had limited resources to promote it or didn't prioritize its promotion with what resources it did have. Reissuing *Lotusland* is a welcome chance for me to try again, and after having the copyright returned to me and establishing Painted Veil Press – a new imprint for this and possibly future publications – I was free to do with the novel as I pleased, and it's been good to have creative control of the novel for a second run. *Lotusland* has had more editing, a new design of its interior, new endorsements, and a beautiful new cover. We'll see where this takes the novel in 2025, but there's no doubt that, for a time anyway, it will receive new life and find new readers – which is what any writer wants.

Also, the 50-year anniversary of the end of the Vietnam War falls on April 30, 2025, and with it fast approaching, and international media attention soon to spring up around the event, reissuing the novel seemed like a way to attract more readers to my novel. I expect 99.9% of media references to novels about the war to skip over *Lotusland*, which is fine, because my novel isn't about the war. But then will the media, if they discuss Vietnam as it is today, 50 years after the war's end, mention my novel? In 2015, during the 40-year anniversary of the war's end, hardly any media did – even though the *New York Times*, the *New York Review of Books*, and *The Atlantic* had writers who requested and read my novel – so I expect that will be the case again. I'm trying to achieve a better outcome in 2025, but I'm not famous and don't have that kind of pull.

6. Is the publishing industry more receptive now to novels set in contemporary Vietnam or does it still prioritize novels about the war and the refugee experience? Perhaps I'm under-read, but I

have a hard time naming any literary novels set in contemporary Vietnam.

There's a reason you can't, and I doubt you're under-read. The publishing industry remains stubbornly resistant to novels set in contemporary Vietnam; novels and memoirs about the war and Vietnamese diaspora remain highly sought-after, it seems. But novels about Vietnam today, a half-century after fighting between the US and Vietnam ended, continue to have difficulty proving their value to publishing's gatekeepers. Since *Lotusland* was originally published, one has trouble naming even two or three literary novels set in post-war Vietnam. This myopia only contributes to the unhelpful equating of Vietnam with a war and painting the country and people as belligerent, rather than allowing for the truer depiction of a country with a deep culture and fascinating history (of resisting wars, in part), and a people as friendly and intelligent and optimistic as in any country you'll find.

7. What do you hope to see in the next ten years where novels written in English about Vietnam are concerned?

As I said, I hope to see more novels that depict contemporary life in Vietnam. It seems important to document, in ways only fiction can, the seismic changes that Vietnam has undergone since *Đổi Mới* – widescale economic reforms initiated in 1986 – and even more recently, since the world's interest in Vietnam as a tourist destination and investment opportunity has taken off. Already, the 1990s, 2000s, and 2010s have passed by with only a handful of literary novels written in English about post-war Vietnam being published, and we're on track for the same to happen in the 2020s. I think future generations of readers will be worse off for this lack of representation of what Vietnam was like during these times. Of course, Vietnamese fiction translated into English can fill some of this void, but there's too little of this happening now, and no indication this is about to change. Until now, the only literary fiction about Vietnam that's been made available from a non-Vietnamese perspective are accounts of the war. Now here we are, fifty years since the war ended, and this endless stream of Vietnam War-era fiction has grown tiresome and – despite the brilliance and importance of some of it – of more limited value, I think.

Where fiction about Vietnam is concerned, contemporary stories are potentially of great and lasting value to the relationship between both countries. That might sound grandiose, and also self-serving, but there's an undeniable truth in this. After all, literature should do more than merely allow publishers to rake in profits, which seems to be the only model at work now. Literature should also accomplish the important task of capturing a culture as it changes and grows – capturing the cultural zeitgeist between its blooming and fading and the development of a new and different one. Those pursuits don't have to be mutually exclusive.

8. What advice do you have for people writing novels in English about Vietnam now?

Write what you feel driven to write. The field is wide open and virtually untapped, and at some point the publishing world will take notice of such writing, which could change the publishing landscape forever. And one doesn't have to be with a Big Four publisher to make an impact. Smaller publishers are more willing than the Big Four to take chances on such fiction, though smaller publishers normally don't have the reach or resources to get books in front of readers, so the burden on writers to find readers on their own is much higher and no less difficult than it's ever been. But I've always thought that persistence is the most important quality that successful writers have. If you write something of high enough quality, it will find readers.

9. Since the original publication of *Lotusland* in 2015, you've had two other novels published, both set in Japan. Why didn't you write more novels set Vietnam after 2015, and do you plan to set more novels there in the future?

Since moving to Japan in 2015, I've had few chances to return to Vietnam, and that's hindered me from writing about it. In fact, I continue to work on the first novel I ever set out to write, which has never been published – except for an excerpt in *The Ontario Review* – that I started in 2001. It's set in Vietnam's Mekong Delta, but also in Phnom Penh and Kratie, Cambodia. Maybe I should have shelved it permanently by now, but I'm still too attached to do that. But because

I continue to work on it from time to time, I think it shows I haven't given up on writing more novels set in Vietnam.

As I've said, in the future I hope to spend more time in Vietnam, and I think this will give me confidence, as well as material, to write again about the country. Now I'm focused on writing my third "Kanazawa novel." After that, I may feel compelled to step back from Japan and re-focus my attention on Vietnam.

10. What do you think about *Lotusland* ten years after its original publication, both its initial reception and its likely reception after being reissued?

I doubt the reception to *Lotusland*'s reissue can be any quieter than in 2015, so that's already a positive outcome! Although I'm obviously biased, I think *Lotusland* still has great relevance today, and I think it continues to portray Vietnam authentically. It's still a debut novel despite its reissue and slight revisions, and I recognize that the faults it had before are scarcely less apparent now. But it's as unique as ever in portraying Vietnam at a time of great change and renewal and captures human relationships that are deeply affected, in good and bad ways, by the country's dynamism. I think this uniqueness, and this authenticity, are what make the novel worth reading. I hope it finds a wider audience because of these qualities and continues to be read and shared. And I hope that anyone who reads this interview will do just that.

Birth of a Vietnamese Novel
September 21, 2015

The following essay was first published in
Diasporic Vietnamese Artists Network (DVAN).

David Joiner, author of *Lotusland*, shares how living in Vietnam inspired his journey to become a writer.

My "writing life" and my "working life" have intersected off and on for roughly half my 10 years in Vietnam. People often ask me, "What do you write?" and, even more, because I'm an American, "Why Vietnam?" Well, I write novels, mainly. Or at least I've written one that's going to be published. But I couldn't have written it without having spent so much time in Vietnam. In fact, Vietnam is the setting for my novel, and many of my characters are Vietnamese. But this doesn't exactly answer the question "Why Vietnam?" Let me explain.

To start, I never considered becoming a writer until I was 25. Not until I turned 24 and found myself living in the Vietnamese country-side - the only American and one of only two native English speakers in Dong Nai province - did I become a serious reader. There was little else to do during those 12 months but immerse myself in books. In 1994 there was no Internet in Vietnam, I didn't have a TV, and I lived 12 km by one-speed bicycle from the center of town. Naturally, I turned to books. I'm convinced that had it not been for that year volunteering in a slow, countrified environment, where I had few distractions and the life most familiar to me was contained in novels stacked on a small bedroom bookshelf, I never would have become a writer.

But the odds were perhaps greater than that. I come from a family of scientists; I was an underachieving student most of my life; I majored in Japanese Studies; I never took either a creative writing or a literature course in college; a graduate school professor failed me in a literature seminar and told me repeatedly that I'd never become a writer (and then harassed me until I graduated); I've lived in publishing hinterlands for most of my adult life; queries to literary agents have been ignored by the dozens; I've been rejected by the publishing industry too many times to count; I was married to a woman who admitted to trying to sabotage my writing career. My list goes on. Clearly, I wasn't born on an easy path to literary *anything*.

I have lived and worked in Vietnam seven separate times and have spent more than ten years here. I visited the country on four other occasions, usually while on holiday. The first time I lived in Vietnam, from 1994-95, I brought from America two suitcases filled with clothing, health supplies, cassette tapes, teaching materials, and books. I must have packed more than thirty books - novels, essay collections, and story anthologies.

With little to do in my free time, and occasionally needing to retreat from an intensely foreign setting, I sailed through my reading material in half a year. When I traveled in Vietnam, I acquired used and photocopied books from sidewalk vendors and hotel lobbies and devoured them. By the end of that year I had also filled a notebook with similes and metaphors that I imagined were brilliant (they weren't) but had little use for since I had come up with them outside the context of any narrative. Filling this notebook, "useless" though it was, represented another important step in becoming a writer. I was *imagining* myself as a writer, and though I look back on that effort with some embarrassment, there's no denying that I began to feel more confident expressing myself on the page. I even began to believe that with hard work I might actually publish something.

Each time I have been to Vietnam, the country has given me something different, something more, something valuable. Although there were Vietnamese novels and poetry collections that I came across and relished reading, it was life in Vietnam that influenced the writing of my own novel. By this I mean, in addition to my own lived experiences, the people I got to know, the stories they were kind enough to share, their attitudes and behaviors that I came to understand and respect, and certain aspects of their culture that over time I absorbed. And of course there have been causes in Vietnam that I have supported, one of which - the horrific legacy of Agent Orange - found its way into my novel.

But looking back, I see that what Vietnam has given me most of all are *chances*. Chances to live on my own in a foreign country; to see America from as far away as one can get from it; to read, write, and develop a serious appreciation for stories and the written word; to explore the country with one eye open to the land I wanted to describe and another eye open for stories I could tell; to make my living as an editor and writer, and to develop ideas for novels; to write those novels; to find a publisher; and to consider any number of new starts for myself.

In my 21-year relationship with Vietnam, I have gained knowledge about the country, its people, and its culture, and I hope I have given back, even beyond my early years as a volunteer teacher. And I hope my book is another way to give back - a way to share with others a Western perception of Vietnam at a specific point in its long, tumultuous, but always fascinating history.

No country is perfect, and Vietnam is no exception. But given my interests in novel writing, I can think of no better place where I could have spent the bulk of my time creating. Writing a novel takes time. More than that, it requires mental energy, and Vietnam gave me the chance to earn just enough to focus my real attention on writing.

Will Vietnamese people like my novel? It's hard to answer that since my novel will be published in English, but hopefully some will if one day they have a chance to pick it up. If the book touches them, that will be the greatest gift I can offer - an author's expression of gratitude for so many opportunities extended to him over the years.

"An intimate, rewarding novel of people linked by misfortune who search for redemption, wholeness, and purpose. Joiner evokes his protagonist's inner world vividly among descriptions of the life, culture, festivities, and natural environment of a small hot-spring town near Kanazawa. *The Heron Catchers* is an engrossing sojourn in one of Japan's most charming off-the-beaten-path destinations."
- Jeffrey Angles, translator of Hiromi Itō's *The Thorn Puller* and author of *My International Date Line* (Winner of the Yomiuri Prize for Literature)

"*The Heron Catchers* is at once a novel about a particular place, but is also a novel for us all, as our fates and feelings are intertwined with the natural world. Joiner's deeply felt and sensitive rendering of the inner lives of men and women in midlife, who are more affected by the place they live than they are aware, shifts in subtle waves, like the ocean that borders the town of Kanazawa where much of the novel is set. Closely observed and with care paid to emotional nuances, Joiner has written a book about adult life, and the endless striving we feel for meaningful connection."
- Marie Mockett, author of *Where the Dead Pause, and the Japanese Say Goodbye: A Journey* and *The Tree Doctor: A Novel*

"This slow burn of a novel sears itself into your consciousness with equal parts tension and poignancy. *The Heron Catchers* skillfully captures one blended, broken family's experience of growth and healing amidst the beauty and precariousness of Kanazawa's natural world."
- Leza Lowitz, author of *In Search of the Sun: One Woman's Quest to Find Family in Japan*

"Joiner reels the reader in with characteristic fine plotting, carefully crafted writing, vivid imagery and descriptions of life in the Japanese countryside, and a tone of authenticity belonging to a writer who knows and loves Japan. A riveting and worthy follow-up to *Kanazawa*."
- Amy Chavez, author of *The Widow, the Priest and the Octopus*

"In *Kanazawa*, David Joiner delivers a slow-burning family drama reminiscent of a film by Yasujiro Ozu or Hirokazu Koreeda...Each scene is quietly painted and, even in distress, holds some comfort... [Joiner's writing] treats language as sacred and uses it with delicacy and respect."

   - Tina deBellegarde, *Books on Asia*

"The greatest strength of the book is the way it unfurls, slowly but surely, like tendrils of warmth from a cup of sake that spread from your hands to your soul...Joiner has achieved an incredible feat in making a story whose lifeforce is art seem so effortless and devoid of artifice...the novel is the literary equivalent of superimposing a map of the human condition over a map of the city of Kanazawa. It is a story to come back to time and time again, since each reading can reveal a new layer, a new motif, a new passage that rings out beautiful and true."

   - Viktorija Blazeska, *My Murmuring Bones*

"There is a zen mastery in the writing here, a complete control over the characters and story, but not enough to dry it out. The few surprises that change the characters' directions are gentle, minor, but fascinating in how they ripple through [*Kanazawa*]. There is a bit of Henry James here, where progression and movement are released as if through a sluice, gently raising the water-level so as to allow the narration just the room it needs to maneuver into your subconscious."

   - Erik Raschke, author of *To the Mountain* and *The Book of Samuel*

"*Kanazawa* produces with words a similar effect to wandering around an old city; even if it's unfamiliar territory, the texture of the textual space that David Joiner has created thrums with this history as the plot slowly and deliberately unfolds...Joiner's patient attention to the interiority of his characters and a strong sense of place create a moving portrayal of the messiness of relationships and the ways that all the things we hope to bury in the past stay with us."

   - Reid Bartholomew, *World Literature Today*

"In *Kanazawa*, David Joiner has written a book not unlike its titular city, with great historical depths hidden beneath a deceptively tranquil surface. A story of misunderstandings, miscommunications and family secrets centered around a marriage that seems doomed to fall apart under the weight of unspoken resentments. Above all, *Kanazawa* drips with a sense of place, the setting much more than just a back drop to the action; Joiner shows that there are plenty of stories taking place outside the vortex of Tokyo. Tense, moving, and subtly gripping, *Kanazawa* is a welcome addition to the books-about-Japan shelf."
 - Iain Maloney, author of *The Only Gaijin in the Village*

"[A]n homage to Japanese culture, the city of Kanazawa, and the Kanazawan writer Izumi Kyoka."
 - Dontaná McPherson-Joseph, *Foreword Reviews*

"Joiner manages to craft a nuanced story...[It's] a Kawabata novel, *The Sound of the Mountain*, that comes to mind when reading Joiner's work...*Kanazawa* is an enjoyable look at an interesting city and the problems faced when people have different expectations."
 - *Tony's Reading List*

"*Kanazawa* isn't just a story about an American man in Japan and his wife. It is a tribute to the city of Kanazawa...Joiner's passion for the places and authors within the novel is obvious."
 - *A Basket of Words*

"*Ephemerality* is exactly the intangible essence that Joiner mystifies and sentimentalizes in his writing – a cultural quality that few non-Japanese writers understand so well."
 - Ella Kelleher, *Asia Media International*

"[A]n enjoyable read that moves along quite well and gives a satisfying sense of this corner of Japan."
 - M.A. Orthofer, *The Complete Review*